Praise for *Impers*

"A book that fires up the synapses . . . Pitlor's voice is witty and brisk, bringing warmth and light to questions of identity, independence and, yes, intellectual property. Who owns your stories? How much are they worth? Allie Lang's answers are complicated. Watching her reach them is like sitting down with a refreshingly honest friend who skips the part about how great her life is and dives right into the real stuff. We need more friends like this. Authors, too."

—*The New York Times Book Review*

"By turns revealing, hilarious, dishy, and razor sharp, *Impersonation* lives in that rarest of sweet spots: the propulsive page-turner for people with high literary standards." —Rebecca Makkai, Pulitzer Prize finalist for *The Great Believers*

"*Impersonation* highlights what's important in life, parenthood, and ambition in this compulsively readable story."

—*Good Morning America*

"With refreshing humor and an endearing charm all her own, Heidi Pitlor channels the narrative slyness of Rachel Cusk and the political acumen of Rebecca Solnit to deliver this zeitgeisty novel about the struggles of anonymity, accountability, modern-day mothering, and making ends meet in the gig economy. As both loss and possibility swirl around our lost but scrappy heroine, you can't help but root for her to claim her own voice and personhood. A smart behind-the-scenes tour of the murky world of publishing, politics, and the good people who get caught in the crossfire." —Christopher Castellani, author of *Leading Men*

"Pitlor's genius is that *Impersonation* doesn't resort to pitting two women against each other . . . *Impersonation* isn't just a critique of the 'white feminism' of privileged women who prioritize money and success in existing power structures. It's also more than a critique of the publishing industry, which only cares that Lana seems 'maternal' enough to sell parenting books. *Impersonation* is a critique of our society's fragile social safety net for so many vulnerable women, full of satirical humor and a lot of harsh truths."   —*BookPage* (starred review)

"*Impersonation* brilliantly deals with class, misogyny, and parenthood, all in a compulsively readable story. We'll never look at a celebrity memoir the same way again."   —Apple Books

"In dealing with issues of gender, class, parenting, and the #MeToo movement, *Impersonation* is both timely and timeless."
                    —*The Boston Globe*

"For our heroine, Allison, this is her story of survival and endurance in these maddening times. She goes to extraordinary measures for her son and her work, yet the path is not always clear, and far from easy. A gifted storyteller, Pitlor is also not afraid to ask the tough questions. What does it mean to raise good boys? Good people? What does it mean to be a woman, a feminist, a believer in others and, above all, in yourself?"   —Weike Wang, author of *Chemistry*

"Smart, funny, and provocative, *Impersonation* tunnels through our current politically charged American landscape with humor and empathy. It's a story of parenting—and surviving—in a time when the messy realities of everyday life often clash with ideology. As page-turningly readable as it is relatable. I'll be recommending to my book group."
                    —Jessica Shattuck, author of *The Women in the Castle*

"Heidi Pitlor has written a wonderfully rare thing: a comedy of manners set in the twenty-first century that brilliantly grapples with some of the more thorny issues of class, privilege, and parenting. Smart, funny, and generous in spirit, *Impersonation* is an engaging meditation on who controls the narrative and why it matters. A terrific read that will have you hooked from page one." —Kate Walbert, author of *A Short History of Women*

"Finding a balance between hopelessness and bitterness . . . *Impersonation* asks who we expect women to be in order to be real feminists, and if it's possible to maintain the supposed tenets of feminism when you're dead broke." —*Bitch Media*

"*Impersonation* is the book we need now: an unflinching look at our current moment, and at questions few of us dare to ask. If our personas do good in the world, does it matter what we did to create them? How much hypocrisy are liberals willing to tolerate? Can women raise good men? Provocative, heartfelt, and often hilarious, this is a novel I'll be thinking about for a long time to come." —Anna Solomon, author of *The Book of V.*

"Thought-provoking, funny, and engaging." —*Largehearted Boy*

"A captivating story . . . With Allie Lang, novelist Heidi Pitlor has created a character in whom I became so deeply invested that I was, at times, infuriated for her and by her, much like one could be with a best friend or sister. And if I'm being honest, the times when I was frustrated that Allie wouldn't stick up for herself were because I could see myself responding the same way. These are the best kind of novels: the ones that draw you in and make you feel connected to the characters and yourself." —*Writer's Digest*

"Pitlor's third novel is set during the lead-up to and the aftermath of the 2016 election; she dryly and sometimes poignantly channels the zeitgeist through nuanced characters, settings, and just-right details. Both the story and its resourceful heroine are fresh, intelligent, and charming."
—*Kirkus Reviews* (starred review)

"Smart and thought-provoking . . . Fans of Meg Wolitzer's *The Female Persuasion* will want to take a look." —*Publishers Weekly*

"A witty and unnerving glimpse behind the pretty pages of celebrity autobiographies." —*Manhattan Book Review*

"*Impersonation* has so many rich layers for readers to fold back and appreciate. Writers will find themselves chuckling at many of Pitlor's observations about the realities of their craft; parents will recognize themselves in Allie's blend of fierce love and outright exhaustion; and readers with an eye for politics and social movements will appreciate Allie's growing confusion and disorientation about finding her place— and a place for her son—in this increasingly alienating country. Allie's bittersweet story offers a nuanced portrait of a woman coming to terms with all different sorts of imperfections—and learning to relish moments of grace whenever she can find them." —Bookreporter.com

"Heartbreaking and empowering . . . *Impersonation* manages to cata-logue every important gaslighting moment of the Trump presidency without being overly political or distracting from the main story, an incredible feat that makes Allie's story a timeless one, but also one brave enough to break some rules, to show a flawed character gaining awareness of those things she could do better for herself and her son, while also serving as a worthy record of this moment in all our lives as women." —*New York Journal of Books*

"In a novel that's smart, surprising, thought provoking, and bound to set a few readers on edge, making for good book-club debate, Pitlor offers an astute study of what it means to be a woman today."

—*Library Journal*

"In this searing and nuanced exploration of identity, Allie slowly includes more of her own stories in Lana's book, grappling with how much of herself she must give away and setting the stage for a powder keg of revelations should the truth come out."

—*Booklist*

Impersonation

ALSO BY HEIDI PITLOR

The Birthdays

The Daylight Marriage

Impersonation

A NOVEL BY

HEIDI PITLOR

ALGONQUIN BOOKS
OF CHAPEL HILL
2021

Published by
Algonquin Books of Chapel Hill
Post Office Box 2225
Chapel Hill, North Carolina 27515-2225

a division of
Workman Publishing
225 Varick Street
New York, New York 10014

First paperback edition, Algonquin Books of Chapel Hill, July 2021. Originally
published in hardcover by Algonquin Books of Chapel Hill in August 2020.
Printed in the United States of America.
Published simultaneously in Canada by Thomas Allen & Son Limited.
Design by Steve Godwin.

This is a work of fiction. While, as in all fiction, the literary perceptions and insights are
based on experience, all names, characters, places, and incidents either are products of the
author's imagination or are used fictitiously.

LIBRARY OF CONGRESS CATALOGING-IN-PUBLICATION DATA
Names: Pitlor, Heidi, author.
Title: Impersonation / a novel by Heidi Pitlor.
Description: First edition. | Chapel Hill, North Carolina : Algonquin Books
of Chapel Hill, 2020. | Summary: "A single mother is hired to ghostwrite
a memoir for a successful woman"— Provided by publisher.
Identifiers: LCCN 2020009728 | ISBN 9781616207915 (hardcover) |
ISBN 9781643751085 (e-book)
Classification: LCC PS3616.I875 I47 2020 | DDC 813/.6—dc23
LC record available at https://lccn.loc.gov/2020009728

ISBN 978-1-64375-144-3 (PB)

10 9 8 7 6 5 4 3 2 1
First Paperback Edition

For Amelia and Milo

"To the extent not assigned, Writer waives all 'moral rights of authors' with respect to the Work."

—Intellectual property clause of a ghostwriting contract

Impersonation

PART ONE

2016

CHAPTER ONE

I once saw a woman in a library pick up a biography of Mother Teresa. A few seconds later, she returned it to its display, and next, she reached for a Kennedy nephew's memoir. The title, *The House that Uncle Jack Built*, was printed in a faux handwritten scrawl above the nephew's name, itself set in a bold Baskerville twice as large as the title. The book could have been called *Why I Love Pants*; it was the man's last name that would move copies. After eyeing the front and the back, the woman tucked her hair behind one ear and read the first page.

I took the woman to be in her early forties, like me. Dressed in athletic pants, a Fendi T-shirt, and salmon-colored sneakers, she may have been just summering here in the Berkshires. I stayed less than a pace away and tried to catch a glimpse of her reaction to the moment that Peter Kennedy, as a child, stuck his hand into the eternal flame, "immediately searing three fingers. A cemetery official marched over, called me a 'little brat,' and ordered my whole party to leave, not knowing my relationship to the deceased."

What ineffable quality made people want to keep reading a book after only a paragraph or two? At the time, I was reading this how-to book on teaching your baby to sleep. My goal was for my son—and me—to get more than three hours of rest without waking. I was also halfway through a book on the ins and outs of single parenting.

In my arms, my son chose that moment to eject his pacifier and shriek in a manner both rhythmic and alarming in its goatlike tenor. The woman glanced up, and what she saw was a short, bleary-eyed woman staring back at her, a woman with shoulder-length, unruly brownish-graying hair and an inconsolable baby dressed in a Red Sox T-shirt and a diaper. Cass had spit up on my jeans ten minutes earlier, and the left leg was still wet where I had rinsed it in the bathroom. The woman's eyes went between me and my son while I tried to quiet him. I bobbed up and down, and made pressurized wave noises in his ear, but to no avail.

In order to give her some peace, I headed to the front lobby, at last reinserting my son's pacifier once I found it lodged in the neck of my hoodie. With Cass settled, I turned to see a librarian checking out the Kennedy book for the woman. I was pleased, nearly triumphant. She headed toward the entrance, where we now stood, and a man bypassed her, making her stumble against us.

"Excuse me," I said, although it was she who had bumped into me and my son. "I hope you like that book. I hear it's good."

"I don't have my wallet on me." She kept her eyes on my old flip-flops.

"What?"

"I can't give you anything."

"What? No." I laughed a little, so taken aback that I could not think of what to say next.

She reached for her phone in her handbag and hurried out the door.

I stood there with Cass in my arms.

Had I not signed the nondisclosure agreement, I like to think that I would have asked her to please, in the future, try to avoid these snap judgments of people. Maybe I would have asked her to check her assumptions about class. I don't know. At the very least, I would have informed her that I was the one who had written the book in her hands.

What reason would she have to believe me, though? For all I knew, she was not what she appeared, either. She could have been a Kennedy herself—or maybe she once had a violent encounter with a panhandler. Maybe she even had some financial troubles of her own, although when I saw her sail past in a Mercedes SUV, I guessed not.

At the time, I had ghostwritten a handful of books for an assortment of minor celebrities, one billionaire oilman, relatives of the famous, and the once but no longer famous. Few of my clients were natural storytellers, but they were each dear to me in their own way. They had opened up to me, a few considerably so, and in turn, I had learned to omit any unflattering facts and highlight that which would benefit their personae. I kept in touch over the years with several of them. When Clyde Elliott, a former astronaut, passed away, I sent his widow irises, her favorite flower. She had written me a kind note: "You took an old man's ramblings and turned them into music." I replied with my own note. "Your words touched me deeply, as did my time with Clyde." I didn't tell her that, despite my best efforts to rebuff him, he had been a dogged flirt, or that he had complained to me about how, for the safety of other motorists, his wife should be prohibited from "driving while female." My work to hide or recast the truth—something that had become second nature to me—often had to move beyond the printed page.

I should mention that what follows began not long ago, but before the #MeToo movement and the much-contested confirmation of Brett Kavanaugh to the Supreme Court. Before countless children were separated from their parents near the Mexican border and four congresswomen of color were told by the United States president to "go back and help fix the totally broken and crime infested places from which they came." As always, much of the past looks different from the vantage point of the present or, more specifically, the first day of 2018, when I am writing these words. We lived in a different country, of course, even that recently. I mean this not as justification.

IN JANUARY OF 2016, my agent called me about a new book. I may as well have won a lottery; the money was multiple times what I had earned for any of my previous jobs. And Nick Felles would easily be my most well-known client. I hardly believed Colin at first.

"It's true," he said over the phone. He himself would take home 15 percent. "Now go buy yourself a spa weekend."

I did not tell him that I had more pressing needs than a pedicure and a facial. It was approaching two years since my last book, a memoir for Connecticut congresswoman Betsy McGrath. What savings I had were fast disappearing. I had my side jobs landscaping and substitute teaching, work I did to fill in the gaps between ghostwriting jobs, but it had become tough to cover costs. My car had recently died. I woke each morning with thoughts of doom.

After we hung up, I went for Cass. "We can finally buy you a big-boy bed!" I held him tightly, as if to press all of my relief into his small body and soft face.

"Okay. That hurts. I have to pee," he said.

We had just begun potty training, and I raced him to the bathroom.

A MONTH OR so later, I drove a beautiful preowned Toyota Tacoma with a double cab off the grounds of the car lot, Janis Joplin's "Get It While You Can" blasting from the speakers. I had left a straitjacket of a corporate writing job in Manhattan a decade earlier in order to move back to my hometown in the Berkshires and become a freelancer. I worked in my kitchen; I made my own hours and rules. If I wanted to, I could wear an old T-shirt and pajama bottoms every day.

I had never settled into a mediocre relationship. I had a sweet, lovable son all to myself. I was living life on my own terms, and as I came to a stop at a red light, I thought at long last, I was reaping the benefits.

I was the only person I knew who had never seen *Skinwalker Ranch*, Nick Felles's TV series about shapeshifters, UFOs, cattle sacrifice, and a coven of bombshell witches. Before we spoke, though, I watched a season, and while it was more violent than my usual fare, *Ranch*, as Nick called it, did hook me with its cliffhangers, its seamless meshing of the ancient with the futuristic, its attractive cast that was frequently shown nude.

"How did you come up with the idea for the show?" I had asked him on our first phone call.

"I've always been into the supernatural," he said. I began to record our conversation, as I had told him I would. "I inhaled Tolkien as a kid. And I'm fascinated with primitive violence, I mean, what raw force really looks like, domination and justice between two people, you know? Are you a real warrior if you just push a button or tell someone else to drop a bomb? So I thought, 'Get rid of the guns and the bombs and the drones,' and on my show, I'd just have pure human power. Mano a mano. It was important to me to braid this violence with a lot of fucking." I was about to interject "Why?" but he quickly continued: "Can I be real? What's more objectively beautiful than two bodies doing it? Hello, why do you think the great artists painted so many nudes? Picasso said that sexuality and art were basically the same thing. He's one of my muses." Nick paused again briefly, as if to allow me to ask, "Who are the others?" but then he went on. "Picasso and Tolkien, and Bukowski and Kerouac. Oh, and women. Can a whole gender be a muse? Why not, right? But, you know, I'm no sheep. If you asked me which actress I would do from any time in history? I'd say, *Hell no* to someone current like Dakota Fanning or Kristen Stewart, I mean *before* she switched teams. Give me Linda Harrison back when she played

Nova in *Planet of the Apes*. Give me Mia Farrow from *Rosemary's Baby*."
He cleared his throat.

I tried to clear mine and think of how to suggest he consider ways
to shroud his id. It might have been more effective to joke with him
in a pointed manner, but he hardly sounded like a person who would
laugh about himself.

"I guess I just wanted to get at the dotted line between sex and violence, you know, love and hate. I had this idea of a story that put man
against woman against animal against self against the occult in a hot
pandemonium. In my earliest visions of *Ranch*, Ancient Rome met this
kind of futuristic frontier territory. I could see it all in my head before I
met with the suits at the studio. The rest, as they say, is history."

I thought of Cass, and the fact that human beings required food and
shelter. The money from this book would give us one very good year—
even more if I was careful. If nothing else, I reasoned, Nick spoke as if I
were already his friend, and his openness would only make writing the
book easier.

No one could claim that Nick Felles suffered from a dearth of
audacity or good luck. He had gotten into TV soon after his video
game franchise, *Honor Code,* had exploded onto the marketplace,
outselling even some *Grand Theft Auto* games. With the hope that
I might see a different or at least more nuanced side of my new client, I tried playing *Honor Code* on a friend's son's PlayStation, but I
couldn't even pass level one. Within seconds, a woman soldier in a
black bikini appeared, the words *sexy cherry572* floating above her
head, and ripped off both my arms and exploded my head like a ripe
melon against my opponent's fortress wall. She then stomped all over
my brain matter.

"Your parents let you play this game?" I asked Connor, who was
eleven. "How are you able to win?"

"Maybe you just need to practice more or be, like, younger," he said.

By the time Nick was twenty-seven, he had won three Video Game Awards, three Emmys, two Hugos, and had bought himself a modern five-bedroom in Malibu with an infinity pool and views that stretched from the Santa Barbara Islands to Point Dume. How many other people, he said, could claim to have done any of these things before the age of thirty?

He sent the thinnest of drafts for me to fill out, and on the page, he came across as even more shameless than he had over the phone. I got to work and tried to make him more likeable wherever I could. I gave him a larger appreciation of his vast fortune. I played up his relationship with his mother and dialed down his many public escapades with a South American model. I opted not to include the monologue that he had delivered to me about the ideal nipple size.

Over the following weeks, I was relieved to learn that Nick had another side, a surprisingly kindhearted one. He donated big money to the NAACP and Boys Town, as well as Planned Parenthood. He was curious about me and how I had gotten into ghostwriting, and about Cass, too. We had a long conversation about the need for more diverse characters in certain children's programming. Most of my previous clients treated me more like a therapist, a husk of a person whom they could trust to be gentle with their truths. Very few asked anything about my son or my life.

After I sent him a few chapters to make sure that I was on the right track, he texted: *Dude, u made me sound like a twinkle bitch.*

Can I ask what you mean by 'twinkle bitch?' I replied.

He wrote, *A douche-nozzle. An ass-hat. Just keeping it real Allie cuz we are friends, right? The part about my fans was good. But u probably wouldn't use the words "twinkle bitch" just like I would never say "My life has been a series of precious gifts" or "As I look out over the ocean sunset, a glass of wine in my hand . . ."* I told u I'm a whiskey guy. Can u add a huge amount of sack?

Any response that is less than stellar about your writing can, in the moment, be diminishing. Once the sting of his blunt criticism passed, I tried to think of how to reply. I had already written for a man whose oil company was later sued for actively covering up climate-change science. Was Nick any worse for this planet than Bob Smelnick? Finally, I texted, *Tons of sack coming right up!*

I could not have had less in common with Nick: I was a newly solvent forty-three-year-old who preferred British TV mysteries to *Skinwalker Ranch*, weed to whiskey, Bob Dylan to Kanye, books to video games, privacy to ostentation. But ghostwriting is a form of acting, method acting really, as well as improvisation. You must become your subject, whether they are a Kennedy, a congresswoman, or a guy who espouses anarcho-primitivism and might frequent urbandictionary.com.

I had to start thinking more like a man. No one was asking for grace or modesty here. I had a son to support, as well myself. And I had never worked with Nick's editor, and for all I knew, he was cut from the same cloth as Nick.

I downed a mug of black coffee and returned to the so-called drawing board.

I am living the life I have always wanted. I've been called a "wunderkind" and a "ratings machine." My shows can be seen in Japan, Australia, on airplanes, and at American military bases in Iraq. I've got a candy red Ferrari Enzo, a first edition of *Dracula*, and Axel, my reticulated python, has his own climate-controlled bedroom with a killer view of the Pacific. But I never take my success for granted. I still sign every autograph and talk to every fan. You have to keep it real.

Sustaining this amount of sack for a whole a book would be challenging. Maybe, I thought, I should go back to Nick and suggest that just a hint of douche-nozzle might not be the worst thing for his memoir. Of course sack was who he was, and who he was, for better or worse, was a major success.

I thought ruefully of other clients who had shackled me with their fears of exposing the slightest unflattering truths. Most panicked about coming across as too cocky, too lucky, slutty, overly opinionated. Invisible electric fences were everywhere. The congresswoman's memoir had to have been my most frustrating book. I'd had to downplay her wealth, avoid any mention of her sister who had killed someone in a drunk driving accident, avoid her first two marriages, cut a long section recapping her critical thoughts of a sex-trafficking prevention bill. I might as well have been writing marketing copy for the state of Connecticut itself.

I have to admit that, with time and practice, sack came to feel liberating. Very little of Nick's life was off-limits to me; the work almost seemed more like transcription than anything else. He was enthusiastic and forthcoming and consistent, and soon enough I could even predict some of his answers to my questions. He liked to philosophize with me about human nature. He tended to overuse the words *primitive* and *transformative*. We had long phone conversations about Abraham Lincoln, the creative process, family relationships, skin care, and the versatility of avocados.

The writing went fast, and in a matter of weeks, I finished several more chapters. He liked them so much that, in return, he sent me a pink Gucci handbag and Cass a samurai sword, and although I was more of an any-color-but-pink backpack kind of person and the sword nearly decapitated my son when he got ahold of it, I was touched.

When I had finished half of his book, Nick invited me to meet him for coffee before an upcoming gaming conference in Albany, about an hour away from our house. I did not often get to visit with my clients.

What time and where? I texted.

Only after I pressed Send did a soupy ambivalence form within me. I would get to meet him in person—but he would also get to meet *me*. I am not proud to say that I had been coy with Nick about my age. I knew he would respond better if he thought I was younger, and possibly hot. When he had asked to Skype, I told him that my computer's camera was not working. If he had googled me, he would have found nothing; I tried to keep the lowest possible profile. I had done so for over a decade, as long as I had been a ghostwriter. Before then, I wrote marketing copy for an equity firm in New York. How wildly different my life had been, although on consideration, Nick may well have fit in with some of my coworkers there. Back then, I went out regularly with my male colleagues, who were in general far more receptive to me than the other women in the office, two mid-level workaholic lifers and one brilliant but aloof junior analyst. One evening, I almost won an after-work drinking contest. The following week, they invited me to lunch at a tony American bistro, where I was the only woman at the table. As they discussed classic Bruce Springsteen set lists, the fuckability of certain A-list actresses, Enron, the axis of evil, the New York Knicks, I quietly worked at my turkey club sandwich and sweet potato fries.

"You are the first girl I've ever seen order anything but salad for lunch," one said approvingly.

Being "one of the guys" was a kind of safe harbor. After all, they would not critique *my* fuckability if I was sitting right there with them. And to be frank, I liked having access to these secret conversations. A few women nearby glanced over at me. I became a different person in that moment, a woman who had something that other women desired. I was not used to this sensation, and over time, I admit that I may have milked it too much. When they began to flirt openly with me, I brushed them off, but always gently and with ambiguity. They nicknamed me Little Tiger because of my preference for a shot of sloe gin with a similar name. In less than a month, I was offered a raise and moved from my cubicle to a small office, and even got to handle correspondence and some research for one of the managing directors. Life was pretty good for the moment.

At dawn on the Tuesday that I would drive to meet Nick in Albany, I carried my sleeping son across our front yard. The ranch house that I had been renting, going on six years now, was situated on a cut-through that led to the Mass Pike, and cars and trucks were audible at all times, even from inside. I tripped over a tree root and my neighbor's dog broke into a bark and I whispered to Cass, "Please don't wake up, please don't wake up," because if he did, he would detonate. He was no good with separation.

Bertie met me at her screen door. "I've got him," she said quietly, her dentures not yet in, and reached for Cass. But she was too frail to carry him, so I gestured for her to hold the door as I went inside and set him on her couch.

I hated to leave my son while he slept. He had no father who might watch him today. His Tigger sweatshirt was too small. Bertie's house smelled of incontinence and there was a long gash in her screen door, not that my house was in much better shape. My front steps were crumbling, an accident waiting to happen, and the roof leaked when it rained. Jimmy Pryor, my landlord and neighbor, was frustratingly slow to repair such things. Thanks to Nick's book, though, I had started looking for a nicer place.

I kissed my forefinger and grazed it past Cass's cheek. "Bertie, you're a lifesaver," I said.

Back home, I pulled my hair into the neatest bun I could manage and changed into the professional ensemble that my friend Maggie had helped me find the other day at Ann Taylor. The first pair of gray pants that I had tried on had lining that moved like cream against my skin. The buttonhole was thick and reinforced, and the zipper slid right up, bringing to mind the pricier clothing I had worn back in New York. I thought once again how I should have kept those outfits instead of donating them to Goodwill when I started working at home. At the time, I had been so glad to part with those stiff, constricting business suits and toe-pinching heels, those trappings of a person who had come to seem less and less like me.

It took me about an hour to reach Albany, and I found Nick in a private booth toward the back of Wellington's, a swank restaurant in the hotel where he was staying. A brawny guy about Nick's age sat next to him and both tapped at their iPhones. A Lakers cap on his head, Nick appeared younger in person than in the pictures I'd seen, his face the shape of a plate. Blond stubble dotted his chin. He looked up at me with his glinty blue eyes and said, "You're Allie?"

I nodded. "Hi, Nick."

"Sit, sit!"

The other guy kept his eyes on his phone but coughed into one fist.

"Nice place," I said and lowered myself into a weird metal bowl of a chair across from them.

He squinted over at me. "Dude, you are way hotter than I thought you'd be."

"Oh, thanks." I may have chuckled and picked at my nails. "You have a good flight? When did you get in?"

"Like an hour ago. I slept through most of it." Nick kept his eyes on me. "It's so weird—I pictured you as kind of frumpy. Bigger and kind of, you know, softer. Maybe it was just that first time I read your stuff, when you sounded all lame. I guess first impressions stick." He shook his head.

I blinked over at him and forced a smile. I did not want to come across as uptight.

"No offense, though."

"None taken. Maybe we should write a book together," I tried to joke.

Our banter halted when a statuesque twenty-something with a red bob and jade green eyes appeared at the table to take my order.

"Just a cup of coffee, please," I said.

"You're Shannon?" Nick said, his eyes on the name tag pinned just north of her right breast. His friend looked up at her and slid his phone into his back pocket. "Shannon, can you fill me up?" Nick said. He raised his coffee mug to his mouth and gave the rim an almost imperceptible lick.

"I think I can do that." She flashed a smile, her face pink, and she turned to take another table's order.

The friend muttered something like "Tasty."

Nick looked back at me. "So Allie, I read the chapters you sent. It was wild. It's like I got cloned and my clone wrote this incredible book about me. It turned me on how much you got into my head. I got a boner just thinking about it."

"Great!" I said, my eyes on the table as I reached for my notebook.

He made a few minor suggestions: he wanted me to cut the bit about his bully neighbor when he was a kid, as well as his pet rabbit, Buttercup. He did not think I needed to use the name of the bougie town outside Chicago where he had grown up. "No one wants to hear about all that boring shit."

I took notes as he spoke.

We got to talking about the next season of *Ranch*, his python, his sister's new twins. The day before, I had started writing a scene between him and his mother. She had struggled a lot since being laid off, and Nick was about to tell her that he was going to buy her a condo.

"How's your mom's lupus?" I asked.

"She had a flare-up last week and sacked out on my couch for a couple of days. I hired my massage therapist for her. Maurice does all the older ladies on set. He's my birthday gift to them." Then he asked me about Cass's separation anxiety and whether I had yet tried avocado toast with cilantro and fried egg.

His friend said, "Felly, I've got to split. I'll be at the booth with Jim and Jim." They fist-pumped and a moment later, Nick and I were alone.

He explained that Curtis and the two Jims were here to promote *Honor Code: Execution Time,* the sixth installment in the series. "I do so little for my game these days," Nick said with the regret of a divorced father toward his child. "Life gets mad busy. Hey, I brought you something." He opened a leather folder on the table. "I got Fufu Muhammad's autograph for Cass. She's the actor who does the voice of Doc McStuffins." He handed me a slip of paper on which she had hand-written, "Dear Cass, Don't forget to stretch and flex! Your friend, Doc."

"Oh my God."

"It's no big thing."

My son ingested on average three episodes of *Doc McStuffins* every day. He sang the theme song constantly. Cass saw few characters on TV who looked anything like him, although I suspected the stuffed animals had a lot to do with his love for the show, too. "Nick! He. Will. Die. You have no idea."

Nick shrugged.

"This is fucking dope," I said.

"You sound like me again!" He beamed.

"I'm kind of a sponge, I guess. It's my job."

TWO MONTHS AFTER I went to Albany, I stood watching Cass ride his new balance bike around an empty school parking lot. We had just come from visiting a renovated two-bedroom, two-bath bungalow for rent in Stockbridge. It had a screened-in front porch, an attic that could be used as a playroom or an office, and was located just a block away from Beartown State Forest. It even had a sweet little pergola on the side that was frizzy with clematis. "I'm in love," I told the real estate agent, and she said she would go get started on the lease.

"You got this! Don't keep leaning to the side!" Kurt called out to Cass, and took my hand. Kurt and I had been together-ish for about four months. He had his faults—ambition and money were not currently his things—but he was great with Cass, a kid who liked to draw and listen to music rather than wrestle with friends or play catch. Kurt was also easy on the eyes and, to be frank, gifted in bed, all reasons I had agreed to let him move into my basement. At the moment, Kurt worked part-time at his friend Pete's hardware store and was trying his hand as a sculptor.

"Not so fast!" I hollered, just as Cass tipped over onto a bike rack.

We rushed to help him, and then my cell phone rang. It was Colin's number, so I answered, and Kurt gestured for me to take the call, that he would tend to Cass.

"You might want to sit down," Colin told me in a funny voice. "I've got some news."

"Okay." I glanced around, but there was nowhere to sit.

"Nick Felles is in a bit of trouble."

Kayla Hokin was a lead on *Ranch*, but I did not recognize the other names. There were multiple charges of sexual assault, as well as three other anonymous allegations of attempted sexual assault.

"Wait," I said. My heartbeat zoomed. "Rape?"

Colin went on to tell me that Nick's book had been canceled. Production on *Ranch* had halted, and a press conference with the prosecuting attorneys was taking place as we spoke.

As if by instinct, I wondered if the police had the right person. Of course they did. I had been writing for Nick, *as* Nick, for nearly six months now, and inside my chest, alongside my shock was a fast-wilting flower of sympathy or empathy or something.

"You do not want to see the cover of the *New York Post* tomorrow," Colin said.

I made a pained grunt. An image came to me of Kayla, who played Mai, the eldest daughter of Ahiga, one of the two shapeshifters. A very pretty girl with spirals of black hair and yellow-green eyes, Kayla could not have been older than twenty-three. I thought of Shannon, the waitress in Albany and Nick's boner at my ability to channel him. Every cell in me wished for the obvious not to be true.

There was a stone by my foot. I hurled it with everything I had across the parking lot. It seemed like some piece of this was my fault, although at the moment, I could not define exactly how. "Is Kayla all right?" I said slowly. "And the others? What about them?"

"No clue. I think it all happened like a year or two ago."

"Oh, well, I'm sure they're doing terrific by now."

"Hey you, don't blame the messenger," Colin said. His less-than-grave tone chafed at me.

I was not naïve—I had never thought Nick blameless or puritanical. What percentage of men in show business were? In any business, really? Even eighty-six-year-old Clyde Elliott had interrupted his monologue over the phone describing his first circumlunar flight to tell me I had a voice like Lauren Bacall and that he'd wager I had her figure, too. Men pushed limits. But Nick had *raped* someone? Multiple women? Everything inside me shifted and then plummeted.

Colin went on. "You'll get paid for what you already did, Al."

"I was almost done with his book."

"Oh, okay. Well, you'll get paid for half. I didn't know you were so far along. Still, that's not bad, right? This was the lead title on Assembly's spring list. They are taking a bath on it. Let's be grateful they're paying you at all, right?"

"'Grateful'? Assembly can absorb the loss," I said. I, however, would have to say goodbye to our Stockbridge rental. The week before, I had enrolled Cass in a preschool that would start soon, and had finally gotten us a decent health insurance plan. I had even booked a trip to Disney World for Cass and me, assuming that these expenses would be easily covered by the payment headed my way. We were scheduled to fly to Orlando in only a few days. "I feel almost homicidal," I said.

"Yeah," Colin said. "Chin up. I just got a line on a new book for you. It's early stages—I can't tell you anything else right now, but if it comes through, it'll make you feel way better about this whole mess. And I'm not just talking about the money."

"I can't think about writing another book right now."

"Well, get over it," he said, half-joking.

"Your compassion is touching. Really. Your compassion for me, and also for Kayla and the others."

"I should let you go digest this news."

"Yeah." I cursed myself for snapping at the one person who brought in the majority of my income. "Thanks for, or sorry for, you know. Please do call me when you hear about that new job."

I stuffed my phone in my back pocket. With a shudder, I remembered a scene from *Skinwalker Ranch* when Kayla, in the form of a human, had been made to bare almost everything for an orgy with the witches and man-wolves atop a mesa. The eye of the camera inched up Kayla's body, stopping at the dip of her waist and the upward curve of her breast. It slid up her neck to her young face, pinched in a combination of fear and ecstasy as a man-wolf and a gorgeous white-haired witch dressed in a see-through caftan had their way with her. The eye veered to Kayla's hand, her fingers clenching the hand of her mother, Ahiga, then to the small of the witch's back, the soft flat of someone's stomach, and back to Kayla, or Mai maybe, and Ahiga as they both shapeshifted into snarling foxes.

I thought of all that I had written for Nick about the beauty of the nude woman's body, about Picasso and Bukowski and *Planet of the Apes*, the inherent relationship between sex and violence (had I really written that?), all that garbage he had wanted me to write about his net worth and model girlfriend and Axel, his spoiled snake. All the garbage that I had willingly written.

"Everything okay?" Kurt asked. "You look weird."

"Yeah." I wanted to tell him what had just happened, but I had learned to abide by my nondisclosure agreements long ago. Plus it seemed preferable for Kurt not to know of my writing for—and as—a guy like Nick. "I just lost a really lucrative job."

Around Cass went, making *vroom vroom* noises and squeezing the horn on the handlebars. I would have to tell him that the new house and Disney World were off the table. He had already planned where every one of his stuffed animals would live in his new bedroom. We had made a paper chain, each link representing a day before we would fly to Orlando. It might have been easier to tell him that I contracted a flesh-eating disease.

Kurt said, "You'll figure it out, Hon."

"I don't know," I said. Maybe I could write Kayla a letter and apologize, an idea that made no sense, of course. "I need to figure out if I can still afford that new health insurance."

"It can't be that bad," he said. "How about if I cook tonight? I'll make you guys homemade pizza or something."

LATER, AFTER I put Cass to bed and Kurt had gone out for a drink with Pete, I paced the kitchen, ate three-eighths of a leftover pizza and two ice cream sandwiches, regretted it, ate my son's last Fla-Vor-Ice, saw myself as if from above, and grew disgusted. I would give up sugar, get a real job and stop freelancing, exercise, take Cass to a museum or two, force him to eat more vegetables, eat more vegetables myself, read more.

I considered how long it had been since I had read a great book, some-thing that made me feel substantial. Likely the amount of time that my son had been in my life. I selected my old favorite Virginia Woolf novel, *To the Lighthouse*: " 'Yes, of course, if it's fine tomorrow,' said Mrs. Ramsay. 'But you'll have to be up with the lark,' she added.'" But my thoughts immediately veered to Nick and Kayla Hokin, and that scene on the mesa. I vowed to set fire to that Gucci bag. Better yet, I would donate the bag and the sword to some charity that helped women, domestic violence victims or a similar population. But I'd already had the Doc McStuffins autograph framed for Cass and it had clearly amplified my value in his eyes. Maybe I would just leave that one be.

THE NEXT MORNING, I checked with the airline and hotel and learned that the last-minute cancellation penalties for our trip were so steep that it made no sense not to go. I looked through my finances: there was little I could do about my truck, which I used for the landscaping work I did. The money coming for Nick's book would hardly net enough to cover my debt payments, along with basic expenses and Cass's new preschool over the next few months. And who knew when Colin would actually come through with that other project?

Nick's book had made it easier to digest Kurt's limited contribu-tions. And Kurt made up for this in other ways, not the least of which were being a calming presence in our house and a second pair of eyes on Cass. I thought back to that morning I had first seen Kurt, sleeping on a wooden bench not far from the bus stop in Great Barrington. I had assumed this leggy man in a pinstripe suit and silk burgundy tie was either a salesman or a meth dealer. He opened one eye and I said, "You're pretty dressed up for that bench." He had perfect teeth and impish blue eyes. He admitted that he had just been let go from his job as a financial adviser in New York. He and his wife had worked at the same firm for over ten years, but while Birgitte had been promoted to director of global market strategies in the midtown office, he had been handed a lateral move to the Newark satellite. His clients had called his cell at all hours, moaning about every downturn in the market. His combative, perfectionist manager began to downgrade Kurt's incentives. And then he lost a big client the same day he learned that Birgitte had been sleeping with the global chief investment officer for six months. Poor Kurt melted down. He called his manager a "cheap, greedy tyrant bastard" and was ushered out of the building. That same day, he left behind his Murray Hill Condo, his Siamese cat, 99 percent of his belongings, and finally Birgitte. He boarded the next Greyhound scheduled to leave the Port Authority, disembarked at the last stop, Great Barrington, and began to walk in the dark, aimless. He would give nearly all of his money to Birgitte. "I don't want any ties to Wall Street and its toxic greed and addiction to wealth. I want no more part in the rise of conspicuous consumption that is killing our country. This is the most cleansing thing I can do right now," he told me as he sat on the bench, and I nodded, and congratulated him on his escape.

I now began to wish that he had held on to at least some of his assets.

I called the real estate agent and told her we would not be taking the perfect house in Stockbridge. A few weeks ago, my landlord had given me a new lease. I signed it, and went to pack our suitcases.

BECAUSE DISNEY WORLD was to be our dream vacation, I had booked a room for Cass and me in one of their deluxe hotels. We stepped off the shuttle bus from the airport and were greeted by a handsome bellhop who introduced himself as Slade or Slate. He scooped up our suitcases and led us into the huge lobby painted a pleasant chowder color. "There's a Great Big Beautiful Tomorrow" blared, and I sank into the comfort that came with being somewhere entirely child-focused. Cass could have a temper tantrum or break a vase and theoretically people would not care so much. The many cozy but lavish seating areas teemed with children wearing mouse ears and shouting at their frazzled adults. Giant blue pots spilling with flowers sat on marble side tables. I thought I smelled cotton candy.

I had never been to any Disney property before, despite my frequent begging when I was a young kid. "Be glad we can't afford Disney World," my mother had said. "It's tacky."

I must have been eight or nine. "Have *you* ever been there, Mom?"

"Grampy actually took us for the grand opening when I was about your age. It was so loud even in the cheesy hotel, and the lines were horrible. But it was nice of him to take us, I guess." Even then I knew how my grandfather, a philandering small-town lawyer and professional blackjack player, amassed a minor fortune and then lost it all soon before he died, when my mother was eighteen. Over the years, she had developed a variety of defense mechanisms against the shame of her financial limitations: denial, disassociation, snobbery.

So far, nothing was as awful here as my mother had described. Our hotel room was neutrally attractive in the manner of certain doctors' waiting rooms, and I went to close the door against the sound of "There's a Great Big Beautiful Tomorrow" in the hallway. On the walls hung several watercolors of children sleeping in fields of flowers that, oddly, resembled poppies. Two high beds were made up with soft, white comforters and feather pillows, and there was a plush tan carpet on which Cass tried to do a somersault. "I love this rug. I love this bed. I love this room," he said.

"I think our house is just as nice," I lied. I had at least opted out of the pricier water view. Our room looked out over a row of sedans and a dumpster.

I had fantasized about the two of us holding hands as we strolled past Cinderella Castle, nibbling on ice cream cones and waving hello to Goofy or Doc McStuffins, Cass telling me that he had never been happier. But five minutes after we arrived at the Magic Kingdom, he collided with a pale, lantern-jawed boy holding an enormous turkey leg. The boy got right in Cass's face and said, "Two lanes, asshole."

Cass ran behind me. I told the boy that he was being rude and should take his ugly meat and go.

Buzz Lightyear approached and we said hello, and made our way past the stores of Main Street USA, where Cass asked to buy a lollipop, penny candy, a T-shirt, a pin, a magnet, a lanyard, a stuffed animal, a pencil, mouse ears, unlimited photos of us for $200.

"We are here to have fun, not just to buy stuff," I finally told him.

"Why can't we do both?" he said.

"Hey look, there's someone else from Massachusetts," I offered lamely, gesturing toward a man in a Celtics shirt. When I looked, I saw that he, too, held a huge drumstick.

That night, Cass wanted to know why we had not seen Doc McStuffins.

"Good question," I said, and went to google the character. We had crossed paths with almost no characters roaming the park, and it turned out that most were now hidden away at various meet-and-greet locations. Apparently they were getting harassed by tourists constantly demanding to take pictures with them—although wasn't that the point of the characters being here? Doc McStuffins could only be found at some big breakfast event for which you needed reservations. And none were available. The resort recommended booking up to 180 days in advance. Sometimes the foresight and capabilities of other parents stunned me.

I decided to take Cass to the breakfast event anyway at the tail end of seating the next morning, and just wait outside so we could at least say a quick hello to Doc as she was leaving.

But the moment we approached the hostess stand at the restaurant, a woman with short beige hair was on us. "No standing here, folks."

I could see Doc in the distance by the omelet station, her large plastic head bobbing around with those signature brown pigtails and her white lab coat. She was hugging a toddler girl. I heard the sobs of a dozen babies, a dozen babies who had likely never seen the show and would never even remember being here.

"Come on," I pled with the woman. "We came to Disney World basically just to meet Doc McStuffins. She's my son's favorite. Look, Cass, there she is!"

"No can do," said the woman. "Let's move it along now." She stepped out from behind the stand as if we might rush the place. She had a square face and substantial earlobes.

"Can't we wait until breakfast is over and then say hello? Is it really against the law to just stand here?"

"You'll need to make reservations for another day." Her eyes went from Cass to me and back again.

"You guys are booked for the next goddamned year."

She glared at me.

Cass began to whimper and I grew desperate. "Fine. What will it take?" I asked, reaching for my purse. We would probably never come back here. I had little to lose.

"You and your boy need to leave, ma'am. Now."

A voice inside me said, "No."

She turned and called out to someone else.

"Doc, hey, Doc!" I yelled.

But Doc did not hear me, and another woman appeared and the first woman's fingers were tight around my arm, pushing me back.

"Motherfucker," I said.

Cass began to cry.

I shoved the first woman away from me and she fell backward against the stand.

The other woman helped her regain her footing. "Ma'am," the second woman said, adjusting the lapels of her blazer. "You need to leave or I will have you and your son forcibly removed from the park. Do you understand me?"

Later I would learn that cussing alone was grounds for removal. It hardly seemed possible to vacation in a place like this with young children and not blurt out a single "fuck."

"Doc!" Cass called out desperately. "Please!"

Doc McStuffins finally turned and headed toward us. At last we had won out over these heartless women. Doc would set them straight and we would all laugh at how riled up we had gotten. She would give Cass a hug and I would snap a photo and he would remember this moment forever, the magical time his mother took him to Disney World to meet his favorite character. In that big plastic costume, she waddled toward us and when she was maybe ten or fifteen feet away, I leaned down and whispered to Cass, "Get ready, here she comes." He jumped a few times in his excitement and said, "What do I say to her?"

"Anything you want!" I was giddy now too. "Tell her she's your favorite character on TV!"

Doc stopped. She went to high-five a teenage girl, but the girl recoiled and lifted her iPhone to her face before Doc's hand could make contact. Her plastic face frozen in that grin, Doc turned and headed back toward the omelet station.

"Oh God," I said.

Cass called out one last time in a voice now choked with tears.

"Doc," I called out. "Can we get a quick hello?"

"Michael. Code six at Play 'n Dine." The second woman had a walkie-talkie.

I grabbed Cass's hand and stormed off. In my rage, I explained to him that Doc was a fake anyway, just some jerk dressed up in a costume, and that certain restaurant hostesses got high off of whatever miniscule power they had.

Of course none of this helped. "What?" he cried. "You ruined every-thing. You ruined Doc, you ruined this trip, you ruined my life," he said. He was inconsolable all the way back to the hotel. "I just want to go home."

"No. We are going to enjoy this place. Tomorrow is a new day," I said, possibly because that song was playing again in the lobby.

We walked in silence back to our room, and I admit that on the way, we stopped at the gift shop and I bought him a lollipop the size of his face to make him feel better, and it did.

In the following days, the number of times I said "no" to my son—"no" to the pricey Typhoon Lagoon, "no" to renting a poolside cabana, "no" to any item in our minifridge—put a real damper on things. I tried to encourage him to stay focused on enjoying what we did have. We were in Disney World, after all. How many kids got to say that? (His answer: "Every kid." My response: "*I* never went as a kid." Cass: "You don't count. You're not a kid.")

Cass got to meet Cinderella toward the end of our trip. We even got to do a last-minute meet and greet with Sleeping Beauty in the France Pavilion at Epcot. Both princesses were friendly and kind, and I hoped they would partly make up for our experience with Doc. I asked them questions like, "What's it like to ride in a real pumpkin?" and "How much do you sleep?" in order to buy more time for Cass. Through smiles, they answered in silky voices—"A real pumpkin is magical, but it's better with two slippers!" I watched them perform the same act for each child, even one awful girl who told Aurora that she was obviously wearing a wig and had on "too much hooker makeup" to be Sleeping Beauty. "Where did you ever get that idea? Why, of course I'm Aurora," said the princess without missing a beat.

"I am the only boy here," Cass said as we turned to leave. He was right; we were surrounded by throngs of girls and their sisters and mothers. Even the Disney staff there were all women.

"So?"

"Aren't any princes here?"

I said, "Let me see if we can find some," and approached a younger woman dressed in a crisp white blouse and skirt that looked as if it had been made of a circus tent.

"Hmm," she said. "There's Prince Naveen at Tiana's Garden. Oh, and Gaston is at Belle's Village Courtyard."

"But aren't those places back at the Magic Kingdom?" I said. We had already used up our passes to that park. "We're heading home tomorrow. Are there any princes here at Epcot?"

She looked kindly at Cass. "How about Chip and Dale? They'll be here later this afternoon." She explained that they were funny chipmunk brothers from classic cartoons.

He shook his head. He tended to prejudge anything from a time older than he was as boring and valueless.

After the woman walked off, he begged me to take him back to Magic Kingdom.

I refused but he kept at me. I'd had enough. "Please do not ask me for one more thing," I said. "You need to learn to stop when I say, 'No.' Got it?" He welled up, and I softened. "How about we get crêpes for lunch?" and I marched us toward the kiosk for Crêpes des Chefs de France.

Afterward, we wandered to Morocco and Japan, and then the fountains at the American Adventure, where an a cappella group named Voices of Liberty took their places nearby and starting singing "This Land Was Made for You and Me." They sounded incredible, but because they were dressed in old-fashioned clothes and were not Doc McStuffins, Cass had no interest in them.

We continued on to Italy and took in the replica of the Doge's Palace, the Columns of San Marco and San Teodoro. We went to Il Bel Cristallo shop, a place made to resemble the outside of the Sistine Chapel. "Maybe someday I'll be able to take you to the real Sistine Chapel," I told Cass. If there was something I craved most, it was the ability to travel with him. "You never know."

RETURNING HOME WAS the psychic equivalent of drinking newly spoiled milk. I picked up a landscaping job, which would only last a few days. As it was summer and school was out, there were no substitute teaching jobs to be had.

Kurt upped his hours at the hardware store and that was a help, but he soon cut back again when he started a new sculpture. He had been collecting various items from the dumpsters next to houses in town that were being renovated: patches of vinyl flooring, several toy Furbies, a broken Cuisinart, a cracked non-flat-screen TV. He had begun to build a ten-foot-tall chair, a thing far too wobbly to even climb, which was the point. He named it *Throne of Waste*. As he had with his other sculptures, which lay half-finished in my backyard, he named them before he began. One evening after dinner, he explained that this one would be a statement about materialism, global warming, and greed.

"Okay, cool," I said, standing to clear the table. "Listen, I'm about to drain my checking account on rent and utilities."

"Jimmy charges you twice what he should for this place. We should all just barter. Did you know that last year, barter transactions in the U.S. alone were fifteen billion dollars? It's all about community, and creating value with who you are versus what you own. Money is corrosive to human interactions."

"Maybe we could barter your sculpture for rent when you're done," I said before I could stop myself.

"I mean, we could—" he said. "I'll see if I can get more hours next week at Pete's."

"If you wouldn't mind."

I EMAILED COLIN to ask if he had heard any more about that new book, but he did not respond. I emailed him again a week later under the guise of chit chat: "Can you believe that the host of *The Apprentice* actually got the Republican nomination? Tanya Dawson told me that she is already looking at apartments in Toronto." Tanya, a comedienne and character actress, had been my client years ago, but we still kept in touch.

I heard nothing back from Colin.

I started *To the Lighthouse* again. " 'Yes, of course, if it's fine tomorrow,' said Mrs. Ramsay. 'But you'll have to be up with the lark,' she added." It was hard to focus on the Ramsays.

Things in my life had been so promising once. I had won a few national writing contests in high school, had been named salutatorian of my graduating class, and was granted an almost full scholarship to Dartmouth. I moved up to Hanover, got good grades, and published a couple of poems in the school's literary journal. My adviser, a young-ish Brit Lit professor and the faculty adviser of the journal, was an avid champion of my writing. In a campus full of students who had come from New England prep schools and who were avid skiers and lacrosse players, Professor McCoy was a kindred spirit, a fellow outsider from Pittsfield who graded papers at the same diner in White River Junction where I often went to do homework and write. Sometimes we sat together and talked about Western Mass or Shakespeare. And then midway through my senior year, after class, he brushed his hand across my ass, muttering something about "so many giddy offenses." I chose to think that he had accidentally touched me and that I had misheard him. But the next week, after I turned down his plainly audible offer to visit his "ample personal library," he gave me a course grade of D. Shaken, I registered a complaint with the English Department, but was never contacted in response. My GPA plummeted, both because of this grade and my state of mind. I even lost part of what remained of my scholarship. The whole thing was so dispiriting that I never regained my enthusiasm for writing poetry or my pride of Dartmouth.

WHEN COLIN FINALLY called me, his voice nearly bounced as he described the new client and book. "And it's one of Gin's books." I had worked with this same editor on Tanya's memoir. "You're her first choice," he added.

"Really?" I was flattered. Virginia, who went by "Gin," had requested several major revisions and was hardly the sort to dole out praise. A legend in the industry, her authors ranged from edgy women entertainers (like Tanya) to leaders of the Democratic Party to Pulitzer Prize–winning nonfiction writers. She had recently been given her own imprint at an exalted publisher, Countenance Books. I was used to larger, less discriminating houses. I took in all that Colin had just told me: the thrillingly impressive client—Lana Breban—and Gin and Countenance. "Wow, if this isn't karma after Nick Felles." I had come to think of his book and that whole debacle as "Project Fuckface."

"I know, right? We'll do the usual terms."

"Okay," I said. I thought a moment. "But should you push for more up front? As a kind of insurance? You know, in case the book gets canceled for whatever reason?"

"Have you ever had another book canceled, Al? You don't need to worry about *this* client. And it's a great offer. Come on, take it."

"It is pretty good," I said. I estimated the differential between what I would have earned for Nick's book and what this new project would bring. The two were apples and oranges, of course, and Nick was more widely known, but at the moment, given who my new client was and all she stood for, the sizable differential was tough to ignore.

Still, the offer did exceed what I was typically paid. I could hardly afford to be greedy. "Okay, I'll do it," I said. "Of course I will."

CHAPTER TWO

Lana Breban had come onto my radar a year earlier, around the time she was a guest on *The Late Show*. I had liked her immediately. "Please welcome powerhouse lawyer, and the person responsible for the congressional Task Force on Women and Poverty, columnist at the *New York Times*, feminist rabble-rouser, and the woman you don't want to offend on Twitter," Stephen Colbert had said. She appeared onstage, tall and unslouching in her slim, pavement-colored suit and chunky eyeglasses, her hair buzzed short and dyed royal blue. She brought to mind Annie Lennox. Lana strode toward Colbert like a storm promising to explode everything in its wake. She took her seat and they began to banter, and I soon learned that she had been the one to coin a phrase that I had been seeing lately on T-shirts and bumper stickers: NEVER APOLOGIZE, NEVER COMPROMISE, NEVER RATIONALIZE. "I got the idea for my battle cry from Julia Child. She refused to say she was sorry, even if a dish turned out terribly. A chef has to 'grin and bear it,' she used to say." Lana had immigrated from Romania as a teen, and her accent was still detectable, although barely.

Colbert asked her to describe her recent exposé on *60 Minutes*, "A Day in the Life of Wanda Lesko." I had happened to watch it the previous week. Lana said, "I asked a young homeless woman, the mother of a toddler, to wear a hidden camera that we'd had mounted on a pair of eyeglasses. I wanted viewers to see the world as Wanda did. We look *at* poverty, or at least some of us do from our privileged vantage points, but we need to start looking *from* it." The viewer got to see what it was like to be called a "smelly whore" outside the Times Square TGI Friday's; to learn that the OCFS would take away her son, Christian, if she didn't move her "sorry ass right now"; to get struck in the eye by a half-eaten slice of pizza and then turned away at the Bowery Mission; to fall asleep on the Z train, and then get robbed at gunpoint. The segment was both harrowing and heartbreaking. One expected Wanda to emerge from this day filthy and bruised on every level, but when she finally turned the camera back on herself, she was the same green-eyed waif with the same serene expression. "Listen," she said, her son held tight against her chest, "I'm not in jail and me and my baby Christian are alive. You have to keep your eyes on the sky so that you can see the rainbows when they come out." This particular day had left her no worse off; every day was this horrible for her.

I was thrilled to write for a client who cared more about women's poverty than women's nipples. From my cursory research, I knew that Lana was forty-five. Born in Bucharest, she had immigrated at sixteen to New York on the eve of Ceaușescu's fall. Her father had died when she was eight; maybe the food shortages from the austerity programs had something to do with this. But her mother soon fell in love with an American reporter and, with her two daughters, escaped Communist Romania and moved to Queens to be with him.

Now Lana had a twelve-year-old son and a research-scientist husband, the sole inheritor of his pharma-magnate father's estate. Lester

Harding kept a low profile; from what I could suss out, he was an unremarkable-looking man with a goatee. He studied zebrafish and depression, and had done a lot of work in China.

In addition to practicing law, Lana taught at Columbia, although she was currently on sabbatical. Her op-eds for legislation around non-discrimination and increased protection of women who worked out of the home ran regularly in the *New York Times*, as did her interviews on CNN and MSNBC. She had just been voted Person of the Year by one of the progressive magazines that I used to read when I had the time and energy. On Twitter, she had over three hundred thousand followers, and countless trolls. Just yesterday, she had silenced an arrogant tax accountant with: *Mansplaining blocked. Need emoji for that.* About twenty thousand people had "liked" the tweet.

As the presidential election approached, Lana had become one of the go-to voices for the disenfranchised. She had even just introduced Hillary Clinton at a campaign stop in New Hampshire. Lana had brought along Wanda Lesko, now a married mother of two and stepmother of four, living in Hoboken. Wanda appeared exhausted, a new baby in her arms and Christian running in circles by her side, but she gazed lovingly at Lana as she approached the podium. "Every single woman in our country," Lana said, "deserves the same great life that my friend Wanda has now. Every single one." Christian halted and jammed his thumb inside his nose. He worked hard at whatever was stuck in there and when he finally removed it, flicked it in the general direction of Lana. Footage of the moment went viral at first for its comic value. But things took a turn when certain antifeminist factions tweeted that Wanda's life "didn't look all that great" and that Lana was using this poor woman to "extend her own fifteen minutes of fame."

Lana had published a book already, a lofty and, I had thought, unnecessarily wonky tome outlining the myriad ways that welfare law screwed over black mothers. But this had been nine years ago, and the university press that had published it had allowed it to fall out of print.

I had been hired to ghostwrite a second book, a departure for her, a memoir of motherhood that first had been titled *Oh Boy! Adventures in and Lessons from a Feminist's Attempt to Raise a Feminist Son.* Someone had just deemed the word "feminist" problematic, so now the title was a work-in-progress. To refer to Lana as anything *other* than feminist seemed ludicrous, but I rarely had a say in this sort of thing.

I was scheduled to meet her in Manhattan on a Tuesday in September. I had planned to take the bus from Great Barrington, and Kurt would watch Cass for the day. I got dressed and located my shoes under Cass's bed. I grabbed *To the Lighthouse* from my bedside table: the bus ride would be a good opportunity to really dig in, finally. I considered what lay ahead of me. What if I blurted out something unwittingly offensive about women or gender? Long ago, I had worked for a small feminist magazine, but at this point in my life, I could not have defined the difference between Material and Marxist feminism. I went to retrieve what was left of a scraggly joint that I had been nursing for weeks, and looked around for my Zippo. We would make a stop in Poughkeepsie and I could find some private spot to smoke there.

In my truck, the voice of Charlie Barleycorn, a Canadian children's singer who now lived in Vermont, poured from the speakers: "Red, yellow, brown or black? You're my pal, I've got your back! Puerto Rico, Mexico? My mom's from Ontario!" Charlie let loose with his banjo and harmonica, and an autoharp joined in. I remembered that Cass was not seated behind me and hit the Eject button. Maggie had given us the CD—all songs about race—back when she had learned that Cass's father was of Indian descent. I had taken it, a little awkward about the naked gesture, but Cass loved the music and knew every word.

My section of the Berkshires was bipolar, more so than it had ever been. In my town alone we had a vegan cafe and McDonald's, a Peruvian restaurant and a Subway. Outside Goodwill, two athletic-looking women jogged by a man passed out on a bench, a cigarette butt hanging from his mouth. I could have done without the summering moms at the playground giving me the stink eye whenever Cass enjoyed some Doritos or Oreos, the only snacks he would eat for a time, but I tried to appreciate the multitude of trees and the wildflowers in spring, the cottony meadow behind our neighborhood, the leaves—our famed foliage—already turning yellow and amber, and glowing in the morning sun. And the way the horizon appeared closer and broader than anywhere I had been. The stark Mass Pike cut through the verdant hills toward the marbled morning sky. If I did not have a perfectly beautiful home, I certainly lived in a beautiful region, the place that had inspired the writing of *Moby-Dick* and *The House of Mirth,* numerous musicians and visual artists.

On the bus to New York, I pulled out my book and began again. "'Yes, of course, if it's fine tomorrow,' said Mrs. Ramsay. 'But you'll have to be up with the lark,' she added."

My eyes moved to my bookmark, a photo of Cass and me—our tiny family—on a hayride the year before. There were his expressive eyebrows, his plush toddler lips, his silky hair. My love for my son could feel like sadness, threatening and rich. I thought a moment. What if Kurt left him alone for a few minutes and something happened? What if Cass went downstairs and tried to climb *Throne of Waste,* which now reached the ceiling? Kurt had no car. He used my truck if he needed to go anywhere, and of course I had parked it at the bus station back in Great Barrington. Did he even know where the nearest hospital was?

In Poughkeepsie, I disembarked and huddled behind a dumpster near a ropy man in a gray suit smoking a cigarette. I waited for him to finish and leave, but he was in no hurry. I decided that the benefits outweighed the risks and searched my bag for my lighter. He watched me in a way that fellow smokers never did—with judgment—and so I informed him that his fly was down. There was only time for one drag, but this was my friend Virgil's excellent Purple Haze, and soon I was thinking that Kurt could handle whatever came their way. He was a grown-up, after all, and Cass was no longer a toddler but a preschooler. The feminist theory I once knew would come back to me. Why had I worried about how I'd come across to Lana? I was a reasonably intelligent woman with decent social skills. Everything would be A-OK. The bus driver honked the horn and we had to get going.

In Manhattan, Colin—handsome in a trim, steel blue suit, his hair gelled but not petrified—stepped from a cab just as I approached Lana's building off Central Park West. Old friends of a sort, I reached up and we hugged.

"Check you out," Colin said. "All professional. Last time I saw you, you looked like you had been digging graves." He had been staying nearby at the Canyon Ranch spa and had picked me up from my landscaping job to take me to lunch. Before I could respond now, a uniformed man opened a glass door for us. He so resembled Captain Kangaroo that I vowed to google the actor to see if he was still alive and for some reason now a doorman in New York.

Colin and I headed inside toward a white marble front desk, three waterfalls streaming down the craggy cement wall behind it. I stood next to a potted yucca as Colin told the concierge, a serious, small-nosed man, that we were here to see Lana.

In the elevator, I said, "Any sense of when I'll get the first payment for the book?" It was technically due on my signing of the contract, and I had done so two weeks earlier.

"It'll come when it comes."

Sometimes I thought he found even the mention of money unseemly.

"You're both here," Lana said when we had reached her condo. "Amy, hi. Lana Breban." She extended her hand, which was both warm and hard.

My chest thumped with excitement as I took it. I did not want to embarrass her so soon by telling her that my name was in fact "Allison" or "Allie," as most people called me. Apparently Colin felt the same.

She had lively, kind eyes and a strong jaw. In person, she looked different, though. She had on those chunky glasses, but she may not have been as tall as she looked on TV, or maybe this was because she was wearing flats now. She had such presence, such magnitude on TV and in interviews, and of course she would seem smaller in real life. Her blue hair was now a short bob, and given its density, had a weighted Prince Valiant look. Only she could get away with this, I thought fondly.

She led us through an airy foyer, past a painting of a man whose face appeared to be sliding off his head and a framed sketch of Ceaușescu waving a wand at a group of screaming children. The three of us entered a narrow dining room with a stone fireplace and a canted bay window that overlooked the trees of Central Park. This was an opulent address, but if anyone deserved it, Lana did—and certainly more than Nick deserved his spread in Malibu. There at Lana Breban's enormous oak table lit from above by a feather and glass chandelier, as I unfolded a heavy napkin and draped it over my lap and Colin described the fevered buzz over Lana's new book deal throughout the New York publishing world, I felt a surge of hope for my life.

Working with Lana would mark a welcome return to my younger, purer values. Years ago, after Dartmouth, I had driven out to San Francisco with some friends and found a job as an office manager for a small feminist magazine. I had gotten to research an article about Bill Clinton and Monica Lewinsky and public voyeurism. It was easy to fall in love with San Francisco, that charismatic if fast-gentrifying reminder of a freer, more idealistic decade. I had shared my lunch break at taquerias in the Mission with sharp, principled women writers. But I earned nearly nothing. Since then, my principles had taken a back seat to the need to pay bills.

An attractive, petite woman maybe in her sixties, her chin-length hair black with silver highlights, hurried into the room. Gin. We had never met, but had spoken several times over the phone. She wore an ivory blouse with a gold and black wrap around her shoulders. "Sorry to keep you waiting," she said. She had a cast on her pinky finger and appeared flustered. "Hideous traffic jam in midtown."

"Too much editing?" Colin joked, gesturing to her cast.

"Too much gardening with my granddaughter. But don't let me interrupt. Keep going—I'll catch up," she said, taking a seat. I struggled to envision this polished woman with her hands in dirt alongside a child.

"I'm eager to hear about how this process works," Lana said. "But I should tell you before we start—I only have about an hour. I have to run to a meeting in Lower Manhattan as soon as we're done. One day I will learn to say no to at least some requests—but that day is not today." She laugh-snorted, and her hand flew to her mouth as if to return the snort to its hiding place. "I know this was addressed before we all signed on, but I need to emphasize that what is said here today—and from now on—stays between us. I don't need it getting out that I had to hire someone to write about my life as a *mom,* of all subjects."

"Of course," Colin said. "Without a doubt."

"Always," Gin said.

They turned to me, and I said, "Definitely." I could feel their desire for me to provide them with more words. "You've got my full discretion. I've been ghostwriting for over ten years and I'm used to keeping quiet about my clients."

With a nod in my direction, Colin said, "She's invisible. No online presence, no publications to her name. She hardly exists."

"Wonderful," Lana said. She released her shoulders as if from a too-high hanger.

A pretty, youngish woman wearing maroon cat-eye glasses appeared and filled our goblets with water. Lana, of all people, employed a house-keeper? Or was this woman a cook? She described the lunch we were about to enjoy and fiddled with her earlobe as she spoke. I nodded as if I could define—and had, of course, many times before enjoyed—*quenelles* and *dorade*.

Lana turned to me. "How do we get started?"

"It'd be good if you could give me all the raw material that you have," I said. "Sometimes my client writes me a long email or a letter, or we Skype or talk on the phone, and I take tons of notes. You tell me about your life with your son, all your adventures as a mom, a feminist mom of a boy, of course . . . everything you've learned and what's surprised you over the years. Don't worry about giving me too much—people usually do." I tried to convey the air of a seasoned veteran.

She reached for her water. "Can we make room in the book for some new data about parenting, too, you know, and maybe some studies about economics and gender identity in children? I know a wonderful sociologist in Oakland. She is doing this fascinating research on gen-dered curriculum in public schools."

"Absolutely," I said. I craved the opportunity to write something less personal for once, something outward- instead of inward-looking.

"Did you read those books I sent you?" Gin asked her, waving her pinky in its cast.

"I can see why they became bestsellers. They were wonderful." I noted that Lana had used the word *wonderful* now three times, and filed this away for use in her book. "Those women had so many stories to tell and, I mean, such well-defined missions. They gave their whole lives to being moms."

I assumed that she and Gin were referring to the two books she had also sent me, one a memoir about an American mother who had moved her family of eight onto a decrepit houseboat in Amsterdam, the other the semi-comic account of a Maine woman who had integrated the rules of military boot camp in her family's daily life.

"You don't think *you* have a mission?" Colin said.

"Oh, I have a mission. I'm made of missions! But I am also a work-aholic. I burn pasta. I couldn't even make it home for Christmas last year. And I am terrible at laundry. It really does take a village, right?" She nodded in my direction. "I openly admit I'm not going to PTA meetings or baking my son his favorite cookies every day."

"I'm hopeless with laundry too," I told her. With everything she said, I liked her more. Why had she even wanted to publish a memoir of motherhood in the first place? People sometimes had unexpected reasons for hiring me. For the congresswoman, I had written a book about her life along the Connecticut River. For Jenna Rose, a bridal contestant on the reality TV show *I Thee Wed*, I had written *The Smart Girl's Guide to Finding Lasting Love*. The congresswoman had confided to me that her book was meant to be an extended personal letter to her grandchildren. Jenna Rose had likely wanted the public to view her as an intelligent woman, not that she would have openly admitted it. I understood these motivations. I had supported these women; they were each noble in their way.

"Who was it that said, 'Every life is fascinating'?" Gin asked. "Don't sell your own life short. Motherhood—parenthood—is more than just cooking or volunteering. If anyone knows that, it's you. Certainly don't feel that you have to fall back on research. Can I be frank?"

Lana nodded.

"Readers *want* the personal and the messy. They like to read about real life and struggle, certainly more than economic studies. People want to see you living out your research and your knowledge."

Colin said, "We want to see how you manifest your ideals. What it looks and really feels like to feminist-parent a boy."

His clunky wording made me itch.

"Yes, you are probably right." Lana looked at me anew. "Do you have children, Amy?"

"I have one son, just like you. But he's four."

"Great!" she said. She kept her gaze on me.

Colin went on. "Listen, people will happily read whatever you want to tell them about your life. They want to know more about this brilliant woman who fights for them. They want to know that you are imperfect, just like they are. We're not asking you to rewrite *The Year of the Houseboat* or *Bootcamp Mama*. Remember—this will be *your* book. It should reflect you and your family and what you believe and what you have been through, in all its messy, singular, Lana fabulousness. We would never have asked anyone else to write it."

After I had signed the contract, I had read that Lana's advance was in the "high six or low seven figures." Colin and Lana both had mentioned that she planned to give 2 percent of the book's proceeds to Planned Parenthood. Maybe I should have pressed Colin harder to ask for more. If anyone could understand the need for women to be paid fairly, it was Lana.

The conversation turned, and she said that her son had just started sixth grade.

"What's his name?" I asked, chastising myself for not googling this.

"Norton," she said.

"My son is named Cassidy," I said.

"He's adorable," Colin lied. He had never met Cass.

"Four is a wonderful age," she said.

The youngish woman returned with four plates of food, dollops of something that resembled mashed potato atop fluffy greens, maybe arugula, with tiny peas scattered about. She refilled our nearly full goblets.

"You could also include suggestions for teaching boys how to navigate our gendered culture," Colin said. "What if you don't want to dress your boy in blue or your girl in pink? For a lot of people, competitive sports are the only acceptable activities for their son. They raise their boys to value aggression and achievement instead of health and peace." An image of Nick's round face appeared in my mind. "My nephew—he's ten now? He spends eight hours a day on his computer because—and I quote—'I'm not a jock and I'm not a bully and my laptop doesn't make me embarrassed for not knowing about the Yankees.' Who is telling these boys that it's okay to feel their feelings or have a good cry once in a while? His mother, my sister-in-law, runs a branch of one of those pyramid companies. Wooden jewelry or something. She tells him—and herself—that she *chooses* to work from home, even though she couldn't find a job to save her life after taking off six years when her kids were born. All Ryan has is what he sees—a woman at home tending to his every need and inviting her friends over to buy exorbitantly priced necklaces whose profits go almost entirely to other people."

The mashed potato was a kind of fish that had been ground with something else, maybe eggplant.

Lana said, "Women who take time off to have kids and then want to go back to work have a hell of a time. Just yesterday, I got asked by the NYCLU to head up a panel on ageism and sexism in the office. I swear, I need to clone myself." She took a long sip of water. "You know, there are plenty of alternatives to big chain stores, plenty of wonderful shops right here in the city that sell gender-neutral clothes and toys."

Eager to avoid hearing about Manhattan's pricey children's boutiques, I thought to say, "I could write about *Free to Be . . . You and Me.*"

Colin groaned. "That old thing came out in, what, 1975?"

"1972," I said, my face turning hot. It was the year I was born. As a kid, I knew almost every word.

"Marlo Thomas is a wonderful woman," Lana said. "I did a fund-raiser with her a few years ago. People still play her album for their kids, you know. She told me it still sells."

"It's still relevant," I said, pleased to have her on my side. "'*William's Doll?*' '*It's All Right to Cry*'? My son loves those songs." One day when I was maybe seven or eight, my overplayed *Free to Be* album disappeared and was replaced by Prokofiev's *Peter and the Wolf*. My mother had read that classical music could stimulate children's brains.

"Just look who the Republicans nominated," Colin said. "And look who's backing him: out-of-work coal miners, men in manufacturing who've lost their jobs. And they're blaming immigrants for stealing them. They're demonizing Hillary Clinton. They're essentially feeling emasculated by women in power. Who's to say that if they had gotten a good education in empathy and equality and respect, things might be different for them?"

Lana furrowed her brow.

"You really think one book has that much power?" I had to ask him. Gin gave me a look.

"What if their mothers, or their fathers, had read a book like the one we are going to publish?" Colin said. "What if they really understood feminist parenting? And what if, as a culture, we finally accepted real male emotion? I think we have a chance at creating the holy grail here—a bestseller with a heart. And a brain, and a soul."

I had a hard time imagining even one emasculated man buying this book to learn how to raise his son. "You don't need to convince us," I said.

"No, you do not. Can we talk logistics?" Lana said and flicked her bangs from her forehead. "Should the book cover Norton's birth until, what, until now?"

"I think you should structure it chronologically," Gin said. "Start with pregnancy, and you can talk about self-esteem, body changes, all that. Each chapter should cover one period of time in Norton's child-hood—his birth and infancy and then toddlerhood. I'd keep the focus on your life as a mother just trying to raise a good, sensitive son. Allie, you can send me a few chapters once you've got them, okay?"

I nodded.

Lana gazed down at her right hand for a moment. My eyes met Colin's. The earth seemed to stop. It was an odd sight, her statement hair color alongside her simple tailored white blouse and silver chain necklace. For the first time that I had seen, she wore matching earrings. Two small silver birds dangled just a half inch from her lobes.

"All right," she said at last, and fixed her glance on me. "I guess you and I can work one chapter at a time. I do want to include some infor-mation about the teenage years—you know, technology and every-thing, maybe in an afterword since we won't get there with Norton." She said she would email me soon with some thoughts about the first chapter, and that again, she wanted to approve each one before moving on to the next. "Email is good for you?"

"Sure," I said. Typically, after my client sent me the raw material for a book, I worked on my own for a time. I pictured Lana and me becom-ing friends: getting in touch regularly, working in tandem, confiding in each other about our frustrations with patriarchy.

"You could come over here after you've finished each chapter, and we could go through it together, make sure it's what it really needs to be. Gloria could even watch your son if you need to bring him."

Who was Gloria? I was about to tell Lana that I did not live in New York when I heard the brief strumming of an electronic harp. She reached for her iPhone beside her plate and rose to take the call.

Colin said, "Need to use the restroom," and he followed her out of the room.

Gin reached for her own phone and began texting.

Alone with my food, I glanced out the bay window at the lush greenery of Central Park. I thought of Robert Benchley's comment about this place, "the grandiose symbol of the front yard each child in New York hasn't got."

I had read that Harding White, Lana's father-in-law's pharmaceuticals company, had been the firm to develop Acclivia, a Viagra-like medication with fewer side effects, and Fortia, made for male pattern baldness. Now they were working on a treatment for male infertility. It seemed noteworthy that Lana's wealth was attributable in large part to male anxiety, so prevalent as to afford Norton his grandiose front yard.

I pictured my own Ikea kitchen table, and its view of my patchy front yard. At that moment, Cass was probably in my living room, coloring or watching *The Octonauts*, now that *Doc McStuffins* had been sullied during our vacation. I thought ahead to tomorrow, when Bertie would watch him again while I began work on Lana's book; she babysat three days a week. She had long ago retired from running a home daycare. Her beloved husband died just after she had retired, and she had a son living in Wichita, a pompous-sounding guy with an unpleasant wife and two grandkids whom she rarely saw. Lately, Bertie did not remember everything, and I waffled between fretting about and denying this fact.

Next to Bertie lived Jimmy, borderline obese and alone. His wife had left him years ago, and his two kids were grown and gone. He owned and rented out a handful of small houses like mine in various conditions of disrepair in Lee and Pittsfield. His shepherd mix, Bruin, had diabetes. Last week, as I lugged a trash bag to the end of my driveway, Jimmy drove past in his Buick Encore and called out, "Hey! Town left your recycling box and a mess of cans all over my lawn last week." This was how he saw his whole life: *Someone left me a mess and nobody knows. Nobody cares.*

Out the window at Lana's, I saw an unusually tall, thin man walking alongside a woman across the street. The man jabbed at the screen of his phone. He stopped and threw his head back in what looked like anguish. She recoiled. Another man tossed a cigarette butt onto the sidewalk, and a third man gave him the finger behind his back. Sometimes I wondered if men were less capable of finding happiness. I did worry for Cass.

As his mother, I would read Lana's book even if I'd had no part in writing it. More than once I had been dismayed to overhear the term "little girl" used as an insult. I had seen boys at the playground wrestle with each other like tiger cubs jacked up on steroids. Cass was what some would call a "mama's boy," and in my heart, I savored this fact, but living it was another matter. He could be a little clingy, and I could imagine him getting teased one day.

In that first conversation about Lana's book, Colin had described what they wanted: "You're supposed to try to broaden her audience, and make her seem more relatable and appealing to whoever might not know her yet. Try to make her seem less edgy and severe, more warm and fuzzy, and a little less foreign, too, I guess. Make her seem more feminine. Shirley's words, not mine. Shirley's a consultant, I think, or manager. She asked all about you—she was glad to hear that you were a mom of a boy, too. She wants you to write about Lana coming home from court and changing into mom clothes, running a bath for her son, you know, singing him lullabies, kissing his head, playing catch with a baseball, sharing a hotdog or some other American-seeming stuff. Basically add some 'good old American mom' to the mix. This should be easy for you."

I was used to these candid directives. He had once asked me to dumb down a supermodel's memoir: "People want to know what kind of makeup she wears, not her opinions on Nehru and the independence of India." I had challenged him at the time, but he would not back down. He claimed that he was only passing along another manager's suggestions.

"All right," I said over the phone. "More mom, less edge. You think of me as feminine?" I immediately regretted it. We used to talk this way, but had not in years.

"Yeah. No. I mean, I don't know," Colin said. His voice changed to that of my friend: "I think of you as a hot mess. But a cute hot mess of, like, Chapstick hetty and stoner hippie MILF."

"*MILF*?" I was flattered, despite myself. "Chapstick—what does that mean?"

"Whatever," he said, returning to his employer's voice. "Who cares what I think of you?"

My thoughts returned to my new client. "God, Lana Breban is everywhere you look lately," I said, overjoyed at the idea of working with her.

"You can send a signed copy of this book to Nick Felles when you're done."

I laughed bitterly. "Hey, Col. Would you have given me Lana's book if it weren't for that whole mess?"

"Yes. Gin asked for you. She wanted a mom for this."

"Why didn't she get someone who does more high-brow stuff, like Polly McCardle? Wasn't she going to write that new one for Sheryl Sandberg? I heard Polly was the one who did the poetry collection for the ambassador to Denmark." I had found it kind of weird and dishonest, ghostwritten poems. Polly lived on her own in a one-bedroom in Boerum Hill. When we met once through Colin, she made it clear that she was uninterested in any kind of work-related friendship. Maybe it was my admission that I had never heard of the fashion designer who was seated at the next table in our café—or, embarrassingly, Patrick Modiano, who had just won the Nobel Prize for Literature.

"For starters, she just took a full-time job at *New York Now*. Either way, we wouldn't have gone to her for this one," he said. "I've been trying to get you something better for a while. You remember when you and I first met?"

"The pool hall night?"

"The pool hall night. You were griping about your job at that equity firm? You told me some awful stories about some college professor and that guy dumping you in San Fran. And your father dying when you were a baby. You'd had a tough road. We both had."

"I told you all that? I don't remember."

"I do," he said.

That night, a couple of guys had approached me and my friend after we sat down at the bar, bought us daiquiris and challenged us to a game of Six Pocket. Back then, Colin had a mop of black hair, paper-white skin, and translucent eyes and, like us, had just gone to the Joni Mitchell tribute. We had bonded over our love of Joan Didion and Mary Gaitskill.

"You've always felt like you owed me something," I said.

"Could be."

Although I did not recall confiding in him, I would not forget ending up at his decaying but huge loft on the Lower East Side. With the intensity of two people about to finally leave behind their youth, we went at it in his shower and then in front of the window overlooking a Judaica shop. Although Colin stood several inches taller than me, he was slight and pale. His wrists and fingers were the size of my own. His movements were sharp and precise, correct and responsive in a way that I had never known. Patti Smith played; his hair smelled of beaches; I must have come ten times.

Early the next morning, he got a call from his father with the news that his mother had just died of ovarian cancer. After he hung up, we lay side by side in bed, Colin silent.

I had no idea what to do with my body. He did not cry. "Should I leave?" I asked him, but he said no.

We got dressed and wandered around his neighborhood, the garbage trucks clambering like mammoths down the street, the sun brightening the asphalt sky, Colin eventually teary and contrite about not having seen his mother in over three months. He explained that they had never been close. Originally from Ireland, she had been devoutly Catholic and had, he'd thought, favored his older brother. We walked to a diner and talked some more. We went to Duane Reade. To the East River Park. To a newsstand. He seemed to want only to keep walking—until he did not. We headed back to his place and he crawled into bed. I followed and lay next to him until he drifted off, and then got up and tidied his loft and brewed a pot of coffee.

Sometimes you find yourself without warning at another person's critical juncture. A week later, he came out.

GIN SIGHED AND continued texting. Lana returned and took her seat. We smiled at each other and resumed eating. I had the urge to admit to her that I had watched two seasons of *The Real Housewives of Orange County* and was currently unable to get past page one of *To The Lighthouse*, that I had lost contact with Cass's father, and that for the past six months I had been sleeping with a semi-vagabond who did not pay his fair share of anything. That I had named my son after a Grateful Dead song and that beneath my rayon Target blouse, across my lower back and right side, I had gotten the lyrics of this song tattooed by an old high school classmate and had, the whole time, apologized again and again for the small but notable bulge of flesh that he had to press flat in order to finish the tattoo. I had the urge to lay my entire imperfect, mostly-feminist-but-not-always self before this woman and ask if she approved of me before we continued on together, the two of us issuing forth in one voice. I hated the thought of something slipping out later, when it might be perceived as a lie of omission or even betrayal, some fact that might erode her confidence in me.

"I love your op-eds," I said.

"That's kind of you."

Once I had finished my food, I set down my fork, and massaged one hand with the other. "The work that you're doing is so important. I think I'm more excited for your book than I've been for any other jobs. This one feels more necessary, I mean, given the state of this country right now."

"Oh. Well, good," she said, looking surprised and maybe taken aback by my mention of other projects. "I should tell you I've been getting push-back lately. I have to be pretty forceful to get my message across, and this can seem threatening to some people, even if I don't mean it to be. Growing up under Ceaușescu, I was not raised to just sit quietly and do nothing. Americans might not know much about true Communism. In fact, it seeks to liberate women from domestic life, which is not to say good old Nicolae really liberated anyone in the end. But my mother was—and still is—a powerful woman. She taught me the importance of fighting for what is right." I could have sworn I had heard her say these sentences verbatim to some interviewer. "But Shirley, my adviser—and I—have decided that I need to deepen my image and that I need to be 'warmed up.' More people will respond to my message if I appear a little more, well, vulnerable. I hate to call it 'feminine.' You know?"

I nodded enthusiastically. "Why should warmth and vulnerability equal femininity?"

"Exactly right."

I flushed with pleasure at the validation. "I'm no expert, but from what I've seen and read, you already seem really effective out there."

She thanked me.

"Are you thinking of running for office?" I asked. I could not help myself. The congresswoman had also been eager to "deepen" her image. Maybe they'd had the same adviser.

"No. I mean, not right now," Lana said. She folded her napkin and placed it at the center of her plate. "Let me ask you a question. I assume you have help with your son?"

This may have been a test. "Some, well, not every day."

"But you know what it's like to take care of him at home?"

I nodded.

Gin finally set down her phone.

Lana went on. "So, hypothetically, say I wasn't the one to potty train Norton—I mean not the only one and not every day. Say I was no good at breastfeeding. In this book, you might be able to expand on some topics like that, you know, fill in if I needed it?"

"Fill in?"

"You're the writer," she said. "You're the expert!"

"Sure," I said, still unclear just what she meant, but also glad that in her eyes, I offered some kind of expertise. "Or you could turn to a growing genre of mom-moirs," I joked.

"Who has time for all those?" She laugh-snorted again, but this time let it hang in the air.

Gin chuckled as if she herself had not been the one to send us two such books.

"I think we only need to write about potty training if it involves teaching Norton about feminism," I said.

"Right, of course." Lana went silent when the woman I took to be Gloria came in to refill our goblets once again. After she left, Lana said, "I'm glad you understand about the need for discretion."

"If it makes you feel any better, that nondisclosure agreement is airtight," I said. The agreement stated outright that during the process of my writing Lana's book, I was not to mention her name, that I was "to behave as if [I had] never heard of Lana Breban." Some clients could be paranoid, although after her having been trolled mercilessly on Twitter and the way that Wanda Lesko had been weaponized, I could understand Lana's desire to keep some things private.

When Colin returned, she said, "I've got to wrap up here. I have that meeting soon."

We gathered our things and made our way toward the foyer. A sleek charcoal-colored dog, some kind of small greyhound or terrier, loped across the hallway and disappeared. How strange that we were only seeing it now.

"Well, I can tell I'm in good hands," Lana said, as we reached the front door.

"Lana, can I just say—you are absolutely the rock star that I hoped you'd be?" Colin said.

"Stop. Go on." She set her hand on his elbow.

"Oh, believe me, I could and for hours if you'd like, Darling—"

"Hours? Let's see, I'm free tomorrow," she said with a laugh.

I had seen Colin turn on this fawning persona before in the presence of clients.

Gin's phone rang, and she glanced down at the screen. "I have to take this. We'll talk soon." She touched Lana's arm and hurried toward the elevator.

After we had said our goodbyes and Lana had closed the door behind us, Colin turned to me. "This book is going to rock the world, Allie."

"Or is it Amy?"

He just rolled his eyes. "She'll figure it out."

We rode the elevator without saying any more. It was stuffed with highly groomed, very attractive people. A woman to my left tried to comfort a squalling baby. I noted a couple of people subtly covering their ears. The woman followed us past the front desk, the baby still wailing, and outside, when Captain Kangaroo held open the front door.

Colin said, "A cab! Mind if I grab it?" He flung out his right arm and the car swerved over to meet us. "Give me a kiss goodbye." He pecked my cheek and trotted toward the car.

I stood in front of Lana's building for a moment, trying to assimilate all that had just occurred. I breathed in the smell of charred meat and cigars. A horse-drawn carriage clopped past, followed by another. The summer light was honeyed, the day far warmer here and now than when I had left home that morning. A town car pulled over and stopped before me, and Captain Kangaroo called hello to the man who stepped out, someone familiar-looking. It took me a few seconds to identify him as Alec Baldwin, and I quickly bowed my head and turned to walk the other direction.

I had read that in Bucharest, Lana and her disabled sister had witnessed their father's heart attack in their kitchen. Soon afterward, their mother moved them in with another family of four. She had been a schoolteacher across the city, and had to leave Lana to tend to her sister and the other children in the apartment most days. Across the country people stood in food lines for rations of canned sardines and bread. Austerity measures dictated the rationing of electricity and heat, and residents burned soft coal in the winter, making the air thicken with soot. It was illegal to heat an office above fifty-seven degrees Fahrenheit. So many things were illegal. Thousands of women died from back-alley abortions. Hundreds of thousands of orphans were housed in rundown warehouses, some children even left chained to their bed frames. Lana had once described that time and place in an op-ed as, "Hell upon hell upon hell."

Last year she had been invited to speak at the Library of Congress during Women's History month. Two months ago, she had interviewed Ruth Bader Ginsburg for *The New Yorker*.

I would have loved to hear more about Lana's childhood, those dark days in Bucharest and her move to New York. This sort of material was gold for a memoir. I wondered just how she and her mother and her sister managed after her new stepfather left them for another woman only months after they had arrived in the United States—and not only managed, but thrived. Lana got into Yale, attended law school at Stanford, worked at a law firm fighting workplace discrimination and harassment, married Lester, began publishing op-eds in local papers, then national papers. She had triumphed, really, and on her own blue-haired, pasta-burning, incompetent-with-laundry terms.

CHAPTER THREE

Nearly four weeks later, I opened Lana's first email with her notes for Chapter One, *Pregnancy and Childbirth*.

> Hello! I hope you and your son are well. Please start chapter by encouraging reader to use midwives, doulas, birth plans (we had midwife, birth plan). Then a discussion of corporatization/medicalization of birth in U.S. For a thorough history with stats, see Cahill and Drum's study @ Stanford, 2013; for recent overview, NEJM, Valentine, 2015ish. My assistant Valerie <u>Val @LanaBreban.com</u> can get you links. Happy writing, and all the best, Lana.

Each morning over the past few weeks, I had logged on, hoping to see an email from her so that I could get started at last. I still had yet to receive my first payment. Apparently the publisher was backlogged. No schools had called me to substitute-teach in weeks, and I had not gotten any landscaping jobs in over a month now.

I reread Lana's note. This had to be the least amount of material a client had ever given me at the start of a book. I typed: "Great to hear from you! I'm eager to get to work. I'd love some anecdotes and memories about Norton's birth and your pregnancy. Clients usually give me too much at first! If it's discretion that still worries you, please be assured that you are in good and professional hands. I do think everyone wanted the book to be more personal and less academic?"

She switched to instant messaging. *I carried to full-term. Labor went relatively quickly and birth was natural. I can find out Norton's size if you want. He was a big baby.*

Maybe she would be more forthcoming if we spoke. *Can you Skype or talk on the phone?*

She wrote: *Sorry, busy day. (Busy life!)*

I reread her initial email, and predicted Gin's response to a detailed recap of our country's corporate-driven medicalization of labor and delivery: "Zzzzzzz."

Ok, I wrote. I tried to think fast. *Just a couple little questions, if you don't mind. What was pregnancy like for you? What did you do to prepare for the birth—any classes?*

Lana: *No classes. Lots of morning sickness, thrombosis, insomnia, but I got through it.*

Me: *Did you learn the sex before Norton was born?*

Lana: *Yes. Pls. remember to advocate for birth plans. Very empowering for women. Have to go now. Can't wait to see Chap 1. Good luck!*

The chat box disappeared.

On my counter, the jacket of *Bootcamp Mama* showed a photograph of the author, an attractive, athletic red-haired woman dressed in army fatigues and a cap. She balanced a crying baby in one arm and a sleeping red-haired toddler in the other. A silver whistle hung by a cord that rested above a centimeter of cleavage.

In general, I tried never to rely on Google when writing a book. I was hired to write what readers did not already know or could not easily learn, but in desperation, I googled Norton, Lester, and their family. I came up largely empty; Lana had given birth before becoming so well-known. Almost everything I found related only to Lana's and Lester's work or Harding White. There was little evidence of Norton online, just a few pictures of him on Facebook at other children's birthday parties, one with a woman who may have been Gloria, but the snapshot was too blurry for me to be sure.

I myself had learned I was pregnant when I was home alone. It was just me and a pee stick one wintry morning five years ago. The first person I told was Jimmy, who at the time was crouched up on his roof, chipping away with an axe at an ice dam. He said, "With whose kid?" "A guy I met last summer. It's not relevant." "Whoa. Al, you've got to think this through." He lowered the axe and two poles of ice fell through a snowbank right next to me. The next person I told was Maggie, who said, "Is this a joke?" To Jimmy, I said, "I'm keeping it." To Maggie I said, "Why would it be a joke?" To my stunned mother, "Enough! Enough about how hard this will be. Enough about what your friends will say. Just tell them that the baby's father won't be a part of our lives. How about, 'Congratulations'?" And then I began weeks of cycling through fear, exhilaration, and aggressive self-doubt.

I considered tracking down some nugget of Romanian wisdom about love or pregnancy or motherhood, but any sort of stereotyping might prove dicey with Lana. I recalled my work with Tanya Dawson. Years ago known for her dead-on impressions of Scary Spice from the Spice Girls and Janet Jackson on *Saturday Night Live,* Tanya had asked me more than once to sound funnier, looser, "in general, less like you are a white person trying to sound black." I was mortified, and asked if she would be more comfortable with a black ghostwriter, but she reassured me that she had heard worse imitations of her. "And the only two black ghostwriters that anyone seems to know of are working on other books right now. Your agent said you're a chameleon, but if for some reason you did sound too white, I should just tell you. So, that's what I'm doing." Eventually I did learn to better reproduce her voice and sense of humor—at least this is what she told me.

At my kitchen table, I began what seemed like a journey in a row-boat to the middle of the ocean with no map or compass:

> It was time for our first ultrasound, and in moments, we would learn whether I was carrying a girl or a boy. I tried to get comfortable on the examination table. The technician came into the room, squirted gel across my abdomen and flicked on the screen. Having endured everything from morning sickness to thrombosis to insomnia, I felt

She felt what? I had fattened up plenty of moments before, but past clients had at least given me the basics of these moments. I had written at length about walking in platform pumps in a runway show and sitting with Congress, listening to the State of the Union address. Hell, I had described the feel of a girl's nipples through her shirt during a first kiss in Winnetka.

I turned back to Lana's book:

> Having endured everything from morning sickness to throm-bosis to insomnia, I hoped that the worst had now passed. In a moment, I felt

I excised the word *felt*, and recalled the afternoon I learned that I was carrying a boy.

> The rhythmic thumps of the baby's heartbeat provided a soundtrack for the gray clouds ebbing and flowing on the

monitor. It was impossible to make anything of what I saw. The technician nodded with the knowledge of our baby's sex. Lester and I knew that this woman would not be the one to tell us, so we waited eagerly for our ob-gyn to join us ten eternal minutes later.

"It's a boy!" the doctor said, and I laughed, because for some reason I had expected a girl. "He looks healthy," he added.

I was growing a boy inside me! What did I know about little boys? I had no brother, no

"I had a dream that we hitched up to Newfoundland." Behind me, Kurt cracked his knuckles.

"Give me a 'heads up' if you plan to be gone more than a week," I said.

He had come to love road trips and solo camping, and went away sometimes for several days on his own. This arrangement was not a terrible one. When I needed to dive into work, he disappeared. When he began to miss me, he came back and helped out with Cass. The casual nature of whatever we were may have been the reason I had forgotten his birthday last month. I often chose to go check on Cass or shower instead of cuddling naked with Kurt in bed. He called me the guy in our relationship. I told him that this was sexist. "I mean that it's a breath of fresh air after Birgitte," he said. She had apparently been insatiable with his time and money, although who knew how she might describe their lives together. I had the thought that a lot of men secretly wanted women to behave more like them.

Kurt went into the kitchen, and I tried to concentrate again and think of ways to accommodate Lana's few requests for the chapter:

For too long, a woman's body has been public property. (Add quick bit of history.)

You have the right to be as private or public with your pregnancy as you wish. Sometimes, well-meaning strangers will
approach you and touch your belly without asking. It may be wise
to develop a stock response to this situation: "Hands off! It's
mine," you could say. Or simply smile and respond, "I'm tick-
lish," and back away.

No one has the right to touch you without your permission.
If we draw boundaries when we are pregnant, we empower
ourselves.

The tone was off. From across the room, Bootcamp Mama watched
me, compelling me to be sassier or warmer.

Kurt walked by again and squeezed my shoulder and then stretched
his long, freckled arms to the ceiling. He headed off to get dressed and
finish rebuilding Jimmy's carport, in exchange for half of our rent.

I finished the ultrasound scene, then herded Cass out of the house
toward Bertie's. He stopped to examine an empty Happy Meal container on the lawn.

"Come on, no dawdling," I said. I took the box from him. "I've got
to get back to work."

"Dawdle, bottle, waddle. Can't I stay home today?"

"No. Sorry." A Pathfinder splashed a mud puddle on us and sped
off. "Thanks, Ron! Appreciate it," I muttered. Ron Garbella and his
wife had recently moved into a house across the street. With my bare
hands, I did my best to wipe the mud off of Cass, but he began to
whine.

"It's just rain," I said, taking Cass's hand and nudging him forward.
"Hey, Love, please keep walking. I have so little time to work."

"I can't go to Bertie's today. That car got mud in my mouth."

"Then spit it out."

"You always say no spitting." Maybe he would become a lawyer someday. And then he could support me.

Out of desperation, I offered to take him for a Happy Meal at McDonald's later if he reached Bertie's house by the time I counted to twenty. He made it there before I had reached ten. When I saw Bertie waving a spatula from her front door, I turned to head back home, relieved, then felt guilty about having resorted to a bribe, and one whose primary appeal to him consisted of French fries and a flimsy toy.

Back at home, I opened my laptop.

I may not have known much about boys, but I did know that our son would have our love and best intentions and unconditional acceptance. *Our son!* What a wonderful sentence.

After our doctor and the technician left us alone, I looked over at Lester. "What if he only likes sports? What if he is aggressive?" I said.

He chastised me for assuming that a boy would automatically like or be any particular thing at all.

"You're right."

We decided we wanted to try natural childbirth. Births in our country have become overly and unnecessarily medicalized, institutionalized, and doctor-driven. We wanted an experience that

I went online and clicked on a website about natural labor and delivery. I opened a page to find several gruesome and graphic accounts of unnecessary, ultimately disfiguring episiotomies and C-sections. The pictures began to transfix me—was there no injustice women had not sustained? Who had taken these photographs? Who were these women who had allowed it?

We wanted an experience that reflected our own values, that honored our

Another dead end.

Across the street, Jessica Garbella lowered herself onto a yoga mat in her bedroom and stretched into cobra pose. I watched her for a moment. Ron had been brought here recently from New York to start a new summer theater, not that the Berkshires needed another cultural venue catering to the people who summered here. The Garbellas had bought the three-bedroom Cape from the Newtons, a couple who had moved to be closer to their college-aged kids, or more precisely the Garbellas had bought it from a builder who had flipped it. Maggie and I had gone to an open house and had gawked at the gleaming quartz counters, the black clawfoot tub in the master bathroom and the in-ground pool surrounded by Japanese silver grass and blue hydrangeas. I could taste my own envy. Jessica taught Ashtanga yoga in the back room of a food co-op. We'd had coffee once, and she had given me a 10 percent–off coupon for her yoga class. She was nice enough, but went on a little long about Ron's controlling sister and mother. She stayed in cobra pose as I watched now, going nowhere for an impressive amount of time. The Garbellas did not have children.

Motherhood changed everything. You could no longer practice yoga consistently—consistency itself was no longer a predictable thing. You could no longer get high so often or drink milk from a carton—you were a role model for someone else now. You could not blast Janis Joplin in the kitchen without causing your son to scream at the noise. Janis Joplin sounded different to a young child. She sounded awful. You could not go skinny-dipping with your tenant/partner in Goose Pond late at night unless someone was at your house, watching your kid, and even then, as the warm water held you and the sky blinked with stars and the black pines smelled of freedom, even as you moved through the dark water with this man inside of you, the man whispering how good you felt, how right this was, how your wet skin drove him crazy, your thoughts turned to your son in his bed and your elderly neighbor probably asleep on your couch and the way she coughed as if a brick were lodged in her neck and how she forgot your son's name the other day and you worried that she might die right there in your house, and then what would you do?

Later, when Kurt came home for lunch, I was glad for the chance to take a break from failing to make progress on Lana's book. He tugged me up out of my seat and we kissed for a good long while, which made me want to slide my hand inside the back of his jeans. Something stuck out of his jeans pocket there, and when I grabbed it, I saw that it was a folded map of Northern Maine.

"That's Pete's," he said, and took it from me. He leaned in again, but I had lost the mood. I saw that he had a rash on his neck, angry, raised pimples strangling him.

"You touched a raspberry bush," I told him.

"I don't think so. There were just dead trees around the carport."

"You did," I said. As a landscaper, I had spent far more time around raspberry bushes than he had. In general, I worked far more hours than he did. "Go look in the mirror. That's raspberry."

"What does it matter?"

"You should wash it off with warm water and soap. It'll get worse unless you wash it off right now." I looked over at him. "You're not really thinking about going all the way to Newfoundland, are you?"

"I don't know. It was just an idea, but a good one, right? Pete and Sandra went last summer and said it's incredible. You can see icebergs and even the Northern Lights sometimes. Want to go?"

He should have known better than to ask me such questions. "I have to go pick up Cass soon. And my mom and Ed are coming later."

Kurt shrugged. I imagined him at the edge of some cliff, gazing out over the Atlantic at chunks of white ice floating under the vast green and purple aurora borealis, some rugged and gorgeous fisherwoman at his side. I was not simply jealous of her; I wanted to *be* her—unencumbered by debt, newly beloved, somewhere exotic. "You can come out to dinner with us if you want," I said.

"I told the guys I'd shoot hoops this evening. You want me to meet up with you all afterward?"

"Maybe," I said, and then, "Don't worry about it."

My mother and Ed (technically my stepfather, but always just "Ed" to me) were about to move fourteen hundred miles south to live with her cousin in Sebastian, Florida. Lottie owned a duplex, and her longtime tenants had just moved out. Kurt had not yet met my mother or Ed, and all they knew of him was that he was subletting my basement and that Ed had not been able to find his name on the national registry of sex offenders. I could not seem to form a mental image of these three people together.

"Think you should ask Pete if you can put in a few hours at his store, you know, when you're done with Jimmy's carport?" I said.

"He's all staffed up right now. How's the latest writing project going? Better than the last one?"

"That bar is pretty low." I restrained myself from saying anything more specific. "But yeah, it's okay."

"You want me to cancel with the guys tonight?" he asked.

I looked at him.

"Maybe I should meet your mother and Ed before they move? Or no?"

"I don't, I mean—" This was our dance; neither of us initiated forward motion. Maybe we both secretly feared rejection or being alone, and at our age, there was a lot at stake. It was not easy to find someone with whom you had chemistry, someone without a debilitating addiction or an unmentioned spouse and who was not some kind of, in Nick's words, "douche nozzle." In the end, I knew that Kurt valued his newfound freedom too much to want to make any commitments, and I hated for Cass to grow attached to someone who might just up and leave us one day. "My mom and Ed can be kind of a challenge," I said.

"How long have they been together?"

"They met a year after my father's aneurysm." Kurt knew that my father had been a cabinetmaker and the three of us used to live in Brattleboro, that he had died when I was two. "We moved down to Lenox a few months later."

"That was fast."

"Yeah," I said. "I have no memories of my father."

"You don't call Ed your father?"

"No. I probably glorified my biological father when I was a kid, and Ed as 'Ed' just stuck." My father had sounded great to me. He had marched on Washington against Vietnam. He had played banjo in a bluegrass band and had volunteered regularly at a soup kitchen.

I went to throw away a wrapper that Cass had left on the floor and took stock of our place: the gunk-covered plates and bowls balanced on the counter, the plastic cups everywhere full of water that had dripped from the ceiling.

What would come of this place once my mother and Ed had moved to Florida, when they were no longer here to judge me? Also, they had been babysitting Cass most Mondays. Sometimes my mother slid me money if she could afford it—a twenty or two here and there, not a ton, but enough to make a difference at the time. What would happen when Bertie was no longer able to watch Cass—and if Kurt moved on?

I HEARD THE old Mercury Sable in the driveway. "They're here, they're here," I told Cass in a vampire-y voice, an attempt to establish a fun tone for what would likely be an un-fun evening. I play-bit his neck, but bore down harder than I had intended and Cass started to cry.

"What's wrong with him?" Ed asked as he came in. Ed was an opinionated man with a pillow face in which was buried a trace of handsomeness. An insurance adjuster, he was primarily interested in railing against high taxes and their neighbors, an artist couple who led drumming circles in their condo complex. "Is he hurt?"

"He's fine," I said.

"He doesn't look fine." The subtext: *You are the parent. Toughen him up. Get him a good father already. You have no one to blame but yourself for his behavior.*

"Everyone ready to go?" I asked.

"Maybe he just needs to eat," my mother said. "Did he nap today?"

"Off we go," I said, and guided everyone outside.

Ed drove us to Lenox, down Church Street, past the patisserie, the wine bar, the Gifted Child toy store, to a farm-to-table place called Tabitha's that a celebrity chef from New York had recently opened. The restaurant had moved in where a local bank used to be, but one would never know this. The walls inside had been stripped and covered in rough wood paneling. Everything was striking and elemental: the exposed concrete floor, the metal tables, the paintings that hung on the walls, black canvases each with a slash of blue or green paint at the center.

A hale, college-aged woman seated us at a booth beneath an industrial lamp. "My name is Serafina," she said, handing us menus attached to slabs of heavy slate. She wore a floor-length dress that resembled an abstract painting.

"Can you guys really afford this place?" I said after she left and I got a look at the prices on the menu. They had been saving and living frugally for years in order to move south.

"It's a special night," my mother said. "We don't move down to Florida every day." She ran her fingers through her mahogany-colored hair. She was a tidy, attractive, intelligent woman. She had just worked her last day at Tanglewood. Her predilections for contemporary

Japanese art and ephemeral food trends had never stopped grating on me. "Don't you have any nicer clothes?" she asked, eying my army jacket. I'd had it since college.

"No one dresses up to go out to eat anymore," I said.

"Maybe you could find a blazer or a pretty blouse. They've got some cute stuff at the outlets right now."

I reminded myself that concern was how my mother conveyed love. I was not all that different.

"How's that new preschool going?" Ed asked Cass.

"He just started. Might be too soon to tell," I said.

"Are you making lots of friends?"

"No," Cass said.

"Not even one? Sometimes it just takes one, kiddo," Ed said.

The preschool teacher had told me that on his first day, Cass had thrown sand at a little girl named Maribel and hoarded all the plastic shovels in the sandbox.

"You love the clay and the coloring," I said, and I nudged Cass to add more.

"Yeah, I like clay. I got to finger-paint. I made an elephant."

"Terrific!" my mother said. "What kind of elephant?"

"I don't know," he said.

"What was its name? Did he have a job?" she tried. I looked at her. She had no natural ability to make conversation with a four-year-old.

"What's everyone ordering?" I asked.

My mother said, "I think I'll have the quail." She had more lines around her mouth now. I would have those lines someday. I already had a few.

Cass crawled onto my lap, a tight fit in this booth, but I wrapped my arm around his chest and took in his warmth. I would miss this when he grew too big to sit on my lap, too big for me to hold and pretend to eat his hair.

He began to shake salt across the table. A man seated next to us turned to watch him.

"Cass. We don't do that." I took the salt shaker from his hand and set it back on the table.

"Do you want our bed?" my mother asked me. "Lottie's got one there. No use paying to move ours."

Their old queen-sized bed probably would not fit in my bedroom. "You should donate it to Habitat for Humanity."

"Habi-what for what?" Ed said. "The Vadhrises' son will take it if you don't want it. He's moving to Boston soon." The Vadhrises had been their neighbors for decades. The two couples had united in their frustrations with their drumming-circle neighbors.

"Cass, what are you going to have for dinner?" my mother asked.

The children's menu had two items. Thankfully one was mac 'n' Gruyère, and although I guessed that Cass might take issue with a cheese that was not heavily processed, I held out hope. "He'll have the mac n' cheese," I said. If he didn't hear the word *Gruyère*, maybe he would eat it.

"And what about some veggies?" she said to him.

"Unlikely," I said.

"Cass, when was the last time you ate your veggies? Let's see, there are green beans that were grown on a farm right down the road from here. Or cauliflower gratin or yummy roasted squash."

Cass grabbed the salt shaker again and hurled it at Ed's shoulder.

"Hey!" I said. "No throwing."

"I didn't," Cass lied, and dropped his head. Maybe he had been aiming for my mother.

Ed slammed the table with his fist. "He could have gotten me in the face."

This would be the image that they would take to Florida: Cass behaving like a pill in a nice restaurant; my responding ineffectively.

I considered giving him a time out, but where? I burst from the booth with him in tow. "Do you guys have coloring pages and crayons or anything?" I asked Serafina, who was leading a young couple between the tables.

"Yes, sorry, okay," she said, maybe more to the couple than to me. After seating them, she stood by their table and chatted for a time. The man, who looked to be in his twenties, had what might have been an ironic beard that thinned to a hairy cloud at his chest. The woman's head was shaved, and her pretty face was somehow made more so by a dark gap between her front teeth. Both wore jeans and oversized, lumpy sweaters. Maybe they were two of the farmers who provided their crops or whatever to this place, and Serafina felt that she had to dote on them. The crayons and paper never came.

The meal progressed in this way. Ed was given a ribeye instead of the swordfish he'd ordered. My mother complained that the quail had been "brutally overcooked." Ed again pressed Cass about preschool and his loser status there. I spilled my glass of lemon water across the table. Ed asked how Bertie's health was, did Cass have any friends in our neighborhood, was I dating anyone, was I subbing these days?

When our waitress asked if we would like coffee or dessert, I answered for all of us: "No."

My mother said, "Allie. You seem stressed out. Do you have any work right now?"

"It's okay to admit if things are tough," Ed said, rubbing the place on his shoulder where the salt shaker had made contact.

"I want to go home," Cass said.

"We need to wait for the check," my mother told him. "The check tells us how much we have to pay for our dinner. And then we'll pay it and sign what's called a receipt and then we can go home. What else did you paint at preschool?"

"I drew a lion."

"What kind of lion?" she asked.

"Mom," I said. "Give me a break."

"Allie," Ed barked.

Serafina brought an unlabeled bottle of wine to the farmers' table and swept her long hair behind one shoulder as she filled three glasses.

"Does your lion have lion friends and a job?" my mother said, undeterred.

"The lion is very popular. He's an architect and his favorite color is blue," I said.

"Don't take that tone," Ed said.

Cass reached for the pepper shaker and I snatched it from him. "I have a new project," I said. Tomorrow they would be gone, and I hated to leave off with them on such a sour note. I hated for them to think that I was a mediocre parent and that work had stalled out again. "A new book."

"Oh?" my mother said.

"My client is really one of the most important women in this country right now." I understood this was already too much information. They knew that I was a ghostwriter, but rarely, if ever, for whom or for what pay, despite Ed's best efforts at uncovering this information. Sometimes I gave them very vague clues about my clients, maybe more to satisfy the gnawing isolation that came with anonymity than their curiosity.

"Hillary Clinton?" my mother asked earnestly.

"She said 'important,' not 'annoying,'" Ed said, laughing.

I shot daggers at him. He did not love "the bloviator"—Ed had been hoping for Jeb Bush—but he truly despised Clinton, and I feared attitudes like his might win out in the end. Thankfully the polls had her winning. "You think someone would be writing a book for Hillary Clinton less than two months before she becomes president?" I said.

"You are in a real mood," my mother snapped.

Loud but gentle music came on, a slow, lilting classical guitar and cello likely composed with the sole intent of relaxing its listeners. Miraculously, it seemed to work on Cass. He turned his back on the salt and pepper shakers and leaned into my shoulder.

"Not that anyone asked, but I'm thinking I just won't vote this year," Ed said. "To be honest, I can't stand the sight of either one of them."

"What? You have to vote," I said.

He waved me away.

At long last, Serafina left a small wooden folder with the bill on the table.

"So what's the book about?" my mother asked.

"Mom."

"Is it really going to matter if you tell us?" she asked. "Who's going to find out?"

"It's a memoir of, well, it's about parenting." I had to change the subject. "Who did you hire to move you?"

"Adam Carmichael. Wasn't he a year or two behind you in school? He has a moving company now."

I nodded. Adam had been a coke dealer when he was sixteen. The thought of him shooting the breeze with my mother gave me pause.

Ed looked over at me. "I hope this very important woman is paying you well."

"Is it Michelle Obama?" my mother asked. "Or that lady who runs Facebook? Sounds exciting whoever it is."

"It's a good project," I said.

We rose and walked past the farmers, now enjoying a plate of shriveled mushrooms, and out of the restaurant.

The evening sky was the deep wild blue that I had only seen in Western Mass. The moon was a coral marble. I squeezed Cass's soft fingers and began to whistle, "Oh my darling, Clementine, " our bed-time song when he was a baby.

"Soon you won't have to deal with my last-minute pleas for babysitting," I said to my mother and fastened Cass into the car seat.

"Do you have anyone who can come to stay with him overnight if you have to go away? Any friends in town?" Ed asked. We'd had this conversation before.

"Bertie can. She watched him when I had to go to New York for a meeting last month."

"Anyone else?" my mother asked gently. She was well aware of Bertie's age and her waning memory.

There was Kurt, but I did not want to explain him and what he was and was not. I could hardly explain these things myself. "We'll be fine," I said.

The darkened, jagged trees sped by on our way back to Lee. The car bumped over a few small potholes as we passed Laurel Lake. A memory came to me of a trip I took with them when I was eleven, my first and last plane ride with them. The three of us had flown to Jamaica for my uncle's wedding. Uncle Nathan had dropped out of college to follow the Grateful Dead and no one heard from him for a few years, not until he called one day and told my mother that he had become a tour guide in Jamaica and was engaged to marry a tourist he had met there. We stayed near Montego Bay in one of a handful of tents in the woods across a two-lane road from a spit of beach. In the large tent where I would stay with my parents was an air mattress, a wine crate, and a plastic baggie of incense.

Nathan and Setti, his bride-to-be, organized a dinner picnic on the beach that first night. Even now, I remembered someone playing guitar and a small group of people singing about kinky reggae and Jah love. Adults danced near a crackling bonfire. Feral mutts chased each other into the low waves, and I saw a few people with dreadlocks swimming naked as the sunlight oozed purple and copper into the water.

Nathan and Setti had on all their clothes and sat together by the fire. I could not help staring at their long and tangled sun-bleached hair, their fingers or toes always touching, her crystal eyes, his dark eyelashes.

"Time for bed," my mother had said immediately after we had finished eating.

When I protested, Setti offered to keep an eye on me and walk me back to our hut soon. My mother pulled her cardigan tight around her shoulders as she and Ed headed back across the road, his arm through hers.

Setti stood and came to me. She leaned in and whisper-sang "Freedom," Richie Havens's mesmerizing incantation on the state of being a child without a mother.

She returned to Nathan and wedged herself between his knees, her back against his stomach. He reached his fingers around her face to feed her pieces of grilled breadfruit. He wiped something from her chin and she jutted forward to lick his thumb and encase it with her mouth. Laughter rose from the waves, the sky now everywhere speckled black. Someone turned on a radio. *Sugar Magnolia, blossoms blooming.* People were smoking all manner of things—I swear I saw someone raise a lighter to a pineapple—and there came the smell of sour sweat. Something was thrown into the fire and it popped and spattered in the air. *Singin' sweet songs of melodies pure and true.* I looked around and saw that I was the only child there now. Even my teenage cousins had gone. I was thrilled.

The wedding ceremony the next morning brought a small band, as well as a gangly friend of Nathan's, a recently declared Marriage Officer whom people called Stone and who wore an orange silk shirt, linen pants, and flip-flops. It brought Nathan with his long hair brushed out and girlish and a sky blue button-down shirt and a heavy beaded necklace. It brought Setti in a green-blue wrap dress, her thick, pale hair in long waves around her tanned face, a soft sheen of nude lipstick, an unwavering smile. "I do," they both said, and kissed in a way that made it seem to me they might ingest each other.

I later learned that they had only gotten married for my grandmother, who had stomach cancer and would die a month later. She had been pleading with Nathan to settle down. "If it hadn't been for her, and if Nathan hadn't met Setti," I overhead my mother say to Ed. "I mean, really, he would have already knocked up every girl you see here."

At the beach reception, a skinned, glistening goat hung on a pole. Young girls, a few with long, pretty dreadlocks, slow-danced in imitation of grown-ups. My mother and Ed remained seated at the table until someone pulled them toward the band. I watched them dance politely, and watched Nathan and Setti dancing, too, chest to chest, crotch to crotch, and then, only three songs in, they were gone. Back at the table, my mother said, "Why didn't they just elope?"

I decided that when I grew up, I would live like Nathan and Setti. I would not become my mother—tired, muted, and resentful. I would not marry anyone like Ed—judgmental, moody. I might not marry at all.

Soon after we returned home to Lenox, I stopped brushing my hair in order to try to form dreadlocks. I insisted that my mother buy papaya and coconuts at the grocery store. At dinner one night, I told my mother and Ed that from then on, I would only answer to the name Marley. "Bob Marley was a Rasta reggae singer. Setti told me about him. She said he believed we are all holy and that people just need to relax and not worry so much about money and what everyone thinks of you, Mom."

Ed let forth a slow leak of air from his mouth and said, "Ho, boy."

My mother had reheated leftover meatloaf. Dinner as an only child with them had always been a quiet, utilitarian affair.

My mother said, "Meat okay?"

"Meat's good, Lauren," Ed replied.

"That's all you have to say?" I asked. I thought of the dinners at my friends' houses, when their brothers and sisters tussled with each other and slipped bits of food to family dogs. I thought of all the complaints, puns, jokes, the adults swapping double entendres, the kids pleading for dessert. "Why didn't you two ever have any kids? I mean together."

My mother looked at me. "Our family is just fine the way it is."

"It's not a family. It's a few people."

"Don't say that," she said in a hurt tone.

"I can't help it," I said. Jamaica was so far away. I had no idea when or even if we would ever go back. "I wish I had a brother or sister."

"I'm sorry, but that is not going to happen, Allie," my mother said, drizzling additional salad dressing on her lettuce.

"*Marley*," I said.

"You're not black, you know."

I wanted to object, but how?

The rest of the meal passed without a word. "You can clear your plate if you're done and start the dishes," my mother said.

"I don't want to. I don't want to wash the dishes tonight. I don't want to wash dishes ever again."

"Pardon me?" my mother said.

I rushed into the kitchen, grabbed a sleeve of Saltines, and headed out the back door. I thought I would spend the night in the woods at the end of our street and hatch a plan to leave these two polite adults and this tidy, passionless house, and even return to Jamaica. I would somehow, in some way, become Nathan and Setti's child. I moved swiftly past the other townhomes and cars.

After a short while, my mother found me sitting in a patch of ferns. "Come on, Allie—I mean, Marley. You know, I wouldn't call myself that at school. You might offend some other kids."

"You offend *me* by being so conformist," I said, full of assurance and ignorance.

She rolled her eyes. "Honey. I'm tired and I have to make a few phone calls and then I want to go to bed."

"You have to call your *friends*?" She had a small group of well-off summer friends, administrators or volunteers at Tanglewood who spoke daily on the phone about their husbands and each other, and it incensed me. I still cannot say why. She herself worked in the gift shop at Tanglewood, as well as for a local caterer. "You never answered me. Why don't you have more kids?"

"I'll be inside when you are ready to behave again."

"That's going to be a LONG time because the last thing I want to do is behave like some prissy little doll for you."

"I don't think anyone's worried about that happening."

"Cunt." It was the worst word I knew. I had overheard my babysitter speak it once to another girl on the street, a real snot of a girl who went limp at the sound of it.

"What just came out of your mouth? You do not use that filthy language. My *daughter* does not say things like that."

"I do now," I said, maybe glad to see any light go on inside her.

"You really want to know why you don't have a brother or a sister? Ed can't. Edward is unable to have children. You happy?"

I swallowed. "Then why did you marry him?" I was not ready to admit defeat.

"Because I loved him," she said.

"Fine," I snapped, but a part of me wondered if what she loved most was his ability to keep us housed and fed.

"Listen, Allie. You need to start calling that man your father. He's not going anywhere. I married him almost eight years ago. He is your father now. You hurt his feelings, still calling him 'Ed.'" She did not wait for a reply before turning and storming back home.

I was furious. Why did she not care about the feelings of her own child, or betraying my real father? The man inside would remain "Ed" to me long after it would have been more natural to call him "Dad"— and of course, I would remain Allie to them. Even now, my eleven-year-old's obstinance remained surprisingly accessible in their presence.

WHEN ED PULLED the car into my driveway, I saw the basement light cast a small stripe on the side lawn. Kurt had returned, and I was glad not to come home to an empty house.

We stepped out of the car and as I scooped an almost sleeping boy into my arms, I said to my mother, "I guess this is when we say goodbye."

"I'll miss him," she said and reached for Cass's head. "I'll miss you both. Go, get him to bed."

Ed stepped forward. "We'll talk." He engulfed us in a hug.

"This isn't goodbye," my mother said.

"It isn't?"

She licked the pad of her thumb and wiped something from Cass's face.

The two made their way back inside the car, these people now in their seventies, these medium-sized, careful, essentially kind people who had raised me, who had loved me and Cass the best that they could, these people who were now closing the car doors and driving away.

CHAPTER FOUR

I sent Lana a draft of the first chapter. I had filled the pages with data about the disproportionate physical, psychological, and economic impacts of pregnancy and childbirth on women versus men. Childbirth was of course an overwhelming prospect for any woman, so I tried to infuse the chapter with hope for an experience free of dogma and guilt. I included a quote from the writer Elizabeth Noble: "However much we know about birth in general, we know nothing about a particular birth. We must let it unfold with its own uniqueness." And I closed on a note that I hoped communicated wonder:

> We carried our new son into our home for the first time— and only then did this massive endeavor come into focus for me. We had created Norton Breban-Harding and brought him into the world, but now we had to lead him through it. We had to teach him how to eat and sleep, how to sit and crawl, how to be kind and respectful, how to navigate this patriarchal American society and resist getting co-opted by the patriarchy, no matter its appeal. No matter how it would punish him for resisting, or

how it would reward him for conforming again and again. But for now, Norton was just a baby asleep in his bucket seat and we were just two new parents. I set him down, and went to Lester.

Conjuring their experience had been a challenge, and not only because Lana had told me so little. From pee stick to ultrasound to the various discomforts, indignities, and joys of pregnancy throughout the onset of labor with Cass, I had been alone. I had hoped for a natural birth, but at the hospital I had quickly folded in the face of eviscerating labor pain. When I first carried Cass inside my house, Ed, who had borrowed a friend's video camera, yelled, "Hold on! Don't move. The goddamn lens cap won't come off. Christ almighty. Okay, now go back outside and bring him in again." I did, and this time, the record button was stuck. "Ed! Jesus, Ed," my mother said when he realized the batteries had died. In the time that it took to get his camera working, a bolt of pain shot through the scar across my abdomen, Cass grew unbearably heavy, and I crumpled to the floor. Thankfully my mother was able to catch him before he hit his head. This was the only moment of Cass's entry into the world that had been caught on camera.

How different it might have been if I'd had a partner or the psychic energy to pontificate about my son's role in the world of boys and men after returning home, where unlimited help awaited us.

I was proud of none of my self-pitying thoughts. If nothing else, I was at least used to envy and self-pity. I had been a ghostwriter long enough to know that I had to elbow past these things in order to get the job done.

Unfortunately, I had been unable to think of a way to feminize or Americanize Lana's first chapter. Was I supposed to provide recommendations for makeup that would not run beneath the sweat of labor? Describe how to keep from moaning while pushing the equivalent of a bag of potatoes from one's embattled birth canal? Integrate a love of country into the whole thing—write her, what, pledging allegiance as she held her new son? I had done the best that I could with so little.

In the days that followed, I googled Lana in order to learn what she was doing other than reading the chapter and responding to me. She spoke in Chicago at a summit of CEOs about gender balance in the workplace, and at Wellesley College and MIT. Apparently she had also spent some time in a salon. I was saddened to see that, in the footage of her in Chicago, her signature blue hair was now a flat, dark brown.

The next day in Washington, D.C., she introduced the president of NARAL at a fundraising luncheon. My mother would have been so impressed; she leaned more left than Ed, and had once attended a NARAL fundraiser with a group from Tanglewood. I set up a Google Alert that would notify me each new time Lana's name appeared online.

I began *To the Lighthouse* once again. "'Yes, of course, if it's fine tomorrow,' said Mrs. Ramsay. 'But you'll have to be up with the lark,' she added." I read slowly, letting myself float along the pleasant ambiguity, the absence of a linear plot and consistent narrator. I had always found reading Virginia to be a good exercise in mindfulness.

A WEEK PASSED.

In addition to Connor, Maggie had a younger son, Liam, who was Cass's age, and although there was little chemistry between the two boys—not that we had ever openly discussed this—we decided to meet up at a playground that Monday. Liam raced around with some other kids, swinging easily from rung to rung on the monkey bars, striding up the long metal slides, climbing to the top of every structure. Cass remained in the sandbox, building a kind of fortress around a toy bulldozer.

"I'm sorry he's not interacting with Liam more," I said.

"Don't be! We can never get Liam to stay in one place. He's an animal." Fifteen years younger than I, Maggie had waist-length red hair, and today she wore a Bohemian wool wrap atop black leggings. She wandered over to talk to the mother of two older boys who were now, alongside Liam, chasing a squirrel in a nearby field.

Thirteen days had now passed since I had sent Lana that first chapter. I began to worry that she had in fact read it and hated it. I imagine that for most writers, the time spent awaiting the first reactions to a new piece is filled with anxiety. But when a ghostwriter anticipates the first reaction of a client, she awaits answers to different questions: "Did I sound enough like you? Did I portray you as you wished?" Or in the case of Lana's book, "Did I guess right? *Did* you in fact give birth in a hospital?"

One of Liam's new friends was now in the sandbox with Cass and looked ready to demolish his fortress. Cass appeared terrified. "Hey!" I yelled over. The ruddy, rabbit-faced boy lifted his sneakered foot and in less than five seconds, stomped out the entire thing. I knew what was coming, and it did: Cass burst into tears. "Hey!" I called again and marched over to them. "Cass, it's okay, you can build another one."

My son made a weird sound, a cross between a hiccup and a sob.

The boy, who had to be about nine or ten, began to snicker into his palm. He had feathery, unruly eyebrows.

"You want to tell me what your problem is? Where's your mother? Where's your grown-up?" I added, remembering the correct term.

He shrugged and kicked a bunch of sand onto Cass.

"Quit it," I said, but he just stood there, smirking down at Cass, who was now whimpering and picking sand from his hair. I looked the mean boy in the eyes. "You feel big and tough now? You want to go terrorize more innocent squirrels, you little turd?"

Maggie approached us. "Allie, he's just playing."

Cass stepped out of the sandbox and moved beside me. "We don't have to tolerate this sort of playing, do we?" I said.

"I think we kind of do. They're boys. They like to destroy things."

"Not all of them," I said. I brushed the rest of the sand from Cass's shoulders.

"That is true. And thank god, right? We need at least a few to be kind so they can grow up and become artists and doctors and—" Her voice trailed off. We watched Liam and the mean boy begin to joust with large sticks. "Liam can turn literally anything into a weapon. The other day, he and Connor stuck some of those corncob holders into the tops of our pool noodles. Then they loaded up their Nerf guns with pebbles and almost murdered each other. Liam's left butt-cheek is totally black and blue right now. I'm so proud," she said.

Although I knew she meant her last comment sarcastically, there *was* a hint of pride in her voice. After all, as she herself had said, this sort of thing was not abnormal, and for most parents, myself not always excluded, normalcy was a kind of holy grail.

THUNDEROUS POUNDING AT the front door shook my house. I had just come out of an icy shower and I scurried, naked and swearing, around my bedroom, searching for clean clothes. The pounding continued. I pulled on a T-shirt and pajama bottoms.

Jimmy Pryor stood in an unzipped raincoat and too-small Patriots shirt on my front stoop, the rain soaking the world behind him. "Where's Kurt? He told me he'd start painting my shed today. It's nine fifteen. Don't either of you work? You know it's a freaking weekday?" His Boston accent mashed down his consonants.

"It's pouring out there." I ushered Jimmy into the front hall and shut the door behind him.

"He can work on the inside of it," Jimmy said. Drops of rain ran down his face.

"He's painting the inside of your old tool shed?"

"You want to hand over the rest of this month's rent, Al?"

I had finally gotten my first payment for Lana's book. After Colin had taken his cut and I set aside a chunk for taxes, after I paid for a new fridge for Bertie—given how little I paid her to watch Cass, it was the least I could do once hers broke—and everything else that I owed, it was far more prudent for Kurt to work off half the rent than for me to pay it outright. But now, Jimmy Pryor—who watched dogfights on YouTube and blew God knows how much of his tenants' rent money on regular trips to some casino in Schenectady—had gained dominion over my life. Why had I let this happen?

"I'll go wake Kurt," I said at last. "I'll send him over when he's ready."

"Trashman left your box on my lawn again," he said.

"*Bin*," I said. "It's a recycling *bin*." Cass had come up and was hiding behind my legs.

"Call the town. How many times do I have to ask you? Register a freaking complaint." Jimmy reached forward and tweaked Cass's shoulder.

"When's he going to leave?" Cass asked. "I want breakfast. I'm *star*-ving."

"Don't be a girl," Jimmy told him.

"Hey. Don't say that," I snapped.

"Why not?" He screwed up his face at me. "You tell Kurt I came."

Cass and I watched Jimmy move through the downpour across my front yard, a sway on one side of his body and his arm that swung low on the other to compensate. Jimmy lived alone with Bruin, who now required daily insulin shots. This was about the fourth time over the years that he had agreed to barter for rent. It was difficult, though not impossible, to stay angry with him.

"Why did he call me a girl?" Cass said.

"Because girls are wonderful." I kissed his head, glad for my ready response. "Let's go get you something to eat."

I checked my email as he ate. At long last, Lana had gotten back to me.

I have to admit that I like having a professional write for me. I would not call myself a natural writer. It can be hard work!

Nice job with the first chapter. I do wonder about the passive tone—esp. that Elizabeth Noble quote. As I'm sure you know, a basic tenet of feminism is agency—becoming the person to make the biggest decisions about your own life and wresting that control from the patriarchy. So much about our medical establishment is patriarchal.

Please also address the big business of infertility. And I'd love you to discuss the history of medicalization of birth—this topic should be a gold mine. You might more assertively promote at-home birth, natural childbirth. And I think there could be more focus on midwives, doulas, birth plans. Birth plans are key to maintaining control, power, etc.

Could you write something about how birth can actually be empowering, to make it more upbeat and readable? Don't some women even reach orgasm when they deliver?

I resisted the urge to reply that I had done the best I could with the nothing that she had provided me. That my mandate was to make her seem more relatable, not more academic. That climaxing while delivering a baby seemed about as likely to me as singing opera while drowning, although a hat tip to any woman who was granted the experience. That no one I knew would describe childbirth as "upbeat."

My hands hovered over my keyboard.

Per the advice of my doctor, I labored at home for four hellish hours. After I managed to drive myself to Berkshire Medical, I curled up on the floor of the waiting room and screamed through the next contraction. Someone who worked there came over, and I begged her for an epidural, but she did not or could not find an anesthesiologist. I handed her my birth plan and never saw her again. I was wheeled into a room, and realized I had forgotten to bring my MP3 player that I had loaded up with relaxing but empowering songs. When I showed the nurse the lavender and the diffuser I had brought to help calm me, she just nodded as she ran out of the room to help someone else. She came back, though, and rubbed my back a little and told me the detailed story of how she had given birth on the floor of a ferry en route to Block Island. I told her to go find the anesthesiologist—I needed an epidural or I would die. My mother and Ed appeared in the doorway. My body felt as if it would split in half. It took forty minutes for the man to come—forty minutes of burning, searing pain and my parents snapping at each other to do something, anything, while trying unsuccessfully to find a nurse who would page a doctor and my telling them all repeatedly to go to hell. Eventually it was decided that Cass was too big and I too small to provide safe passage, so I was taken to an OR and had a C-section and passed out and did not meet Cass until someone roused me maybe fifteen minutes later. Most of the experience felt like warfare. Most of the time, I did not entertain one thought about trying to wrest control—if I had any thoughts at all, they were about survival.

Kurt was now puttering by the kitchen sink. "You almost ready?" he asked.

What was I doing, writing this? "Yeah," I said. I had promised Kurt—non-owner of a car—a ride into town this morning, and Cass was due at preschool soon. "Jimmy came by to see if you're going to work on his shed today."

"But it's pouring out there."

"Yeah, well, he wants you to paint the inside of it," I said.

"Are you kidding? If that isn't busywork."

"I know," I said, my eyes on my laptop. "But I guess it's also rent money."

"I'm aware of that."

My phone rang. My mother. "I only have a minute," I said.

"I have a new one-upper story for you." My mother had told me all about Patty Copeland the last time we spoke. Apparently "the one-up-per" talked incessantly about her family. Patty had twelve grandkids, more than anyone else in their condo complex, and this was a sym-bol of status, I guess. "Remember my friend Louise? She moved down here about a year ago?" She went on to detail a spat between Patty and Louise.

Kurt gestured to his watch. Cass had to be at preschool in five minutes.

I held up a finger—*one more minute*—and he led Cass toward the door. "Mom, I have to go. Can I call you later, after I get some work done?"

"On your book for that important woman? I know you can't tell me outright, but maybe you can just say something like, 'I cannot confirm or deny it,' if I'm right. Is it Meryl Streep? You know that I've seen every one of her movies?"

"I'll call you later."

I ran to the truck, but I still ended up drenched from the downpour, sidling in next to Kurt. I turned the key and Charlie Barleycorn came on and Cass began to sing along: *Sing it now, sing it wow, black and brown together, pow! In the land of Canada, I have friends from Africa!*

As I drove, I wished that I could I tell Kurt or even my mother about Lana giving me almost no material for her book. I had no colleagues, no comrades in the trenches. As I drove, I catalogued all the subjects that I had kept encased in silence over the years: the identities of my clients; my vacillating but often alarming levels of debt; from my parents, my relationship with Kurt and my fears of being an inadequate mother; my infrequent if consistent enjoyment of marijuana; my worry that working alone and being a single parent was turning me into a narcissist. If it were possible to x-ray my anxieties, my interior would have appeared as an opaque mass.

In the narrow parking lot outside Little Rainbows, Cass stalled by asking to hear one more Charlie Barleycorn song. A couple of mothers trudged through the rain carrying babies, lunchboxes, backpacks, jackets, boots, diaper bags, and their tiny daughters in tow. Some women's ability to multitask was astonishing.

The director, a pious woman in her sixties with cropped gray hair, stood at the front door and waved at us. I reached back and pushed open Cass's door. "Cass, Sweetheart," she called. "Hello! It's off to work we go, right? Come help me set up for circle time!" She wore a lilac-colored corduroy jumper and her signature rabbit slippers. Susan Ferrell was her name, but the kids called her Suze. She had the ability to put me completely at ease just by standing before me. I knew not to stay and make sure that Cass settled in. Suze had taught me this: my presence only made him more anxious.

I had wanted to send Cass to the Montessori preschool two streets over from our house, the small, red colonial where children climbed mulberry trees and sat criss-cross-applesauce next to a vegetable garden. I thought a small, individualized program might be better for a more creative kid like Cass. He and I went for a tour one day, and I took note of the low tables that held thematically organized tools and art supplies and maps. The ten children quietly moved from activity to activity whenever they felt they must. Afterward, we followed the director to her office and talked a bit, and I inquired about the tuition. When she told me the number, I said we would be in touch and marched Cass right back home. I ended up enrolling him at the cloyingly—and inaccurately—named Little Rainbows, part preschool, part daycare, all white children, a sprawling room in the basement of a Methodist church in town. The children ran amok at Little Rainbows with just an occasional organized activity. I had thought Cass would like the relaxed spirit of the place, but so far, he had found it a mixed bag. He did enjoy the arts and crafts, and Suze herself, but not so much Barton Haller, the kid who wiped his hands all over the walls after peeing or, in Cass's words, the "footy, farty" smell of the Cheez-Its Suze gave them. So we bumbled forward, me hoping that Cass would grow to like Little Rainbows, and that Bertie would continue to watch him for criminally low pay the rest of the time I had to work.

I pulled up to Pete's store. Kurt got out, but I stayed in the car and saw a blond guy that I recognized from my high school walk in after him: Sean Strum, or Strummy as he was called back in the day, had been on my bus and had been the first child that I heard swear and use horribly sexist slurs. His presence used to feel like a loaded gun to me. I had not known that he still lived here.

Beside the store, a stray dog squatted and released a heap of shit, then trotted off.

I was not supposed to still be here. After Dartmouth, I had imagined finding a great job writing under my own name, moving somewhere like Paris or Barcelona, traveling, learning to scuba dive and play guitar. I would meet some foreign writer, have a kid or two. Then, when Cass was a baby, I daydreamed about the two of us living near the ocean. He would spend his childhood digging around in the sand and playing in the surf, learning to ride the waves, and maybe later he would catch fish and snorkel. I envisioned a close group of smart, witty, artistic friends who also had kids. Some of these friends would be single like me. We would all own small beach houses near each other and the kids would travel in a pack, in and out of our homes and around the beach, the older kids minding the younger ones, the adults taking turns overseeing the group when needed, and in this way, we would raise each other's children when they were not raising themselves. We would have lives outside parenthood. We would have balance.

And then Ed had had a heart attack on my seven-year-anniversary at the equity firm in New York, and I had left my job and moved back home to help my mother. We were told that he might not make it, and I knew that she would need all kinds of help if he did not.

This was about ten years ago, and every now and then I contin-ued to research different places for Cass and me to live. With each year of motherhood that passed, though, moving came to seem more complicated and unlikely. Still, I sure as hell did not want to stay put forever in the same town where I had grown up, where I ran into for-mer classmates, a few who were now struggling to find work—like me sometimes—or tragically hooked on painkillers, most who spoke to me with disdain, as if I thought I was too good for them. If any of them had asked me and Cass to get together, I would have said yes. Not to Strummy, of course, but yes to most of the others. I really could have used more friends.

Kurt hefted three cans of Benjamin Moore paint into the bed of the truck and climbed back up beside me. I brushed the raindrops from his face and saw that the rash on his neck had mostly disappeared.

"I picked up a can of white that was on sale," he said. "I figured I could plaster up the ceiling in your hall and then paint it. Maybe this will earn a few brownie points with Jimmy." He set a hand on mine.

"Thanks, Kurt." I felt gratitude, almost choked with gratitude, for him. "That'd be great."

"And I'll ask if he has other work for me. Maybe I can cover half of November's rent."

"That would be a huge help," I said. "You know that Benjamin Moore is one of the pricier brands, right?"

"Jimmy thinks the cheaper stuff won't last. I went through this with his carport. His old, makeshift, half-rotted carport." Kurt raked his fingers through his hair that had grown almost to his shoulders by now. "This work—this life here was supposed to be soul-enforcing."

"Yeah." I could not remember the last time I had used the word *soul*.

I reminded myself that, for over a decade, Kurt had worked eighty-plus-hour weeks managing a stable of demanding clients while married to a gruff, two-timing Danish woman. He was still in recovery.

The cab of the truck smelled of soil, an odor I had come to like. It was dry and cozy in there, and we sailed through the rain. I felt the satisfying splashes whenever the tires cut through deep puddles.

He said, "Let's get pizza and watch *The Muppet Movie* with Cass later. He's never seen *The Muppets*, has he?"

I shook my head.

"And after he goes to bed, you and me?"

"Deal." I smiled over at him and pictured the day ahead, Kurt out painting Jimmy's shed, me holed up in my kitchen sipping a mug of coffee as I forged ahead on Lana's book.

Back at home, I opened my laptop to see my earlier rant about Cass's birth. I reread it, selected the whole passage on the screen, and clicked "delete."

CHAPTER FIVE

S ometimes I kept the radio tuned to the news in the kitchen. This is how I first heard the *Access Hollywood* tape, while playing Go Fish with Cass: "When you're a star, they let you do it. You can do anything. Grab them by the pussy. You can do anything."

"What's wrong?" Cass said to me.

I hoped he had not heard the radio in that moment, or if he had, that he was too young to understand. "I don't—nothing. I'm fine," I managed, my face hot, and I rose to turn off the radio. "Go fish."

That afternoon, I happened to see Strummy again at a gas station. The sight of the mudflaps on his old Ram pickup, those naked girl silhouettes that I had seen plenty of times before, made me recoil now. At Price Chopper, I eyed every other person that I passed. Had they heard the tape yet? The cashier, an older man, winked and kept his fingers on mine as he handed me the receipt. I jerked my arm away and hightailed it out of the store. What had always seemed like a persistent virus now resembled a cancer.

I ADDED TO Lana's first chapter a discussion of infertility and the medical establishment's pigheaded insistence on "fixing" the woman's body, despite the fact that 30 percent of fertility issues could be traced to the male partner. I wrote:

> We women are our own best advocates. We know our bodies better than anyone else. We are the ones to give birth—not our doctors, not our anesthesiologists, not our partners. My birth plan allowed me to create my own experience, and to exert a measure of control during a time that can feel chaotic at best. We must each be the author of our own story.

I sent it to Lana, and hearing nothing back, I wrote her a few days later to confirm that she had received the pages.

Yes, thanks, she finally replied. *Will take a look when I can.*

Google Alert kept me posted on her comings and goings. She was the keynote speaker at a fundraiser in Miami for Emily's List. She engaged in a Twitter war with an outspoken Texas congressman. She spoke at a Planned Parenthood luncheon in Seattle, and a snippet of the event circulated on social media, this footage of her recapping the beginnings of the movement for birth control one hundred years ago: "A young pregnant woman named Sadie Sachs, who already had three children and did not have the money for a fourth, gave herself an abortion. Her children were the ones who found her passed out in her own blood. When Margaret Sanger met Sadie, she said, 'I was resolved to seek out the root of evil, to do something to change the destiny of mothers whose miseries were vast as the sky.' 'As vast as the sky,'" Lana repeated, and set both of her hands on her heart. I saw that, without realizing it, I had just done the same. Her eyeglasses had been replaced by contact lenses, and as she went on, she blinked constantly. "We cannot wait for men to do something to make the lives of women better. We must act now to starve the roots of evil. They grow deeper and stronger every day. Each person here must act. Every one of us has to vote in every election. We have to teach our daughters to do the same."

What an enormous gift, I thought, to be writing for this particular person right now.

A couple of days later, she published an op-ed about the big business of treating infertility and in the first paragraph, utilized my phrase "the medical establishment's pigheaded insistence on 'fixing' only the woman's body." The rest of the piece was a barely tweaked version of what I had sent her for her book, and she closed with this: "We women are our own best advocates. We must each be the author of our own story."

I clicked out of the *New York Times* website, with thoughts of dashing off a passive-aggressive email to her congratulating her on such a well-thought-out and well-written op-ed. But I was just going to have to pretend I had never read the piece, and continue to await her response. At this rate, I would be lucky to finish Lana's book by the time Cass started elementary school.

"COME ON, LET'S you and me go find a bear," I said to Cass on our way home from Bertie's late one afternoon. *We're Going on a Bear Hunt* was his latest favorite book. We found some sticks by the new stone birdbath at the end of the Myerses' driveway and there we were, armed and marching around, ready for anything. Cass suggested that we think more about how to protect ourselves. "We need a plan," he said. "A bear can be anywhere. Those people in the book should have come up with a plan." The characters in the story encountered all sorts of difficult terrain and weather, although in the end, only one bear.

We ran behind Bruin's plastic log cabin doghouse, crossed the street and passed the Scannellos' wildflower garden and the Myerses' driveway. We debated whether it was best to freeze like statues or fight or run away in the face of a grizzly. A dog barked and a car screeched in the distance.

"I'm scared," Cass said.

"That was just a dog and a car."

We crouched behind a row of dried-out rhododendrons.

"What if it wasn't? Maybe it was a bear." He looked terrified.

I imagined him saying things like this when he was a little older, and I imagined other boys—and girls—mocking him. "This is just make-believe. Try not to be scared. Try to be brave," I said.

"How?"

"Pretend. I do it all the time," I said.

Maggie drove by, and when she saw us, she pulled over and got out. "What are you guys doing behind that bush?" she asked.

"Hiding from bears," I said, winking.

"*Oh*, I see. Good idea. There are bears everywhere in this town."

I motioned for her to say no more.

"Do you two want to come over for dinner?" she said. "Kurt's welcome to come, too. Liam's having some friends over and Brian's making quesadillas."

Although I liked the idea of sitting around with Maggie in her pretty ceramic- and South-American-textile-filled living room, sipping a drink while Brian made dinner and the kids ran off and played, I knew that this latter part was unlikely, given Cass and Liam's experience at the playground. Brian loved nothing more than the Celtics and cigars, and had little in common with Kurt. The only time they had met, the two had gotten into a charged debate about gun control. "Thanks," I said, thinking fast. "Let me check with Kurt?"

A door slammed somewhere and Cass grabbed my leg.

"Come on," I said. I took his hand and we ran behind a big oak, a grand, old sprawling thing that poured above us like a cloud. "We're safe now."

"I'm really scared." His voice wavered.

"Cass, listen, there aren't really any bears in Western Mass," I lied.

I set my hands on his shoulders and started to sing "Rock Around the Clock," a song he liked.

Maggie, who had a terrific voice, joined in. She taught music at the middle school where I sometimes subbed, and the students adored her. Then we all danced around the bush, picking dead dandelions and blowing their fluff into the air. I did savor the moments when another adult helped me parent.

Cass gazed kindly over at me. I made an air kiss.

"Who's my dad?" he asked.

It was as if a record had scratched and stopped.

"Oh." A parent could never, not for one moment, rest. I reached for a plate-sized leaf on the ground and crinkled it in my hand.

"I should head home and help Brian with dinner," Maggie said, taking Cass's cue. "Let me know if you guys are coming?"

"Will do." I watched her head back to her car, and led Cass over to our front yard. "Remember I told you about that man who came to see us once when you were a baby?" My spiel thus far had been: *Your mom and dad met nine months before you were born. We loved each other for a moment and then decided that we would always love you, but that we could not live together if we wanted to be happy. The end.*

Cass jammed the toe of one of his faded Keds into a tree root.

"Your father lives in Chicago now. He's a very nice man. We met nine months before you were—"

"Why can't boys have babies? What if a boy *wants* to have a baby?"

"If they really want to, I mean, there might be ways now."

"What's my father's name?"

"Daniel," I said, the name bulky in my mouth. I had googled him several times over the years, but could only find a few brief mentions of his small advertising agency. "Daniel Sikdar. I'll tell you anything else you want to know."

"Is he ever going to come back?"

"That, I don't know," I said. And then I lost my nerve. "But maybe we can go meet him one day."

"When?"

"Hey, how about we go to McDonald's for dinner tonight instead of Liam's house?"

He nodded enthusiastically.

I RARELY IF ever spoke of Daniel to anyone.

He had been spending a summer in the Berkshires when we met. Initially, I thought he was years older than he was. I myself was thirty-seven and had been hired to landscape his grandparents' rental house, a Queen Anne–style with a jaw-dropping view of the Berkshires.

I first noticed him lying in the sun on the back grass, reading *A Death in the Family.* He had a shaved head and wore wire-rim glasses, running shorts, and no shirt. We peered over at each other, me high up on my ladder by the top of the pergola trying to brush Japanese wisteria vines out of my face, him supine on a canvas beach lounger, and I thought that he was handsome, objectively handsome. He had a nice chest, smooth and fit. Embarrassingly, his smile made me blush. When I stepped down off the ladder and went for my lunch, I nodded over at him.

He said, "Hey."

The thought of sex presented itself. I had never before and have not since had this particular experience.

I went to sit on a hammock nearby. I peeled back the Saran Wrap on my cheese sandwich and saw that he was watching me. How to proceed? It was a cloudless day in July and I had not had sex in over a year. He set down his book and removed his glasses. There was a tingling in my stomach, and I could not manage to eat my sandwich, although I did try. He finally stood and approached, and then we were on each other right there beside the hammock between the elms. "Your parents aren't here?" I pulled away to ask, and he shook his head and I looked up at this face, his kind eyes, his deep dimples. We kissed and kissed with real force, and I let my hand explore his naked chest, and he lifted off my grubby tank top and jean shorts and his own running shorts.

"Do you have a rubber?" I whispered into his ear. A grackle above us made a chipping sound.

"No, sorry. Should we stop?"

"No," I said because, frankly, I was about to come. It made all the sense in the world in that moment and in the moment afterward.

We held each other and caught our breath, and I had the thought that the best sex I'd ever had was free from the bounds of long-term relationships. A woolly bear caterpillar crawled across my abdomen and he picked it off and set it with great care on the grass. I ran my fingers over the rise of his bicep.

I told him that I had promised to finish this job by the end of the week and should probably get back to work, and once I did, we kept looking over at each other, grinning and shaking our heads. Just how old was he? What was his name? What if I got pregnant? I was lucky that I had never gotten pregnant before, despite stupidly neglecting birth control a few times. I thought of friends my age currently struggling with infertility—and what about disease? Anyway, it was too late to undo what was already done.

He was there the next morning, this time with a picnic blanket to lay beneath us and protection, which broke at one point, bringing an end to things that day.

When I finished the landscaping, we said goodbye, awkwardly wishing each other good Augusts. A number of months later, I learned that I was pregnant. There came dumb shock and momentary excitement and confusion. I tracked him down, this person—this college senior,

Lord help me. I had guessed him to be in his later twenties; he would soon admit that he had guessed the same of me. I wrote him a letter—I suppose I felt that an email was too casual for the occasion—informing him what had happened, and I told him that I expected nothing from him. I had decided to keep the baby. There was no need to explain my reasons, although I did; I was not so young anymore—who knew if I would get another chance at this? I gravitated to children—I confessed that I understood them, sometimes more than adults. And I wanted the experience of being a mother; I had in fact begun looking into the grueling and exorbitant processes of freezing my eggs and adoption. So this was serendipity. I said that I felt up to the challenge of raising a child on my own. I felt more than up to it; I was elated.

Daniel corresponded tentatively. "If my parents or grandparents knew about this, they would disown me four times over. This is your decision and I respect it, but if you change your mind, I will support you. Either way, please let me know how you would like me to continue." Occasionally I thought back to this note, wistfully wondering if by "support" he meant something more than emotional reinforcement.

I reassured him that I had made up my mind. He wrote back that he felt reassured. He asked me if I wanted or needed anything at all, and I answered that I only wished to learn more about him so that I would know what to expect from this baby as it grew. We continued to trade letters; he told me that he did not believe in email, that handwriting was a "dying art" and that he enjoyed receiving something other than bills in his mailbox, and I was charmed. We told one another all about our lives and families. His grandparents were from Guwahati, a city in Assam, and came to visit his family about every five years. Daniel's father had come from India to attend Yale, where he had met Daniel's mother, whose own parents had immigrated to Toronto from West

Bengal before she was born. Both of Daniel's parents were lawyers, and they had raised Daniel in a strict but loving home. They had taught him the basic facts about the Vedas, the Upanishads, the sacraments called the Samskaras, although they never joined a Hindu temple or burned incense. ("Mom thinks sandalwood smells like rot.") Daniel had grown up in Greenwich, Connecticut. He was allergic to tree nuts and was not a fan of spicy food, although he did like his grandfather's catfish curry. He had a brother named Michael, and Daniel himself was a business major at Ithaca College. He had at one point considered changing majors to political science in case he ever wanted to apply to law school, but the course load had been too much. He had never had a girlfriend. He had recently discovered Ayn Rand. He rode a moped. He had recently bought a new dresser. After a while, I had no idea how to respond to his revelations.

I came to think of him as a sperm donor, a lovely, gentle, curious, free sperm donor.

The pregnancy was mostly and blessedly uneventful, and I grew so used to people like my ob-gyn nosing around for information about the father of my baby that their questions no longer bothered me. Each time, I obfuscated and quickly changed the subject.

As Cass's birth approached, Daniel admitted he was overwhelmed by the thought that he was to become a father, and I told him that I did not expect him to come to the birth—I could not imagine him at something so personal and raw, and I did not expect him to visit us afterward if he did not want to. I felt increasingly guilty. Had I used him? Was I discarding him? And what about the baby, who deserved a father?

Around the time that Cass had begun to sit up unassisted, Daniel did come to see us once. He appeared so young in his pale yellow button-down and khakis, his black hair, now grown out, combed in a razor-straight part. I watched him take in my small living room that looked as if a large gang of babies, not just one, had set up camp. I had meant to clean up before he came, but between tending to Cass, writing Jenna Rose's book and subbing, I had been flat out. Daniel held a small gift wrapped in paper that I recognized as being from the Gifted Child in Lenox. He stared over at Cass, who was seated on a towel, busily sucking a spoon. Cass looked far more like Daniel than me, and I could see him taking in this fact. "That's him?" he asked.

I overcompensated for his obvious unease by blathering on about what Cass ate and how he slept and cooing in Cass's ear in an attempt to make him respond to this man, to at the very least acknowledge him. "You want to come say hello?" I asked Daniel.

"Sure," he said. He stepped toward the center of the room and knelt down. "Hi there." For all I knew, he had never met a baby before.

Cass turned his head the other way to face the wall.

"Let's open the gift you brought," I suggested to Daniel.

We helped Cass tear off the shiny wrapping paper to reveal a blue rattle shaped like a dog. We watched as he brought it to his mouth and, as if reacting to a horrible taste, tossed it aside.

"Cass, no! That's not food," I said.

"It's okay," Daniel said.

"But it was such a nice gift."

Daniel rose and his arms hung limp from his body.

After he left, we wrote less and less frequently. I kept him apprised of milestones in Cass's life. Daniel kept me apprised of his new job in advertising and, eventually, his engagement to a nice girl who worked in human resources at Fidelity. Her parents were Hindu; her grandparents had lived in West Bengal.

The last time I'd seen Daniel was about a year ago, when he was traveling from Cambridge to Los Angeles for work and I happened to be in New York for the day. We met up at a sports bar near LaGuardia and ordered nachos and glasses of Sam Adams. I told him that Cass was turning into a good artist, that he had separation anxiety and loved music, and Daniel listened and nodded blandly.

"I have some news, too," he said finally.

"Oh?"

"Aadya's pregnant."

"That's great!" His reason for meeting me that day came into focus. "She doesn't know about Cass."

"No."

"Or me?"

He gently shook his head.

"All right." I took a long sip of my beer.

Later I regretted that a Knicks game was blasting from the TV mounted on the wall just behind his head and that he might not have heard me say, "I won't get in your way. Please know that I only want the best things for both of you and for your baby." I leaned closer to him. "You've been so sweet."

"To be honest, I haven't known how or, like, what to be during any of this."

"Who would have?" I said. "I'm glad for you."

"Are you?"

"Yes," I said, and I was. I think I was.

Still, as we said goodbye, I knew that Cass would in time grow to crave this man and suffer his absence. I nursed my Sam Adams as I watched Daniel hurry off toward his gate, his leather briefcase swinging in one hand.

AWAKE IN BED hours after our dinner at McDonald's, I ruminated over the fact that Cass had no Indian men in his life. Kurt had fallen asleep about an hour earlier, after we had watched two episodes of our favorite British spy series. He turned over now and grunted quietly.

I went to find the Woolf book. " 'Yes, of course, if it's fine tomorrow,' said Mrs. Ramsay. 'But you'll have to be up with the lark,' she added."

I put the book down and picked up my laptop. My mother had been urging me to join Facebook like she recently had, so I decided to create an account, but to only "friend" her, and to use a fake name, Amy Cassidy, in case any nervous clients came across me there. I explored other people's pages, and quickly located my ex in San Francisco, now married with three kids. It was a shock to see him this way and to see him so much older and thinner now, although why should it be? On Lana's public page was an article from *The Washington Post* about a demonstration that morning. A group called Women Vs. Feminism had protested a global economic conference about women and children taking place in Washington, D.C. Several delegates from other nations had pressed for the United States government to overhaul a welfare reform law that had proven harmful, primarily to poor black mothers. An Austrian delegate told a reporter, "Your racist policies are weapons that kill." In a photograph, a group of women, some younger with children, some older, brandished signs that read REAL MOTHERS STAY HOME WITH THEIR CHILDREN and CAN'T FEED 'EM? DON'T HAVE 'EM! A few held homemade signs that read LOCK HER UP! When asked by the reporter about these protestors, Lana said, "These women who are not feminists might not understand what the word 'feminism' means."

I scrolled down to the comments from her followers and took in one lewd GIF involving a photograph of Lana and a crossed-out hammer and sickle, as well as two entries—"Go back to your country, Lana. Don't talk down to American women!" and "Fe-men like Lana oppressing real men and real womenz who want real men cuz fe-men can't get laid bitch"—before closing my computer in disgust. I crawled back beneath the sheets and tried to gently rouse Kurt. He stirred, but did not wake. I turned to face the ceiling and a water stain that had, I could tell in the dim light, spread into the shape of a clover. I recalled a poll I had seen earlier that day; the numbers were close, but Hillary Clinton held the lead. The election could not come soon enough.

CHAPTER SIX

*C*hapter One looks good! Once I get my thoughts together I'll send you something for Chapter Two.

Lana had not written, "Thank you for providing me the material for my op-ed." Nothing like, "Maybe we can cut some of the business of infertility section since I already used it in the *New York Times*." I wondered if her not thanking me, her never apologizing for using my words or for taking so long to respond, were actually functions of feminism. What did we really owe anyone, after all that we had endured? Didn't we all have more important things to do than worry about niceties and timeliness? Especially now that we had our new president.

My mother had been calling several times a day since the election, and together we thrashed around in the news, alternately reacting to and venting about the promise of mass deportations, the announcement that more Facebook users had engaged with fake articles before the election than real news, the swastikas found in schools, the racist slurs on park benches. Something toxic had been released and was continuing to mobilize in the country. I began to wonder about Cass's safety amid the eruptions of racism nationwide, and found myself watching vigilantly anyone who looked at him in the grocery store or on the street.

As a prominent feminist immigrant, Lana was in higher demand than ever before. Google Alert flooded my inbox with links to TV, radio, and podcast interviews, more op-eds, videos of what had to be three or more speeches each day. She spoke with a kind of weariness, as if she had seen our current situation coming years earlier, but she also tried to impart hope. "We will come together at last. Poor women and rich, black women and white, *even* women and men if we have to," she said to a crowd in Burlington, Vermont. "You just watch us!" I was pleased to see the return of her chunky eyeglasses, at least for the day. She tweeted more regularly. She was everywhere, in multiple time zones each day. She even made a cameo appearance on *Saturday Night Live*.

I told Colin that I worried she might not want or have the time to publish a book anymore. "Oh, I'm sure nothing's changed. But if you want me to, I'll call her manager just to ask." Shortly after, he called back to tell me that we were a go. "Shirley was even ready to talk about Lana's book tour."

"Great!" I said. I wondered how long it would be before I got my orders for Chapter Two.

We were deep in November now. The air bit at any skin left exposed, and the ground was slick and craggy with ice. On a blustery Wednesday, after I got home from subbing at the middle school, I walked Cass home from Bertie's; rather, I ran, with him riding piggyback through the slicing wind.

At the kitchen counter, I poured a glass of milk for Cass and asked about his day.

"Bertie slept all morning," he said. "I watched TV."

Apparently he had gotten to watch two episodes of *Dora* and two *Caillou*s, which I estimated as one hundred and fifteen minutes, nearly two hours of being unattended. Afterward, he said, he had crawled inside her washing machine, although he could not figure out how to turn it on, so he got out and built a pyramid of "these little orange bottles that she had on her counter" and then gave himself a snack of chocolates. He was clearly proud that he had found ways to entertain himself for so long.

"When she woke up she made spaghetti for lunch and then you came." He blinked fast, and all of his features pinched together on his face just as he ran to the bathroom. I followed behind and stayed with him while the contents of his bowels rushed into the toilet bowl. He writhed around and let out a sob as another round began.

"Those chocolates—were they next to the medicine bottles?"

"If that counts as dessert I won't have any tonight." A pained expression passed through his face. "I didn't eat all of them."

"Did they come in squares?"

He nodded.

"How many did you eat?"

"I don't know."

When the worst of it seemed to have passed, I said, "Those chocolates weren't just chocolates." He listened, visibly confused that something as delicious as chocolate could hide such horror. "You couldn't have known," I said.

I went to call a local health clinic, and the receptionist gave me the number for poison control. "How many squares did he eat?" the woman there asked.

"I'm not sure," I said.

"You don't, you can't even guess?" The woman's voice was breathy and concerned.

"I was working," I said.

"Why was he left alone with the medicine, Ma'am?"

"I wasn't there. He was with his sitter, and she, she had—Does it matter?"

"Yes. Why did the sitter leave a box full of laxatives within reach of your four-year-old son?"

"Can you tell me what I should do for him right now?"

"Ma'am, you need to bring him to a hospital. I see that you're calling from a Western Massachusetts number. Do you need me to look up the nearest facility?"

"No, I know where it is," I answered. With our limited health insurance, a visit to the ER would cost a fortune.

"If I were you, I'd have a long talk with that child's sitter. You need to make sure to leave your son with an adult who is responsible or an accredited—"

I hung up.

In his bedroom, Cass was curled in the fetal position on his yellow giraffe comforter. "You okay?" I asked him.

"I guess."

"You up for a quick walk?" I helped him into clean underwear and a new pair of pants, and gave him another piggyback ride through the bitter air and back down the street to Bertie's.

I explained to Bertie what had happened in the past thirty minutes.

"I wasn't feeling well this morning and I had to lie down," she said. "I didn't mean to leave him for that long."

"But you did." I held Cass's hand firmly in mine.

"I'm sorry." There she stood with her rust-colored hair in a nest atop her head that sat upon her short neck that rose from her squat torso. She looked at me with guilt, and I felt that all of this—my reliance on her inexpensive labor, our lack of decent health insurance, Cass's gorging on Ex-Lax—was my fault.

"We should go find that box and see how many pieces he ate. I think I took one or two the other day," she said.

We counted six squares missing, give or take whatever Bertie had already eaten. It seemed a manageable number, sort of. I silently blessed the person who had invented the childproof caps that had kept my son from the medicine bottles still arranged in a pyramid on her counter.

I turned to Cass. "Don't ever open a box or bottle or anything by yourself—just don't open anything ever again."

"My stomach feels bouncy again," he said, his face turning.

I ran him to Bertie's bathroom just in time for his next round, although not in time for him to fully remove his pants and underwear. I tried to clean the mess using the lacy peach washcloth that Bertie gave me, all the while comforting him and reassuring her. "I'm so sorry, I'm so sorry," she kept saying, and thrust a bottle of mouthwash at me.

"What is that for?"

"I don't know. I don't have my glasses!" she said.

"Do you have any paper towels, or cleaner, or just regular towels?" I asked, as Cass sniffled, his body quiet now. Bertie moved from foot to foot as if her brain had frozen. "Stay there, Cass," I said, and found some of what I needed in her kitchen and did the best I could to clean and reassemble her bathroom before giving her some half-baked, awkward forgiveness, and finally walking Cass back home.

"I want Hippo," Cass said inside the living room. He'd had his small green stuffed hippo since he was an infant. "Where is he?"

Together, we searched. Cass stubbed his toe and there was a moment or two when it seemed that we would never find the thing, a moment when the cruelty of the world was too much, but in the next moment, I saw a sliver of soft green snout protruding from a lower kitchen cabinet.

"You mean you still have that neighbor lady watching him?" my mother said. I had called her after settling Cass on the couch. "I don't know what to tell you." She offered to consult her neighbor, a retired ER doctor. We hung up, and before long, she called back to tell me to keep a close eye on Cass. Give him lots of water. If the diarrhea returned, I should bring him to the ER.

"Okay," I said. I looked over at my son, now whispering something into Hippo's ear. He deserved to be able to go to the hospital. I was a terrible mother.

I remembered when I had first told her that I was pregnant and planned to be a single mom. Her fingers had gone white around the handle of a spatula. "No."

"Yes," I said. We stood facing each other in their narrow, bright kitchen. "I know. It's a surprise! It was for me, too."

"You have no idea, not one clue, about how difficult this will be."

"You know, you were a single mom for a while. I mean, after my father died and before you met Ed. You handled it okay."

"That was only for six or seven months. And those were six or seven of the hardest months of my life, and not just because you were a cranky infant and threw up all the time. Thankfully, things with Ed moved quickly." She reached forward and fixed my collar.

I tried to convince her to be more optimistic. She would be a grand-mother, after all. I had a baby inside me—a baby! Eventually she smiled sadly and said, "All right, it's your decision." Just before I left, she ges-tured to my flannel shirt and said, "Can't you wear something more flattering? In a month or two, your figure will be gone for God knows how long. Allie, you do have a cute figure. Sometimes, I swear you don't even want to be seen."

Now, I imagined my mother reporting back to Ed about today's debacle. I could all but hear her words: "I told her how hard this would be on her own."

Cass had fallen asleep on the couch. I poured him a glass of water, set it on the floor near him, and made myself a peanut butter sand-wich. The kitchen was silent. I relished the small moment of peace.

Snowflakes had begun to form outside the window, specks of light blowing horizontally in the wind.

I opened my laptop and saw that Lana's notes for the next chapter had finally come.

"Hi. Here are the subjects for chapter 2: circumcision; breastfeeding as a feminist act; the culture of shame around nursing and the sexualization of the woman's body; hiring help—a necessity! Workplace family support in this country vs. other countries. (Talk to Val if you need to.) Happy writing, and all the best, Lana"

I groaned. Was she withholding details about being a mother because the details did not exist? She worked nonstop, especially now, but I tried to cut her some slack. Hell, when we met, she had admitted to being hands-off in raising her son.

Maybe she needed some prompts. I instant-messaged her:

I hope the following questions aren't too personal, but I think personal is what everyone wants for this book, for better or worse! Was Norton circumcised and breastfed? How were those experiences for you? How long a maternity leave did you get and how long did you take?

I can also write about the difficulties of getting infants to sleep—unfortunately I know a lot about this—and the most popular methods of sleep training. Ferber vs. Sears (both men, of course!); and choosing what works best for the individual baby and parents. Did you have any magic solutions for getting Norton to sleep—or were you one of those lucky people who were blessed with a good sleeper? Hiring help might not be an option for every reader, but I'll discuss it, as well as leaning on family and neighbors if/when possible.

Another idea for this chapter: "pink and blue propaganda," or how to dress your baby boy in pink and avoid the confusion of nosy strangers . . . How did you dress Norton when he was a baby?

The theme song from *Caillou* tinkled forth from the next room. I took it as a good sign that Cass was awake and feeling decent enough to want to watch TV. He loved this show about a whiny, bald boy who lived in a nice house with his parents and sister and cat, a boy whose life could not have been more different from Cass's own.

She must have been at her computer—for once, she wrote right back. *I nursed and it was difficult at first. We stuck to yellow, green, and orange.*

I responded, *I had so much trouble getting Cass to latch on—and so much pain! That little jaw could have pulled a finger off my hand at first. What troubles did you have? For how long did you breastfeed?*

Ha! Not long enough. I did try, but it was a no-go. Good idea to write about sleep training and clothing choice. Speaking of choice, I have to go to speak at a pro-choice conference. Look forward to seeing the next chapter. Thanks, Lana

"No! Don't leave yet," I said as the chat box vanished.

In desperation, I wrote to Colin: *Lana is giving me nothing, NO material about herself or Norton, just general ideas for each chapter. I've tried and totally failed to get more from her. SOS!*

He wrote, *Keep trying but don't drive her crazy. If you have to, just write something generic-ish about mothering a boy. You know a lot about this topic! Remember to make her really likable.*

I reluctantly emailed Gin, trying to hide my growing panic: "Having a little trouble getting specifics from Lana! Any ideas or suggestions?" I went for a box of animal crackers, which I emptied while watching Cass watch *Caillou*.

Gin replied: "Lana's probably not used to talking to strangers about her life. She's out of her comfort zone. You could try telling her about your own experiences and see if she loosens up."

I asked if she was able to instant message right then, and she said that she was. I typed, *I already tried talking about myself.*

Gin: *Then try something else. You'll figure it out. Good luck!*

Exasperated, I did some research and wove some of what I had found into Chapter Two.

In a recent survey, 72 percent of passersby described the sight of a woman openly nursing her baby on a public bench as "the opposite of sexy," "lewd," and/or "thoroughly repulsive." But throughout the ages, artists have celebrated the aesthetic beauty of breastfeeding—and not only women artists like Mary Cassatt. Édouard Pingret, Paul Gauguin, and Henri Lebasque painted poignant, loving scenes of mothers feeding their babies. One of my favorite works is Kitagawa Utamaro's woodblock print, *Mother Nursing Child Before Mirror*, a wonderful portrait.

Utamaro was one of my mother's favorite artists—and I remembered glimpsing an Utamaro-like print hanging in Lana's foyer.

The most important thing was, I went on to argue, selecting a method of feeding that made *you*, as an individual with your own particular life and needs, concurrently the sanest, healthiest, and most fulfilled, as well as a method that spared your chest from assault and battery.

I drafted an email begging Lana to give me more and then deleted it; I worried this might antagonize her.

What was also missing was Lana's voice, some essence that still remained elusive to me. There was the difficulty of the wide gap between her earlier image and the "more American, more feminine" woman I was meant to help create, the one with the new hair color and contact lenses. Maybe I had to stop thinking in such binary terms. A woman could be both soft and hard, feminist and feminine, couldn't she?

The door opened, and Kurt was there with Pete, both very stoned. Pete wore an old John Deere T-shirt. His work boots tracked dirt across the kitchen floor. I told Kurt about the laxative incident, and he doubled over laughing.

"I'm glad you find it hilarious," I said.

"I'm sorry, Al. That must have been really . . . shitty," he said, fighting back a smile. I glared at him.

Pete opened the refrigerator and pulled out some leftover mac n' cheese. "Gimme some of that," Kurt said and reached for the container.

"I have work to do. Cass is in the other room. Go," I told them. "Be somewhere else." I ushered them toward the door to the basement. Before long, I heard them head out in Pete's car.

My irritation with those two bloomed into a larger irritation with Lana and this book. To hell with them all. I had bills to pay.

During Norton's infancy, my favorite moment of the day was when I came home from work. I would set down my work bag,

Across the street, Jessica Garbella stood in mountain pose.

change into my yoga pants and head for his bedroom. Feeding Norton made me feel connected to primal women. It was a raw and wild thing at first. Sometimes nursing him hurt, but other times it felt wonderful. Sometimes I could not stand to share my body with this baby, but later, I could not stand to set him down. My mood swings were astonishing, and I found that listening to calming music (Joni Mitchell or Neil Young) helped me relax. Later, when I got the hang of it, breastfeeding actually had the same effect.

I deleted Joni Mitchell and Neil Young. Who knew what music Lana liked?

I often walked Norton in his stroller around Central Park. A group of teenage boys, maybe high school students, caught sight of me feeding him once. Lester had gone off for a coffee. "Put that shit away, lady. It makes me sick," the tallest one called over.

I was unsure that I had heard him correctly, so I asked him to repeat what he had said.

He did.

Well. I walked over to them, Norton in one arm, my other hand on my hip. I informed the young man who had spoken that he likely had suckled at his own mother's breasts as a baby; that no state or federal laws banned women from nursing in public; that women's breasts did not exist for his and his friends' gratification.

I then realized that my shirt hung open and that the whole of my right breast was visible.

The tallest boy made a rude comment about the size and shape of my chest. The others laughed in response. One said, "Damn, son!"

"Clearly you have never seen or held an actual woman's breasts," I said, "or you would be aware that most in no way resemble those exploited in cheap porn, which is, I'm guessing, your only experience of them. Most breasts are not buoyant or perfectly uniform. A normal woman's breasts are soft or fibrous or rashy, and always perfectly imperfect."

I had myself a good laugh as those boys made gagging noises and hurried out of the park.

Back when Cass was a baby, I had gotten a landscaping job near the stables at the Mount, Edith Wharton's house, and I'd had to bring him along. Unfortunately, I had been far less confrontational than in the scene I had written for Lana. After the painters' unwanted comments, I returned Cass to his bouncy seat, buttoned up my shirt, and grumbled some righteous thoughts about the ghost of Lily Bart, words probably audible to no one but me. In his khaki shorts and paint-spattered T-shirt, one of the painters mumbled something about my soil-covered hands and his junk, and the others snorted with laughter as they walked away. My mouth silently formed the words "Fuck you."

I pictured myself responding to them in the way that I had written for Lana. Even revisionist imaginary vengeance had its merits.

What would Lana think of my spinning a full scene about her out of thin air?

I heard the start of another episode of *Caillou* in the next room and, when I went to check on Cass, saw that he had fallen asleep on the couch. Hopefully, the worst had passed.

FOUR HOURS LATER, after one stomach pumping, one nuclear tantrum, one charcoal slushie, and ten minutes of violent vomiting, Cass and I drove home in silence from the Berkshire Medical ER. I told myself not to think about the cost of all this for the moment. The only other people on the road were a few truckers droning alongside us. By now, all the leaf peepers had come and gone, but it was too early in the season for the skiers to arrive. The night sky was blurry and starless.

Back at my house, Kurt sprawled on my couch, a bag of pretzels in his hands as he took in the latest episode of the British spy series.

"I cannot believe you are watching this without me," I said, and burst into tears.

He sat up and flicked off the TV. "Let me put Cass to bed," he said, and he touched my shoulder.

I tried to gather myself and rescued a partial joint from a small puddle of dish soap in the kitchen, but the paper was too wet to hold a light. The house smelled like diarrhea. I felt acutely and deeply sorry for myself. The irony of writing from the viewpoint of a self-sufficient, powerful woman was getting harder to ignore.

Kurt returned. "I only watched about ten minutes. I'll watch it again with you."

"Forget it. I don't have the energy to even watch TV right now. I don't have the energy to move."

He sat cross-legged on the floor next to me. He had eyes the color of pale blue hydrangea.

"Oh, Allie. Oh, Hon," he said, removing my boots and socks in order to begin massaging my toes. He kneaded my feet with his long, warm fingers and relief shot up through my legs. He began to hum some song I did not recognize, and I closed my eyes and took in the sensation of being touched and nurtured. Everything would be okay. The day was over and tomorrow was a blank slate, a whole new beginning. I felt myself start to drift off.

CHAPTER SEVEN

Kurt watched Cass the next morning while I worked. I flipped through the books that my mother had bought me back when Cass was a baby, books that laid out various sleep systems: a parent could choose to listen to their infant wail for increasingly long periods of time or sleep beside their wailing infant. A parent could choose to establish a rigid routine and schedule their life around sleep and/or feeding, or they could choose other highly structured methods. I thought about the word *choice,* and how infrequently some people—I—even encountered the opportunity to make any real choices. Sleep training? Clothing colors? When he was sick or I was too depleted to protest, Cass still slept in my bed. He wore whatever fit him from the clothing Maggie sometimes gave us, clothing that her own kids and nephews and nieces, a huge number, had outgrown. Pink, blue, Club Med Aruba. Sleep was sleep and clothes were clothes.

The doorbell rang, and Jessica Garbella stood before me in a teal ski jacket and yoga pants. She had a mass of blond curls and a kind, healthy face. "Any chance you've got some olive oil? I get mine at the farmer's market, but they're done for the winter."

"Sure," I said. I went to the kitchen for the same bottle of Bertolli that I'd had for maybe three years, and when I returned, I caught her eyeing my living room. Cass had dumped all his laundry in a corner and was now sitting on the pile in his underpants. On the floor, in the center of the room, sat a stack of new stuff for Kurt's *Throne of Waste*: an acoustic guitar, a cracked toilet lid, a cat-shaped desk lamp with two legs missing, and a bunch of unraveling baskets. Jessica had never been inside our house, although I had seen hers at the open house with Maggie and the day we had had coffee. Hers was decorated in oatmeal and ocean tones. It was faintly but not overwhelmingly posh, and was very, very clean.

"Sorry about the mess," I said. "I've been working all morning."

"Don't apologize! You have work to do! You have better things to worry about than cleaning, right? Women should *never* apologize."

"Yeah," I said, wondering if she knew of Lana and her signature phrase. I held forth the small bottle. "Is this okay?"

"I just need it to condition my scalp." She eyed the bottle. "You know what? You keep it—I'll just go buy some at that Natural Foods place in Lenox or wherever. No big deal."

"You sure?"

"Totally. Do you need anything?"

I thanked her, but said no.

She looked behind me, maybe toward my kitchen. "If you're working all day, I could pick up some prepared food for you guys for dinner? That place has incredible tahini lentil wrap sandwiches. I bet Cass would love them."

At the time, Cass loved three varieties of foods: Kraft Macaroni & Cheese, almost anything from McDonald's, and Papa Gino's cheese pizza. There were a handful of other items that he tolerated, despite my best efforts to broaden his palate. "Don't worry about it," I said.

"It's on me. It's no trouble if I'm already going there, right?"

"Thanks, but he's kind of picky." What more to say? I smiled down at her feet. "I should probably get back to work."

"Of course. You're busy—I'm being such a pain. Oh hey, my yoga classes are full, but if you ever want to try it, I'll make space for you. Just say the word, okay? I'll even give you the 'friends and family discount.'"

"ALLIE?"

It was two in the morning, and I had just been out cold.

"This isn't the best time," Kurt began. He rested on his elbow beside me. "But, I guess, I mean, I have to tell you something."

I opened one eye and trained it on him.

"Don't worry, it's not so bad," he said. He gathered the sheet around him and sat up in bed. "It's just that I've decided to go hitch around Northern New England before winter really comes. My cousin up in Manchester invited me to housesit for him for a while. And I might try to hit Montpelier and Acadia. And even Labrador and Newfoundland, too, if I can find a way. There's a storm coming this weekend, so I'm thinking that I'll head out in a day or two. I haven't gone anywhere in weeks. Months?"

It took less than a moment for his words to form a small, hard pit inside me.

"Huh," I said. My eyes focused on his worn copy of *Walden* atop *We're Going on a Bear Hunt* over on the bedside table. Since finishing Jimmy's shed, he had painted the Garbella's basement. That was a week ago, a week of sleeping late and reading, rather rereading— and frequently quoting to me—Henry David Thoreau's chronicle of self-discovery, a week of watching Cass for a total of maybe an hour, of shooting hoops and getting stoned with Pete and watching TV and sleeping. "You shouldn't hitch. Just take the train or something."

"Trains cost as much as planes these days. I want to hitch—I've never done it before."

"What about *Throne of Waste* and all the stuff you've been saving for it?"

"I'll finish it when I get back," he said. "Come with me."

"What, and bring Cass?"

"Why not?"

"Because he just poisoned himself while Bertie slept in the next room, and because I have to work. Because I have a job. I have to pay rent and I have to be a mother and I have to stay here and be the grown-up. You know, we still owe Jimmy the rest of November rent and December is about a week away."

"I'll see if I can make some money when I'm traveling, okay?"

"Doing what?"

"I'll figure it out."

I could have thrown his dog-eared copy of *Walden* in his face. Technically, he was doing nothing wrong. He had never promised me more than he was currently giving us. He and I had explicitly agreed to the same freedoms, and he was merely setting off to enjoy them, something he was able to do as he had no real responsibilities, only his soul's desires to direct him. I was tempted to ascribe this enviable condition to his gender, although I knew that would have been inaccurate.

"Don't hitchhike. It's not safe," I tried again.

He reached in the drawer of the bedside table for a joint.

"I could use some help with Cass," I said. "Bertie shouldn't be watching him so much. Obviously, she can't handle it anymore."

"What about asking Sandra to come sit for him?" Sandra was Pete's wife. She managed a new microbrewery in the next town.

"Why? Because she's a woman? She already has a job." Sandra had told me that she never wanted to have kids, that there was too much to enjoy in life without "that sort of straitjacket."

"No. What the hell? She was good with Cass when they came by here the other day. She played Hide and Seek with him."

"Just go," I said, but not before I grabbed the joint out of his hands.

"I won't be away forever." He looked over at me. "One quick smoke?"

After he had gone back to sleep, I lay there awake. I finally went to find my book. " 'Yes, of course, if it's fine tomorrow,' said Mrs. Ramsay. " 'But you'll have to be up with the lark,' she added." I glanced out the window at the world, black and cold. I hated being so needy, although maybe *needy* wasn't the right word. I was something less overt, less invasive. I refused everything and required nothing and so here I was, just about alone with my son, still in Jimmy's old house in the town next to the one where I had grown up.

I set down the book and reached again for the rest of the joint, now on my bedside table. It took but a few inhalations for me to assure myself that I was doing the best I could, that at least Cass was on the mend now, and that it was time to go to sleep.

When I told Bertie that she no longer had to watch Cass three days each week, that for now one day would be plenty, she said, "You don't trust me anymore."

We sat at the card table in her kitchen. "No, that's not true," I lied. A better mother would have stopped this arrangement altogether and kept her son by her side until she figured things out, but with Kurt leaving so soon, I needed any coverage I could get. "I'm working on this new project now and I'm home a lot more," I said.

"You can't work at the same time that you watch him. You've told me this again and again." Soon enough, Bertie would be the closest person to a co-parent that I had. Despite everything, she loved Cass, and he loved her.

"I'm really sorry." It was all I could say.

"All kids have their accidents. If they don't get into medicine, they get into the house cleaners or the cat food, believe me. At my daycare I once had a kid eat a whole container of hamster food. Another kid got into my gin."

I looked at her.

"It was a home daycare. The kid went upstairs into our apartment. You said Cass was feeling better today."

I had not—and would not—tell her about the hours that we had spent at Berkshire Medical's ER last night. There was little point. My eyes on her pocked green linoleum floor, I grew angry at something that I could not name.

It occurred to me that, with her new hours, we would see her less and that she would be alone far more. I might not be able to check on her regularly. "Why don't you give me your son's phone number?" I said. "You know, just in case of emergency."

"But we hardly ever talk. To be honest, I doubt he'd come running if I needed him. He's not what I'd call a good man. Anyway, he lives in Wichita."

Jimmy came by that evening for rent and leaned into the doorway, sniffing around. "Smells good in here." Kurt was preparing something Mexican in my kitchen.

I hated to ask. "You want to stay for dinner?"

Jimmy gave me a weird look and shrugged. "Why not?" He followed me inside the living room.

Thankfully Kurt had moved all the items he had collected for his sculpture down to the basement. In the kitchen, Jimmy glanced over Kurt's shoulder at the chocolaty chicken broth simmering and softening the chunks of onions and tomatillos. The counter was covered in new glass containers of anise and coriander seeds, cloves and cumin, wrappers from stone-ground Mexican dark chocolate.

"Looks like mud," Jimmy said.

"You guys don't know this, but back when I was in college, I thought about becoming a professional chef for a while," Kurt said.

"There are lots of things I don't know about you," I said. I did not know how he had been able to pay for all the ingredients of this meal, for example. I did not know when he would come back from this trip, or if, while hitchhiking, he would be picked up by a psychopath and left robbed and dismembered by the side of Interstate 91.

I watched Jimmy hoist up his silver track pants and take a seat at the table. He removed a toothpick from his shirt pocket and poked deep between his molars. His eyes scanned the cluttered kitchen, the dishes packed inside the sink, the overflowing trash can, the smear of something—chocolate?—on a cabinet door. This was his house. This was his stove on which our dinner was cooking.

He yanked the toothpick from his mouth and looked with curiosity at something he had extracted.

In the corner of the living room, Cass sat on the floor, arranging his crayons in a rainbow before him. I went to retrieve my laptop and put on "Rock Around the Clock" at full volume in order to drive out all the little sorrows rustling around inside me. Cass and I danced around the room, singing every word. This song was our game changer. Music often was, for us—we both liked the Ramones, the Jackson 5, Queen. Cass howled with laughter as I spun him up in the air and into the kitchen, barely missing Jimmy's back. The song ended, and Cass brought his crayons to the kitchen table, where he drew a picture of the ocean, complete with a curl of moon overhead and wooly clouds and, I thought, a prodigiously rendered dolphin leaping in an arc from the water.

"Kurt tells me he's going on a long trip?" Jimmy said, eyeing me above Cass. "You'll cover December yourself? You got enough work these days?"

I nodded and kept my eyes on my son, as he added some purple to his water, some orange to his moonlight.

Back in the sleep-deprived, emotionally volatile, but also reverie-filled early days of his life, I began writing an essay about being a single mother. I wrote about the blunt and occasionally offensive questions from strangers ("What country did your baby come from?"), the unsolicited advice, but also my unprecedented affection for this boy. I had heard so much from Maggie about postpartum depression. When Connor was born, she was hardly able to get out of bed for weeks. Her doctor had put her on medication. I prepared myself for the worst, but my connection with Cass was immediate and so overpowering and physical that I wondered if I was actually experiencing the love of two parents for this soft, mewling, frightened-seeming little boy. "Welcome" had been my first word to him. I slid my finger inside one of his fists. It curled around me like a shrimp.

At that point, I had been ghostwriting for about seven years and had produced little personal work other than a few stunted tries at prose poems about the joys and frustrations of anonymity. I had published seven, almost eight books, but not one word under my own name. I had the notion that I had begun to absorb all these voices that I was ghosting, that they were beginning to saturate my consciousness, and that my own voice, whatever that was, had begun to atrophy.

I ended up drafting about half that essay during the strangely calm first weeks, when Cass slept well and often. I wrote of the double-edged sword of single-motherhood: Such joy! Just a year earlier, I had feared that I would never have a baby. Now I had this beautiful, healthy boy all to myself. *I had this beautiful, healthy boy all to myself.* I wrote about eight pages that culminated in thoughts that would be interesting to no one but me, thoughts like: "Dear Cassidy: What if my car finally dies or my landlord decides to sell this house or you grow sick and we run out of food and there is no one to stay home and watch you while I run to the store?"

Cass handed Kurt his finished picture and—bless him—Kurt set down his spatula and swooned. "Someday your art will be in a museum." The most direct way to my heart had to be through my son.

Jimmy reached out and socked Cass on the arm, grinning. Cass yelped, came running to me, and buried his face in my chest.

"Don't be a pussy," Jimmy said.

"*Jimmy*. Jesus," I said.

"You've got to teach him to take it," he said.

"Why? So he can grow up to be like you?" My son had no one other than me to advocate for him.

"This is the world. The world isn't soft. Allie, no one else is going to coddle him like you do, or let him wear a pink I LOVERMONT T-shirt."

"To hell with the world these days."

"Dinner?" Kurt said loudly.

We took our places around the table. I poured the water and bit back the desire to continue berating Jimmy. The chicken mole was sweet and piquant and velvety, the salsa crisp and tangy.

"Not bad, Kurt," Jimmy said. He mentioned a ranch home across town that he was considering buying. This would be his fourth property—paid for at least partly with the rent money that we gave him. "It'd need a facelift. Some new bushes out front, for starters, so maybe you can help out," he said, looking at me.

"Yeah, sure," I said.

"You hear stocks are up? Maybe our new president isn't so bad after all, hey, Allie?" Sometimes Jimmy enjoyed taunting me about the fact that his "side" had won the election.

"You hear that he's averaging twenty lies a day?" I said.

Kurt glared at me.

"Give him a chance," Jimmy said. "He's not even in office yet and the libtards are all crying their eyes out."

"I'm sorry, '*libtards*'? I find that term infantile and moronic, if you want to know the truth." I was well aware that I had just now sounded like the "coastal elite," and I opened my mouth to say more when Kurt cut me off: "Who wants more wine? Or food? I made a ton, so everyone has to have seconds."

"I'll have more," Jimmy said.

"You know what's also moronic?" I said. "The fact that he's still talking about Hillary. The election is over."

"Listen," Kurt said, his eyes moving between us. "I am about to say something that you both need to hear. Repeat after me: 'I will not talk politics with this person, at least while Kurt is out of town.'"

"This isn't just everyday politics," I said. "This is the future of our goddamned democracy."

"ALLIE," Kurt moaned. He flashed me a look that said, *Jimmy is your landlord and you are only screwing yourself right now.*

"Say it with me, Hon." Jimmy grumbled, laughing.

But what I really wanted to say was, "What exactly do you admire about the new president? Was it the time he told an interviewer, 'It doesn't really matter what [the media] write as long as you've got a young and beautiful piece of ass,' or when he said that a female opponent was too ugly to win votes? Was it his comment about Mexicans being rapists or his birtherism? Was it his comment about dating his daughter? Or the one about Megyn Kelly?"

But I had a son who needed a home and lived in a town where rent prices were on the rise. My cash flow was so unpredictable that no other landlords would have put up with me for this long. I reluctantly repeated the words alongside Jimmy: "I will not talk politics while Kurt is out of town."

"We need some booze," Jimmy said. He reached for his wallet and handed me a $20 bill. "You want to run out and get a six-pack of Coors and a bottle of chardonnay or whatever for you?"

It seemed a kind of olive branch, an olive twig. "Sure. Be back in a few," I said, and headed out.

Still riled, I allowed myself to sit in my truck outside Discount Liquors and listen to Sarah Vaughan singing "Mean to Me." I took my time in the store and tried to center myself. Jimmy was hardly the only person in the country who had voted the way he had. Getting through a day meant alternately enduring and rejecting patriarchy.

Back home, I set the Coors and a six-pack of Guinness for me and Kurt on the counter.

"Jesus," Jimmy said, peeling back the tab on a can. "You drink that tar? I bet it gets you hammered after three sips."

During Cass's bedtime, I struggled at first over what to tell him and eventually just blurted it out: "Bertie's going to start watching you less—just one morning a week. And remember that Kurt is going away tomorrow for a while. You and me, we'll get to be together a lot more during the week. But sometimes I'm still going to have to work like I do when you're home on Mondays."

"Then why can't Bertie keep watching me?"

"It's getting hard for her. She needs her rest."

"Where does Kurt have to go?" It was all too much at once for Cass.

"He's going away on a trip. But he'll be back."

"Why don't you two get married?"

"Come on. It's time to sleep," I said, lifting the sheets and guiding him beneath them. "Kurt and I like things the way they are."

"I wish I had a baby sister or brother," Cass said.

I kissed his forehead and gazed down at his hair. It needed a trim. "Yeah?"

"Why don't you two have a baby?"

Being an only child was not easy. You felt different from most of the world. Sometimes you worried that your life might be less fun, less dimensional. Your parents were sort of your siblings, and a lot of limits and disappointment came with that. "I'm probably too old to have another baby, to be honest."

"Oh."

"I'm sorry." I could think of nothing to add, nothing hopeful and true to say that would ease this moment for him.

The baby in him was still apparent in the roundness of his cheeks, but I swore his neck was longer than it had been even yesterday. His fingers were bigger, too. He did not drool in his sleep anymore. He no longer broke into a grin when I first came into his room in the morning.

I pulled Cass's door shut and went to find Kurt. He was not in the kitchen, my bedroom, or anywhere else that I looked, not even the basement. He spent most of his time upstairs with us now, and it had been weeks or longer since I had been down here. I had forgotten how spare it was: just a futon, a trunk, and one fold-up chair. That morning after we had first slept together, Kurt and I sat amid the bunched sheets and early sunlight from the little windows and presented each other with what I suppose were our terms, which were identical, for any future sex and cohabitation: no expectations, no demands, no commitments. He had, after all, just left a cage of a life and craved freedom. And for my part, Cass was the only person I felt able to tend and nurture. We congratulated ourselves on so easily reaching an ideal arrangement. How strange, I later thought, to launch this discussion that early, to even attempt to address and define something that was less than twelve hours old.

We had revisited our arrangement a few times since then, and after some heated exchanges, agreed not to alter much other than our patterns of communication. Soon after our first night, he disappeared for one night, and then a week later for another, and so I had asked him to just let me know before he went away. I wondered whether he had met someone else or had a couple of one-night stands, which was mostly fine with me because it meant that I could do the same if I wanted. But after that, Kurt never again disappeared without telling me—and he eventually asked me not to assume that he would always be game to provide large swaths of childcare when I had to work or had other plans.

"I was outside putting new wiper blades on your truck," Kurt said now from the top of the stairs. "I picked up some new ones yesterday. Yours were shot. I don't know how you could see anything when it rains or snows."

"That was nice of you."

On my couch upstairs, we took turns with his briar pipe, and I sucked in well-being and buttery contentment. I thought I could actually feel my skeleton soften and my brain begin to relax. We talked about Jimmy and Cass and Bertie, and then our biological families. "I wish I'd known my real father," I told him.

"Yeah, that's rough." Kurt had been adopted, something he had mentioned only in passing a few times. "A few years ago, I tracked down my biological mother. She's Scottish. She was an au pair in France when she had me. Now she builds boats in a small town outside Aberdeen. She has a family, so she didn't really want to be in touch with me. I thought it was so cool that she worked with her hands."

"What about your father?"

"He's an attorney in Westchester who was in France for a month. My biological mother said that he never knew about me. Obviously, she didn't want me to contact him."

"Oh. That's sad." Outside, wind blew the loose snow upward, sprays of white dust that moved toward the treetops and were visible in the light that shone out from the kitchen. I stood up and wobbled on my feet. "You'll have a good trip and then you'll come back here and everything will be A-OK. And this book will come out and Project Fuckface will become a distant memory. And, you know what? Congress will impeach that guy. The country will get back to normal. Everything'll be great."

"Project What? You are higher than a building right now."

I nodded.

We ignored the mess of dirty dishes on the table as we spread bath towels on the floor and lit some old votives in a wide circle around them. Kurt grabbed another can of Guinness and joined me on the floor, and I kissed the nape of his neck. We shared the beer and it felt like an adventure, like teenagehood, a finite piece of time in which we could do and say whatever we wanted. He reached around and coaxed me closer to him. I wanted to tell him that I loved him, something neither of us had said yet, but I did not want my words to wreck the dream of the moment if he answered them with silence.

I had the thought that I had let this person too close to me, and to us.

At last he turned to face me, and pulled his T-shirt up and over his head. "Come here, Al," he said, and positioned me on top of his lap.

"Wait," I said, and I rose to blow out the candles. The room went dark.

Despite the bath towels, the kitchen floor was not a forgiving surface. We kept inadvertently hurting each other, mashing the other person's hipbone against the hard vinyl or leaning too hard on a hand or a knee. He bunched up a towel to use as a cushion beneath his elbow, and he put all his weight on that arm and it collapsed to the side, he and his rib cage landing hard against the vinyl. "Ouch," he said. "This floor is going to kill us."

I laughed, but stopped myself. "We're going to wake up Cass," I said, and he said, "This will help keep you quiet," and covered my mouth with his, the sure push of his lips and tongue returning me to myself. Finally, we got into sync, and the floor and my awareness of my thoughts fell away.

Afterward, I lay against him, both of us tacky with sweat as we gathered our breath. There was the odd sensation of a train having blasted through the room, leaving only silence in its wake.

I rose and went for a glass of water, and when I came back, Kurt gazed up at me with a strange look. He wrapped a towel around his waist and moved into a seated position.

"You want some?" I passed him the water and he took a sip.

"Thanks," he said. "I saw a picture of her the other day."

It took me a moment to even think of the correct question. "Birgitte?"

"Confession—I googled her on your computer when you were out." He used my computer every now and then when he needed it, since he no longer had one. The only piece of technology he had kept was a Samsung flip phone.

"You did?" I thought of our first night together, when again he had mentioned her a beat too soon after our bodies had parted.

"I don't know why. I went to her Facebook page. She's already moved in with this guy, a restaurateur. She posted a picture of them with his new Jeep." He made an expression of disgust. "It was weird. I don't know what made me do that."

"Oh?"

"I almost wrote to her." He began to worry a lock of his hair between his fingers. "Everything that happened to me before I came here? Birgitte, the firm, my life in New York? Sometimes it's like I imagined it all. I can't seem to connect myself to it. I don't know why."

I hated that he could access his past and slip into this sort of thinking just by typing a few words into my laptop. "Do you miss her? You miss your old life?"

"No. I guess—it's still just disorienting. If you could have seen me there . . . I guess that guy wasn't really me. But I don't know if this is me here either, I mean, playing father and responsible partner and everything in some random town in Western Mass?" He caught my wounded expression and added, "I'm not talking about you, though. You know what I think of you. And Cass, too. I'm not explaining it very well."

"Birgitte and I—we're really different," I began.

"That's an understatement. She never learned to drive and she couldn't change a lightbulb. She shopped at Barney's and Bergdorf. She went to New York Fashion Week shows with her friends." He looked down, and maybe to justify himself, added, "But she was whip smart. And she worked hard. She intuited the gyrations of the global markets in a way that I never could."

"There had to be a reason that you were with her, right?"

"Yeah." He bent forward to gather a few of the candles.

"I'm going to check on Cass," I said, a little blue.

"Come back when you're done, all right?"

I nodded.

My son was starting to look more like me than his father, I thought as I looked in at him, or maybe I just secretly hoped for this. When Cass was born, everyone told me how little he looked like me. I knew that they did not mean this as an insult, but I was taken aback every time. I never had a good or ready response.

I wondered if Daniel ever thought about Cass or me. I tried to remember Daniel's voice, his hair, his eyeglasses. What was his facial expression when I first saw him, five years ago? What was mine? If only I could retrieve these things and hold them beside the moments of my life as it was now, and know that I was continuing along the correct path, that I was where and who I should be, that Cass was, too.

It had to be an hour before I headed to my bedroom and found Kurt asleep on his side of my bed.

THE NEXT MORNING, I sat on the futon watching Kurt zip up his duffel bags. As he chatted about his plans, I wondered when and if we would see him again, and if there might be anything I could say to stop him. I wondered when I would next have sex; when I would next fall asleep beside a man, if ever; what it would feel like that night to sit at the dinner table with only Cass, and to watch the British spy series by myself. To make myself feel better, I reminded myself of Kurt's naïve rejection of money, and this helped, at least in the moment.

An hour later, we kissed each other goodbye, and he trotted across the front yard to catch a ride with Ron Garbella to Fitchburg.

PART TWO

December 2016 – March 2017

CHAPTER EIGHT

I f I had written an account of the time after Kurt's exit, Colin would
have cut it back. He would have told me that the reader wasn't
interested in the day-to-day life of an overtaxed single working
mom. Five years ago, when I was deep in the middle of Tanya's book
and he had balked at what I'd written, I'd asked him who this "reader"
was that he imagined. "A middle-aged, Oprah-loving, wine-drinking,
suburban mom with a bachelor's degree, a part-time or nonprofit job,
and an active book club full of similar women," he said.

"That is impressively specific," I told him.

"Good. Maybe you can keep a specific picture of this person in
mind when you revise Tanya's book."

In the draft, I had described, with no shortage of the frank detail
that Tanya had given me, her happy if chaotic toddlerhood followed by
her repeated molestation over a stretch of eleven years by her great-uncle; her subsequent bouts of depression; and her suicide attempt that
resulted in her stay in a psychiatric ward. Flash forward to her first
stand-up show in New York, her appearance on *The Daily Show*—before
which she had an anxiety attack—and her successful career, although
she often felt like an imposter. The book ended with a comic—okay,

macabre—fantasy of Tanya castrating her great-uncle Hands, as he was called, in front of his poker group.

"Allie," Gin said, soon after I talked to Colin, "this is a really uncomfortable read. God," she said half to herself, "why didn't I ask to see it earlier?"

"Tanya's not exactly known for her light, breezy humor," I said. "And her uncle died years ago, so I figured we were on okay legal ground there."

"Where did you put the feel-good part?" Gin asked. "We need more overcoming struggle, a lot more catharsis, and WAY less violence porn. Make that none." She informed me of the ratio she preferred in memoirs: 30 percent background, 30 percent struggles and formulation of personal philosophy, and the rest overcoming of struggles, arrival at fame and fortune, enjoying of fame and fortune, name-dropping, gratitude.

"That ending doesn't count as catharsis, at least?" I joked.

Gin just sighed. "You skipped everything important: the time between the mental hospital and her success. Wring some forgiveness from her. Get her moving on to a healthy relationship, even if it's with her dog. And end with gratitude rather than this crazed and not funny daydream about murdering a family member." Gratitude was big for readers, she explained.

"I know—gratitude, hope, a glossier finish. I get it. But she doesn't like animals," I said meekly. Still, I agreed to try again.

I called Tanya, and she hated every one of Gin's ideas. "This whitewashing is bullshit," she said, and I had to agree.

But the next morning, she called me back. "Just write whatever you have to finish this thing," Tanya said. "I need the money. I don't make as much as you probably think I do."

"Are you sure about this?"

"Yes," she said.

In the end, she begrudgingly okay'ed even my replacing her revenge fantasy with a scene of her taking her young niece to see *Brave*, a movie Tanya told me she had secretly found "lame and suffocatingly white. They couldn't shoehorn one token black person into a crowd scene?"

"I know," I said, feeling awful, realizing only then the large flaw of this movie that Cass and I had so enjoyed. Our first draft had to have been a far more entertaining and intelligent read than this book version of vanilla pudding, and I told her so. "I'm sorry about all this. Gin is underestimating readers."

"I'm used to vanilla pudding calling all the shots."

I apologized again and offered to go back to Gin, but by then Tanya just seemed annoyed with me. Understandably. My guilt was my problem.

For memoirs like Tanya's, I had been asked to write (and shape and augment) more—and ghost less; I had to be far more present on the page than I had ever been. It would never come easier or more naturally to me—and Lana's book had begun to demand a new level of fabrication. I reminded myself again, I did need the job.

With Bertie watching Cass far less, and without Kurt pitching in for rent, I had to cut back on Cass's time at Little Rainbows. Good friend that she was, Maggie took Cass along with Liam and her other son to the playground a couple of afternoons. But from Cass's postmortems, I knew that the rabbit-faced boy had been there, and that Liam and he had ignored Cass save the two or three times when they—both of them, I was saddened to learn—smashed his sand buildings.

Still, almost a week after Kurt left, I was lucky enough to get a subbing job at the middle school. After a trying day (I enjoyed the kids, but they had no qualms ignoring everything I said and texting each other LeBron James memes), I picked up Cass from Little Rainbows, put on *Go, Diego, Go!*, and sat down on the couch beside him. I reached for my book—" 'Yes, of course, if it's fine tomorrow,' said Mrs. Ramsay. 'But you'll have to be up with the lark,' she added"—and drifted off to sleep.

I woke to the sound of a woman's voice. There on the screen, seated in a hot pink leather armchair, was Jenna Rose, my former client. She wore a white lab coat, her highlighted chestnut hair sculpted into a tight orb, her lips a glossy mauve. "This one-of-a-kind makeup has been formulated from Bahamian seashell dust. Are there any colors more beautiful and sensual than those found on the beaches of the Bahamas? Look at this lush bronzer made from the Emperor Helmet and the Roller Conch, two of my favorite shells." She looked incredible and sounded authoritative.

I had liked working with Jenna. She was nothing like the chirpy, weepy contestant who had won first runner-up on *I Thee Wed*. She approached me and the book with the cautious air of a woman whose public image had been whittled into a princess figurine. She questioned a few of my ideas, as well as my revisions of the handful of passages that she herself had written, although she eventually accepted them. A client's approach to her book often stemmed from her station in the world—or her perceived station. Jenna had a lot to prove, and together we crafted what I thought was a fairly intelligent guidebook to creating one's own definition of attractiveness and worth. It became a manifesto for maintaining integrity as well as interdependence within the context of love.

On TV now, she adjusted her reading glasses as she rose from her chair. "Our scientists vaporize the crystals to create the purest colors straight from the ocean. Let's go on a tour of our high-tech lab and meet some of these scientists, or as we call them, 'colorizers.'"

I remembered reading that she had married one of the production assistants from *I Thee Wed*. I was glad that she had continued to find work, something she had confessed to me worried her after the end of the show, and that she had achieved seemingly all of her personal and professional goals. At the moment, this was more than I could say for myself. Even finishing half of Lana's book had come to seem unlikely.

I opened my laptop and saw a new message from Lana, her response to my draft of the second chapter: *Any way for you to treat breastfeeding as more of a revolutionary act? You (I) come across as neutral, even anti-nursing at times!*

I replied: *I hear you. But to be honest, don't a lot of people breastfeed these days? Isn't it more revolutionary to bottle-feed your baby loud and proud?* I may have been justifying my own failure to breastfeed Cass. *Nursing may be best for those who don't work and have the resources for lactation consultants, breast pumps, and all those gadgets out there to make the whole—uncomfortable!—process more comfortable.*

Nursing had come to seem like a privilege to me back when Cass was younger. To work full-time and to be available full-time as your baby's sole food source was no simple thing.

Lana wrote, *This may be so, but I'd like to take a more overtly PRO stance. Also you used the word 'wonderful' four times in the chapter. Oops! And if you were thinking of the woodblock you saw in my hallway, it was a Hashiguchi, not Utamaro.*

Ack, sorry! I shuddered.

In some ways, it had been even easier to write for Nick Felles than for Lana. I had not heard his name in a while, and annoyed, I googled him. Two more young actresses had just come forward with accusations of sexual assault. One had a small part as a witch on his show, and I did not recognize the other. There in a photo was his smug baby face, his arm draped around the actress I did not know, a cigarette between his two fingers that dangled just above her breast.

I immediately toggled back to my conversation with Lana. *I'll redo this section.*

Lana: *Thanks. I did like the part about nursing in the park and those rude teenagers. LOL. (Could you tone it down tho? Don't want to turn off readers! Less profanity if you wouldn't mind, even if it's meant to convey male anger.) How did you come up with this?!*

Me: *Something similar happened to me once.*

Lana: *What creeps! Yes, by all means, feel free to fill in where necessary with more of this sort of thing!*

Me: *Ok. I think readers would rather hear your stories, though!*

Lana: *Did Val send you Ned Boyle's contact info? He's an old friend and he's on the board up at Columbia Memorial, Child Psych. One of the most impressive docs out there. You could talk to him about sleep and attachment parenting. He'll have some good data on boys' neuro, etc. I'm remembering a study about the mother's voice, response in male child. Also would you look into the marketing of binary-gendered clothing and toys?*

Me: *I know from raising my own son how hard it is to find gender-neutral toys.*

Lana: *Great—go with that. You hardly even need me! (Except again please redo breastfeeding and Utamaro and tone down language.) FYI, I'm out of commission the next few weeks. Have a conference in Melbourne. If that flight alone doesn't kill me, what follows will: lecture in London, meet cousin in Barcelona, quick vacation in Paris, summit in Geneva.*

Me: *Ok. Wow.*

I made a quick mental assessment; I had yet to finish two chapters in four and a half months. I would have to show Gin double this, and soon. The final manuscript was due in two months, although maybe this could be pushed out if Lana talked to Gin. Still, I owed Jimmy rent money, and I would be unable to pay utilities soon. I had already left my electric company two pitiful phone messages.

Me: *Good luck with all that traveling.*

Lana: *This is my life!*

You should see mine! I wrote and quickly deleted. And then, I don't know why, but I typed the following: *Lana, I need to tell you that my name is Allie, not Amy.*

Lana: *It is?! Why did it take you so long to correct me?*

Of course this was my fault. Of course there was no *My bad!* or even hint of shame on her part. How meek she must have thought me. I typed, *Better late than never, right?*

She wrote, *Well, yes!*

THAT NIGHT, I helped Jimmy move a minifridge that he had found on the side of the road into my basement. He planned to use it in the new house that he had just bought, after he converted the basement into its own rental unit.

"Any sense of when you'll be able to get me some rent, Hon?" he asked, breathing heavily as we set the thing down in the corner of the now largely empty space.

"I can give you part of it now," I said. "Or soon, I think."

I saw his face manufacture both pity and skepticism. "I've got this, I swear," I said. "I might be able to pay you a few months all at once. Just not right now."

"When's Kurt going to get back? You sure you can cover for him?"

I glanced down at the rusty minifridge on the floor. "I made do before he moved in, right?"

"I've been good to you," Jimmy said, squinting as if trying to see me in some different light. A toothpick emerged from between his lips. Apparently it had been inside his mouth the whole time. "With this new property, I don't have a lot of wiggle room right now."

I said what I knew that I had to: "You *have* been good to us. You've been amazing. Jimmy, I don't even know how to thank you. You were so easy about Kurt moving in downstairs and letting him paint in exchange for rent. And you know, you're like—you're like a second grandpa to Cass." Was it too much? I had found that flattery rarely was, that it could be more effective than anything with certain people, even if it made me feel like a verbal prostitute right now.

"Aw," he said, waving me away. He moved the toothpick toward the side of his mouth. "Just by the end of the month, okay?"

"To BE HONEST, I try to caution parents against assigning too much import to a baby's sex in terms of its predetermining behavior. Excuse me." I could hear Dr. Boyle put the phone down as he began to cough and hack for a good minute. I was about to suggest we try this later, when he came back on. "Genetically, boys and girls are 99.8 percent the same." He went on for a while about the cells in the anterior hypothalamus.

I asked him about Ferberizing and about Dr. Sears (Dr. Boyle told me they were old friends, and I detected no small degree of competition). I had some questions about attachment parenting and he responded blandly, without giving me his own take on it. I imagined that he had lived through multiple fads in parenting. Each generation was so sure of its choices, only to be refuted by the next.

We moved on to teaching boys empathy. "Modeling compassion is always a good idea. Modeling feminism in the case of this book," he said. "And a good marriage—an egalitarian one, I guess."

"What if you're not married?" I had to ask.

"Then modeling good relationships, I guess."

We discussed boys' capacity for empathy. "It depends on the child and his environment. Nurture, nature, you know. A boy raised with a significant amount of external stressors will have a harder time learning anything," he said, and began to cough again. "I'm talking about poverty, abuse, disease, alcoholism, divorce, you know. We all shut down in the face of immediate stressors, or at least most people do. The fight-or-flight instinct kicks in. A boy dealing with these kinds of problems might not be as empathetic. He might act out. He might even develop depression or anxiety."

"Or separation anxiety?" I asked carefully.

"Sure."

"And the absence of a father? What impact would that have?"

"Again, it depends on the household." He went on to give another blurry answer that gave me little to go on for either Cass or the book.

"So you could say that just the existence of alcoholism or divorce— or the absence of the father—doesn't automatically cause stress." He did not agree or disagree. "What's the best way to help your son with his anxiety?"

"Honestly, I'd just say to love your boy. Hold him and comfort him when he seems to need it. Try to make sure all his basic needs are met. Teach him that people are there to help him, and that the world around him is manageable and caring."

"What about moms who aren't able to always do that? I mean, for reasons of time or money. Or disability or what-have-you?"

"No one is always able to do anything. We all do our best," he said magnanimously.

"HOW'S THAT FAMOUS woman's book going?" my mother asked over the phone.

"Slowly," I said.

"Lottie had some of us over last night, and five minutes in, Patty Copeland got the news that her daughter-in-law had a baby. So then the whole night revolved around Patty. This is grandchild number thirteen, but you'd think it was her first. And then we got to hear all about her son meeting some big NBA player, and now the two are best friends and planning a vacation to Cuba. I finally told Patty that *you're* writing something for one of the most famous women in the country right now. The mystery just killed her. She would not stop asking me who it was."

"What?" I said. "Why'd you do that?" I was almost impressed by my mother's resourcefulness in turning her own nagging curiosity into social capital.

"I didn't tell her anything. I just had a little fun with her, and believe me, it worked. She stopped talking about her new granddaughter and her son," she said with a laugh. "Anyway, we've gotten the condo almost all set up. I found this Japanese woodblock print at a—get this—a yard sale down the street. It looks like an original, so we're going to get it assessed."

I glanced over at my screen. Google Alert had sent me a link to an article titled "Breban Bares All at European Women's Lobby." "Mom, I have to get to work," I said. "Let's talk more in a few days?"

I clicked on the video. Lana stood at a podium on a stage; behind her a line of maybe twenty women breastfed their infants. Apparently Lana herself had not bared anything. The juxtaposition of all these slender, somber-faced women wearing business suits, a few holding briefcases, and the diaper-clad babies was really something. "Never Apologize!" Lana said into the microphone, as did everyone else in the room. "Never Compromise! Never Rationalize!"

One of the babies slipped, and the mother's breast came into full view. The woman may have been too busy adjusting the baby in her arms to care, and why should she? The video had already been liked 57k times and disliked 109k times. I could only imagine the tweets to come. This speech struck a different chord from recent ones Lana had given. Maybe she and her people had finally rethought their efforts at diluting her image. Maybe now that the battle lines had been drawn throughout the country, she had decided to actually provoke the trolls in order to galvanize her supporters.

I checked Lana's Twitter feed and Facebook page to see what she might have to say about all this, but she had not posted anything yet.

Was I supposed to now include this in the book—even if it had nothing to do with raising Norton? Surely there were other ghostwriters who had dealt with similar clients. I had not come across more than a few of us over the years. We always spoke haltingly about our work, strapped as most of us were to our nondisclosure agreements. I did a search, and in a heartbeat, there it was, a support group. Everyone had an alias; I went with AMLCAL, my initials together with Cass's. *Ghostwriters Talk* was a private mutiny, a chorus of anonymous voices comparing payments and terms and snarky anecdotes about unnamed celebrity clients.

It was a relief to see that what I was earning for Lana's book was about average for similar projects. There was talk that the top earners and biggest name clients could bring in as much as $500,000 per book. Everyone spoke of their clients in code, BM (Boss Man) or BW (Boss Woman).

SILENTPARTNER wrote: *I once did a novel for a has-been country singer BM, and he bitched the whole time that the writing wasn't literary enough. He wanted it to be, and this is verbatim, "Surrealist and broad-canvas, like Gabriel Garcia-Marquez." I was like, Dude, you are (hardly still) known for your tired songs about your ex-wife and cold beer.*

Someone said that they had maintained a Facebook page for a rage-prone sit-com actress. There was a business book for a verbally abusive media tycoon; a young adult novel for a speed-addicted teen pop star. I had to restrain myself from googling the country singer BM and the sit-com actress, and almost chimed in about Nick, but he would be instantly recognizable, given the widespread news coverage. For all I knew, allegations continued to gather against him.

The ghostwriters discussed their favorite jobs, which really meant their favorite clients, those who had become like family over the years, also those who had put them up at the Beverly Wilshire or the Mandarin Oriental for a week, those who brought them along to a dude ranch or on Caribbean vacations. I began to feel sorry for myself. Congresswoman McGrath had offered me and Cass the use of her cottage on Cape Cod for a weekend, but that and the Gucci bag and samurai sword that Nick sent had been about it.

But I was being petty. Weren't there other more meaningful perks to ghostwriting? Both Jenna Rose and Tanya Dawson had become friends, although I had not heard from Jenna in a while now. Still, I was no longer writing about tax breaks for the extraordinarily wealthy or listening to my colleagues fantasize about Halle Berry and the office manager's hot daughter. My schedule was somewhat flexible, which helped with Cass. I worked in my pajamas. This was not nothing, I told myself.

CHAPTER NINE

Three weeks after he had left, Kurt called me from Montpelier. Labrador and Newfoundland were a no-go, he said. He had been having too much fun in Vermont and had decided to stay put for a while. "I've been helping rebuild part of a barn with some people I met." He went on to tell me about the reclaimed wood they had found at another old barn nearby, the many stables, the cabin nearby where they had set up camp and slept. "I'm thinking I'll come back once the barn is done, in a couple weeks or so. It's spectacular country up here," he said.

"It's nice country down here, too." It was late, and I suspected that he might be about to tell me something I did not want to hear. "Who are these 'people' you've met?"

"Oh, there's a carpenter and a builder and the guy who bought the barn, he's a kind of farmer. And his father, who has a few goats and pigs that will live here. Everyone is so kind and interesting—and real."

I waited for him to go on about any one of these people. When he did not, I said, "Cass misses you."

The quiet on the phone was a heavy cloud between us, something theoretically permeable but still intrusive.

"I've been letting him watch too much TV," I said.

"It's okay. You're doing the best you can."

I did not want to crave Kurt's physical presence like I did right then. I did not want to be jealous of a barn or a carpenter, or anyone else. I certainly did not want to sound piteous. "I should get back to work," I said.

"It's eleven-thirty at night."

"I've been trying to work when Cass is sleeping. It goes better that way."

"Jeez, that's got to be tough," he said. "I think about you guys, you know."

"We think about you, too. Anyway, onward," I said. And then, "We miss you."

"Yeah, me, too." He added that he would call again when he knew more about his return, and that he would send Cass a postcard.

I went outside into the frozen night. The dark sapphire sky was unusually clear, and stardust hung everywhere. I could just make out the Berkshires, a blueish rolling at the bottom of the horizon. I looked across the street at the Garbellas' house, the small farmer's porch and the ceramic pot near the stained wood door, all its lights off.

Things were hardly perfect for me and Cass, but we were getting by without Kurt. And writing this book was a good thing to be doing. Women needed it. Mothers. Single mothers. And boys, and men, fathers, stepfathers, all of us. No one needed another *Bootcamp Mama* or some new screed that guilted us into teaching kids to make their beds military style or throwing away our iPhones and all our friends and comforts so we could experience a simpler life on a houseboat. Ideally, Lana's would be a book that empowered mothers.

Back inside, I saw a new text on my phone from my own mother: "It's Oprah, isn't it?!"

• • •

Two DAYS LATER, Lana instant-messaged back. She had read my revision of the second chapter, where I had added in, per her request, a discussion of gendered toys and clothes, and then described certain shopping experiences with Norton, who had for better or worse become a version of Cass. My mother and Ed had given me a stack of onesies when Cass was born, blue garments emblazoned with sayings just right for Lana's book: "I cry and her top comes off," and "My Mommy thinks she's in charge! That's so cute."

I told Norton that colors did not have "private parts." He was too young to understand the reasons that clothing and toy manufacturers segregated their products in order to promote power to one gender and beauty to another, thereby maintaining a cultural patriarchy that financially benefited them.

When Norton was three, he decided for a time that he liked "girls' clothes" better. Although to be honest, I did worry about other children teasing or bullying him. I reminded myself of what Frederick Douglass said: "If there is not struggle, there is no progress." I bought Norton one pink party dress and a couple of skirts, as well as a Barbie doll, for which he had begged for weeks. He carried his Barbie wherever we went. One day, when we stood in a checkout line at a supermarket, a woman approached us and said to him, "I hope you're holding that thing for your sister."

It had all come back to me: the woman's pointy, glossy face; Cass, in the seat of the shopping cart at Walmart, hugging his Barbie in her bridal gown to his chest; my own feeble response—"Yep, it's his sister's." And what followed, Cass's blinking fast as he tried to make sense of what I had just said. He was even then—most children are—attuned to the hardest truths. And although, after the woman walked off, I tried to explain myself and told him that his toy preferences were nobody's business, the damage was done. "Why did that lady laugh at me?" he said. I admit that I changed the subject and off we went.

Lana wanted me to cut the bit about toy manufacturers segregating products by gender for financial gain. *Not sure we can actually prove this and I don't want to inadvertently rankle any execs who happen to read this. Otherwise looks good. Toddlerhood, here we come!*

Me: *I'm already on it!*

Lana: *How about picking up on the theme of pink vs. blue? (Let's keep it to parents and kids, rather than investors' motives.)*

Me: *Will do. Any favorite stores?*

Lana: *I'd rather not use store names—just say "children's clothing store" pls. Between you and me, some of those execs are also big donors to important causes, and have nothing to do with inventories anyway.*

She was starting to sound like Betsy McGrath. Betsy had insisted that I include the following in her memoir: a history of the native tribes that once lived along the shores of the Connecticut River; its Dutch and Puritan settlements; its industrial past. My first draft of her book was over six hundred pages. "The editor thinks there are too many detours," I reported back to the congresswoman. "He said that people want to hear more about *you*."

"I'm not sure how much more I have to say about myself."

Betsy was mild-mannered and agreeable. She had married her high school love and had emotionally if not financially supported him and their children for decades before stepping into his congressional seat after his sudden death from a heart attack. Her favorite subjects of conversation were her grandchildren and a new bill that she was cosponsoring, a bill that would limit the estate tax in Connecticut. In the end, I trimmed some of the detours and pulled a few more memories from her, but the book was what it was.

Most reviews were courteous and tepid. One said, "Rep. McGrath gives us Connecticut in all its Connecticut-ness. Her memoir read like a beloved great aunt's high school research paper about her home state."

"Mom." Cass hovered in his pajamas in the doorway of my bedroom. "I had a nightmare. Can I sleep in your bed?" He yawned wide.

"You want me to turn on your closet light?"

"No. I just want to be in your room with you."

Letting him sleep with me when I was too tired to argue was not going to strengthen his ability to be apart from me. "Hold on. Let me finish what I'm doing and we'll figure it out."

I wrote to Lana that I would get something back to her soon and awaited her response before logging out. Cass had already crawled on top of my sheets. "When is Kurt coming home?" he asked.

"I'm not sure," I said. I looked at Cass's shiny hair and his robot footsy pajamas. Although he had grown attached to his Barbie, he had never much cared about wearing pink or blue. He did tend to prefer clothing with images of robots or animals to those with tools or sexist sayings, thank God, or maybe it was really me that preferred these things. "I actually talked to Kurt tonight. He said he misses you."

I leaned over to tuck him beneath my sheet, and lay down beside him. I knew that I should walk him back to his bedroom, establish boundaries, and teach him independence, but he was warm and sleepy and felt so good next to me. I always slept better with someone next to me.

You shouldn't use your child to fill your loneliness, some voice within me said.

It's just for one night, another answered.

THE REVISION WENT quickly the next morning.

> We were looking for an outfit for him to wear to an upcoming wedding. To the left of the store were clothes for boys, and to the right, girls. I guided Norton toward the display of blue blazers

and khakis, the small striped ties hanging on a rack in the corner. I tried to find a blazer his size, but when I did, he was gone.

I found him leafing through a rack of puffy white dresses. "This is the girls' section," I said.

"Oh," he said, and his eyes dropped. The navy blazer in my hands was so plain, so uninspiring and adult compared to the soft lacy fabric with the enormous satin sashes.

Sometimes I imagine a children's clothing store arranged like this: a large, open area segmented by age and size only, with affordably-priced blue skirts and pink blazers and green and yellow pajamas and blank T-shirts on which children can determine whatever it is that they want to say: "I Want Candy" or "I Need a Hug." Bins of stuffed animals, a corner with bean bags and shelves of books, colorful maps of various countries on the walls. I might call the place Be You.

I HAD AGREED to transport a washing machine across town to two of Jimmy's other tenants. Jimmy and I struggled as we heaved it into the cargo bed of my truck, and afterward, mopping sweat off his forehead, he said, "You see that he's officially in? The electoral college gave him the green light?"

"We aren't supposed to talk about the news," I said. I tried, sometimes in vain, not to think much about the election and its possible impact. It seemed that for Jimmy, the whole thing had been a sort of game, that victory had not only been sweet, but the only thing that mattered. Not whether Russia had interfered, not whether the president himself would do a decent job or be a decent person or really anything else. Jimmy's team had won and mine had lost.

It turned out that the two tenants had been in the year ahead of me at high school, but we had starred together in a production of *Oklahoma!* Jen and Gary were now a couple, but he was off at work at the Sunoco in town, where he was manager. Outside of their place, a mint green bungalow in better repair than my place—although not by much—she and I caught up on what we had been doing over the years. "I work at a nursing home in Pittsfield," she said. "My true calling is fostering rescue Greyhounds, though." Jen had put on a little weight and gone blond. Both suited her, I thought. We laughed about being "Jimmy Pryor's suckers," and then gingerly lowered the washing machine from the back of my truck onto a dolly. We rested a moment before rolling it into the house.

THAT NIGHT, AFTER I got Cass into the bath, I lowered the toilet seat and sat down across from him. He lay on his back and let his hair float in the water. He said, "Look, my peanut is getting bigger."

"Peanuts will do that." In this moment, I wished that I had one so that I could talk about this stuff from a place of greater intuitive understanding. "Sometimes they get bigger, but then they go back to their normal sizes."

"Why?"

I tried my best to explain how blood circulates and what happens when pressure builds inside of veins.

"Barton Haller told me I have a girl's name."

"So what if you do?"

"Why did you give me a girl's name?"

"Your name is Cassidy, not Cassandra. But there are lots of names that both boys and girls can have. You know, if I wanted to, I could have named you Cassandra or Emily or Lisa."

He looked like he was not buying it.

"Anyway, I really named you after a song. 'Ah, child of countless trees. Ah, child of boundless seas, What you are, what you're meant to be,'" I sang. "It's from this band called the Grateful Dead."

"What does Grateful mean?"

"Glad," I said.

"The Glad Dead?"

"I guess so, yes."

"Who is Iron Man? Barton hit me because I didn't know who Iron Man was and then I didn't want to go on the big slide with him. Then he broke my hair."

"Oh, Sweetie." I wondered just what he meant by "hit" and "broke."

"I started to cry and then he called me a fag."

I swallowed hard. "Where was Suze? She is going to get one hell of a phone call from me tomorrow," I said quietly. I stopped myself from launching into a full-blown rant, which would only upset him more.

Sometimes I felt as if, in raising Cass, I were introducing a small, perfect alien to the terrible planet earth. *Here are the earthlings who will make fun of you for looking the slightest bit different. Here are the feelings—sadness, fear, inadequacy—that, as a male, you will be expected to only rarely admit. Here are the very few interests that boys are expected by most people to have. Here is the sort of earthling that you are supposed to be, an earthling who is nothing, not one tiny bit like the being you really are.*

"Sometimes people aren't nice," I began.

"Then why are you always telling me to be nice?"

"Because someone has to break the cycle. Kindness can be contagious. And it has to start somewhere, right?"

He grew quiet. I may have raised more questions than I had answered.

We were unprepared for Norton's early questions about gender and sex. I suspect that children wait until their parents are least anticipating it to broach these topics. Norton's first came when I was helping him with his bath one night. I could find no words. My mind was an instant traffic jam, and I spoke haltingly in biological terms, and of physiology and physics, verbiage of course too sophisticated for a four-year-old.

Afterward, I worried that he detected a degree of shame in my answer, something I was loathe to impart. Would he think that women were cowed by such things, that maleness had the power to shame even his own mother? I had in mind for him a more European and open, less puritanical attitude toward the body. I filed away my concern under the heading "One More Subject I Would Have to Untangle as a Feminist Parent of a Boy."

"I'M SO SORRY, Allie. I'll have a talk with Barton about the word 'fag'— and about being kind to other children," Suze said over the phone.

"That'd be great. And maybe you can say something like, 'Not every boy loves Iron Man or going down the big slide like you do.'"

"If only that were true!" She had a laugh with herself. "Listen, Allie, Cass is in good hands here. We have very strong, clear kindness rules."

I had seen the kindness poster that hung above the rows of cubbies near the front door. Although well-intended, the rules seemed vague and unenforceable to me: "Always be nice! Make a new friend today! Be kind to your planet! Remember to smile!"

"Suze, Cass told me that Barton doesn't wash his hands after using the bathroom. I think he's been wiping them on the walls and on some of the other kids, too," I said. I sounded uptight, like a helicopter mom. And a snitch.

"Boys!" she said. "What can you really do but laugh, right? Another one peed all over the caterpillar slide today. I'm telling you, I saved at least three other kids from getting drenched. Unfortunately, I did not save one of them from throwing up on the same slide about ten minutes later. It was a day!"

"Oh my god." I wondered why anyone would choose this sort of employment.

At least Christmas vacation was approaching, and then Cass would get a break from Barton. As the holidays approached, so did cold and flu season, which meant it was also substitute teacher season. I picked up shifts in both the middle and high schools. Even so, my bank account came close to being overdrawn just after I paid a steep heating bill. Bertie loaned us her old fake Christmas tree and the three of us hung ornaments and draped it with multicolored beads from Maggie's trip to Bolivia. I had written and printed up for Cass a children's story about a boy who lived underwater with a school of fish, and thought that he was one of them. At Walmart I charged a few toys and a pair of pajamas.

Bertie came over on Christmas day with a frozen pot pie and, for Cass, a coloring book and some new markers, as well as a tiny stuffed lion. He was excited and went to find Hippo. "Dad and his baby son," he said, smashing the animals together.

I nodded. The absence of a flesh-and-blood father in the room could not have been more apparent. "But aren't they different species?"

"Parents can have babies that are different," he said.

Bertie's eyes flashed between us.

"Of course they can," I said, nervous about what he might say next.

"Hippo loves his lion son," Bertie said, nodding.

Jimmy brought us a box of Munchkins and another of salt-water taffy just for Cass. I grew teary with gratitude for them—and maybe also exhaustion.

"Oh, Al," Bertie said, squeezing my hand between hers.

We sat around the living room and even sang some Christmas carols, and I tried not to compare this day with the Christmases of my own childhood, when we would make the long drive to my aunt's townhouse in Norwell and enter to the aroma of something roasting and the sounds of my cousins chasing each other in and out of the kitchen and bathroom. I would join the two of them in their bedroom, where we played Twister or watched *Miami Vice,* happily awaiting the "Ho, ho, ho's" of my Uncle Nathan, who dressed as Santa Claus the years that he came with my Aunt Setti from Jamaica, where they still lived. He would pull from his backpack gifts like beaded T-shirts or carved wooden masks or blue fish-shaped glasses of sand. He and my aunt had always smelled faintly of skunks, a smell that took me many years to identify.

SOMEHOW, WE HAD eked out a nice Christmas, but things were getting so tight that I considered pulling Cass from Little Rainbows or even cutting Bertie's one day of sitting for him, although losing even the small amount I paid her each week would, I knew, be hard on her. I thought about asking Colin to advance me part of my next payment, but echoing in my mind was something Ed had told me long ago: "Don't ever tell your employer that they are responsible for paying your bills. You're there to add value, not take it away."

"But my value is my skills, not my bank account," I'd said.

"Not everyone can differentiate between the two," Ed said. I resented it, but he was right then, and unfortunately, he still was.

WITHOUT ANY WARNING, a filling in one of my teeth apparently broke. I took a sip of coffee and yelled out in pain. I had done some landscaping last summer for Aaron, a nice guy I had known back when I was a kid who was now a dentist, so I called him to tell him about my tooth. Reluctantly, I confided that I was temporarily short on cash.

"Just come on by and I'll take a look," he said brightly. "We can set up a payment plan if need be. Not to worry."

In his waiting room, I apologized to him up and down for having brought my son. "Being a single mom isn't always easy," I said, maybe to garner sympathy and a better deal.

"Okay," he said vacantly. He appeared disappointed in something, and it dawned on me that his friendliness both last summer and over the phone may have been tinged with flirtation. He had asked me to meet him for coffee last summer, but I'd had other plans. Maybe now that Aaron knew I had a son, I no longer qualified for his payment plan. Sure enough, there was no wedding ring on his left hand. "I'm running a little behind, so give me twenty minutes or so," he said.

I arranged some toys in front of Cass. He played with a wooden abacus and a fire truck happily for a while, then not so happily. A few other patients waited, and then Cass began to kick an empty chair. A woman shot us both looks. "Hey," I said, and tugged him closer to me.

Twenty minutes passed. Thirty minutes. Cass began to march in circles and then behind the reception desk, and accidentally knocked a stack of files onto the floor. I raced over to him, apologized to the receptionist, and led him back to the chairs.

Forty-five minutes passed. An hour. I read to him from a torn copy of *The Wind in the Willows*, my jaw twinging with pain as I spoke, and after a few pages, he wandered off. Seconds later, he returned with a replica jaw from one of the patient rooms. He dropped it in the large fish tank in the corner of the room with a loud *plunk*.

"Cass! Oh God." I rolled up my sleeve and retrieved the jaw from the murky tank, the tetra shooting off to the sides. "None of you saw that, right?" I feebly joked to the other patients waiting as I set it on the receptionist's desk.

One man half-smiled, and a woman only raised her eyebrows in response. I knew her from somewhere. *Barbara Kinzer*, I remembered. The director of the Berkshire Gilded Age Society, a foundation that oversaw the preservation of the many local historic mansions. Long ago, my mother had established a fair-weather friendship with Barbara. She had a daughter my age, an unpleasant and clingy girl named Sandrine whose sole interesting trait was her uncanny ability to recite passages of Stephen King's books from memory. Barbara appeared not to recognize me in my adult form.

What if Aaron changed his mind and asked for full payment today? I felt like a child among adults here.

At last Aaron appeared and said he was still running late. He suggested that his sister come pick up Cass. "She's at home with her baby Dylan right now anyway," he said. Vanessa lived a few houses down in a renovated Victorian that a decade earlier had been an art gallery. I had met them when we were kids, back when I used to hang around Tanglewood while my mother worked in the gift shop. Their parents had had a summer home here and season tickets.

"Thanks, Aaron, but I can handle it." I pulled Cass past the reception desk and into the restroom.

"You are not allowed to touch a fake mouth or anything else in those patient rooms ever again," I said to him. "You are not allowed to put anything in that fish tank. Those are living creatures. You could have hurt the tetra—you could have killed them. I need for you to behave perfectly right now. Do you understand?" Others could probably hear me. I lowered my voice and said, "Don't you want my mouth to stop hurting? If you keep this up that nice dentist won't want to help me."

He nodded, big-eyed.

Vanessa showed up about ten minutes later, "glad to help out," Dylan in a Baby Bjorn on her chest. She did not look glad. "This motherhood thing is no joke. Dylan sleeps for at most an hour at a time. I'm so tired I drove over my cell phone yesterday." She stood there across from me in a batik headband covering most of her short black hair, a smear of something white on her cheek, and sighed heavily as she waited for me to hand over my son.

"You don't have to take Cass. Your hands are already full."

Barbara Kinzer coughed into a fist. Cass wandered toward the fish tank and began tapping on the glass.

"What's one more kid?" Vanessa said.

"Maybe he can help entertain Dylan," I offered meekly.

After they left, I headed to the bathroom, where, sitting on the institutional toilet, I tried to gather myself. If I had been able to make an appointment like everyone else, I would not still be here, waiting and panicking about the bill. In my mind, I ran through my poor life choices. Why on earth had I wasted all that time earning nothing at the magazine in San Francisco? Why hadn't I stayed at the equity firm in New York, ill-suited work and my questionable after-work persona notwithstanding? Oh, the life I—and Cass—would be able to enjoy now if only I had been more Machiavellian then. Integrity—and real feminism—were clearly for people more financially secure than I.

An uncomfortable question formed in my mind: did I regret having had Cass? The answer was immediate: no. He was nothing that I regretted even slightly. Not for a second, not even after today's behavior. He could be an unbelievable pain. He could push me to limits I had been unaware that I had, but he was Cass, my Cass, my sweet kid, as close to me as my own breath.

I RAN MY tongue over my new filling, which needed some sanding, as I read Lana's text message. She wanted me to discuss discipline in the chapter about toddlerhood.

Last night we went to dinner at Daniel, and a boy next to us had a huge temper tantrum. His mom just sat there texting the whole time. It took all the restraint I had not to walk over and ask why oh why she had brought her son to this not exactly kid-friendly restaurant.

Sounds rough, I wrote. Whenever possible, I made a point of offering praise or support to mothers in that situation. At least I had been doing so since I'd had Cass. Not that I frequented restaurants like Daniel, which I could not resist googling. Its website showed photos of artful morsels dotting plates and three-figure prix fixe options. *Did Norton ever pull something like that?*

Lana: *He had his moments.*

Me: *What were some of the harder moments for you?*

I waited several minutes for her reply. Had Norton really never had a tantrum? Perhaps he had only done so with Gloria or some other person who was tending him.

Finally, her response came:

Once he used a Sharpie to draw all over a framed Annie Leibovitz of Lester and me that she, Annie, had given us as a wedding present. We were livid. We had to get it reframed.

Me: *Wow, that's a good one!* I cringed with sympathy. *Did you punish him?*

Lana: *I'm sure we did, but we also tried positive reinforcement and whatnot. I can't remember much more. Sorry.*

Me: *Any memories of disciplining him? Were you "time out" people, or did you take away privileges or screen time or something like that?*

Lana: *Let me think about it. Have to run. I'll get back to you.*

But she did not get back to me that day, or the next, and so I had little choice but to return to her book and again stretch what little she had given me.

A parent must determine their own style of discipline. Norton once found a Sharpie marker and drew all over an original Annie Leibovitz photograph, a gift from Annie herself. Another time, he ate a handful of a neighbor's laxatives and we had to rush him to the hospital, where he endured the grueling stomach pump. At his first dentist appointment, he grabbed a replica jaw from the display counter and dropped it with a great PLUNK into the fish tank in the corner of the crowded waiting room.

I have never felt less like a powerful woman than I did in those moments. Parenthood can profoundly deepen and texturize a woman's life, but also, if I am to be perfectly honest, can diminish it, at least temporarily.

I would change the laxative and replica jaw things later, maybe make up some other examples. But for now, I needed to research "positive reinforcement" and other methods of discipline that worked for parents. I had yet to find a method that consistently worked for us.

CHAPTER TEN

With every book, I had given small pieces of myself to my client: to Jenna, a knowledge of Adrienne Rich's poetry; to Tanya, a fondness for the movie *Brave*; to Rick, a love of portulaca and snapdragon plants. But Lana's was coming to require more of me—the whole foundation, so to speak, rather than just a roof shingle. I emailed Colin and Gin again to seek their advice. A day passed, and then Gin texted back.

Should I ask Colin about finding another writer for Lana?

No! I replied, stricken. *I'll figure it out. Sorry to bother you.*

Gin: *Will you send me what you've got so far? You do know that Lana just asked for an extension, right? That you have until April 15? Our production team is not thrilled, so if you could get me the final manuscript a few weeks before then, that would be ideal.*

Me: *I didn't know. Wonder why she didn't tell me.*

I agreed to send the first three chapters in a few days, a week at most, and got right to work.

We give away what we have to in order to survive. It seemed counterintuitive at first, but when I thought in anthropological terms, I understood something essential: in prehistoric times, of course, when men ventured out to hunt and bring home their rewards, women remained home. They ceded their love and energy and time and gathering skills to their families. We cede our bodies during pregnancy, at least temporarily. But once we hand off too much of ourselves, women inevitably grow hollow. We shrivel.

I am aware that I may be justifying the lengths to which I next went. But I grew increasingly angry that without going to the well of my own experiences, I would have been unable to write Lana's book. Between the withholding of information and the subtle, sometimes passive pressure that came both from her and Colin to fill in the many gaps with my own thoughts and material—it had the feel of gaslighting. Lana never outright refused to answer a question; instead, she just had to rush off to a meeting or a rally. I had tried inventing anecdotes for her, but the leap from my mind to hers, from my life with Cass to hers with Norton was too great. What did I know about world travel and restaurants like Daniel, about interviewing people like Ruth Bader Ginsburg and being friends with Annie Leibovitz? What did I know about teaming up with a husband as well as one—or more?—nannies to raise your son? My patience was shot.

It was a Monday, and I knew that Lana would be in New York because she had told me as much. I reluctantly called Maggie. "Any chance you could take Cass today?"

"Oh, sure," she said. "Liam's got a friend here and we were going to head to the park, but maybe we can, I don't know, find an art class or something else to do."

"You're the best, Maggie. How can I thank you?"

There was a beat during which I considered how little I could offer her, especially since our sons did not mesh. "No need to thank me," she finally said.

I gathered a few things, drove to Great Barrington, and caught the early bus, nearly full this time. A piercing body odor came from the man seated behind me, an exceptionally hairy person who may well have been covertly masturbating against the back of my seat. When the bus got going, I reached in my bag for my copy of *To the Lighthouse.* "Yes, of course, if it's fine tomorrow,' said Mrs. Ramsay. 'But you'll have to be—" and I lurched forward as the man slammed against my seat, saying, "Jesus God." I exchanged wary looks with a young woman next to me and another two across the aisle, as if we were all four united in battle. I closed my book. Oh, to just get up with the lark and go for a sail.

I stepped off the bus in Manhattan and walked to Central Park. The late morning was brisk but not as bitter as it had been at home. I set up camp behind a large, snow-covered boulder across the street from Lana's building, and I pulled my ski cap low on my forehead. Maybe I should have brought a disguise—a wig even, or fake glasses just to be safe. Although the thought only reinforced the absurdity of my mission here. I wrapped my scarf around my mouth and nose and tried to ignore the glances of a jogger passing by. Soon I spotted Captain Kangaroo. A woman cleaned her taco truck nearby. Two men fed their horses and adjusted their harnesses. I waited.

Captain Kangaroo gazed up at the sky. No one exited the building. If nothing else, I would know that I had tried my best here.

Finally a good hour later, Gloria and a boy who I assumed was Norton stepped past Captain Kangaroo and headed north. My pulse thumping, I crossed the street and followed them at a distance onto West Ninety-Fourth. He was of course taller now than in those old pictures I had seen online, a bean of a boy, with shaggy dark hair and less-than-stellar posture. He wore athletic pants, a navy snow jacket, Nike Air Max shoes, and had a duffel bag slung over one shoulder. He and Gloria entered a deli and, a moment later, came out with a girl of about five, a girl with long black braids. She marched between them, grabbed both of their hands, and the three turned and headed a couple of blocks north. I was twitchy and alert, trying to avoid oncoming pedestrians while keeping the three of them in view. They soon stopped outside a small market, and like an ambush predator, I darted behind a delivery truck, and then across the street. Gloria went inside the store, but Norton and the girl hung back by the flower display. I hovered in the entryway of an apartment building, trying to appear unremarkable, and waited for something, anything, to document. A keen sense of purpose and fear buzzed in my gut. Norton lifted the girl into the air and swung her around, and she screamed in Spanish at him. He set her down and she swatted up at his chest. I guessed that she was Gloria's daughter, but I could not be sure.

Gloria emerged and the three continued onward to the next block. They approached BIG APPLE AIKIDO, a small storefront beside a housewares boutique. I slipped behind a car and watched Norton give the girl a high five and talk for a minute or so with Gloria. It may have been an argument; I swear I heard him say something like, "You're not my damn boss," and she replied in Spanish. Norton pivoted and headed inside the dojo, leaving Gloria to curse something in the direction of the sky.

When her gaze drifted to mine, I took off, walking hastily down Ninety-Fourth Street, veering left and right at people and cabs. *Get it together*, I told myself. Gloria would never recognize me after having met me only once.

I stopped at a crosswalk outside a Starbucks and unraveled my scarf. The café was crowded, but I found a seat in the corner and caught my breath. A Bonnie Raitt song played. The smell of dark, earthy coffee beans hung in the air. I ran my hands through my hair, took a few deep breaths, and focused on an empty paper cup someone had left on the table. The logo of the two-tailed mermaid siren grinned back at me. She was both seductive and motherly with her ample chest, her arms and posture open. Vulnerable, but hidden at the same time, she posed with her hair covering her chest, the logo cutting off just above the place where her navel would be.

I reminded myself of the reason that I was in New York.

Gloria and the girl had left by the time I returned to the dojo. I leaned against a Duane Reade and waited for Norton to emerge across the street.

Just after two, he came out with some friends, all of them talking at once, and I trailed them to a nearby Turkish café, a charming place where I would not expect to find a group of boisterous tween boys. Inside the café, I glanced around at the narrow space, its uneven wood floors painted gold and its walls covered in ornate tiles. I asked the host, a kindly small man, for a table of one and he led me to the far corner of the place, five tables away from the booth where Norton and his friends were now seated. "Enjoy yourself," the host told me as he handed me a menu.

A few people came through the front door, one an attractive older man with a shaved head and a gray goatee—Rick McClatchy, for whom I had written *The Contemplative Gardener: The Joys of Urban Planting and Cultivating Quiet*. He was a daytime talk show host. We had met a couple of times, and at the moment, I wished this were not true, as I hardly wanted to explain why I was in New York. But now as he passed my booth, he looked down at me. "Allie?"

"Oh, Rick, hi!"

"What're you doing here?" he asked.

"Seeing a friend," I managed. How natural lying had become.

He half-nodded and ducked his head, and I understood that he, too, was at a loss as to how to handle this situation. Introduce me to his friends, who may well have known nothing about me? "You look good. Everything all right with you?" he said. We exchanged awkward pleasantries and he said, "Well, I've got to use the restroom and get back to them."

"Of course. Nice to see you, Rick," I said, and reached for a menu. If they did not know he had worked with a ghostwriter, how might he identify me to his friends—a neighbor, perhaps? A cousin?

I ordered tea, and watched Norton and his friends. The fact of their choosing a rather cosmopolitan café told me plenty about his level of taste, although nothing that I could not have guessed. The acoustics here were poor, and all the voices joined in one murky din. Norton socked a friend on the arm, but mostly the boys just laughed and ate and made gestures with their fingers. I could only imagine Lana's reaction to Norton flickering his tongue between his fore and middle fingers. Maybe I would drop that into our book.

I had to improve my attitude, to shed my bitterness.

I followed Norton and his friends out and trailed them as they headed to a brick apartment building two blocks away. They disappeared inside, and I bought a hotdog from a nearby food truck, then paced the block. I wandered around a stationery store and ogled the letterpress cards, the wood-scented candles. I cradled a heavy paperweight in my hands, melted obsidian that looked like a small human brain within a glass globe. The woman at the register watched me as if I might steal the thing, and a little defeated, I decided to call it a day.

On the bus ride home, I assessed what I had seen: Gloria, Norton, and a girl who may have been Gloria's daughter behaving like an average family. A sibling tussle followed by a mother-son tiff. It was not unimaginable that Gloria was more of a mother to Norton than Lana. I guess I did not blame Lana for training her gaze on loftier goals than motherhood, but a part of me resented all that I was expected to provide in her reaching said goals. Would she have become *the* Lana Breban without people like me? And what about Gloria? Would Lana even have been able to raise a son or work half as much without her?

Over the years, I had turned Betsy McGrath, a pro-business, regressive congresswoman, into an environmental historian. For a good six months, I had impersonated Nick Felles. If nothing else, it was better to impersonate Lana Breban than these others.

Maybe she was secretly ashamed of being a hands-off mother. When I considered the possibility, I thought it unlikely. Shame—certainly shame about motherhood—seemed distinctly un-feminist to me, and anyway, Lana had dozens of reasons to be proud.

SINCE SHE COULD not give me any real time, I would have to spend some virtual time with Lana the woman, the human being behind the public force. The first video I found on youtube showed her three years earlier, speaking before a congressional committee. Her hair still close-cropped and a rich blue, she sat rod-straight in a silver blazer, her hands planted on each side of the microphone, a row of zoned-out white-haired men behind her. She had no notes. Here was the magnetic presence that I remembered. She thanked the committee and, leaning forward, began: "We live in a time of bifurcation. Racial bifurcation; the haves and the have-nots. Our government has become strictly bifurcated along party lines. But I'm not here today as a Democrat or a Republican, or a rich or poor person." She shook her head for emphasis.

Oh, really, I said aloud.

"I am here today as a woman. I am speaking to you today as a feminist, a person who wants better things for all women. Now, some people don't like the word 'feminist.' They hear only negative connotations: 'aggressive, bitter, short-sighted, elitist, man-hater.' Some women would like to rename feminism 'womanism' or 'humanism.' I am here to tell you that labels do not matter. Because lives are at stake. Families are at stake. The lives of our women and children. The lives of our mothers and babies, and poor people in our country—poor women and poor children." She addressed a new income-assistance program that had just been passed, and her voice rose with certain verbs: "oppress" and "provide" and "nurture." She exuded an easy and consistent assurance and, with it, rock-solid authority. "And your program that supposedly sets out to enhance the 'welfare' of poor people? Your program that saddles women with rules about every minute of their time and work? I tell you—you've gotten welfare rolls down, but poverty is up. Way up. Because of the limits and some other short-sighted choices, there are women who cannot even afford enough food or doctors for their children, or medicine or childcare that would, in fact, let them work more and earn more money. And so women are forced to juggle an infeasible amount."

Focusing solely on her style and mannerisms was impossible. This was her talent; her message *was* her style. Strength and authority and power were, of course, the goals she set for other women.

"And we get caught in a punishing cycle that cannot be broken. Some women have turned to crime, to drugs. Some women, because they are unable to be in two places at once, have lost their children to the states, to foster care."

She broke to take a sip from the glass of water before her. After she set it down, she drew a deep breath in and looked all around the room. She was in charge right now, and she was in no rush. *Never Apologize.*

I gazed down at my hands, a little chapped and pale, now resting by the keyboard. A long, white scar cut across between my left thumb and forefinger from the time I grabbed a hoe by the wrong end on a job planting azaleas.

Lana went on to speak about entitlement reform for the wealthy, and ended with the story of a woman who worked as a dental hygienist during the day and at McDonald's at night, a woman whose four-year-old son was taken from her by the state after she'd had to leave him home alone for ten minutes to run down the street and give her landlord a rent check.

I sank. "By the grace of God . . . ," I began, never a religious person, and closed my laptop.

Here was Lana Breban, a woman who was all but directing the national discourse on gender equality, the person regularly featured as a foremost expert in law and discrimination—and I was being asked to portray her singing lullabies to her son? Maybe she had been convinced to alter her image in service of some future electability—or maybe not-so-future electability, in the wake of November 8. The country, the electoral college at least, had opted for Hollywood celebrity and disruption over relevant job experience, nationalist values over globalism. We had chosen a man with a longtime history of "locker-room talk" over a woman he had accused of playing "the woman card." I hated to think that reductive insults like the latter may have swayed voters. Some mornings I still woke having forgotten about the election, newly stunned by the results.

I wanted more for Lana than manufactured likability and the joys of hands-on mothering. And I guess I wanted more for the country, too.

I clicked on the Fresh Air website and listened to Lana being interviewed about her childhood in Bucharest and the restrictive food decrees, but also about the thrill of hearing with her sister a stolen Blondie album on a neighbor's record player. When asked about her father's death and growing up without him, Lana answered, "A lot of my friends in America did not have dads either, because of divorce or their being gone at work so much. We moved to Queens after my mother's husband left her. The families we met there were little matri-archies. My mother was sad to be alone, but she made a lot of friends in our new building. The women helped each other and really became each other's families. Sometimes I wondered, and still do, what it would be like to have two parents and what would have come if my father had lived? Would we have stayed in Bucharest? But we can never fully envision or understand what we did not have." She, her sister, and her mother had learned English soon after arriving in New York. Lana had a paper route as a teen: "I would ride my bike down the cracked

sidewalk and see lights flick on one by one in the apartment buildings,
all those women up so early. I would look in at the women who lived
on the first floors, cleaning and folding laundry before the night even
ended. There was one woman who, when she saw me, would run outside in her bathrobe and give me half an apple or some bread. She said
I was too skinny and she always had advice. Always advice. She'd say,
'You've got the right idea, working already. Don't ever stop working.
Never assume somebody else is going to take care of you even if they say
they will.' Things like that." Terry asked, "Was she the first feminist you
met?" "That woman would *never* have labeled herself a feminist," Lana
said. "This was just her life. She also brought me books—she worked
in a library." Lana described reading *Roll of Thunder, Hear My Cry* and
Anne Frank's *The Diary of a Young Girl* by the humming light of the
small pantry, where she slept so that she would not have to listen to her
younger sister kick the wall in palsied spasms.

There was a new reserve in her voice, and something raw just beneath
the surface of her words as she went on about Anita. I'd had no idea that
Lana's sister had had cerebral palsy, or that her sister had died when she
was only fourteen. I often tried to make connections between my subjects' past and present lives. People who had nothing as children usually
wanted something as adults. People who had been bullied, of course,
tended to become bullies themselves.

I watched one last video. "You have been wronged," Lana told the
Asian American Women's Council just last week. She listed the standard gender pay gap for various subgroups within the council. Burmese
women earned almost half of what white men did. Cambodian,
Vietnamese, and Indonesian women got less than seventy cents for
every dollar that white men did. "You have been wronged and you, and
no one else, will make it right unless you act. Now."

I found where I had left off in her book, and began:

You—and no one else—know exactly how to parent your particular child.

Did this work? I thought it did. I gazed out the window at a tube
sock in a tree flapping with a breeze.

There will be those who say that the world is just the way it is,
that boys will be boys. These people will say, 'You can't change
biology and nature!' They may whisper to a friend if he cries,
try to hide a laugh, or call him terrible names. It is within your
power to ignore them.

I found a close-up of Lana's face, a photo taken during her speech at
a healthcare conference a few months ago. Her bob haircut had already
begun to grow out. Her face had been caught in a laugh, and she may
have been wearing a little lip gloss and some mascara. She glowed, I
thought, maybe even more so than in person. I looked at it. I stared
at it in order to decipher something. Maybe she in fact enjoyed this
new image. Maybe this, more than her blue hair and all that Twitter-
shaming, was who she felt she was meant to be, and a grand condo on
Central Park West was where she had long ago felt she was meant to
live. Since the election, she had become ubiquitous. Even Jimmy Pryor
mentioned seeing her "get her ass kicked" on Fox News the other night.
Maybe ubiquity and influence were really what she was after in the end.
    I printed out the picture and taped it on the windowpane that faced
me, and got back to work.

"WHO'S THAT?" CASS asked the next morning.
    "My boss."
    "What does she make you do?"

"She doesn't really make me, I mean, she's not *exactly* my boss." We looked at her together. Who would he even tell? "I pretend to be her. I'm writing her book for her. I write as if I *were* her."

"Why doesn't she just write her own book?"

"She's too busy. She wasn't really trained in writing this kind of thing."

"You pretend to be her?"

"Yes. Only on the page, though. Not in person."

"Her name goes on the front?"

"Yes."

"And yours does, too?" he asked.

"Nope," I said. "It's okay. But it's just how my job works."

"Isn't that lying?"

"It's confusing, I know." I sank a little. How would Lana have answered these questions if she were me? And how would she keep the answers from diminishing her in his eyes?

Cass shoved Hippo beneath his sweatshirt and said, "Look at me! I'm pregnant." He waddled and lumbered around the kitchen, bumping into everything.

I said, "Don't make fun of pregnant women."

He turned to me. "Did it hurt to have a baby in you?"

"Sometimes. And it's a lot of work to make the baby come out. That part really hurt."

"I'm sorry." He slid Hippo from beneath his shirt.

"It's not your fault," I said. "Not really."

Maybe someday, Lana would tell Norton that she alone had written this book about him. If I were her, I might. The alternative would be confusing for really anyone.

AT THE LAST minute, I omitted the laxative and replica jaw incidents. I reluctantly left in the breastfeeding-in-the-park and Barbie-shaming episodes and cobbled together enough pages to send to Gin.

She responded quickly: *Good stuff so far. But I think you need WAY more anecdotes, less policy wonking and philosophizing about stuff like circumcision and the infertility industry. After all this is memoir, not History/Poli Sci or Gen'l Nonfiction. If Lana isn't forthcoming, then make it work some other way.*

Can you be more precise? I wrote.

Expand whatever she gives you, she replied. *What exactly are her struggles as a mom, and where does she find her gratitude and hope?*

Absorbing Gin's question, I grew exasperated. I clicked onto *Ghostwriters Talk,* which felt like a kind of solace or at least a momentary escape. INVISIBLEWRITER62 complained that a BM was "too busy" with some press junket to read the final draft of their memoir. They also feared that their teenage daughter may have started smoking pot; she had come home from school with hooded, red eyes and ate almost all of a blueberry pie. When INVISIBLEWRITER62 approached her and tried to engage conversationally, the girl had leapt backward, *obviously to stop me from smelling her. Unfortunately, she has experimented with alcohol in the past.*

Another ghostwriter answered: *Search her bedroom the next time she goes out, and if anything turns up, confront her as soon as you can. The issue has to be addressed head-on. Pot is a gateway drug, and if you don't lay down the law now, she might end up addicted to cocaine or opioids.*

I sighed. *She's just experimenting,* I typed. *Weed is probably the least addictive and most benign mind-alterer out there. It's legal in more and more places, right? Maybe just let this be?*

SILENTPARTNER responded. *No offense, AMLCAL, but you have pretty loose boundaries!*

The week before, I had admitted to paraphrasing a few E. M. Forster sentences in a short historical novel I had written years ago for an Olympic gymnast (it was fair use, legally). I had made a politician sound as if they really did care about the environment, while they had

taken a good amount of money from some of their state's biggest pol-
luters. I had even, I told them, slept with my agent once. This had been
part of a thread called "Confessions." I had been disappointed in their
lesser sins—someone had wadded up a photo of a demanding client
and thrown it in the trash; another person made (but did not use) a
voodoo doll of a client.

Doesn't INVISIBLEWRITER62*'s daughter deserve some boundaries and privacy?* I wrote.

Not when it comes to drugs! SILENTPARTNER replied.

Kids need parents, not friends, someone else wrote.

She's just a child! another person added. *Children crave limits.*

Children? I wrote. The daughter was seventeen. *Okay, subject change.
Who here is able to support themselves solely with ghostwriting?*

Me, wrote SILENTPARTNER.

I am, wrote INVISIBLEWRITER62.

No one else replied.

INVISIBLEWRITER62 added, *Of course it doesn't hurt that my spouse
is a pediatrician.*

Someone responded, *Lucky you* with an eyeroll GIF.

People began listing the additional work they did to make ends meet:
teaching high school history, bartending, catering. Others worked at
Banana Republic, Outback Steakhouse, a DMV, and Petco. Someone
was a cheese monger at Whole Foods.

GEEZERWRITER, a new voice at least to me, wrote, *I used to make a
living ghostwriting Hollywood diet and exercise books. I was able to buy a
little vacation place when I was twenty-eight. We sent two kids to college,
and one to grad school.*

What happened? someone asked.

Who did not know the answer?

*Let's just say that there's more than enough information online now
about diet and exercise.*

I had to ask, *Do you still have that second home?*

GEEZERWRITER said, *We had to sell it five years ago to a young family from Tarrytown. But I'm not bitter. I'll tell you—the high that came from writing for the stars? Priceless. Not that any of you would recognize anyone I wrote for! Enjoy your youth while it lasts, folks!*

I logged out a little deflated, as if I did not entirely belong here. From what I could tell, I was the only single parent, the only person who had never published anything under my own name, the only person who had read even a few pages of *Fifty Shades of Gray*.

The phone rang and I saw Kurt's number on the small screen beside me. I perked back up.

"Hey," he said.

"Hey."

"It's getting really cold up here."

"It's cold down here, too," I said. This ridiculous rhythm.

"You know what I was thinking about today? Remember that huge storm that night last winter when we were at Jimmy's, the night we watched *Good Will Hunting* and drank way too many Old Milwaukees?" Kurt had only been living with me for about a month, and things between us were new and electric. Halfway through the movie, we sneaked out and fooled around against a snow bank behind Jimmy's shed.

"It's a miracle we didn't get frostbite," I said.

"You should've come up here for New Year's. There was a big potluck and a barn dance. A bunch of people brought instruments and we just jammed. I haven't played guitar in over twenty years, so I was a little rough."

"Sounds fun."

"Yeah, it was. A few of the guys are talking about driving out to someone's cousin's ranch in Wyoming for the rest of the winter. But I don't have the cash for that kind of big trip, so I guess I'll be back down there in about a week."

I was underwhelmed by his decision, made by default more than anything else. "Don't rush. Come back when you're ready," I said. I may have sounded resentful.

"All right," he said. "Do you want me to come back?"

"You want to come back?" I said, but then changed the subject. "Cass pretended he was pregnant with a stuffed animal the other day. I feel like he's getting more and more curious about his dad."

"Is Cass around?"

"Love?" I said, and handed him my phone.

I logged back onto the group chat. SILENTPARTNER and SECRET-SCRIBBLER were now recommending addiction counselors and a family intervention.

INVISIBLEWRITER62: *What if she refuses to listen or even stay in the room and hear what we have to say? She can be really stubborn. It's a trait that I'm proud of, to be honest. She's a very strong woman in the making!*

Then just let her be, I wrote, and logged out.

CHAPTER ELEVEN

"You don't have plans tonight, do you?" Jimmy asked. Bruin tugged at his leash on our front stoop. In Jimmy's other hand he held a big bag of dinner from Boston Market. "If not, I figured you could use some company."

"Thanks," I said. "No plans, just Cass and I, as always."

"You and Kurt should get married," Jimmy said.

"I'm not sure I believe in the institution."

"Why?" Jimmy unfastened the dog's leash and together we set out the tubs of chicken and cole slaw and mashed potatoes. Bruin lunged up, hooking a chicken wing into his jaws.

"LEAVE IT," Jimmy hollered. He pried apart Bruin's mouth and fished out the thing. The presence of the dog almost canceled out the surprise kindness of the food. Jimmy had seen Cass cower in the face of Bruin's teeth-gnashing and unpredictable but frequent urination.

"What the hell's wrong with the 'institution'?"

"For starters, it's not always beneficial to women. I don't want a legal promise to be the thing keeping me with someone—and keeping that someone with me."

"Good lord, listen to you and all this cuckoo crap," Jimmy said.

I inhaled hard. "Marriage ties you down. I don't know very many happily married people. Do you?"

Bruin rose onto his hind legs and set his front paws on the counter. He growled, bearing his fangs in the direction of the food. "Git, Boy." Jimmy snapped his fingers before the dog's face.

"Any chance we could put him in one of our bedrooms while we eat?" At the moment, Cass was coloring in his own room. I hated to say what I had to next: "It's just that Bruin can be a lot for Cass."

"That boy will be fine if you get out of his way. Let him get used to dogs—and to everything else that scares him."

Jimmy may not have been mistaken.

"Maybe. Cass, dinner," I called. "Jimmy's here." I heard some movement in the hallway. "And Bruin," I said in what I hoped was a voice coded with warning, but it was too late; Cass stood in the doorway, and when he saw the dog, he tore back to his bedroom and slammed the door.

"Well, good to see you too, kid," Jimmy said. "I'll go stick this guy in your bedroom, Al." He looped a finger around the dog's collar and tugged him out of the room.

I heard a slap of wind and then the clicking and squeaking of the walls. A proper blizzard was coming, apparently a fast, dry snow. The sun had recently set and pinkened the sky low on the horizon.

I cajoled Cass out of his room, and finally, the three of us took seats around the table.

"You've got to let Kurt know that you need him," Jimmy said, lifting a drumstick to his mouth.

"But I don't," I said. "Need him."

Jimmy gestured toward the stack of mom-moirs and books about parenting boys on the chair beside him, then over at the piled dishes on the counter, an unfinished macaroni necklace on the floor, and over at Cass. "Baloney."

Here was the advice of someone from a different generation, igno-rant of the variety of ways that a person could live her life now: inde-pendently, freely, with consideration and choice. I did not need Kurt blazing in and out of our lives. I did not need his erratic and limited financial contributions to this household. I would figure things out soon enough.

I heard a scratching and whining behind my bedroom door. "Dogs don't like to be shut away in rooms," Jimmy said.

"Yeah, well," I began, but stopped myself from being defensive. I reached for more food.

No one said anything for a while. What a scene this was: Jimmy wiping grease from his chin with his arm, Bruin now howling, Cass making a face of his mashed potatoes and then using his fingers to make the hair. I knew that Jimmy had meant to cheer me up, so I said in as upbeat a voice as I could muster, "Hey, did Gary and Jen tell you that I was in a play with them in high school? *Oklahoma!*" We chatted about them and some of Jimmy's other tenants, and although I was not hungry, I made myself eat a few bites of chicken and cole slaw.

AFTER THAT BLIZZARD, snow continued to fall for the next three days in alternately gentle and aggressive passing storms. We had made a snowman, but he quickly disappeared under more snow. Stuck inside with me, Cass watched too much *Dora* and ate too much of the peanut brittle that my parents had sent us for Christmas. He made a mosaic of the seashells that my mother had collected from a beach near their condo. Whenever possible I worked on Lana's book. Cass and I went sledding a few times. We Skyped with my parents. I finally made it to page 14 of *To the Lighthouse*; "'No going to the lighthouse, James,' he said, as he stood by the window, speaking awkwardly, but trying in deference to Mrs. Ramsay to soften his voice into some semblance of geniality at least."

It was only a matter of time before cabin fever took over. My parents had sent us a gift card to the Norman Rockwell Museum in Stockbridge for Christmas, and I suggested to Maggie that we could all go. She offered to drive us all in her van, and on the way her sons watched *Sharknado 3: Oh Hell No!* on the little screen that hung from the ceiling. "Cass, look what happens to that kid's leg," Connor said. From the passenger seat I could hear characters screaming with terror and the rapid popping of bullets. I glanced over to see Cass burying his face in his hands.

"This is their favorite movie right now. This and *Robocop*. World's best mom right here," Maggie said, laughing.

I wondered if I should "accidentally" switch off the movie. I also wondered whether I should start exposing Cass to something other than Nickelodeon Junior.

The museum was set on thirty-six acres of snowy lawns and woods that children were encouraged to explore. Maggie's friends from Northampton, Cecil and Wendy, met us near the gift shop with two more boys, one around Cass and Liam's age, and a tween or young teenager. Cecil and Wendy looked strikingly similar to each other, with their long blond ponytails and brown barn jackets.

"Should we let the boys go off on their own?" Wendy asked, although her two had already disappeared.

"Be good," Maggie told Connor and Liam, as they turned and sprinted after their friends.

Cass hovered behind my legs. "He'll probably just stay with us," I said. "He's a little shy."

"That's totally fine," Wendy said. "Every child is different, right?"

I nodded. Out the window, I saw the boys begin to climb a bare apple tree. There was a particular loneliness in watching other children happily frolic while your own held back. This fell away when I saw the older boy yank Connor, who had to be half his weight, from a branch, and slam him on the ground. The older boy jumped down from the tree and twisted Connor into a chokehold. It looked like he might be crying. "Mag," I whispered and gestured outside.

"He's fine. It's always a wrestling match when these guys get together."

The older boy flipped Connor onto his back and mounted him.

Maggie and Wendy began to chat about some other mutual friends, and we wandered the museum, taking in the many *Saturday Evening Post* covers, all those doll-like children's faces caught in innocent moments of daily life, the adults hovering over them or belting out songs in a barbershop quartet, eagerly playing baseball or taking a break from playing Santa (while a little boy looked on, stunned). Life before the tyranny of iPhones and the Internet, before the existential dread of autocracy and climate change. We got to the Four Freedoms paintings, and I stopped in front of *Freedom from Fear*, the cozy scene of a couple tucking their two children into bed, the father grinning almost smugly. He held a newspaper with a headline about the Blitz. Here was his family, safe and sound, while across the Atlantic, bombs lit up the night sky in London. Rockwell had painted the series after Roosevelt's speech, the one that was meant to galvanize American support for the war. Though intended to promote democracy, the paintings now seemed, from this particular moment in history, more like a celebration of American exceptionalism and the nuclear family. Of course, everything was tainted now.

The four boys came back inside, grabbing at each other's heads. "Cole, Max," Wendy said, "not here, not inside. Quit it." She caught me looking at them and Cass keeping his distance as we made our way toward some other rooms.

I hated to be seen as a prude. "How old is Max?" I said.

"Twelve. This one loves his mommy, doesn't he?" she said, her own eyes on Cass.

"He does," I said. Lana's words rang in my head: *Never Apologize.*

Onto the awkwardness brewing between us, Maggie said, "Wendy and Cecil run an incredible store called Music with Conscience. They sell recycled instruments and all this cool stuff that benefits African charities. I bought my favorite necklace there. It's made from recycled paper beads. Wendy works with a group of Maasai women in Kenya, and the money goes to bringing in water."

"Wow, nice," I said.

We had made our way to *The Problem We All Live With*, the famous picture of Ruby Bridges on her way to an all-white school. What real progress had been made since this moment captured in the painting?

The boys piled on top of each other and began to yank each other's hair only feet away from the painting. Max and Cole made noises like grunts, or small sobs, and the tangle of boys rolled left and right.

I called, "Hey, guys! Kids!" Worried they might take down the painting, I moved into a defensive squat, my arms flung wide, and hustled my body between them and the wall. Where were the museum guards or docents? "Watch it!"

"You and Cass should come to Northampton for a concert some time. We sponsor all kinds of kids' shows," Wendy said magnanimously, indifferent to the scene before her, although she then raised her voice so I could better hear her say, "Charlie Barleycorn is playing next week. Does Cass know him?"

"Actually, he loves Charlie Barleycorn," I said, taking quick lateral steps as I shadowed the boys. I had so many questions for Wendy. *How much are tickets? Will your sons be there and do they tend to wrestle during your concerts? Do the kids get to meet Charlie Barleycorn? What would Charlie say if he saw these boys permanently damage that painting of the civil rights movement?*

She told me that tickets were fifty bucks each. I reminded myself that I was sick of his music anyway, and intercepted Cole's arm just as it was about to graze the frame. "Back off," I said to him, and he winced when I briefly dug my nails into his skin.

Max mounted Liam and farted in his face, and it had the effect of loosening the tangle of boys just as a museum worker finally appeared and clapped his hands. "Ok, kids, take it outside. Let's go!"

THAT WEEK I got a call to sub at the middle school, and Bertie agreed to watch Cass for the day. But when she answered her door, she said, "What are you two doing here?" She had forgotten to put in her dentures again.

I reminded her of my subbing job, swallowed away an acid dread and guilt, and on the back of a ripped envelope, wrote down the phone numbers of the school, the Garbellas, the hospital, poison control, and my cellphone, which she already had, but what could it hurt? "Don't forget your teeth," I whispered to her before I left.

On my way inside the school, Maggie and I met up and chatted for a moment. "So we'll be gone by the end of the month," she said.

"What?"

She looked at me. "I didn't tell you that we are moving? To Bolivia? Too much on the brain right now—we only found out the day before yesterday, right after we got back from the museum. It's only for six months. Brian's firm transferred him—some guy down there just quit and they need someone to fill in for him right away. I cannot believe I forgot to call you! Who knows what else I've forgotten to do."

"Wow," I said. "Wow!"

"You have to come visit! You would love it. We'll be close to Copacabana and Lake Titicaca. There is even a treehouse on the property! The guy from Brian's company who's helping us relocate said that our neighbors have alpacas. I'm going to have to homeschool the boys, but honestly? I'm kind of excited. They need less time sitting on their butts inside all day. Wendy sent me the name of an ex-pat artisan she knows there, a woman who homeschools her kids, too, and she's going to help me get started."

I blinked fast. I could not manage to take it all in.

"You and Cass have an open invitation. You can even sleep in the treehouse! Liam would love to have a friend there."

"It sounds incredible," I said, but we both knew that Liam and Cass were as compatible as a squirrel and a shark, and that flights to South America were not exactly feasible for me. She was my one close friend and the news hit me hard. Another person gone.

"Hey, did the school get another teacher to fill in for you?" I asked as we made our way to the teacher's lounge.

"No. And get this—they're not sure they are even going to. They might fold music in with band or something."

"Do they need a sub?"

"I don't know, but if they do, I'll tell them to call you. I'll say that you're the best sub in the system!" She shifted her canvas bag on her hip and said, "Promise me you'll find some way to come visit us. I'll cook salteñas and we'll sip piña coladas and watch our sons run around and play in the trees."

I had no idea what a salteña was, but I guessed that it was delicious. I tried not to betray a coil of envy inside me. "How can I say no?"

She blew me a kiss and headed off to her first class.

Her family had to be over the moon with excitement at the thought of such an adventure—who would not be? I let myself fantasize about filling in for Maggie when she was gone, then visiting them at their utopian lakeside property, gossiping about the middle school teachers, going for hikes and spotting alpacas and Incan ruins or whatever.

I was emotional all day, and that afternoon, when I stopped at Bertie's and found her and Cass peacefully playing Candy Land, I found myself awash in gratitude. Why not celebrate the small things in life, like my son not overdosing on Ex-lax and Bertie not passing out while on the clock? I was writing a book for an amazing feminist woman; I had Cass, and we both had our health. We were not headed to Bolivia for six months, but things could be worse. We drove directly to the grocery store and splurged on ingredients for a red velvet cake, his favorite.

"I thought you could only have cake for birthdays," he said.

"I just feel like celebrating how lucky a mom I am. You can actually have cake whenever you want, except not every day because it's not that good for you."

Back at home with *Highway 61 Revisited* playing in the kitchen, I mixed the batter and let Cass lick the extra frosting from the spatula.

He said, "Bertie is alone right now."

"Oh, Sweetie." I was raising an empathetic son—something else to celebrate. "We should share our cake with her," I said.

After we had frosted our rather lumpy pink-and-white finished product, we headed back down the street. I knocked on Bertie's door, but no one answered, so we let ourselves in and peered all around.

"Bertie?" I called.

The place was stone silent.

"Come on," I said to Cass, a little uneasy, and left the cake on the counter. "Let's check Jimmy's house." Sometimes he drove her to doctors' appointments.

But Jimmy had not seen her. In the dim evening, we made our way around the neighborhood and to her friends—Peg Myers, Sandy Truscello. I suggested to Jimmy that we call the police if we did not find her at home once we got back there.

"Don't freak out. Maybe she just went for a walk," Jimmy said. He had been irritatingly calm since I had first gone to his house.

"After dark? On a cold winter night?"

We returned to her house, which was still empty, and I said, "Do you remember her son's name?"

Jimmy made a pained expression. "Robert? John?"

I was already filing through a stack of little notebooks on the counter, and found her address book at the bottom. "Norm!" I said when I found the correct entry.

"Give him a call in the morning if she doesn't show up," Jimmy said.

"All right," I said, but then I did call 911. The dispatcher was Sandy Truscello's cousin and had met Bertie once or twice, and he let us file a missing person report early.

"Nothing else we can do," Jimmy said. "She'll be fine. Go on home."

"You're not worried a little?"

"I'll worry when I know that there's something to worry about," he said.

I buckled Cass into his car seat and we drove my truck at a crawl toward the lights of the Mass Pike, just visible through the trees at the end of our street. We turned and headed past the Truscellos' and the blue colonial where a couple of my old classmates lived with their four kids. You could see the lights from TVs in the windows of the houses. No one was out walking around. I vowed that when we found Bertie, I would check in with her every morning and offer to run errands—grocery shop or whatever else she needed. I would take her to see a neurologist. Maybe ask her to move into the basement with us if Kurt did not end up coming back, a thought that sat heavily in my ribcage. The truck's brakes clutched as we hit some black ice, and I decided to head home.

Anyway, all those stairs were far from ideal for an eighty-four-year-old with bad knees and mediocre balance.

I WOKE THE next morning and it took a moment for me to remember that Bertie had vanished, a fact that landed on me like an axe blade through a wall. I got Cass, and herded him down the street once again, but Bertie's house was still empty. Again we climbed into the truck and drove a few fruitless laps around my neighborhood.

Back home, I paced my kitchen. I found my book. " 'No going to the lighthouse, James,' he said, as he stood by the window, speaking awkwardly, but trying in deference to Mrs. Ramsay to soften his voice into some semblance of geniality at least." I gazed over at the picture of Lana on my window. She seemed to look back at me standing there, panicking that my friend and only viable babysitter was lost right now, wandering the back roads of Lee in her nightgown and likely no dentures, about to freeze to death. What would Lana do if she were me?

The answer was easy: Lana would tell herself that she had tried all that she could to help Bertie right now, and then open her laptop and focus on work.

When I logged in, I saw that Lana had emailed me last night.

"Ned Boyle didn't have any stats about empathy?" She had only just finished reading the third chapter.

"Well, he did say that modeling compassion was the best way to teach empathy," I replied. "Do you want me to focus on the parent's well-being here? What teaching empathy does emotionally for her/him/them? Might be interesting to zoom in on you for a bit."

"Okay." I could see that she was online right then, and I guessed she would instant-message me soon. When she did, I asked her, *How did you and Lester teach Norton empathy?*

Lana: *Hard to say.*

Me: *What is Norton like? I know so little about him! Do you feel that he's empathetic?*

Lana: *Yes. He's a well-rounded kid, and he gets good grades. He likes martial arts and is currently obsessed with* The Twilight Zone*!*

Me: *So he's into Sci Fi—very cool! Is it the sport or the philosophy of martial arts that he likes?*

Lana: *He's naturally athletic—likes basketball and soccer too.*

Me: *Are you two close?* We were almost six months into working together and still I had to ask this question.

Lana: *Of course! The three of us are close.*

Me: *How does he show empathy to girls and women? Can you remember any times when you took it upon yourself to teach him compassion or empathy?*

Lana: *Hmmm. Once I helped him hold a door for an elderly woman and he carried her groceries to a cab that was waiting.*

Finally we were getting somewhere. *Did you talk to him about it afterward? What did he have to say about it?*

Lana: *This was at least a few years ago—sorry, don't remember much more.*

"Come on," I groaned.

Me: *What do you like to do with him? It might help me if you describe in more detail your relationship with Norton.*

Lana: *Watch movies, play with the dog, all the usual stuff. Sometimes we take him to Yankees games. He really likes Morgenstern's ice cream. Norton is at the age when he just wants to be with his friends, though, not so much his parents any more. Allie, the third chapter looks great overall.*

Me: *Thanks! These kind of details are so, so helpful.*

Lana: *What else can I help with?*

Me: *Has Gloria been with you since Norton was born?*

Lana: *Yes.*

Me: *Would it make sense for me to talk to her?*

No response came for a few minutes. Maybe she had gotten a phone call or something. Maybe she did not like the question.

Lana: *If you need to, you could just write about other places that moms usually take their kids in NY, the places where you take your son and the things you like to do with him, and I can alter or add in more details when you send me the draft.*

Me: *Actually I don't live in New York. I live in Western Mass.*

Lana: *Oh! Really?! Well, I'm sure you'll figure it out. I've got a deadline in half an hour, and then I go shoot* Ellen *this afternoon.*

Me: *Ellen?*

Lana: *Degeneres. The talk show. Apparently she is a fan.*

BERTIE'S SON FLEW in from Wichita that evening. "Norm McQuecken," he said, his hand thrust out. Blond, ruddy, and strapping, he hunched his back in order to fit inside my doorway. He looked nothing like his mother, who was dark-eyed and barrel-chested, but elsewhere petite. From what I remembered, Norm had not visited Bertie in over five years. "You haven't found her yet, have you?"

I shook my head.

We had already combed the area several times that day, and again just an hour earlier, but I offered to drive us all around again. "Your mother has been a lifesaver to me with Cass," I told Norm, as we headed to the truck.

"Yeah, well, and then she just takes off on you?" He kept his eyes straight ahead, one hand around the back of his neck. "You drive that Tacoma? That's a big truck for a little lady."

"It's not so big."

"Watch out. This little lady's a spitfire," Jimmy said from behind us, Bruin trailing along after him on a leash.

I tried in vain to think of a way to invite Jimmy to stay back. We piled into the truck, Norm in the passenger seat, and Jimmy snapped his fingers for Bruin to jump up and onto the back seat. A part of me believed that he was including Bruin in our plans just to spite me. "How about we swing by your house and leave the dog there," I said.

"Mother of Christ, not this again. He'll just sit here with me."

Cass climbed onto my lap, between the steering wheel and me. So that he would not have to sit next to the dog, who was now crackling something in his teeth, I allowed it. "You had to bring the damn dog," I said.

Norm turned, and I saw a look of bemusement pass between him and Jimmy. The sight plucked at a string within me. I shoved the truck into reverse before Jimmy had even closed the door, gunned it out of my driveway, and Bruin flew forward between the two front seats. Cass yelled out. I slammed on the brakes, and pushed the dog over my arm rest. "Go on, get back there."

"Might help if you don't drive like a lunatic," Jimmy said.

"You guys talk to the police yet today?" Norm said.

"Yeah. No news," Jimmy said. "I'll swing by the station first thing in the morning." He opened his window halfway and Bruin stuck his head into the frozen air. The cab of the truck filled with cold, and Cass pulled my sweatshirt jacket around himself. We crept along the streets, passing all the small flags and Christmas lights and inflatable Santas in people's yards, the dark, still woods at the edge of the neighborhood. Soon the only sound in the truck was the engine. The streets were empty, the sky metal gray.

"Have you noticed," I began, turning a little toward Norm, "that your mother's memory hasn't been so good lately?"

"It hasn't?" he said.

"Yes, I mean, should we worry that she might not remember how to get home—or where she lives, you know, her address? You hear about these people with memory loss or Alzheimer's wandering off."

"Alzheimer's?" Norm said. "She's not that bad off."

I knew from Bertie that they spoke at most once or twice a year on the phone. I refrained from telling Norm that you can detect far more about a person by being in same room, that Wichita was 1500 miles away from here, and that an adult only child should visit his elderly mother who lives alone more than once every five years.

The rest of the morning passed with no sign of Bertie, so we left Norm at her place and were home by lunchtime. As I made grilled cheeses for Cass and me, my phone rang. My mother, who skipped any niceties. "I've got twelve 'friends' on Facebook already! But I never should have accepted that friend request from Patty Copeland. Now I have to read daily updates about her oh-so-successful kids and award-winning grandkids."

"Then don't go on Facebook every day," I said.

"I posted my first picture this morning. It's that photo we took when we went to Nathan and Setti's anniversary party in New York?" Nathan and Setti's only child, a daughter, had been a student at Columbia. They had gathered the family two years ago at a hotel in the Bronx. "We're all standing near Times Square, outside *The Lion King*? It's the rare picture where everyone is smiling and looks good."

"I think people usually post newer pictures, Mom. And—we didn't even see the show. That would have cost a—" And that, I understood, was why she had posted the picture. "Mom, why do you want to impress Patty Copeland? Who cares what she thinks?"

"I *don't* care," she protested, and sighed. "How's that book coming?"

"Slow."

"Is it Gloria Steinem?" she asked.

"It's not Gloria Steinem. It might not even be anyone you've heard of unless you watch Ellen Degeneres or read the news these days. We agreed to stop doing that after the election, right?" Admittedly, I peeked at the headlines every now and then to make sure we were not in the midst of a civil war.

"Ellen De—is it that red-haired comedian who did that awful thing with the mask of you-know-who's head? I wouldn't call her influential," my mother said. "What's the worst that would happen if you just told me? Remember when you were writing for the actor—you told us some things. I still remember—'at the Oscars, the winner can't talk for more than forty-five seconds'! Nothing happened to you then, right?"

She was referring to a memoir I had ghostwritten for an octogenarian who had starred in a few epic war films, or Oscar bait. Although he had been nominated twice for Best Supporting Actor, he had never won. "Moving on here," I said.

A prolonged nothing ensued from my mother. I could all but hear her thinking, "Why did you even mention this book at Tabitha's?"

"I should never have said anything about this job," I said, and thought a moment. "Maybe I felt judged by you guys that night. I wanted to show you and Ed that I wasn't a failure."

"What? Sweetie," she began.

"Anyway, Bertie is missing. She disappeared a couple days ago. I'm trying to work and take care of Cass and find her—and please don't remind me how many times you warned me about becoming a single parent." I may have needed a villain right then, someone other than myself to blame for the fact that so much was at stake every minute of every day. It had been since Cass was born.

"Where is she?"

"Missing," I snapped. "We've been looking all over the place for her."

"You called the police?"

"Of course."

"Did she wander away? Has she done this before? Does she have dementia?" She paused, probably letting various implications sink in. "You can be honest—just tell me, Sweetheart."

"I haven't been relying on her as much to help watch Cass. But even once a week was too much, I guess."

"You can't rely on her at all if she's missing. You know, people with Alzheimer's wander out of their homes and forget how to get back."

"You think I didn't know that?"

"Jesus, Allie." Another silence rose up and bled out between us. "What can I do?"

"Find Bertie? Send me fifty grand?"

"Should I come up there? Maybe we should just drive up."

"No." But after we had said goodbye, I wished that I could go for a walk on my own to clear my head, and leave Cass home. Maybe I should have considered saying yes.

ELLEN GROOVED DOWN the aisles amid the audience and up onto the stage. She introduced the day's guests: "Russell Sharpenberger, dog-trainer extraordinaire! Lana Breban, lawyer-activist extraordinaire! Bruno Mars, who needs no introduction!"

Cass, sitting next to me on the couch, laughed as Russell Sharpenberger got a shih tzu to balance a soccer ball on its nose, and again when a standard poodle performed a loose rendition of the Electric Slide.

Then Lana came out. She vigorously shook Ellen's hand and took a seat on the soft white chair across from her. Her dark hair—darkened, I thought—now hung above her shoulders.

"You just got back from Geneva, where you spoke at a summit about international women's rights," Ellen said.

Lana nodded. "Lovely place, Geneva."

"Lovely cookie, too," Ellen said. "Pepperidge Farm, that is. Is that going to make any of my sponsors angry?"

The audience howled with laughter.

The two discussed Lana's work mentoring new women leaders through the Alliance for International Women's Rights, as well as her now infamous speech at the European Women's Lobby. "Did you tell anyone beforehand that those women would be breastfeeding publicly?"

"No," Lana answered with a sly smirk.

"And did you encourage those women, or was it their idea? To do what they did? In front of live-streaming cameras?"

"Let's just say that I didn't do much to dissuade it," Lana said.

Ellen looked flatly at the camera.

"I got to hold every baby afterward and oh my god, was that fun! I miss when my son was that little. What's better than the wonderful weight and smell of a baby? And wasn't it the best, all those women so freely feeding their babies?"

The audience rose to their feet and clapped.

Ellen said, "Some people call you an angry feminist and an elitist. I mean, I don't of course, but what do you say to people like that?"

"The word 'feminism' has gotten weaponized. This doesn't bother me. If women's equal pay and rights are negative things to you, then you are not someone who concerns me."

A few audience members hollered their approval. It occurred to me that what was left of Lana's accent had entirely dissipated. Maybe I was just imagining this.

She went on: "I'm not interested in ignorant people or in their judgment. I am more concerned with supporting women and families by getting better parental leave, and working with the government to raise subsidies *without* raising taxes." Yes, her accent was gone now. "I am concerned with talking to men about why promoting women is actually good business practice. And also why women in leadership is not only necessary but critical to our nation's success."

Ellen nodded.

I thought I heard a woman yell, "You're my president, Lana!"

"So," Ellen said. "Lana, can I get you to do a dance with me?"

She laughed and said, "I am not sure that this is something you want as a part of your show. I have two feet that are so far left they can hardly hold me up."

"Well then, how about we just sing a song? Could you help me sing us to commercial break?"

"I'm no great singer, but I'll try," Lana said.

Aretha Franklin's "Respect" came on, and Lana and Ellen rose from their seats. A man wearing headphones scurried onstage, handed them each a microphone, and the two women began: "All I'm askin' . . . is to give me my *propers* . . ." Lana's voice was imperfect, just as she had claimed, and her accent made a comeback. These things lent the scene a certain vulnerability and sweetness.

Cass, who had wandered off, came back in the room and pointed to Ellen. "Is that a man or a woman?"

"A woman," I said. "Why does it matter? What if she's a little of both?"

"You can't be *both*."

This was what he knew—this was what he was shown every day on Nickelodeon and at Little Rainbows.

I flicked off the TV. "Give me one hour to work and then we can do something fun."

"A whole hour? I hate when you work," he said. "All you do is work."

CHAPTER TWELVE

"I found her," Norm said over the phone. "Outside the Shop 'n Save. She's been staying with her friend Ruth."

I was stunned, and a laugh-cry erupted. "Who is Ruth? I don't think I know any Ruths from around here. You sure this was a friend?"

"She lives over in Becket. They ran into each other when my mother was out for a walk the other day. Ruth's sister is visiting and I guess my mom knows her, too. They had some big reunion—they've been watching old movies, cooking, playing Scrabble. Anyway, my mother came home a few hours ago, and she was out of food, so she walked to the store, and then she forgot how to get back home. I saw her just standing there in the parking lot, asking some random man if he could help her." He sighed. "We're here at her house, if you want to come over and say goodbye. I'm going to move her back to Wichita with me. She can't live here on her own anymore. She needs more eyes on her if she's not going to tell anyone where she is."

"What?" I said. "She's amenable to that?"

"I can't afford to put her in some nursing home."

"A nursing home? I'm sure there are other options," I said. "Do you need to rush to a decision right this minute?"

"Allie, she tried to call you."

"She did?" I remembered one call yesterday—but no message—from a number that I did not recognize. "Listen, if she stays, I'll try to help her out more. Maybe Ruth can come over and pitch in sometimes, too." It was a desperate, self-interested thought; if she moved away, I would have no one else to help watch Cass.

Over at her house, Bertie sat alone on the middle cushion of her butterscotch-colored couch with her eyes on the carpet like a girl who had just gotten in trouble at school. Norm stood beside her, his arms crossed.

"Allie," Bertie said. "I should have tried calling you again. I wasn't really thinking, I guess. I'm sorry." It was heartbreaking to see her so reduced.

"It's my fault," I said. "I should have picked up." I took a seat across from her, and Cass crawled onto my lap. The heft of him made this moment one degree better.

She said, "My friend Ruth and her sister and I did have some fun."

"Oh, Bertie. You got swept up in the moment. It's sweet. There's no need to apologize."

"I wouldn't call it 'sweet,'" Norm said. His hair had caught on a plaster ceiling whirl. I could not take my eyes off the blond lock that stood at attention, firmly tethered now. "My mother almost got in a car with a goddamned stranger at the Shop 'n Save." He stepped forward and his hair finally broke free from the ceiling.

"I did not," she said. "I'm not senile." She picked at a seam on her couch as she spoke.

"Of course you're not," I said. I could feel Norm's eyes on me, but I kept going. "How about we talk about what's next for you? Maybe we can help you decide what's best for yourself?"

Norm gestured violently for me to follow him into the kitchen. He shut the door behind us and repeated everything that he'd already said to build a case against his mother staying put or, as he called it, "courting disaster."

"You don't think she deserves a say in the matter?" I was aware that the situation was more complicated than probably either of us would have liked. There was, of course, Cass's Ex-Lax incident, as well as the frequently missing dentures and the fact that memory loss in the aged so rarely improved.

"It's not just her aging mind or whatever is going on right now. She never had good judgment," he said. "Does my mother ever talk about me or my family?"

"A little," I said. "I take it you two aren't so close."

"She ever tell you about her grandchildren? She has two, a five-year-old granddaughter and a ten-year-old grandson," he said. I was so close to his own age, maybe a little too like a daughter to her, and then there was Cass, whom she actually saw and tended and maybe even preferred to her own grandchildren. Norm may have felt threatened by me.

I shook my head.

"William is nonverbal. He was tough when he was younger—he used to beat on me and my wife, but mostly her. He's a big kid, big like me. He gave his mom all kinds of bruises and cuts, but we tried to keep his condition quiet and to give him privacy. Even when people were sniffing around to try to find out whether I was abusing her. This one day, William took down part of our fence, and then our dog Lulu ran off and never came back." Norm began to massage the back of his neck. "He'd punch through his bedroom wall and smash our glasses and plates. After Natalie was born, things got worse. One of us had to be with William at all times, and the other with the baby. We hired someone—I had to get back to work. But our aide couldn't be there 24-7, and once, when my wife was on her own with the kids, William tried to bury Natalie under a bunch of pillows and some chairs."

I kept my eyes on his face. "I didn't know."

"We had to move him into a group home about an hour and a half away. It was the closest one. That's always the next question—couldn't he live closer?" He made a gruff noise indicating that what he had just told me was the tip of a very large iceberg. "Well. My mother didn't understand or approve of our moving William out of the house. She wanted us to try harder to find someone to help out or even move in with us, as if we could afford that. She kept saying, 'Parents don't just give up on their children.' It was hurtful during an already tough time. Anyway, we should get back to her."

I opened my mouth to say something compassionate and wise, but nothing right came to mind. Natalie and Cass were around the same age. I wondered if Bertie's interest in us was at all colored with misplaced guilt or atonement.

We returned to the living room and stood uncomfortably for a moment, no one saying anything.

Norm cleared his throat. "Mom, again, I'd like you to come back to Wichita with me and move in with us. Monica and Natalie and I, and William, we'd all like it. You could get to know them better. You could come visit William with us on weekends."

I was not certain that I could have been as magnanimous in this situation.

"We can't have you wandering around parking lots, asking strangers for help, you know?" he continued.

"Not that you'd necessarily do that again," I said, but this was not my battle.

Bertie looked up at him. "I'd like to sleep on it tonight, okay?"

He shrugged.

Cass got onto his belly and wriggled underneath the coffee table, and I caught Norm watching him.

Maybe Bertie had said what she did in order to placate her son,

when in her mind, she was already planning her next get-together with
Ruth.

" 'NO GOING to the lighthouse, James,' he said, as he stood by the window, speaking awkwardly, but trying in deference to Mrs. Ramsay to
soften his voice into some semblance of geniality at least."

I had first read the novel at Dartmouth, and had reread it a couple of
times when I was in my twenties. *To the Lighthouse* tells of a big family
with a surly father who, at the start, go to their summer home on the
eve of World War I. It describes the coming of the war, the deaths of
certain family members, the abandonment of that summer house in the
Hebrides, and then the family's return ten years later. It is a story about
the nature of change, flux, and the human propensity for unattainable
ideals, really, a story that was written in a style and language that was in
itself in flux, which made it seem that much truer, but was not particularly calming to me. I had too much flux already, more flux than I could
deal with. Someone had once said of the book, "Nothing happens, and
everything happens." The same could be said about life, I thought.

Back at work on Lana's book, I was glad to be armed with details like
Norton's trips to Yankees games and his enjoyment of the family dog—
details at last, and details that would help Americanize Lana. I wrote a
quick draft of her fourth chapter, "The Preschool Years," but of course
these tidbits did not add up to the memoir of a feminist mother, and I
had to expand what I had been given, once again. I had Norton playing
with the dog while watching *Caillou* (his cooking and cleaning mom,
his working and sporty dad). I had Lana turn off the TV and hand her
son a copy of the book *Daddy Makes the Best Spaghetti*. I also wrote
how Lana managed chauvinist neighbors and relatives—*with people
from different generations and upbringings, sometimes all we can hope for
is baby steps*—as well as the segregation so often found in preschools,
the gendered dress-up and the birthday parties.

On *Ghostwriters Talk*, people were discussing the process of writing for clients who were fundamentally different from themselves.

SILENTPARTNER: *Last year I had a B with a disability. This was memoir.*

SECRETSCRIBBLER: *Did B like the book?*

SILENTPARTNER: *Sight-impaired, but listened to it on tape. Yeah, really liked it, thank god. I just told myself to go for it the whole time. Stop being self-conscious and just become B!*

SECRETSCRIBBLER: *Any of you ever tried to publish under your own names?*

GEEZERWRITER: *I did. A novel. I earned one thirtieth of what I made ghostwriting and the book sold less than 2000 copies. But you can get it on Amazon. LMK if you are interested in confessional sci-fi!*

What was "confessional sci-fi"?

SECRETSCRIBBLER: *I'm getting paid dick for this new book for that tech guy. $21k minus 15% to agent, 30% to taxes and my take home is like $11.5k.*

It was disheartening: yes, we were lucky to have work, but we were almost all of us working multiple jobs while writing for some of the most privileged people in the country.

I typed: *What if we got together and tried to demand an industry-wide rate? Could we unionize?*

GEEZERWRITER: *LOL. Good luck with that.*

SECRETSCRIBBLER: *Isn't there some kind of freelancers' union? There's the writers' guild.*

INVISIBLEWRITER62: *You know how many young wannabe authors would kill for this work and be happy with skimpy pay?*

Someone posted a GIF of an enraged Hulk thrashing a tiny man to the ground again and again.

IN SILENCE, CASS and I helped Bertie pack up her clothes and her Scrabble board. "You're really okay with this?" I said. I wanted to ask if she worried about living in the house where her grandson no longer did. And visiting him in his group home. Had she forgiven Norm for sending him away?

"Don't feel bad for me. I have a hard time remembering some things and that's bound to get worse. Norm is family, despite everything." *Parents don't just give up on their children,* she herself had told Norm.

"Your dentures," I said, gesturing toward the glass on her dresser. I resented the speed with which this was all happening. They would fly to Wichita that evening. Norm had already spoken to a real estate agent about listing her house. This might even be the last time that Cass and I saw her.

I LOUNGED IN my bathtub that night, submerged beneath a weightless layer of Johnson's Bubble Bath. Everyone had left: my parents, Maggie, Bertie. Who knew when Kurt would come back, or if he even would? He was supposed to have returned before now. I poked my toes through the bubbles. Cass was asleep, and I became glad for this moment of quiet, the tranquilizing heat of the bathwater, and the chance to just wallow.

I grew nostalgic for a time in my life when my decisions about men or work or travel were based on nothing but want. I had moved to San Francisco, worked for the magazine for little pay, hooked up with Daniel, had a one-night stand with Colin—all because I had wanted to. But Cass and my career as a ghostwriter were things I had wanted as well. What other work would I even do if I could choose anything at all? I had no idea. There were real rewards in the friendships that I'd had with these large personalities. And admittedly, it was a thrill to write from the point of view of someone more powerful or well-known.

I thought back to Nick again. Of course I never would have agreed to work with him if I'd known what he'd done to those actresses. But: I had not been completely ignorant. I had seen plenty of episodes of

Skinwalker Ranch. I had played *Honor Code*. I had listened to him go on about nipples, Picasso, Linkin Park, the young Mia Farrow. It was as if I had been standing by a fire for months, tending it and feeding it, but in the growing light and warmth had ignored its ability to burn.

There may have been validation that came with the approval of a very famous, very successful man. Yes, I had hesitated, but then had resolved to adopt that "large amount of sack" as my own. And at the time, becoming Nick had been exhilarating, frankly, certainly more appealing than wiping Cass's pee off the bathroom tiles or hauling bag after bag of builder's sand to a client's drainage ditch.

Still, exercising my freedom of choice—to live with independence and authenticity, to write, to avoid settling into bad relationships, of which there had been several; to rely on myself and only myself—had, in the end, limited my choices. Exercising my free will had in essence taken away my freedom.

"'No going to the lighthouse, James,' he said, as he stood by the window, speaking awkwardly, but trying in deference to Mrs. Ramsay to soften his voice into some semblance of geniality at least."

I reached for a washcloth, and my book slid into the water.

CHAPTER THIRTEEN

*A*llie, *I have a speech tomorrow at Mount Holyoke College. That's near you, right? Could you meet for an espresso or cup of tea afterward? Bring your son if you'd like!*

I wrote, *Sounds terrific.* Mount Holyoke was at least a forty-five minute drive, but people tended to think of Western Mass as a smaller area than it was. I pictured Cass trying to sit still in some espresso shop in Northampton. *Yes, Cass will be with me. Any chance you'd be up for a nice walk somewhere instead of a café?*

The next afternoon, I pulled my truck into a small clearing near a trailhead and cut the engine. Bundled in his snowsuit, mittens, and boots, Cass climbed around a low snowbank while we waited for Lana. I had found this trail last summer, when Kurt, Cass, and I had come to South Hadley for a day-long music festival. It had been a great, chaotic day full of bands and dancing, food trucks and Cass's epic tantrum after he grew tired of all the noise and commotion. Kurt had heroically scooped him up and trotted him back to the car while I gathered our picnic supplies. It seemed just days, not months ago.

"This woman you're going to meet is my boss," I told Cass. "Remember that picture in our kitchen? She's a really big deal. I need for you to be well-behaved and kind of quiet today, all right?"

"Why do I have to be here?"

"Because," I said, and I tried to think of a kind way to tell him that there was nowhere else for him to be, and no one else to take care of him.

The daylight was electric, and the air brutally cold. The woods behind us stood sparse and still. Thin tree trunks rose uniformly from the ground. In winter, the woods here could be solemn and beautiful, an X-ray of itself in summer.

"Allie!" Lana hurried toward us, dressed in an overcoat and black tights, a big leather pocketbook slung over her shoulder. She gave me a light hug. She wore immaculate silver and turquoise sneakers, and the thought that she might have bought new shoes just for our walk was touching. A cab idled in the small lot behind her. "Hello," Lana said to Cass, and he dropped his gaze.

I nudged him. "This is Cass. He's still learning how to be friendly to new people," I said.

"No, I'm not," he said.

"I almost never have time to do this sort of thing," Lana said to me. "Just take a plain old walk in the woods. I guess I'm more of a city mouse. I tend to get antsy when I'm too far from New York. My museums and my restaurants and my box and flow."

"Box and flow?" I said.

"It's an exercise—oh my god. Have you never tried it? Allie! It will change your life. You start off shadowboxing, and then work your way up in rumble rounds. It kind of morphs into flow and then some Ashtanga. I have a trainer come to our place, but I think you can take group classes. I'm sure some gym near you offers it. I've been doing it for six months and honestly? I feel so much sharper and after months of insomnia, I'm finally sleeping well."

"Nice!" I said. She was more buoyant than usual today, or maybe it was just that we were discussing subjects other than her book. "Does Norton ever exercise with you?"

"No." She gave me a perplexed look. "Promise me you'll try it."

"Okay. I will," I lied.

"So, I read Chapter Four on my way up here," she said, her sneakers crunching the snow. "I think it's almost where it needs to be, but I might add more about discipline at the preschool age. Even small boys can be tyrants. This topic is ripe for a feminist discussion."

"All right," I said, looking around for Cass.

"Women tend to shrink in the face of male aggression, even if this comes in the form of a child. It's hard-wired for too many women."

"This is true."

Cass sprang out from behind an enormous boulder, sending me face first into a rocky snowbank. I was not hurt, but I was stunned, and then mortified. I tried to casually clear the snow and ice from my face. "Cass, that was *not all right*," I said. I unwound my scarf, now crusted and pressing frozen bits against my neck.

"You sure you're okay?" she asked.

I nodded. "Just about good to go."

Cass yelled, "I'm FREEZING."

"Yeah, it's cold out here, but you'll be fine," I said.

Lana watched us.

"How much farther do we have to go?" he said, wiping at his eyes with his mitten. He began to jump up and down, bored. Something was stuck on my eyelashes, but I let that be for the moment and resumed walking. Lana stepped in front of us and over a heap of what looked to be frozen horse manure, and we followed. "How much farther?" he pressed.

"We just started, honey. You'll be okay," I told him. "He does best with large doses of patience," I said to Lana.

"How long do we have to be here?" he said.

I looked at him.

"My boogers are frozen," he said.

"Cass," I said. I finally brushed a crumb of ice from my eyelashes.

"You are far more patient than I am!" Lana said.

How to respond? "He's just being a kid." Maybe she did not recognize challenging—or any childhood behavior, since she had spent so little time around it.

"I—" She slid on a wide patch of ice. "Oops!"

"Here, take my hand," I said, and she clutched my forearms and tried to balance. Although she was considerably taller than I, she was far less steady, like a hat rack in a strong wind, and I struggled to keep us both upright.

"Any other thoughts about Chapter Four?" I had written of her discouraging Norton from playing with fake guns and toy soldiers, although, for all I knew, he had a collection of BB guns and planned to enlist in the army someday.

"No, just the discipline part."

"Did Norton like preschool?"

"Yeah. He went to West Side Montessori. You know, you might advocate for Montessori in the book. West Side is terrific. Although I'll be honest, I was a little jealous when I heard about the green renovation that happened after Norton left. Every inch of the place is sustainable now. They even installed nonglare lights to help the kids focus."

"Preschool has not exactly been the haven for *us* that I hoped it would be. Sometimes I worry it's because Cass is an only child. He hasn't learned to share like he might have if he had a sibling. We have to be their siblings, right? We have to be their friends and parents and fathers and mothers all at once," I said, prompting her to say more.

"Right," she said. "I like that—'their friends and parents' part. You should put that in the book."

I hid a sigh. "Did Norton have trouble making friends?"

"Not really. He's a personable kid."

Apparently Norton had no real problems, and no real personality.

We continued to walk, Cass stopping now and then.

"How about if we set up a schedule, you know, some goal dates for each chapter? Gin asked if we could get her a draft of the manuscript a few weeks before the new deadline that you two worked out." I tried not to betray my resentment at Gin having been the one to tell me about this.

"Okay." Lana slid on another patch of ice and grabbed onto a nearby birch tree.

Cass sat down beneath a small tree now and looked over at me with a long face.

"You need to get this boy home," she said, although I had the sense that she was the one who was done with this trail. "I've heard that sticker charts can be helpful. People say they can work magic with kids."

"Yes, I've tried them."

"I think you have to do them a certain way. You have to break it all down for the child, offer a sticker for every single thing he does right. And then at the end of each week, he earns something he really wants, like a fun trip to an amusement park or a new Lego set."

"Right, yeah." For a while, I had thought myself pretty smart; Cass curbed his complaining and stopped fussing whenever I left him with my mother and Ed, and in return he got little smiley stickers on a piece of paper that hung on our refrigerator. This worked for about a week or so, until he earned enough stickers to win the big prize, a stuffed version of Lambie from *Doc McStuffins*. The minute I had cut off that tag and handed him the animal, Cass, like some wily con artist, reached for Lambie and said, "I'm not going to Grandma and Ed's tonight. Their food is disgusting. I'm staying here with you and Lambie, and I'm never eating broccoli or peas ever again."

"Things are getting even busier for me, so I can't guarantee how quickly I'll be able to give you feedback on the chapters," she said. "But this morning I had an idea. What's the soonest you could finish a draft of the whole book—without our back and forthing?"

I was thrilled. "Two months? Maybe less?" But did this mean she would give me no more input?

"All right. What if you went ahead and finished on your own, and came to New York after that? We'd comb through the pages together and knock it out as quickly as possible, probably even in a few days or so. We could even ask Gin to come and weigh in. What do you say? You could bring Cass. I'll have Gloria watch him. I can clear my schedule once I know the dates."

"You sure Gloria won't mind?" It seemed like a lot to ask.

"She won't, but I'll let you know if she does," Lana said, getting into her idling cab. "Give me a 'heads up' when you are almost finished and we can make a plan."

I drove home, relieved and excited about moving things along more quickly now.

I emailed Gin to tell her about the new plan, and she asked me to send the next couple of chapters once I had them. When I called Colin, he said, "Wow, that's generous of Lana. When was the last time a client agreed to give you whole days of her life *and* cover your childcare? And this after our lunch in the fall *and* your walk today?"

"She's not giving *me* anything. She's giving her book something."

"*You* are writing her book."

"We both are. Lana's different from all my other clients. She's more hands-on, but at the same time she gives me nothing. And you wanted me to recreate her whole personality, remember?"

"I'm not trying to antagonize you."

"She can sacrifice a few days to work on *her* book. Yes, she's busy, but she has enough time to work out with a personal trainer."

"Who doesn't? Priorities, right? Listen, just bang this thing out. Come down to New York, but don't stay a minute longer than necessary.

I don't want her heading into publication all irritated about how the writing process went. I don't want any negative associations with you and me and the book. People like Lana take on more than they can manage. Please tell me she didn't offer for you to stay with her?"

"No," I said.

"Three nights at a New York hotel aren't cheap. You two need to stay with me?"

I was surprised. "That would be so helpful. You're the best, Col. Even if you are an overprotective mother hen to your clients sometimes."

"You should be the same way."

"How did we ever end up in bed ten years ago?"

"That was the luckiest night of your life," he joked. "You think you'd be working for Lana Goddamned Breban right now if that didn't happen?"

"Jeez," I managed. "I like to think I might."

IT WAS ALREADY January, and I had to deliver in less than eight weeks. That next morning, a Saturday, I woke early and set up Cass with crayons and paper, and then turned back to my laptop. I remembered a reality show that I had watched with Bertie one night after we had put Cass to bed: *Rescue Sitter*. A stern but likable twenty-five-year-old went to a nameless suburb to meet Stephanie, a gaunt thirty-eight-year-old woman, a former paralegal whose husband traveled three of every four weeks. Rescue Sitter—her civilian name was Amber, and she kept her hair in a tall maroon Mohawk, a spiked steel ring hanging from her septum—moved into the family's guest room for a week and her work with the triplet boys began. Video clips were shown of six-year-olds blowing raspberries at the camera, drawing with their mother's lipstick all over the windows of her car, pig-piling on the family's labradoodle. The scene changed to their father. He said, "It's really Steph I'm worried about. The boys walk all over her. I need to have clients over for dinner sometimes and I never know if Matt and Miles are going to break into some food fight or if JJ will start a belching contest at the dinner table. I'd like to have kids I can be proud of, you know? Steph seems really burnt out." He was away on a business trip that week and spoke via Skype, but would join Amber and Stephanie and the boys at the finale of the show. Amber turned off the video on her laptop and faced Stephanie at her kitchen table, reiterating her lack of control in the house. Stephanie simply hung her head and nodded, wiping away a tear. Then came a lot of role playing between Amber and Stephanie before the real journey to tame the triplet boys could begin. Amber told her slumped client, "Stand up straight. Put your hands on your hips. Raise your voice. Really raise it. Steph, repeat after me: "Belching IS NOT allowed at the table. You boys will NOT throw your food. If ANY of you does either of these things, you will be sent IMMEDIATELY to your room.'"

Stephanie tucked a strand of ash-blond hair behind one ear and did her best. "You guys can't just burp or do whatever you feel like—"

"Stand up straighter. Start again." Amber crossed her arms beneath her considerable breasts, lifting and joining them as if they, too, might want to berate this loser woman.

"You boys can't belch at the table, or you'll be sent to your—"

"LOUDER."

Stephanie pulled up the collar of her turtleneck almost to her chin. "You boys can't—"

"Steph! Don't be a candy-ass. Look me in the eye. Emphasize your words," she said. She jutted her head forward and her septum ring bobbed as she spoke. "Really YELL at me! Show me your power!"

After more practice, Stephanie finally channeled Rescue Sitter's volume and stature.

"That's what I am talking about. You go, girl!" Amber shoved two fingers in her mouth and blew a deafening whistle. "Go *mommy*! Go *mommy*!"

Stephanie shrank back to her previous self and giggled into her hand.

When I had switched off the TV, Bertie had said, "I never had to be taught to raise my voice to Norm or anyone else. When did parents become so weak?"

"'Weak?'" I said. Was she referring to me too? "How about 'empathetic'? Or 'compassionate'"?

"Weak," she said. "Afraid. What are a few six-year-olds really going to do to you?"

Several answers immediately came to mind, but I said nothing.

Organizations like Girls Who Code and FearlesslyGirl demonstrate that we are finally learning to empower girls. But what of empowering ourselves? Some of us might still struggle when trying to assert authority in the face of our children. Speaking sternly and definitively may feel unnatural at first. But it is necessary to teach our boys that women deserve respect.

Of course, each of us must determine our own style of discipline. Positive reinforcement can work well for some children. The occasional bribe will not ruin your son.

I opted not to mention the efficacy of a McDonald's Happy Meal. I thought about Cass's separation anxiety; a child's acting out so often stemmed from unmet physical needs like hunger or fatigue, or unmet emotional needs. I hated to teach a person that emotion was a bad thing. Especially boys. They got enough of this just living in the world.

And a gentler tone does not need to be a less effective one. We must experiment and rely on trial-and-error to learn what best suits us and our particular children.

I wanted to caution readers against believing that all discipline problems were solvable. Some might disappear with maturity, I could say.

One never knew. Of course Lana's book was meant to promote authority, not uncertainty.

> The school years are a time of entering society with your
> child, a time of socialization and of making public and standing
> tall behind your decision to enroll him in ballet classes or to
> demand that he not pummel other boys even if another initiates
> the pummeling. 'Boys will be boys' is a phrase we have all heard.
> But it waives culpability for everything from violence to insensi-
> tivity, public and graphic discussion of sex to the abandonment
> of hygiene. Boys will be whatever we help them become.

I wrote with dumb hope, and looked around for Cass, but he had gone
into the other room.

> As parents, we have the chance to teach our boys that every per-
> son, no matter their race, gender, abilities, or class, has value.
> This message is, of course, more important now than ever.
> Simply because a bully is popular or famous hardly means that
> he is a good role model.

I knew enough not to tiptoe any closer to the president. My mandate had been to broaden Lana's fan base, and maybe I had already
written too much.

I heard a strange clunking sound, and went to see that Cass had
made a stairway out of pillows and books and furniture and was now
balancing a lamp at the top of a heap while attempting to grab onto the
shade. "Hold up. Come with me," I told him.

I helped him into his red snowsuit and Elmo hat, and we headed
outside to the truck. Across the street, Jessica Garbella was shoveling
the end of her driveway. She waved hello. "Where are you two off to?"

"The Mount," I said, deciding as I spoke. "In Lenox. The Edith Wharton house."

"Ooooh, I haven't been there yet! I'm dying to see it."

"It's off-season and the house itself isn't open. We're just going to go play on the grounds for a while."

Her face opened wide.

"Do you—do you want to come?"

She nodded eagerly.

In my truck on our way to Lenox, Jessica told us that Ron's mother, who had a house near Ventford Hall, another Lenox mansion and museum, was now in Marco Island and driving Ron and her crazy with constant texts about his sister attending the Women's March in Washington. "His mom's afraid that there's going to be a terrorist attack. I am turning off my phone right now," she said, and reached in her pocket.

"God, inauguration was yesterday. I've been so buried in work that I'm losing track. And the Women's March is today?" I had seen on Google Alert that Lana would be one of the speakers. The battle lines in our country were now etched in stone. What luck I'd had in getting to work with Lana, especially now. Route 20 appeared vacant before us, the tree branches limp with ice. I grew a little heartbroken at being so far from the fast-beating heart of this historic moment.

"I was surprised when Annika first told me she was going to D.C.," Jessica said. "She's a plastic surgeon, and not the good kind that does reconstructive work after mastectomies or injuries. She and her banker husband are Republicans. It's like, 'This isn't your party, girlfriend.' I really wanted to fly down to D.C. for it, but we have to go to a fundraiser for the Red Sox Foundation in Northampton tonight."

I nodded, amazed by the sorts of people who lived in the Berkshires year-round now. I pulled my truck into the empty lot of the Mount, and we rode over the dirt and ice path down toward the road that led to the house.

"Oh my God, is that it?" Jessica said, when the estate came into view.

We trudged through the packed snow toward the white Carolean mansion that Wharton herself had designed after tiring of privileged Newport. She and her husband had lived here for ten years before they divorced and she moved to France. Snow covered the high roof and windowtops, and gave the stately house the look of a wedding cake presiding over the sprawling valley and woods.

"It's incredible. Look at it! I loved *The Age of Innocence*. I loved the movie with Michelle Pfeiffer."

"She wrote *House of Mirth* here, you know," I said.

"Can you even imagine having this kind of money?"

The French flower garden, in season a rainbow of lilies and phlox and hydrangea, was now a rumpled blanket of white. Jessica, Cass, and I wandered between the lindens toward the Italian Garden, its fountain now a still pool of ice. Cass moved to step onto the frozen water, but I pulled him back. We continued out through the snow and along a slick, narrow path toward the sugary woods. Cass lay down on the powder and made a snow angel. "Come on, you make one too!" he said, and both Jessica and I got down, lay on our backs, and made smudgy larger shapes on either side of his as if we were his angel parents. When we stood again, he set stones on all three of them for eyes.

"Perfect!" Jessica said. She brushed off the back of her jeans. "We're trying, you know, Ron and I. To have a baby. We've been trying for years. I've gone through four rounds of in vitro—and I've taken every herb and supplement known to womankind, I swear. I've practiced every fertility asana. I've tried meditation, acupuncture, massage," she said as if to head off any suggestions from me, suggestions she must have heard numerous times. "I carried a baby to three months last year, but then I lost it."

"God. I'm so sorry. That sounds miserable." I was surprised by what she had just said and the fact that she had said it. I thought of the times

I had seen her doing yoga through her window, and wondered if what I had previously thought was cobra pose was in fact a kind of fertility pose.

"If everyone else in the world didn't have a child, it wouldn't be so hard."

"Is Cass, is this too much—?"

"No, I just meant in general. It's like every twenty-one-year-old who still lives with her parents and every junkie single mom in Western Mass pops out babies without even trying." She took off her snow hat and shook out her curls. Something inside me reoriented. "My therapist had me make what she calls a 'grace box.' It's a little corny. But every day, I'm supposed to write down on a piece of paper something that I'm thankful for. I've actually been doing it for over a year now."

"Does it make you feel better?"

"Well, it doesn't make me feel any worse." She sighed and looked over at Cass. "Let's say something we're thankful for. All three of us!"

"Right now?" I said.

"Right now. I'll start. I'm thankful that you guys brought me to this amazing place and that I can breathe the same air that Edith Wharton once did!"

"Nice," I said. I thought that I was thankful to have Cass. Of course this was not the moment for that sentiment, so I blurted out the next thing that came to mind: "I guess I'm thankful to have a truck."

She cocked her head quizzically.

"I've always wanted one. It's really handy for the landscaping work I do. It's kind of silly, I don't know. Anyway. Cass, what do you feel glad about?"

We had followed him back to the Italian garden, and now he was trying to balance on an icy façade. He shrugged.

"What makes you want to say 'thank you'?" she pressed him.

"They actually had to make a collage about gratitude for Thanksgiving in preschool," I told her. "His had a picture of a pilgrim, a turkey, and a cornucopia. I think it was more about cutting with scissors and using paste than gratitude, really. He's kind of young for that concept."

"Honey, you *have* to be thankful for something," Jessica said to him.

"But I'm not," he said.

"He suffers from what I call Extreme Honesty Syndrome," I said.

"Ah."

I wanted to hear more about her infertility, and tell her I knew what it felt like when it seemed the whole world had something you did not. But I also didn't want to dwell on a topic that she had chosen to leave behind.

We wandered the grounds and sang "Frère Jacques" and "You Are My Sunshine" and "The Wheels on the Bus." We played hide-and-seek in the rock garden and headed toward the dolphin fountain. Cass reached for her hand as he balanced on the side of the fountain, and she said, "Got you! Should we see how fast we can walk on this thing together?" She would make a good mother someday.

We headed back to the truck, and my phone rang just as I pulled my seatbelt across my chest. I considered not answering, but then I saw that it was Kurt.

"I have a question," he said after I picked up.

"All right."

"Do you want me to come back?"

I turned on the radio in the truck. "I thought you *were* going to be back by now." Every now and then over the past week, I indulged a brief, maybe petty fantasy of refusing to take him in when he returned, or telling him that I had met someone else and that he had missed his chance.

Jessica looked over at me. I mouthed, "Sorry."

"Okay," Kurt said. "I'll be more straightforward. Sometimes it's hard for me to figure out exactly what you want."

"You know that I could really use your help here." With Jessica and Cass in the truck, I tried to speak softly and keep things brief. I reminded him how hard it was to find enough time to work, especially given my expedited schedule. "I can't exactly leave Cass home alone," I told him and shifted into drive.

"I hear what it is that you need, Allie. But what do you *want*?"

"It's not a good time right now to talk," I said. "And I'm not in that headspace. I can't be—I don't exactly have that luxury."

"Well, I was thinking of coming back in about a week. Would that work?"

"Sure," I said.

Jessica pulled her own phone from her jacket pocket.

"Why is this on me," he said, "to say that I want to be with you? I'd like to know that some of this comes from you, too."

"You were the one to leave. You've been gone for almost two months now. Come back if you want to come back," I said. "Just don't ask me to beg you."

We said a strained goodbye and I hung up.

Cass said, "Was that Kurt?"

I nodded.

"Why were you so mean to him? Is he coming home?"

Jessica looked up from her phone. "Allie, you did the right thing. He can't just take off on his own family whenever he wants. It's not fair to you or Cass."

"Thanks." I could hardly lay out everything that she did not know about us without joining the ranks of the irresponsible people who were easily impregnated.

When we reached her driveway, she said goodbye and hopped out of the truck. She looked different to me now, maybe more sharply drawn. I said, "I'm glad you came with us."

She blew us kisses and trotted inside her house.

Back at home, I turned on *Caillou* for Cass. Prolonged active time outdoors with your child was a form of money in the bank for overextended parents, at least for me. I checked Lana's Twitter page for mentions of the Women's March. She had not posted anything yet, but I found plenty of other photos and videos, footage taken of the rivers of people filling the National Mall in Washington, Fifth Avenue in New York, but also smaller demonstrations in Alaska and South Carolina, and others in Budapest, Kolkata, Lima. It was unlike anything I had ever seen, so many hand-knit pink hats and clever signs, all those women, all those *people*, men and children and people of all kinds, the millions who wanted better things for women and had made their outrage into an explosive, breathtaking, harmonious global event. I filled with something that I can only describe as the opposite of loneliness. I could not look away from my computer screen: the handmade cardboard signs in Tbilisi, girls and their mothers bundled against a storm in Fairbanks, the Eiffel Tower obscured by thousands of kindred spirits. I set my hand on my pulsing heart.

"Cass," I said. "Come here. I want you to see this."

CHAPTER FOURTEEN

The facsimile of truth is created with an abundance of details. I considered who might have grounds to protest my inventions—Gin, who had expressly told me to pad what little I had? The publisher? Colin? Lana obviously had no qualms. And who would even fact-check the manuscript? Authors—or in my case, ghostwriters—were required to be their own fact-checkers. Norton? Norton's friends? Their parents? I threw in enough vague mentions of other kids that surely some of them would see themselves in these pages. From experience I knew that people found themselves in books whether they were there or not.

I invented a friend for Norton, a sweet, bespectacled kid "whom I'll call Zach, to protect his privacy." Zach had a dream of becoming a fashion designer. His parents, a lesbian and a transgender woman, helped him start a line of clothing made from their neighbors' kids' clothes that no longer fit them. Clothes for Fashion-Forward Bros, the line was called, and his parents—along with Lana, who took him and Norton a few times a year to Broadway shows—encouraged him to donate the proceeds to homeless shelters.

But it was too much. I cut the Broadway shows and homeless shelters. I cut the recycled clothing part. What about the lesbian and transgender woman? The country was what it was, post-election—roughly one-half cheering for boys like Zach, the other half apparently scraping backward for its days-of-yore white male power. I reluctantly made Zach's parents heterosexual teachers and his father the coach of his Little League team. I called the boy's clothing line simply Clothes for Bros.

Although it had lost a certain significant something, I did think it would pass muster.

"I'm lonely." Cass had appeared beside me.

I melted. "I'm so glad you can articulate that."

He kicked a leg of my chair.

"Not every boy is as articulate as you are—I mean as able to put words to feelings. What do you love, Cass? What do you love to do?" It was a question I had never asked him.

"I don't know. I guess watch TV."

"What else?"

"Nothing."

"Really?"

He shrugged. He flopped onto the floor and began to slither around.

"Are you being a snake? You like pretending to be animals. You love being outside," I told him.

"No, you do. You always make me go outside."

This was true. What child hated being outside? "You're good at art," I tried. "You are an incredible artist. You draw these beautiful pictures, some of the most beautiful things I've ever seen."

He slithered into the next room and began to build a fort out of the couch cushions and his sleeping bag.

I followed him and said, "See, you like to build things."

"Can you play with me?"

Every time, the question punched my heart. He should have had a sibling, a friend, more preschool, a pet, an imaginary friend, anything in addition to only me. "Let's go outside. You were right—I'm the one who loves the outdoors, but maybe I can do better at showing you why. We'll make a snowman, okay?"

The old snow that covered the front yard was dry, but we did the best we could, scooping with our hands and packing and shaping the snow into a lumpy mass, a hillock really, rather than three neatly stacked snowballs. Cass gave him bottle caps for eyes, and I stuck a carrot where his nose should be.

"You know what I'm most thankful for? You, Sweetie."

Cass nodded, perhaps unsure how to respond, and went to find crayons for a mouth. He headed back to the house, saying, "He needs a pipe." He stepped inside and returned with my favorite blown-glass bowl, a gift from Kurt soon after we met. Cass stuck it in the snow just above the crayon mouth. "Let's skip the pipe," I said and reached for my bowl.

"What should his name be?" I asked Cass when we were done.

"Daddy."

"Oh," I said, swallowing hard. "Okay. Anything else we should put on him?"

Cass went inside once more, found a long scarf of mine and wound it out around the bottom of the snowman. It appeared as if a very large blobfish had fallen onto the lawn.

"I think he looks good," I said. There was something endearing about our very imperfect snowman. "Listen, honey. I'm sorry you don't have a dad."

"It's all right."

We stood there, Cass with one finger far inside his ear now.

"Don't pick your ear," I said.

"Okay," he said. He did not remove his finger, but it seemed cruel to badger him further.

To WRITE WITHOUT stopping for Lana's approval at the end of each chapter was freeing. Time moved more quickly, and before long I sent Gin three more chapters. Again, she said, "Better, but we need more Zach, more Lana, more soft moments between her and Norton. What does it feel like when he graduates elementary school? Is she sad, proud, what?"

I added in whatever came to mind; I wrote things I had heard Maggie say about Connor. I added Little League playoffs and a martial arts tournament. I tweaked stories about me and Cass and wove those in as best I could. To mitigate my unease over all my fabricating, I expanded a rather academic discussion of phones, texting, and social media, and added in research about the impact of screen time on middle schoolers' brains, Gin be damned. It was Lana's book, after all, and she had been the one so eager to include research and data.

I added back another day at Little Rainbows for Cass now that payment seemed within reach. He lost his first tooth and I got to play tooth fairy. I left him a note written in swirly cursive thanking him for trusting "me" with such an important thing. His eyes went wide when I read him her words.

The days grew warmer in a brief respite from winter, and the rest of the snow on our lawn melted. Jessica began to come over some late afternoons with tea for us and hummus and carrots or kale chips for Cass, who unfortunately was not shy about his preference for less nutritional snacks. Still, 2017 was turning into a decent year.

One day, Jessica and I went for a walk around our neighborhood during lunchtime, and she confided in me that she and Ron had begun to consider adoption.

"That's exciting," I said.

"I know—it's exciting and terrifying and a million other things at the same time. I assume you and Kurt adopted Cass?" she said carefully.

"Oh! No," I answered, and I finally explained how Cass had come to be. I may have tried to make it sound as if Daniel and I had shared a prolonged romantic relationship.

"Where's this guy Daniel now?" she asked.

"I'm not sure," I said. "But I'm fine with it. Honestly."

"You are?"

I told her that, in the end, we were not all that compatible. "Things might have been financially easier, and of course it would have been better for Cass to know his father. I guess I'd be lying if I said that I never once wished we *had* fallen in love."

"But now you have Kurt!"

I nodded. "Sometimes."

"He'll come back. You are so brave, Allie. You had a baby on your own! You've done everything on your own."

"It didn't feel like bravery. It felt more like necessity—both sleeping with Daniel and having the baby," I half-joked. "I mean, I was getting older and I'd always wanted a child."

"I know, it's a devastating thought that you might never have one, right?"

Before meeting Daniel, I did not remember devastating thoughts, just a nervous hesitation about what my future might hold, as well as real appreciation for the sudden opportunity. And, afterward, a strange comfort at the idea of becoming a mother maybe, alongside a stew of other more complicated thoughts and feelings. But I kept my mouth shut.

THE NEXT DAY, after I picked Cass up from Little Rainbows and steered my truck into my driveway, I saw a person sitting on my front stoop.

I had to look closer to see who it was. He had a beard now and wore a brown leather hat that I did not recognize.

Cass flung open the truck door before I came to a stop, and I slammed on the brakes and yelled after him. He ran out to Kurt, and I shifted into park and followed Cass. Kurt appeared more solid in his flannel jacket than I remembered, and he smelled like dirt. He looked entirely different with his beard, older maybe, and frayed, and his fair skin was faintly burned and chapped. He had turned into another person altogether from that man in the pinstripe suit on that wood bench over a year ago.

"You two," he said. He shook his head. He dumped his big duffel bags on the kitchen floor, and I worried that he would now tell us he was just here for a few hours, that he had decided to go with his new friends to Wyoming or something. He had been gone for so long.

"You're back? I mean you're not headed anywhere else right now?" I whispered. I hardly wanted to get into anything more in front of Cass.

"It appears that I am back and not going anywhere any time soon."

"Good," I said, relieved to have another adult who could help with Cass. But also something else. I understood then that I had missed Kurt's presence, his body and his deep voice around the house, his slow saunter, his foot rubs, the curve of his legs against mine when we slept, and his mouth, and the pressure of his lips.

I made grilled cheese sandwiches while Cass told Kurt about Bertie disappearing and our driving around at all hours to look for her, my working "every single minute," about Jimmy and our Christmas. "What did *you* do when you were away? Why were you gone for so long?" Cass asked him. "Why do you have a beard?"

"Well, I helped build a barn and I thought I'd try a new look. You like it?"

"A little."

Kurt told us all about the farm where he had been living. "There were goats and cows and chickens. We collected eggs and cooked them fresh every morning. And there was a rooster they called Magpie. He sounded more like a dog howlin' at the moon than a Buckeye crowin'. He woke me up every single morning before the sun rose."

Cass grinned. Evidently he liked this new persona. "What else?" he said to Kurt.

"There was Delilah, the billy goat, and when she got goin' she sounded like a whiny teenager beggin' to go to the mall with her friends."

"You picked up a new accent," I said flatly.

"Might be I did." He lifted off his leather hat, revealing the thinning top of his hair.

I hoped that he was hamming things up just for Cass's sake. I was not entirely sure what to think of this faux farmer shtick, maybe in part because it was a residue of his long time away, and evidence of his happiness elsewhere. "I hate to be a spoilsport," I said. "But I'm on deadline right now. You mind if I go work at the library?"

Kurt agreed to watch Cass, and the two of them headed into the living room. I saw Kurt pull a piece of maple sugar candy from the side pocket of one of the duffel bags. I could breathe again. With his help I might even finish this book with time to spare. I would sleep better at night. I would have sex again. Maybe I could even finally finish *To the Lighthouse*, its pages now dried.

Still, over the years I had thought, maybe fantasized, that Cass and I were a self-contained unit bucking the odds, thriving in our subversion of tradition and its bounds. Me and Cass, my sidekick, the two of us doing just fine on our own. Very few people could single-handedly manage everything in their lives, of course, but for so long, forever it seemed, I had tried to do just this. Independence had been my north star, but I could not single-handedly manage everything in my life. At least not now. This understanding was both a relief and terrifically sad.

Ours is a time saturated with technology, an unprecedented flood of videos and images for which the younger teen boy may not be prepared.

Seated at one of two carrels, I researched the tween and teenage boy's brain and male impulsivity and aggression during these years, as if I had not already seen it first-hand when I had subbed. I wrote of trying to maintain one's parental authority in the face of the adolescent need for independence and choice; ways to teach boys to respect girls and their own and each other's changing bodies; the capacity and function of language, the role of demeaning words that could be heard nearly everywhere lately, particularly in the realm of politics.

So much lecturing. I had to bring it back down to earth. I added a brief scene of Norton and his friends getting a bite to eat after their martial arts class.

When I returned home, the furniture had been pushed to the sides of the living room to make room for a huge floor puzzle. Van Gogh's *Bedroom in Arles* lay partly finished, with pieces strewn everywhere. "I got it up in Vermont for our future painter," Kurt told me.

Cass tried a piece that showed one of the tilted paintings, and it fit. "Look!" he said.

Something inside of me grew and swelled and filled every empty part.

And then, the feeling shrank. I wondered why love so often felt like sadness. "Don't be wonderful," I wanted tell Kurt, and might have if we were alone. "Don't behave like Cass's father unless you plan to be this person for the rest of time. Don't be good to me unless you plan to always be good to me."

"IT'S ME," MY mother said over the phone one morning. Kurt and I were still in bed, and I had been tucked inside a dream that he and I and Cass were hanging out at Lana's house and rearranging her living room for a visit from Aretha Franklin. I resented being yanked back to reality. I heard Cass moving around in the other room, and caught up with my mother, but could not shake my resentment. "Lottie's friend Maura said that her daughter put away a hundred dollars a month and ended up saving over thirty-five thousand," she said. "I wish Ed and I had done something like this for you when you were young. We started saving way too late, and then you had to rely on that scholarship and then even some of that fell through at the end."

"Mom, please," I said. "I don't earn enough to start that kind of account right now."

"You're not twenty-three anymore. And you know, Cass should probably be in preschool every day, not just some days. Believe me, when he's older, you'll understand what it's like to want him to be independent and really thrive so that you as a parent can let go and not worry anymore and just enjoy your own life."

We had been talking for maybe five minutes and I already wanted to throw a brick through a window. "Lana Breban," I heard myself say. "*She's* who I'm working with right now."

"Oh!" my mother said. "She's that famous feminist?"

"Yes," I said.

Behind me, Kurt made a sleepy sound.

"Now forget I just told you that."

"I read her op-eds all the time—and her speech at the Women's March was incredible. She's becoming *really* famous!"

"Yeah, she's having a moment. The time is right."

"You know who's a huge fan of hers? Patty Copeland. She joined Twitter just so she could follow Lana."

I could all but hear the gears turning in my mother's mind. "Mom. This stays between us."

Kurt, now awake, stared over at me. He may have heard everything.

I went to finish our talk in the bathroom and ran my finger along the cracked edge of a floor tile as she spoke.

"I just want to be able to brag a little about you. Sue me for feeling proud of you. Come on, Alligator. Let me namedrop just this once?" she said. She had not called me "Alligator" since I was a kid.

I did not buy this maternal pride. My mother was not a person content to be outdone by someone she envied. "Maybe you just want to tell her I'm working with someone like Lana, someone who's so well-known and influential and everything because in reality, I—and you—are none of these things, and you desperately wish we were. I mean, at Tanglewood, all those times you pretended that you didn't work at the ticket booth or the gift shop, but that you were there as a tourist? Did you think I didn't know what was going on? All that stuff you've taught yourself over the years about wines and art that you can't even afford?"

"That is just nasty."

"I'm only being honest," I said.

"All right, we're being honest now? How about your telling me and Dad about this big, secret job right there in a crowded restaurant? And your being so high-strung about Cass that night? I wasn't the one who was embarrassed in front of all those people at Tabitha's."

"I didn't want to go to *Tabitha's* in Lenox! And I wasn't embarrassed in front of them. I was just feeling judged by you and Ed."

"'Judged?' Why would you feel judged by us? That's ridiculous."

I pressed End.

Fuming, I paced as much as was possible in my small bathroom. I considered the absurd amount of currency that my mother gave to others' opinions of her and stubbed my toe against the baseboard, hollered a few choice words into a towel, and decided to take a shower. I must have stayed a half-hour or more in the steam of the hot water, scrubbing my elbows and feet, working the shampoo into my scalp with my fingernails, and rinsing every last bit from my hair.

Kurt sat up in bed, reading *Shop Class as Soulcraft: An Inquiry into the Value of Work*. When he saw me, he set down the book. "What's going on?"

I told him as little as I could—yes, I had just leaked the identity of my client to my mother. Yes, this client was Lana Breban.

"Get out," he said. "Birgitte used to be obsessed with her column in the *Times*."

This information landed a little off-kilter for me. "Really?"

"Allie, that's awesome!"

"It is pretty awesome," I said. At least I could be sure that Kurt would not spill my news to Birgitte. Mostly sure.

WE ALL KNOW or have met a teenage boy who comes home from high school, grabs a snack from the cabinet, and takes it up to his messy bedroom. Media would have us believe that this is an inevitable fate, that women are the only ones to shop, cook, and clean for our families. Why not teach your son to cook and even encourage him to make dinner for the whole family—and maybe one or two of his friends—once a week? Why not ask him to clean the house in exchange for something, perhaps extra money, thereby teaching him that cleaning is labor and should be valued as such?

I considered writing a scene of Norton cooking or cleaning. The last time I had asked Cass to make his bed, he had said, "Why? You never make *your* bed." I said something about being the mother and the boss and respect, and I probably did not speak with enough conviction or volume, because no bed had been made since then.

A few days after Kurt's return, the Garbellas hired him to do their taxes and help get their finances in order. It was enough to cover some of the back rent that I owed Jimmy, as well as a furniture-making course in Lenox. Kurt had built some Adirondack chairs up in Brattleboro and said, "I think building furniture might be something I'd want to do for a living."

"Yeah?" I said.

"Yeah. If I do say so, my chairs were pretty good. And it felt great to make something that other people might even want to buy, you know? Anyway, I'm going to check out a salvage place, see if there's some old wood I could play around with. Okay to take the truck?"

A voice inside of me said that making furniture had to be about as lucrative as farming heirloom tomatoes. Wouldn't it be better, given his finance background, for him to start up a small accounting or tax firm here in town? But another voice told me to cool it, that furniture-making certainly beat doing nothing, and that finding one's passion was no easy matter. I thought of how my father had been a cabinetmaker and of the pieces of furniture he had made himself: the little desk that had been in my room growing up, the end table that I had covered in stickers. Maybe this loose serendipity meant something about Kurt and me.

I knew so little about my father, and I went to find the old shoebox that I kept at the top of my bedroom closet. Inside were a few mementos of my childhood: my first library card, a favorite *Garfield* comic strip, a postcard from Aunt Setti and Uncle Nathan, one small photograph of my father, Eli Lang, holding me. In it, he sat on a plastic folding chair, wearing shamefully small yellow athletic shorts, a Cat Stevens T-shirt, and round John Lennon–style wireframe glasses. He had a dark beard, a mole above one eyebrow, and was, I thought, a relatively handsome guy. I was swaddled in a white blanket, and the only part of me that was visible in the picture was my wide-open mouth. One of his hands hovered near my stomach and he gazed down at me, his own mouth ajar as if he were saying something, maybe trying to calm me. I was two months old and he was thirty-four. A year later, he would be gone.

I considered calling my mother and making amends. It had been days since our argument, and I still felt sick about it.

Soon, I told myself. Soon enough, if I did not hear from her first.

THAT AFTERNOON, KURT fixed a pipe under the sink that had gotten clogged with one of Cass's socks. Maybe it had been there a while; he was old enough to know better now. Kurt went off to find Cass. I tried to ignore the heavy smell of Drano, and returned to my laptop at the table.

I was nearing the end of Lana's book, and set out to write about separating from your son if and when he went to college. I advocated for allowing him to choose his own path, whatever this might be, and afterward pausing to honor your own accomplishments in raising him. How about a trip somewhere or a nice dinner with family or friends, if possible?

I looked over at the photograph of Lana still taped to my window before launching into the final chapter: "Adulthood." I could see Cass and Kurt through the window, dragging branches and carrying sticks across the lawn. When Cass was twenty-five, I would be sixty-four. I tried to picture myself as an older person and it was hardly difficult; thin creases had appeared on my neck. At some point, my hair had grown coarser and the grays near my left temple had joined in a stripe. There were moments when I grew distressed about aging and the unstoppable passage of time, but others when my changing appearance and Cass's new abilities fascinated me. We got to be a number of different people in one lifetime. What would Kurt look like in the future?

An image came to me: an amalgam of himself, that photograph of my father, and my uncle Nathan. And Cass? At twenty-five? Kurt chased him in a circle around the yard, and they both disappeared from view. When they returned, they tried to build a towering structure from the branches. It was the strangest thing—the two were framed inside the center windowpane right above Lana's picture. They looked as if they had all been caught there, placed just so for my viewing.

I set my fingers on the keys.

"The time will come when your boy is, of course, no longer a boy."

The cursor blinked at me, waiting. In that moment, I could not write any more. I did not want to. I closed my laptop and went outside to join them, to stop them, maybe, and maybe in some way to attempt to stop time.

I PRINTED OUT the whole book, made a neat stack of pages on the kitchen table, and gave myself a moment to take in the sight. The sense of accomplishment that came at the end of a draft, even with this, my eleventh (not counting Nick's), was more profound than any I had known. To finish a book is to reach land after a long and often grueling swim.

I sent Lana, Gin, and Colin the file. I said a prayer that they, especially Gin, would not ask for too many changes and that she would deem it sufficient to release payment.

My mother called. "Honey, I'm sorry about all that I said."

"I'm sorry, too," I said. "I probably shouldn't have called you guys judgmental. Even if you are."

"We are not."

"Maybe just a little?" I said. "And also, I shouldn't have told you about working with Lana."

"It's okay. We'll let it go now," she said. She took a sip of something. "This morning I had to hear about Patty's granddaughter's ability to speak Mandarin. She can also recite almost all of MLK's 'I Have a Dream' speech."

"Get out. How old is this girl?"

"That's not the point," my mother said. "But she's five."

"That is incredible. Cass can't even write his own name yet."

"So what? He's a good artist. His grandmother doesn't brag about him incessantly to her friends. He has this going for him."

"Maybe I should start talking to Cass about people like MLK, and maybe Gandhi or Malala."

"If he's interested in them. Otherwise, just leave him be. He's a sweet boy, a creative, quirky kid and he's doing just fine the way he is. You're both doing great. You've got a really interesting career. You're doing far better than I was when you were a toddler."

"Really? Thanks, Mom," I said. "You know, I think you need a nice long break from Patty."

"Could be."

A MOMENT OF relative ease came. Cass finally made a friend, a shy, polite boy named Carlos whose family had recently moved to an apartment in one of Jimmy's houses on the next street. The boy's mother, Luana, was a translator for various tech firms and, like me, worked from home. She was funny and gregarious; we got along instantly. Carlos introduced Cass to *PAW Patrol*, and at our house, the two played imaginative games in which they pretended to be dogs performing rescue missions on each other or stuffed animals. One afternoon, Carlos found Cass's old Barbie Bride under the bed and held it up, laughing. "Why do you have a girl's toy?" Carlos said.

"Toys aren't like that. They don't have private parts," Cass said as I walked by. "Look—"

After a pause during which I assumed they lifted Barbie's layered satin and crinoline skirt (should I intervene? No, I would not intervene), Carlos said, "See?"

"There's no vagina."

"But she's wearing girls' panties," Carlos said.

"Time for a snack!" I said.

That afternoon, Bertie called. It sounded as if things were going well in Wichita. She had her own good-sized bedroom, she told me, and the weather had been decent. She was getting to know her granddaughter Natalie better. "We play Pretty Pretty Princess a lot. I think Nat has every single Disney princess costume ever made."

"Cool," I said, and stopped myself from asking whether the girl had other less stereotypical interests. There was no need to become the vegetarian who lectured everyone on the evils of meat production. I wanted to ask about Bertie's other grandchild, William, and whether she had yet visited him, and whether her relationship with Norm had improved. Had her memory gotten any worse? Was it difficult to live with other people after living alone for so long? But I just started with "We miss you."

"Yes."

"Kurt finally came home. And Cass made a friend, this boy named Carlos. He and his mom just moved into one of Jimmy's places over on Birch."

"Birch?"

"Birch Street."

"Well, it was good to catch up," she said abruptly, ending our short conversation.

Afterward, I thought about it a while. I wondered if it had become difficult for her to talk on the phone and to find the right words.

I LOOKED DISMALLY at my closet; the outfit that I had bought last fall at Ann Taylor would get me through one day in New York. I had yet to receive payment for Lana's book—or even word that it had been deemed finished. Kurt encouraged me to "shop somewhere other than a big box store. I mean you're going to New York to meet with *the* Lana Breban, right?"

At another store with clothes that I considered appropriate for my trip, if a bit dull, a woman roughly my age who wore navy slacks, a poncho, and heels followed me around at a distance. I noted her eyeballing my army jacket, my old Chuck Taylors. She watched me thumb through racks of identical gray slacks and white blouses, and I finally turned.

"I might need some help in trying to look professional," I admitted.

"Of course. Let's see." She swept around the place, gathering black wool pants, a few blouses and sea-colored scarves. She faced me and squinted, as if trying to see me from afar. "I don't know. Why don't you try them on and we'll take it from there?"

The fitting room was immaculate, a roomy square with a tan cushioned bench and a wood-framed mirror. It smelled of tea. The first blouse I tried on held and lifted my breasts, and the top button closed just low enough to reveal a hint of cleavage.

"The fabric feels so nice, but I think this is too small," I told the woman when I stepped out of the changing room and in front of a three-way mirror.

"No! It sure isn't. That blouse is just right for you. It's okay to accentuate the girls a little. You look *amazing*."

I loved this nickname, "the girls," and I pictured my breasts as identical twins too long hidden beneath sweatshirts, finally given permission to peer out at the world. The saleswoman disappeared for a moment, and returned with a black leather belt, slid it around my waist, and fastened the buckle. She draped a wine-colored floral silk scarf around my neck and said, "Did you have any idea that you were this gorgeous?"

I assumed she said this to every customer, that she worked on commission. "Not, I mean, well, no," I said, tugging at the scarf that felt tight around my neck. I had unwittingly jumped into a well-worn trope, the "before" in a "dazzling" makeover.

"That's because you're used to seeing yourself in old, ill-fitting men's clothes."

I felt the urge to justify something.

"Look at you!" She shook her head. "I would kill for those girls and those toned gams."

Another clerk strode over to me and gathered my hair in her hands, holding it into a sort of bun. She cocked her head. "Jewelry," the women said simultaneously. They dispersed and then brought me five different pairs of sterling silver earrings, a couple of necklaces, and three different bracelets.

It all became kind of embarrassing. I appreciated the attention, the feel and fit of the clothing, as well as the calming aroma of the fitting room, but I also missed the anonymity of Target, the young woman guarding the dozen cluttered changing rooms, her focus more on gabbing with another employee and refolding mountains of T-shirts than on me and my gams.

In the end, I bought one blouse, two pairs of pants, a pair of earrings, and a blazer. The total came to the equivalent of over three weeks at Little Rainbows. "A bargain for all these pieces," the first woman said after she informed me of the total. Two other women stood next to her, along with a well-dressed twenty-something guy who had just showed up. They all beamed with pride as I handed them my credit card.

TWO DAYS BEFORE I was scheduled to go to New York, I got a Google Alert: "Breban announces bid for US Senate." I hurried to click on the link to the *New York Times* and saw that about an hour earlier Lana had filed for candidacy in the wake of the senior Democratic senator's surprise announcement that he would not seek reelection next year, that he would instead retire.

I was at once stunned and unsurprised by Lana's decision. I had detected something like this, but I had assumed that any campaign would be years off. She had never, as far as I knew, held a political office. Maybe the presidential election had been a catalyst.

"Great news, huh?" Colin said on the phone. "We *desperately* need more women in the Senate right now."

"True," I said. He had not sounded at all surprised. "How long have you known about this?"

"Oh, not so long."

"A day? Six months?"

"At most a month or so. I wanted to tell you, but Lana's people asked me to keep it quiet until now. Even with you. They only told *me* because they wanted to double-check something in her contract. They didn't want you to write a book about a future senator. They wanted you to keep writing a book about a regular mom."

"What? Why?"

"Who knows? We're not the political experts. At any rate, a press release just went out. Major first print run. You should be psyched."

"Nice," I said, thinking I would be even more psyched if I were to earn any royalties on this book. "Did you read the draft yet?"

"I've got about fifty more pages. So far, so good. I like it! I mean, maybe a teensy bit heavy on the advice, and a little light on the mommoir, but I've got some ideas to soften up the voice. We'll talk more when I'm done."

I blanched. Trying to balance feminism with traditional femininity had not been easy. Especially with a dearth of material. Even now I did not have a firm grip on Lana's sense of humor, her marriage, her friendships, or really even her parenting style. The only time she had let her guard down, I thought, had been with Terri Gross when discussing childhood.

I emailed Lana to congratulate her, wondering for how long she had known of her campaign plans. Everything that had transpired in the past six months looked different now.

A few hours later, she replied: "Thank you. This book is more important than ever. Lana Breban as gentle mother, kind woman, human . . . LOL. My campaign manager says it could 'win us the women's vote' (as if I didn't already have that, I told her). Let's make it happen, Allie!"

How strange, to refer to oneself in this way, to intimate even if jokingly that one was not in fact gentle, kind, or even human.

PART THREE

April – November, 2017

CHAPTER FIFTEEN

Cass and I rode the elevator to Lana's floor. In the quiet, I recalled the thrill of being here about seven months ago, and the sensation that I was helping to right some cosmic wrong after the fallout from Nick Felles. Finally, so many of us had thought, we would have our woman president. In the months since then, some innocence, some necessary hope or optimism for the future, had begun to drain away. If nothing else, I was ready to move on to a new, more straightforward book and a client who was open and forthcoming, who asked for only my listening and writing skills.

Gloria took our coats at the door and led us into the dining room. I still knew nothing about her, not even whether that little girl had been her daughter. Gloria said Lana was at a meeting that was running late, but would be back in five or ten minutes. "I will come to get Cass when Lana arrives."

"Thank you," I said. "Really. This is such a help."

She smiled and left, and he and I took seats next to each other at the table. Central Park looked different in April. The cherry trees and dogwoods had begun to bloom pinks and whites, and fewer people wandered the paths than in the summer. Cass swung his feet in his chair. He looked up at the wire and feather chandelier. "That looks like archery."

Lana's small dog nosed open the door and trotted over to me. "Hi there," I said, and patted its head. It reared up on its hind legs, *his* hind legs, I now saw, and lapped his gritty little tongue against my hand as if it were something to drink. I tugged away from him and gave him a gentle shove.

"Hello, you two." Lana stood in the doorway in a coat and leather gloves. "Let me go put my things away, and I'll be back soon."

"Great!" I said. It occurred me that I should tell Gloria a few things about Cass, and I went off to find her standing by a speckled black stone island beneath a sea of clear cylindrical pendant lights in the kitchen. "Just so you know, Cass can be a bit clingy with me," I said, and she asked about his preferred activities. I thanked her again, and on my way back to him, I passed by the living room, a square, lofty space, a crowd of paintings and drawings on every wall. I peered over at one that I recognized, a Yayoi Kusama print, *Waves on the Hudson River*. All those white worm shapes with orange dots, their green carapaces, the vivid blue background. This was one of my mother's favorites. I moved closer and realized with a start that it was the original. "Jesus," I said to no one. I looked around to make sure that I was alone before I reached forward and touched the canvas.

In the dining room, Lana was now sitting beside Cass, and the dog had gone. "My friend here was telling me all about Dora and Diego. Cass says he's seen every episode twice!"

"Oh!" I was mortified, and hoped he had not also mentioned his passion for Doritos and Ex-Lax. "Sometimes when it's too cold to play outside, I let him watch—"

"Allie, it's *fine* to watch a little TV!" she said. "I've heard that *Dora* is a good show. Kids learn problem-solving and Spanish, and there's a strong girl lead."

Thankfully, Gloria appeared. "You ready to go play?" she said to Cass. He looked at me.

"I'll be here the whole time," I said. "I promise, Sweetie."

"Okay," he said and nodded, and I filled with pride as he stood and walked to the doorway.

"I apologize in advance if he breaks anything or tortures you," I joked with Gloria.

"He's in good hands. Stop worrying so much!" Lana pulled her chair closer to the table with an expression of distaste. In front of her now were her laptop, two phones, an iPad, and a small cup of coffee. "The others should be here any minute."

Who were "the others"? I knew that Gin would come. But I had expected this meeting to be what Lana had proposed on our walk a couple months ago: Lana, Gin, and I combing through the pages together, while trying to wrap things up efficiently and quickly.

Lana checked one of her phones and asked me, her eyes still on the screen, "So, you're divorced?"

"I'm single. By choice."

"Good for you!"

"Well, not always," I admitted, and tried to think of a way to change the subject. "Oh, hey, I loved you on *Ellen*."

"That was a hoot. Did you know she is the sixth most followed person on Twitter? And she's the fiftieth most powerful woman in the world? This is according to *Forbes* magazine. I got to see her Presidential Medal of Freedom," Lana said, and set her hand on her heart.

"Wow!" I was not hugely surprised by these things, although I was surprised at Lana's adulation. It seemed out of character.

"I still cannot believe she got me to sing on national TV. And get this—I was just asked to do *Jimmy Kimmel*. I hope he's okay with my talking about women's healthcare. I've got a campaign to run now." Her other phone rang, and she excused herself to take the call.

Was the campaign the reason for additional people coming today? More people now wanted to chime in about the book? I hoped not.

When she returned a minute later, two other people followed her.

"Shirley Alexander, Allie Lang," Lana said. "Shirley is managing my campaign."

"The famous Shirley," I said, recalling Colin's mentions of her. I stood to shake the hand of this wiry woman in her thirties with a long blond ponytail and disproportionly large brown eyes who had provided much of the early direction for the book.

A squat man with a sparse goatee and transition glasses, now oddly dark, stood beside Shirley, tapping at his phone. No one introduced us. We all took seats around the table, Lana and the other two on one side and I alone across from them.

"Colin is on his way with Gin," Shirley told us. She and Lana began to chat about some staffing trouble up in Rochester.

Colin, too? I was surprised he hadn't told me he was coming.

The man continued with his phone, and I tried in vain to make out his eyes behind his lenses. Why hadn't the glasses adjusted to the light inside? How could he even see the screen of his phone right now?

Colin blew into the room alongside Gin, who touched my shoulder with either warmth or preemptive pity, I feared, as she passed.

Shirley laced all her fingers together. "So let's talk about our book! Really good work so far, you two." Her eyes moved between me and Lana. "The writing is smooth and smart, and a *lot* of ground gets covered. Lana, as always, your intelligence literally took my breath away. When I was on the subway yesterday, I was reading the part when you imagine your ideal kids' clothing store and I accidentally yelled out 'YES!' Everyone looked at me like I was insane."

The room fizzed with chuckles.

She turned to face Lana. "How are you so well versed about so many topics? You covered everything from gender-embedded language to, I mean, child neurology, the economics of bottle feeding? You had me wanting to go out and have a son just so I can teach him to respect women and girls." She shook her head. "Can I just say that you never stop impressing me? Obviously this country needs a book like this—and a candidate like you—right this very minute."

Colin nodded emphatically.

Shirley turned to me. "This is going to be a really wonderful book. There's a lot here. But overall, I wondered if you might warm up the writing. You went pretty heavy on the academic, which I can understand, since this woman here"—she gestured to Lana—"is so deeply learned. But I'm talking more about the writing than anything else. Lana, you are just too intelligent for the rest of the world! And, well, this book is now in the position of being a campaign tool for us. I want everyone in New York State who reads this to fall in love with Lana."

Gin turned to Shirley. "Yes, I think overall, it could be made into more of a story. Every time we get a good anecdote about Lana and Norton, we cut to some long study or dry advice that sometimes, frankly, came across as a bit patronizing. Many readers will already know about doulas and the business of infertility and why it's so important to breastfeed."

"They will?" I said.

"Right," Shirley said. "I had the same thought. We don't want Lana to seem *patronizing*. Or, god forbid, elitist. It'd be great if we could cut back on all the stuff about European family leave and, oh, gender equality in Iceland . . and that thing about 'communism liberating women'?" She made a spooked expression. "We want to focus more on Lana's love of *this* country."

"I think it could flow better, too," Gin said, her eyes on Shirley. "Actually, and I know this will sound extreme, but I'd cut every piece of data—and even most of the advice."

The man in the glasses pivoted to look at Lana.

"I know, it means rethinking the book we have here," Gin went on. For a small woman, she had the stature of a longtime general. "The story—the characters if you will—get obscured. The book only really moves when we're with Lana and Norton. It just stalls out otherwise."

"Interesting," Shirley said.

I looked over at Lana, who gazed blankly at Gin.

"What do we have, three hundred twenty manuscript pages? At least half of that or maybe more isn't even memoir," she said.

Shirley nodded slowly. "You're right."

"I want to read the story of this revolutionary woman and her son. Period. All the stuff about medical monoliths and mothers in art, blah blah blah—no offense Allie, but you have to know that the reader will lose interest. The study about breastfeeding, Lilly Ledbetter, the income gap. All of that can go," Gin said.

I saw something catch fire in Shirley's eyes. "It really is that simple, isn't it?" She looked over at Gin.

"In terms of the writing itself, the language and the level of discourse, I think it has to be made more accessible. You need to have more fun with it," Gin said, in a tone void of fun. She pulled a laptop from her leather work bag, lifted open the screen, and typed a few times. "Like here—'We had to teach Norton how to eat and sleep, how to sit and crawl, how to be kind and respectful, how to love and lose and win and fall, how to navigate a mostly patriarchal society and how to resist getting co-opted by the patriarchy, no matter its appeal.' I mean, the first part is good, but even the word 'navigate' is fairly highbrow and, well, formal."

Shirley jumped in. "And then we get, 'patriarchal society, yadda yadda yadda, *co-opted*'? A lot of people won't know what the words *patriarchal* and *co-opted* even mean. We don't want this to sound like a textbook for some women's studies course at Smith."

"I don't think the words *navigate* or *patriarchal* are all that challenging," I managed.

"You want us to cut it by half?" Lana said, as if I had not just spoken. "This will be one short book."

"You'll have to do some filling in," Gin said. "But then you'll make room for more of your life. Lester's barely in it. You can talk about how you two met and fell in love, all that."

"Yes, you can talk about becoming a wife," Shirley said, turning to Lana. "We definitely need more stories—like when Norton dropped that thing into the fish tank at the dentist office, or when you faced off against those teenage boys in Central Park. Or when that woman made fun of Norton for having a Barbie Doll? These scenes show you as a regular mom, a vulnerable, likable woman who just loves her son and wants the best for him. *Everyone* can relate to that."

Lana nodded. "Okay."

I waited for her to say more, to even glance in my direction. It did not appear that she was ignoring me as much as blithely continuing on as if I were not here.

I opened my mouth without any sense of what might emerge, but Shirley spoke before I could: "Also, I know you might not like this, Lana, and I say this only as someone who wants you to win this thing and knows that you can: I don't think we should use the word *feminism*. The electorate is too polarized right now, even in New York. Same goes for other terms like that, like *intersectionality* and *microaggression*. Any of that kind of jargon is going to make nonurban voters' toes curl. Listen, I'd like you and Allie to think about two people, two voters when you go off and rewrite this thing: one is a twenty-six-year-old Latino from Utica who just lost his job as a truck driver. The second is a rich housewife in Pound Ridge."

"Republicans?" I said.

"Not necessarily."

"All right, we need less preaching and less data," Lana said. "But feminism and even intersectionality are pretty mainstream these days, right? Look at the Women's March. Beyoncé was singing in front of a projection of the word *feminist* at some award show. Can't we give people a little more credit?"

I nodded vigorously.

"Maybe," Shirley said. "But let's say you win, and let's say in a year or so that you have become what I think you will become—this galvanizing force for good in the Senate, a real leader there. Let's assume— although I'd rather not—that Sir Orange is still in office, and his people pull out this book and wave it around to stir up their base. You see how he treats Elizabeth Warren and Maxine Waters."

"I hope he does come after me. I have a few things I'd like to tell him," Lana said.

Colin spoke up, his eyes on his phone. "Listen, there's no shortage of the feminist spirit in this book. That doesn't have to change. I mean, like this, toward the end, I liked this part—" He tapped on the screen and read:

> The other day, I got home to find Lester and Norton working on a huge jigsaw puzzle, a Van Gogh painting. Lester had been traveling so often and had just returned from another business trip. He later admitted that he had bought the puzzle knowing that it promised plenty of father–son time. I stood in the hallway and watched them sort through the pieces. How lucky Norton and I were to have Lester, I thought. I continued to watch them and let my mind wander toward the future; I tried to picture Norton in high school and later in college. When he was twenty-five, I would be almost sixty. In the end, I could not manage to

visualize him as an older person, and I wonder if this is because I loved him so much the way he was in that moment, happily assembling a painting with his dad.

"That's the tone we need," Gin said.

"You get feminism and the hands-on father without shoving these things in readers' faces," Colin said.

"Yeah, great stuff," Shirley said, tapping her finger against the table. "How about instead of an art puzzle, Lester and Norton are throwing around a football in the park? And now that I think of that other scene, could Barbie be something a little less, well, Barbie? Don't forget about our truck driver in Utica."

"The word *feminism* would have ruined that passage about the puzzle. Remember: show, don't tell," Gin said to me.

I loathed this adage. "Can I ask something?" I said. No one answered, but I went on anyway. "Why does a woman have to be warm and doting and motherly to win office?"

The man in the glasses let out a huff of laughter.

"*Reggie*, stop. She's a civilian." Shirley turned to me and said, "We've learned a lot since November eighth: a whole lot of people won't vote for a candidate they think is a 'militant feminist' or who seems overly ambitious. Secretly, plenty of voters don't even want to vote for a woman who kept her maiden name, let alone someone who dissed Tammy Wynette or slammed stay-at-home moms for baking cookies. A lot of people would rather have a misogynistic blowhard as a president than an intelligent, highly qualified woman they find annoying."

"Well, yes," I said, a little annoyed myself that she thought I could not have guessed these things.

"Listen, I don't like this stuff any more than you do. Believe me," Shirley went on. "I'm a huge feminist. I can't stand Tammy Wynette or baking, and I doubt I'll ever have children, but if keeping this stuff to myself will help Democrats win? If it'll help save us from fascism? You bet that I'll be the first person to wave a flag from my American-made car. You bet I'll be the first person in line at Chick-fil-A." Her hand moved in front of her face for emphasis as she spoke. "You've really got to think beyond your bubble when you go off and revise this, all right?"

"My bubble?" I said.

"Let me guess: you live in Brooklyn. You grew up in Connecticut or maybe the Midwest, maybe Northern California. You went to Vassar or maybe Oberlin. You got your MFA from the Iowa Writer's Workshop, and then you probably taught expository writing for a while. And then you published a couple poems or short stories in some highbrow literary journals. You wrote a novel—something experimental or edgy, something really smart but kind of out there, and then you couldn't sell it, so you became a ghostwriter. You shop at Whole Foods, you try to stick with only local or organic foods, you listen to NPR, you love Dave Eggers. I don't mean to sound cavalier—*I* went to Vassar! I've have read every one of Dave Eggers's books! We're all on the same team here—we all desperately want our country back."

"I don't have an MFA. I don't live in Brooklyn," I said, stepping back through her words. "I mean, I guess I would call myself liberal."

"My point is—"

"I think we know what we have to do with our book," Lana interrupted, clearly ready to move on.

They chatted about some possible cover ideas—a photo of Lana and Norton? Maybe a picture of them walking down a forest path together, hand in hand? They all agreed that whatever it was, the cover had to convey tenderness, love, and tradition.

It all seemed wrong: these efforts to change Lana's image would be transparent to voters. Wasn't it authenticity that most people craved?

Politicians who spoke off-the-cuff? How many polls had showed that people had voted for the presidential candidate who "said what he thought"? It hardly seemed to matter what these thoughts were, in the end.

"As soon as we've got final pages," Gin said, "we're going to want to set up a meeting with you all to talk about a publicity schedule and a tour." They began to discuss media lunches and bookseller conventions.

Still reeling, I gathered my notebook and pen. Lana gestured for me to join her outside the dining room. "Give us a few minutes," she told the others, and I followed her toward the living room, eager to hear what she had to say.

She moved toward a black armchair beside the Kusama painting, and I sat on a crimson leather sofa across from her. The dog appeared and settled at her feet, and she reached her fingers down to him. "This is Liviu. The name is Romanian." Liviu licked her wrist and nuzzled against her arm. "I'd wanted to rescue a dog, some mutt that needed a home. But it was more pragmatic to find a breed that matched our busy lifestyles. We found a wonderful breeder of Italian greyhounds up in Bedford. Liviu has been just right for us. I don't regret a thing."

"That makes sense," I said, trying to discern some latent message. Perhaps the message was that she did not regret her upward mobility, or what had just transpired in the dining room. "You know," I began. "I can hardly hear your accent anymore."

"Between you and me, I've been working with a coach over the past year. Now I can sound more American when I say, 'Vote for me.'" She grinned.

"I always found it interesting that you escaped Bucharest with your mother. I wish I could have heard more about this. We might have been able to put some of it in the book."

She nodded.

I went on. "You had to, I mean, did Shirley want you to work with that coach?"

"It was my idea," she said.

"Oh."

"I have lived here over twice as long as I lived in Romania. It was past time," she said, and shifted back in her seat. "Shall we talk about our book?"

"Or what's left of it." I went for my laptop in my bag. So many pages would have to fall away. Long sections of chapters, so many hours of research that I had done, hours when Cass had been at Little Rainbows or Bertie's house or under my feet. Hours spent online or at the library, writing and rewriting, questioning my words and even myself and whether I was doing a good enough job as a feminist mothering my own son.

"Always expect the unexpected, right? You're clear about our new direction?"

"I guess so." How easily she had just agreed to discard all that she herself had initially wanted for her book. "Will you miss her?"

"Who?"

"Your old self. Your blue hair and your accent. *That* woman." It came out sounding accusatory, but I had only meant to convey compassion, as well as affection for that woman and her chunky eyeglasses (today she wore wire-rims) and her androgynous gray suits, the woman who once tweeted, "Lick your wounds, sharpen your claws, and prepare to maul this goddamn patriarchy. #PussyGrabsBack"

"Why do you think that was the real me? All women are more than one person, aren't we? We have to be nimble, now more than ever." She reached down for Liviu.

"I guess," I said. "You know, with all these cuts, we're going to have to fill a lot of empty pages. And I'm going to need to know what you want me to write." My voice thinned as I spoke.

"Allie, you heard what they said. *Your* stories are what Colin and Shirley and everyone else really want. You are the real writer here—you have that talent. You don't even need me. I spend all my time speaking to foundations and lobbyists, and now that I'm running? You should see my daily agenda. I've spent my life doing far more 'working' than 'mothering.' But the beauty of this whole thing is that with my name and your stories, with my platform and your wonderful writing, we make the perfect feminist mom, don't we?"

I blinked over at her. An image came to me of Cass and his two newly missing front teeth—the soft, fleshy stretch of gums there. He had no say in this. "You want me to give you all my stories? You want me to hand over the few things that I can actually call my own—my life with my son?"

"That's dramatic," she said.

I tried to ignore a tang in my chest. "Isn't that what men say when they are trying to gaslight women?"

"Oh, Allie. Come on. You're not giving up your life or your child or anything else. This is a job. You are getting paid to do a job, plain and simple," she said.

I kept my eyes on the rug.

"All right, how about if we take some time right now? You can ask me anything. And I'll do the best I can to answer. You'll at least come away feeling less martyred."

"'Martyred?'" But this was not nothing, and I raced to think of fruitful topics. It took me a moment to change tacks. "I guess I wonder, how old were you when you realized that girls and women were treated differently from boys and men? What was that like for you?"

"I don't remember any sudden dawning. The difference was everywhere all the time. My stepfather was never at home. He was always at work, and then he left us."

"My father died when I was a baby." I do not know why I said this.

"Oh? I'm sorry."

"I listened to your *Fresh Air* interview—do you remember that one? You talked about your sister. Is it okay if I ask you about her?"

"I guess, if you're just going for context here, but I mean, in terms of raising Norton, it's not hugely relevant."

I filled my lungs with air, effectively enlarging myself, and went for my laptop. "You said, 'My mother, my younger sister, Anita, and I lived in an apartment in Queens. Anita had cerebral palsy. I slept in the pantry so I didn't have to hear her kicking the wall every night. My mother worked so much that I was the one to raise Anita. I brought her to school when I could. I fed her and I did all of her home care. We were very close. But it was hard work and some days—' " I looked up and said, "Sounds like money was a bit tight for your family."

"Why?"

I was taken aback. "Well, you slept in a pantry. And back in Budapest, with all the austerity measures. I can only imagine the contrast between those days and, you know, all that you've achieved now?"

"Our apartment in Queens was quite nice. Anita and I had our own bedrooms and bathrooms, but we did share a wall. I liked the pantry because that's where our cat slept. And, as I said, it was quieter there. And in Budapest? My father was a banker. We didn't suffer like others did. I may not talk a lot about that period of my life, but I don't hide anything."

I had a difficult time believing she was unaware of her image, the penniless, scrappy immigrant who had worked her way to great heights. I could understand why she might not want it known that she, an advocate for underprivileged women, had in fact come from money, that she was not in fact self-made. Still, she seemed a person made entirely of lies in that moment.

"You're disappointed," she said. "Again, women have to be multiple people. We just do. Any other questions?"

I returned to the reason I had broached Anita. "Sounds like you had to be a mother for your sister."

"Yes, I guess that's true."

"Anita was only fourteen when she died. That must have been enormously sad."

She nodded, and I waited for her to say more. But she only looked at her watch again. "To be honest, I'm still not seeing how this is pertinent to the book."

"Your tending to her, your mothering?" I must have been aiming for more of an impact: a show of empathy, the muscle memory of hardship, a softening upon recalling her sister. The smallest detail had the power to evoke a rush of emotions, and I suppose I fantasized that she would blurt out something like, "I spent more time with my sister than I have with my own son" or "My life is so different from what it once was, but what a Faustian bargain it has been! I cannot even tell you Norton's favorite food. We haven't even shared a meal in weeks. I hate to admit this, but Gloria has been the one who's done most of the parenting." And then I would be vindicated, because even with my burdens and my overwhelming dearth of resources, I knew Cass's favorite foods, and the books that he liked, and how well he drew pictures, and so wasn't I in fact a better mother? Wasn't I a better human being?

Then again, I had not been the one to meet with three senators just last week about safeguarding women's overtime pay, military childcare, and retirement. I could hardly seem to manage a household of two, let alone launch a campaign for U.S. senator.

I had the desperate thought that if I revealed some vulnerability, she might do the same. "I don't have the support system that I need," I admitted. "I have to be paid for this book as soon as possible."

"I wish I could help you more," Lana said, as if she had already helped me plenty by allowing me to write this book in the first place.

Giving so much of myself to her book had to merit something more. Gratitude, credit, anything at all. I reached for the last thing I had, almost nothing, really. "Right before I started your book, I was working on another one, but it ended up getting canceled." Without naming names, I went on to describe what had happened with Nick. I mentioned an "enormous" advance, the long-needed chance to crawl out of debt, the sickening phone call from Colin. As I spoke, I became aware that I was dropping crumbs of information that might well lead her to guess Nick's identity.

"He sounds like a real prize. Has he been charged?"

"Yes."

"Did he ever harass you—or anything else? If you need the name of a good lawyer, I can easily give you one."

"No, I just meant to say that I'm still in the hole and—" I heard how feeble I sounded, more concerned with losing a few bucks than having been employed by a rapist. "I don't need a lawyer. The last I read, he was in jail awaiting trial."

"How come you didn't tell me any of this before now?"

"I try never to talk about my clients. Anyway, I signed an NDA with him, too," I said and dropped my head.

"Look at you. You're presenting yourself with the poise and confidence of a frightened deer. You are asking me to help you make money, but at the same time, you are telling me with your tone and body that you don't deserve it. Are you even aware of this?"

"Maybe. I guess I'm not you."

"Did you ever ask Colin for full payment from that awful man?"

"The publisher was the one who canceled the book. I got my kill fee, but it wasn't much."

"You got taken down by that man's horrific behavior," she said, shaking her head. "I assume you're earning partial royalties for my book?"

"No."

"Why don't you negotiate that?"

"I've never earned royalties on a book."

"Then good lord, ask Colin for what you're worth. At the very least, you have to ask for what you need. Hasn't anyone ever told you that before?"

"It's not so easy." I explained the field of ghostwriting: how we could be seen as disposable when celebrity held more currency than writing skills, at least in this country. I looked above her at the Kusama, the abstract lines and dots that to me resembled the chloroplasts inside a leaf as seen through a microscope. I had only ever wanted this work to be fair.

"At least you did the right thing in talking to me. That's the first step. And you know, you weren't entirely off-base," she said, reaching for Liviu again. "I did have to be a kind of mother to my sister. I was the one to get Anita dressed and brush her teeth, use the bathroom, all that stuff. I used to take her clothes shopping. I had to register her in middle school when I was sixteen. I was with her in the hospital after her accident, after, you know. Those were not easy times." She made a strange expression, a sad kind of smile. It appeared as if she was experiencing a memory that she would not share with me. "You aren't even going to try to negotiate with Colin?"

"Maybe for the next book," I said.

"When that time comes, you tell him exactly how much you put into your work. I mean it. Tell him how many hours of daycare you've spent, how many hours of side labor you had to do in order to fill in the gaps. You'll have to estimate of course. Multiply what you've got by 1.5. Any more and you'll lose your nerve. I've seen that happen too often."

I nodded, unable to imagine saying any such thing to Colin. We knew each other too well. He would easily detect a manufactured stance of strength and determination, and probably turn it into a joke, or tell me that his boss would never green-light a raise. And then there was Ed's advice about never talking about your needs with an employer.

"I should go join everyone in the dining room. Listen, you are a writer! Just keep doing what you do best."

"Which is usually memoir, not fiction," I said without thinking.

Her face changed. "You pretend to be other people all the time."

Liviu began to sniff his tail.

"But these people don't pretend to be *me*."

"Do you even want this job? It seems as if you're trying awfully hard to sabotage it right now. It would be very easy for me to walk right into that room and tell Colin that I'd like another ghostwriter, and that you're not on board with this book anymore. Vendrich, Grob has plenty of other writers, don't they?"

"That sucks." It was all that I could manage to say.

"You're not wrong. But do you think I haven't been in your position before? That I never had some privileged person force me to pretend to be something I'm not? Were you even in that other room an hour ago with those people?"

I turned and looked out the window at the park. A horse-drawn carriage plodded between lamp posts.

"I am to thank for writing a bill that, if it passes, will mandate paid family leave for women. I am right now working on another for paternity leave. But the funny thing is that you know all of this already because you know everything about me. Do you want your son to have health-care? You want to be able to send him to college? Every single day, I do something for women just like you," she said. "Do you know how many pro-life bills are floating around congress? Planned Parenthood is on the chopping block. There is no majority support of equal pay. Medicare may well become voucherized. Roe v. Wade may well become history."

I nodded once.

"You can say goodbye to the Violence Against Women Act. No more protection for students or immigrant women. No free lunch programs in public schools. And get ready to pay higher taxes so the government can buy more private jets and vacations. Golf resorts don't come cheap."

"I know. I get it."

"All right." She looked at me, waiting.

I pictured the newly confirmed Secretary of Education, a cartoonishly wealthy woman who seemed to know little about public schools, who had expressed comfort with keeping guns in classrooms as a way "to protect from potential grizzlies." I thought about Carlos and Luana, whose brother had just come to Houston from El Salvador and was worried about being deported. I thought about Jimmy and Strummy and Cass and the cost of college and Pussygate, that awful recording, those ugly words that no president should ever say.

"Okay," I said.

"Okay? You'll do it?"

I nodded, still overheated.

"We'll turn this country around yet, Allie. You and me together, right?"

The Kusama also resembled worms rushing over ice and leaves in different directions. "I hope so."

ON THE F train to Brooklyn, Cass and I found two empty seats next to a woman who was whistling an old Prince song. I once knew every word to "Purple Rain," and I wilted on remembering that Prince had died. She turned to gaze at me as if she knew just how I felt.

Cass moved onto my lap and said, "When can we go back home?"

"Tomorrow." We had missed the last bus to Great Barrington that day. Colin had given me the keys to his apartment.

We headed out of the station and into the chilled late afternoon air. We passed a yoga studio, a record store, a blond woman dressed in a

sari. We passed a homeless couple holding a sign that said LOST EVERY-
THING, PLEASE HELP. I fished a dollar out of my wallet and handed it
to them. Maybe Cass might do the same for someone else one day. The
air in Brooklyn smelled of sandalwood and weed.

Cass and I skipped, not easy in my heels, the rest of the way to
Colin's building. Soon enough, he would be too big for such a thing.

Colin's apartment was located on Tenth Street, and an iron fire
escape obscured most of the front of the building. A shuttered liquor
store covered in graffiti stood next door. We walked up two dim flights
of concrete stairs. The place was more run-down than I had expected,
but his apartment itself was nice enough. His narrow living room was
shrouded in long-limbed, round-leafed plants, and global art covered
nearly every inch of the walls. Several clay and wooden statues stood
beside the plants.

When Colin came home later, he went to change into a T-shirt.
He came back and showed us around a little. "That folds out," he
said, gesturing toward the yellow sectional sofa. "Look at this boy! Isn't
he beautiful?" He went to pinch Cass's cheek and Cass shrunk away
from him.

Colin poured two glasses of wine and took the couch while I sat
cross-legged on the floor nearby. Cass laid across the triangle that my
legs had made. Colin took a long sip, set down his wineglass, and
placed his hand on the top of my head, and despite everything, despite
my sense of defeat, despite the fact that Cass had stood and was now
heading toward a ceramic statue that looked about as delicate as an egg,
I smiled up at Colin and squeezed his wrist. We did not love each other,
and he could have gone easier on me back at Lana's, but we did take
care of each other, mostly, and that was a sort of love.

"You did good back there," he said. "I know it wasn't easy."

"No, it really wasn't."

"Was your talk with Lana okay?" I considered laying out all that had transpired in Lana's living room, but I did not have the energy. It was done now. "Yeah," I said.

At Cass's bedtime, I read him *The Lorax*, that sad and hopeful book.

"'You're in charge of the last of the Truffula Seeds,'" I read, and closed the pages. He was tucked beneath the sheet and blankets there on the fold-out. I held the book against my stomach.

"Can I go to sleep now?" he asked.

"Did you like that book? Wasn't it good? You know, you are one of the people who will make the world a better place."

"Okay."

"What was your favorite part of the book?"

"I don't know. What's a *thneed*?"

"Maybe we'll try it again when you get a little older."

"No, thank you."

"All right," I said. At least he was being polite. "Well, good night, then."

"Will you draw pictures on my back?" he said, turning over on his stomach.

I drew his name and a heart and a tree that he guessed was a lollipop. When he began to breathe heavily, I watched his mouth fall open, his stuffed lion against his cheek.

THE SOUND OF a chirp near my head woke me early the next morning. My phone showed a text from Kurt: *Call me when you get this.* Cass was still asleep beside me, so I took my phone into Colin's bathroom and closed the door behind me.

Kurt answered on the first ring. "Jimmy got a call from Norm with some bad news." He waited for me to say something. "Al? Allie? You there?"

"I'm here." My heart thudded. I sat cross-legged on the cold tile floor, filling the small wedge of space between the toilet and shower. "Kurt, don't tell me yet? Don't say any more right now. Give me a minute. I'm not ready. It's been pretty trying here."

"All right."

I pictured us both sitting there, our phones to our ears. Every breath was a nervous flutter. I kicked at the frosted shower door, and it clanged inside its frame again and again.

"Now?" he said.

"Not yet."

"So it's not going well?"

"I can't make small talk," I admitted.

"Okay."

I pulled my foot away from the shower door. "All right. Just go ahead."

"Bertie had a stroke," he said.

"Did she make it?"

He did not respond, and I said, "I've got to go."

"Allie, talk to me for a second."

"I can't."

"Come on," he said.

A pained noise slid from my mouth, followed by another. I considered hanging up so that Kurt would not have to hear any more, but some sliver of decorum stopped me.

"I know," he said at last. "Me, too."

I sniffled and pressed my palm against my mouth.

"The funeral's next week. In Wichita, though."

I cried a little more, and chokingly told him of our plans to return that night.

"Good. I'm glad you're coming back early."

My first thought after saying goodbye was a question—what to tell Cass? He had never known anyone who had died. My next thought was that Bertie had passed away in her son's home, not her real home in Western Mass, where she had lived for so many years with her husband.

At least in the end, the move to Kansas had been her choice. She'd had a good and long life, I thought, something we always tell ourselves in such moments in order to make ourselves feel better.

I would tell Cass the news later, maybe after we had left New York, and gotten home. Or maybe tomorrow.

KURT PICKED US up at the bus station. He had shaved off his beard, but had left behind a bushy mustache that gave him a sexy, porny seventies look that I quite liked. I went to him and let my head fall against his chest.

"Welcome home," he said into my hair.

It seemed as if we had just returned from some war-torn place, and I held onto him. "Don't go away for a while, okay?" I said. "Stay with us."

"Sure."

"You don't hate me for asking you that?"

"I love you for asking me," he said, his face going pink.

"You do?"

He nodded.

"I do, too," I said, as Cass mashed himself against the back of my legs and hugged us both.

I noticed Jenny Kane, now Jenny Beck, an old classmate, walking toward the ticket booth, glancing over at us and maybe recognizing me. I half-waved at her, but she had already turned away. She must have thought this was my family. I suppose it was.

CHAPTER SIXTEEN

I gut-renovated Lana's book. I cleared out Dr. Boyle's advice, everything about medical monoliths, the fertility industry, Lilly Ledbetter, the evidence of the pink tax—the higher cost of products geared to women—and I made room for the new occupants: the truck driver from Utica and the housewife from Pound Ridge. In came me and Cass's birth and my difficulties breastfeeding. In came barely disguised versions of Little Rainbows, Suze, Kurt, a more athletic version of Cass, and an alternate version of our visit to the Rockwell museum. Whenever I grew reluctant to continue, I would read the day's news: the efforts to repeal and replace the Affordable Care Act, the impending decreased protections for trans people, the president brazenly firing the head of the FBI—and my resolve would reignite. I turned the scene with the Van Gogh puzzle into a game of catch in Central Park. I turned Barbie into a teddy bear. At least I was hiding our lives a little.

Two long weeks later, I sent my revision to Lana, and this time, she read it promptly. She texted: *No birth plan? You didn't have one?*

Me: *I did, but the nurse lost it. Honestly, I know of nobody whose birth plan was implemented the way that she intended. Or at all. I guess we could blame doctors and hospitals and the medical establishment, but there are other culprits too: life, traffic, weather, spouses or lack thereof, etc.*

Lana: *How's this for a thwarted birth plan? I was in San Fran when I went into labor. I'd bullied United into letting me fly. Lester missed the birth of our only child, because Norton came a week early. I felt TERRIBLE. So did Les. (Still does.) (This stays between us, of course!)*

I stared at her words.

Me: *But I bet you were doing something incredible and revolutionary in San Fran.*

Lana: *I was at a friend's daughter's bat mitzvah.*

Me: *Yikes!*

Lana: *How about Norton learning Aikido instead of catch? We just signed him up for one-on-one lessons with the man who used to train Steven Seagal!*

Would the Utica Truck Driver be put off by private Aikido lessons with a celebrity trainer? No matter; this could easily be finessed. I replied, *Super! When's his birthday? Cass's is in a couple weeks! He'll turn the big 0-5.*

Lana: *Tell him I say Happy Birthday! Norton turned 13 a few weeks ago. I cannot believe I have a teenager.*

We chatted a little more about the boys, and she thanked me for my hard work. *I do appreciate all that you've given me,* she wrote. *I hope that I've been able to give you some invaluable things, too.*

My thoughts skimmed back over Nick Felles, and all those dark weeks after I had stopped writing for him, and then Disney World, my mother and Ed leaving. And Bertie. Something rose like a fast wave within me, a sense of the magnitude of all that life hands us, and in such rapid succession. Working with Lana had been disorienting, sometimes terrible, but also, in a larger sense, necessary and good. It had been depleting and confusing and inspiring, and now, somehow, it was done. The book, at least. I had the sense that this mash of emotions would linger in me a long while. I wrote back, *Absolutely. Thank you.*

THAT MAY, CASS graduated from Little Rainbows. He even got a certificate and walked in a ceremony. I was the only mother there without flowers or a graduation gift—who knew that four- and five-year-olds received these things?—but I made up for it by taking him for ice cream afterward.

My final check for Lana's book came through about six weeks later, and Kurt and I celebrated by taking Cass camping up near a lake in Williamstown. As we finished setting up our tent and unfurling our sleeping bags inside, it began to rain buckets. We had little choice but to pack everything back up and drive to a nearby motel, an almost entirely empty two-story place with several American flags out front. We ordered a pizza, changed into our pajamas, and watched *Muppets Most Wanted.* The three of us fell asleep together in bed, our arms slung over each other.

When I woke the next morning, I gently slid Cass's hand from my arm. I left him and Kurt, and went for a walk behind the motel, where a creek ran through a gully and led to a sprawling open meadow. How long had it been since I had just gone for a walk on my own? I let the coarse grass brush my legs and picked a handful of dandelions to bring back to the boys. I watched a butterfly flicker past.

Back in Lenox, Kurt got his first paying job as a furniture-maker: four chairs and a long table to help furnish the barn that Peg and Marv Meyers were now converting to a guest house. They hired me to get rid of some poison ivy and a dead Japanese maple, and plant some ornamental grasses by their steps. Kurt worked in the empty barn while Cass helped me outside, which was idyllic until he became very interested in the poison ivy, and I had to distract him.

When that job ended, Cass and I started going to Sandy Beach most afternoons. We would meet up with Luana and Carlos, as work was light for her, too, at the time. Jessica came along one day in July, and I noticed that her lower abdomen was a little distended. She confided that she was eight weeks pregnant. Luana and I whooped and congratulated her, but Jessica interrupted with, "One day at a time. I'm not going to celebrate until I'm holding a full-term baby."

We both nodded but went to hug her.

That afternoon, Colin called me with an offer for another memoir, this one for a movie actor, a known womanizer who had long ago been named the "Sexiest Man Alive." "This was even before *People Magazine* coined the term," Colin said. "No clue who named him this. I know he's not Lana Breban, but you'll get to write about some cool places at least." The book would describe his time riding his motorcycle through South Africa, Namibia, and Botswana. Colin told me the advance. "Oh," I said. "I got more than twice that for Lana's book."

"I know," he said. "Things are tough in publishing right now. Everyone's reading the news and not much else. Believe me, this is a decent offer."

From the sound of it, this client could well be a geriatric Nick Felles. "What if we asked for a cut of royalties? If I sent you a report of what my costs will be, you know, of what I'll need to live on and for childcare while I'm writing this, would you at least consider it?"

"What, did Lana get to you?" Colin said.

"Yes," I snapped. "So what? You don't need to condescend."

"Sorry. *Jeez*, Al. Lighten up," he said. "You used to be more fun, you know."

"I'm happy to explain how fun it is to work without enough childcare or decent health insurance. I'm happy to explain what it's like to pull a memoir out of thin air because your client all but extorts you, and what it was like to hear the news that six months of work was thrown out because your client raped one or more of his—"

"Okay, all right. I get it," he said. "I can't guarantee anything."

"Thank you," I said, my stomach settling. I had said what I needed to. It felt good and, in a second, a little terrible; what if my exasperation had been too much? What if he deemed me "high maintenance" and decided to finally be done with me and my work? "Anything would be great, Col."

"I'll let you know."

"Did you see that review of Lana's book today?" I had forgotten to disable Google Alert for Lana, and had seen a starred prepublication review from a trade magazine.

"Yes! Nice work! Shirley sent it over. They're all really pleased," he said. "Do you want me to start sending you reviews?"

I was surprised at his offer. "That'd be nice. But only if they're good reviews. You can skip sending me the bad ones, okay?"

The next day, he came back to me with an extra three thousand dollars and half a percentage point of royalties. It would inevitably amount to far less than what I had earned for Lana's book even without royalties, let alone what I could have brought in for Nick's, but it was a start, and I accepted.

I considered the alarming fact that I had earned additional money simply by asking. Lana would say this was also a function of my inherent value. It occurred to me that I could have asked for more years ago. I had always been glad for any offer from Colin, and had taken the payment as something fixed. I had the sensation of discovering some hidden button underneath the seat of my truck, a button that, when properly pushed, had the potential to add horsepower and mileage capability. It had been there the whole time, but I had never known to look.

Admittedly, that three thousand dollars made it more bearable to hear the details of my new client's past affairs with a swimwear model and a smoking hot Dutch biologist whom he had met in Pretoria. After a few phone conversations, after he had gotten used to my questions, and we had gotten used to each other, he asked if I was single. I made a surprised gulp.

"Let me ask you something," he went on. "This will be fun, I promise. Of my films—and you did say that you'd seen them all—which romantic scenes did you like the most? When was I the most convincing? I want to see if you could tell when I was the most aroused, you know, the times when I wasn't acting."

"I'll pass," I said, my stomach tight.

"Oh, Allie, just play along. Not even one comes to mind?"

"I'll pass."

He groaned. "You're not one of those feminists?"

My instinct was to again reply, "I'll pass." As his ghostwriter, I did not want him to think less of me. And after all, he was nearing eighty. He might not have known any better, I reasoned.

You can do anything. Grab them by the pussy. You can do anything. I recalled Billy Bush's laughter. "I might—I guess I am," I finally said. "One of those." I wanted to qualify my answer, to say something that might make him feel better or reassure him, which might prompt him to continue droning on about his virility and success in weightlifting, his decision to turn down the role of Spartacus, but I stopped myself.

From then on, I heard primarily about such topics as the motorcycle repair shop and library in Botswana where he had taken part in a rain-making ceremony and his work advocating against rhino poachers in South Africa. I knew that it would be a far better book—simply because I had refused to pass along my romantic status or my take on the visibility of his lust for his co-stars. How strange that such a quick refusal, such a simple but necessary thing, had ever given me pause. I was well aware that shutting down uncomfortable questions would not always be this simple, but I thanked God that this one time, it was.

SEPTEMBER CAME, AND Cass and Carlos started kindergarten, glorious, free kindergarten.

I first saw Lana's book in the window of a local bookstore the day after I sent the editor the first few chapters of the new travel book. There they were on the cover, Lana in hoop earrings, a cream-colored turtleneck and a navy skirt, and Norton in khakis and a red polo shirt, the two sitting side by side on a park bench, holding ice cream cones and looking beatifically at the camera. *All That Matters: A Story of Love and Motherhood.* How far back in time this book had traveled from its initial conception, a guide to help feminists raise feminist sons. Of course, backward was the direction the country was now moving. Just two weeks ago, white supremacists had marched in Charlottesville, and horrifically, one of them had struck and killed a counter-protester with his car. The president actually went on record to remark about the "good people on both sides."

"There's Lana!" Cass said, pointing at the window. I nodded. "Your name isn't on the front?"

"No, but that's the job."

We walked inside the store and found a stack of the books. I lifted a copy and took in the praise from a list of celebrities, one I swore was a Republican. Surely all these busy people had not read the whole book in such a short period of time. Maybe their assistants had to stay up nights in order to read it quickly—or maybe they had to write these glowing sentences on their bosses' behalf without any access to the book at all.

When we got home, I sent a congratulatory email to Lana. Luana and Carlos came over soon after and the boys played their rescue dog game out front.

The next day, Lana wrote back, "We did it, Allie! *You* did it. Thank you. Truly."

Soon after, my mother called. She had just bought a copy of the book herself.

"You might recognize some, a lot, of stuff in there," I told her.

"What do you mean?"

"I had to fudge a few things here and there," I said. "You'll see."

"Patty said you already made the *New York Times* bestseller list! Is this the first time one of your books has done this well?"

"It is? Wow, great!" I said, excited. Then alarmed. "Wait, what?"

"How does Cass like kindergarten?" she asked in a strange voice.

"You didn't tell Patty, did you?"

"I wasn't—what does it matter now? You're done with the book. You're no longer working with Lana, right? Patty knows to keep her mouth shut. I was very clear about that part."

"Mom?"

She breathed into the phone. "Sweetie. We had that argument, and then I read Lana was running for senate. I was so excited for you! You'll understand someday. You can't help bragging about your child, even after they grow up."

For a brief moment, I was touched, having conditioned myself to expect mostly bafflement and distaste from her and Ed. But the moment passed. "Was anyone else there to hear you?"

"No, I promise," she said. "Allie, how much trouble could a fundamentally insecure old lady in Sebastian, Florida, cause? Try not to worry. I told her that it was totally private information. Let it go."

The book was already in stores, I reminded myself, and, in the meantime, I had written another one. My mother was right; who would care if Lana had used a ghostwriter? I had little choice but to hope for the best and move on. "All right."

"I can't wait to read it!"

After we said goodbye, I stood for a moment, my phone in my hand, my heart sideways. I disabled the Google Alert for Lana, and typed out a quick email to my new editor: "Can't wait to hear your thoughts. I'm really proud of our work. Are we staying with *Uncivilized: Secrets of a Global Adventurer* as the title?"

CHAPTER SEVENTEEN

Kurt and I sat on my couch, our legs intertwined, as he read a nature magazine and I scrolled through *Ghostwriters Talk* on my laptop. I reached over to squeeze his foot. When he set down his magazine, I climbed on top of him. He unclasped my bra, but then Pete called. Kurt kissed my head and whispered, "Love you." "Love you, too," I said gladly, and he went off to talk to Pete in the other room.

Alone now, I thought again of Patty Copeland and went to her Twitter feed. My mother had told me that Patty had set one up solely to follow Lana's tweets. I knew that I was being overly cautious and unnecessarily concerned.

But a heartbeat later, I proved myself wrong. I blinked over at everything on the screen, and had to scroll down to understand precisely what was going on. Two days earlier, someone named John Ashley, whose handle was @deplorablefucker67, had posted: *She had a ghostwriter/ghostmom—A. Lang—cuz LB knows shit about motherhood. Nothing in book is real. Norton raised by nannies. #Breban4Senate.*

Patty had replied: *I know the writer's mother! #Breban4Senate.*

Did Patty think her comment was private? Was she, @GrandmaPattyC, trying to impress other people by having a connection to me? When I clicked on #Breban4Senate, my face—and the rest of me—went numb.

Rich elitist globalist fraud.

Gotta love the coastel SJWs, too important 2 raise there own kids.

Does Lang use nannies too? Or is she one herself? Or a man?

Kill her. Kill them both. Die cunts.

There were hundreds of tweets over the past few hours: one linked to a photograph of a younger Norton standing next to Gloria, her face partially obscured. Another attached Lana's travel schedule over the past year; she had been home, presumably with Norton, for a total of sixteen days. The year before that, another document showed, she had been in New York for only twenty-two days. I saw GIFs of a baby crawling around in piles of money and a toddler photoshopped next to an image of Lana, a speech bubble near his mouth that read "Who the hell are you, lady?" There was a photo of Lana next to George Soros, possibly the most vilified left-wing donor; a picture of two unsmiling women, supposedly but likely not in fact Gloria's sisters, and a host of dirt-faced children seated on the ground against a rotted-out wall. "Oh God," I said. There was a tweet from @BerkshireBabe, someone who had actually seen or heard about Cass dumping the replica jaw in that fish tank in Aaron's lobby, and this one sent a current from my feet to my scalp; a tweet from Barton Heller's mother about Cass, *a sniveling little dork.* And another from her: *This is a book of lies. This is Allison's life, not Lana's.* There was a photo of me in high school from one of the landscapers from the Mount, who proudly owned up to harassing me a couple of years ago.

I forced myself to keep reading. There were rape threats against Lana, me, Gloria, and Norton, wildly graphic and violent fantasies. There were disturbing GIFs, pictures involving KKK insignia and nooses and naked women. There were pictures of Lana's face transposed onto the heads of piled bodies outside concentration camps.

"What?" Kurt asked. He stood nearby, the magazine in his hand.

"What?" he said again.

"Do you think that I'm someone who deserves bad things?" I managed. At best, the general public would think of Lana as yet another politician pretending to be "one of the people" and me as some kind of desperate opportunist and terrible mother. Those who did not know me well enough would think me a liar, a liar who had sold out her own life, and the life of her son.

"What are you talking about?"

I began to hyperventilate. Kurt ran for a paper bag and sat next to me. Now that a hostile cyber-mob was waving their flags and marching toward me and Gloria and Lana, there was no need to hold back. I explained everything to Kurt. I told him all about Lana's reticence and my trip to New York, about the meeting with Gin and Shirley, and the long, tense talk with Lana afterward. I told him about my mother's inferiority complex and Patty Copeland's as well. I had to think that neither of them knew the depths to which things could sink on Twitter, but at the same time, I wanted to throttle them both.

Kurt pulled his whole face back with his hands. "Man. I don't know what to say."

I brought the paper bag back to my face.

"Maybe Lana won't mind that much. She's all over Twitter—she's got to be used to trolls, right? And you didn't leak anything about *her* life, I mean, at least not directly?"

The bag ballooned and shrank and ballooned again from my mouth.

I had told my mother something in confidence, and Kurt was right: there were plenty of worse things I could have done. Still, what would happen to Gloria? And to me, ultimately? I had checked the other day after talking to my mother, and my nondisclosure agreement did mandate that I was to pay back "any and all monies" should I disclose my work with Lana. She herself could not have been more adamant about my keeping quiet. For a moment, I wondered if this Twitter wildfire could even be traced back to me. My mother was not on Twitter, just Facebook. But one only had to google Patty to see that she lived in close proximity to my mother and Ed, and that they all belonged to the same book group at the local library.

I set down the brown bag and yelled for Kurt to go roll me a joint.

"First give me that," Kurt said, and snatched away my laptop. He went to find my phone and hid both. "It's late—you need to get some sleep if you want to have the energy to manage this whole thing tomorrow."

"MORNING, SUNSHINE." IT was Colin. Kurt was bringing Cass to school and I was back on Google, the brown bag at the ready. "Feel like hopping a bus to New York? I take it someone's told you about the fun things about Lana all over Twitter." I let out a pained grunt. I had no idea how much he knew about my involvement. "Her campaign is meeting later this morning and they told me to get you down here. I'll see you at her place—just text me when your bus gets in."

"Why do they need me there?" I asked carefully.

"We'll find out soon enough," he replied.

I checked my email inbox, where a host of new messages awaited me: three from Colin, one from Gin, two from Lana, as well as emails from my mother and Patty even. There was no time to sit and read all these messages; I had to hurry if I wanted to catch the bus. I got dressed, a solid lump filling my throat, and gathered what I needed.

Kurt pulled my truck in the driveway and trotted inside the house. I told him about Colin's call. "Oh man," he said. He and Pete had tickets to see some new band at the Calvin that night. "You want me to cancel and stay home with Cass?"

"But you've been talking about this show for weeks."

"Pete can sell my ticket. This is what people do for each other," he said, as if I were new to the proclivities of interdependence between human beings. I suppose that on some level, I was.

"I'll try to get back as early as I can." I pressed my hands to my heart as a kind of thank you. "What if I never get hired to write again? Oh my god—what if someone does something to Cass?"

"Go. You don't want to be late."

"You didn't answer me. What if some neo-Nazi is on the bus and knows who I am and shoots me in the head? Everyone has guns now."

"Allie, come on," he said. "Just take the brown bag."

On the bus, I forced myself to listen to a meditation app. Afterward, I watched the hills pass by, the clouds like scattered wool in the morning sky. I considered crafting an email to Lana and Colin and just coming clean about what I had told my mother. Wouldn't I at least get a few points for being forthright? If it had not been for Cass, I might have gone ahead and done so. But if there was any chance that Lana and her people had not connected me with @deplorablefucker67 and Patty's tweets, any chance that Colin would continue to employ me as a ghost-writer or that I would not be asked to repay the money I had earned from Lana's book, I owed it to my son and myself to not say anything.

The time on the bus was a gift, a valley between two agonizing moments. There were no discernible neo-Nazis among us, just a handful of businessmen and a group of people evidently headed to see *The Book of Mormon*. I began to read a few emails, but lost the connection, so I just gazed out the window at the Taconic State Parkway. Memories came at me: my seventh birthday, when my parents threw me a Roald Dahl–themed party in our yard. I had dressed as Matilda, my mother as Aunt Spiker, and Ed as a giant peach made from a garbage bag painted orange. The time we drove up to Montreal and Quebec City with my cousins and camped out near Mont Tremblant. On the ride back, my cousin grew carsick and my mother had to pull over, but while we waited on the shoulder of Route 87, we saw a baby moose. The many evenings at Tanglewood, when my mother and Ed sat over picnic dinners with friends and listened to Seiji Ozawa conduct the Boston Symphony Orchestra. I would unlace my shoes and join the other children as we crawled over the low thickset tree branches and chased each other around the endless grass that looked out at Monument Mountain, the Taconics, and Lake Mahkeenac. And years later, that sweltering end-of-summer day when I got dropped off at Dartmouth, at Little Hall, and I met my roommate, a rather shy girl from Oregon. She said she, too, wanted to be a writer someday, but a month later she would move back to the West Coast after hearing the terrible news that her parents were killed in a car accident. My next roommate was an extroverted economics major from Winchester, Massachusetts, a girl who had some faint connection to the Bush family. Over time, it became clear that I was not a good fit with most of the other students at Dartmouth. I would never learn to ski or play lacrosse or join in conversations about European travel or whether Saabs or BMWs were better cars, but I would be assigned a kindly faculty adviser, a man who bought me diner coffee and encouraged my writing and listened to my ideas about poetry and my appreciation of the humor of Shakespeare, and later my gripes about fellow students. "People like you and me are outsiders at Dartmouth," he once said. "But you learn who to trust after a while. You learn who's taking things seriously and who's only here because of luck, family money or whatever. People like you and me need to stick together."

A few days after I had graduated, a friend and dorm-mate whom I had told about Professor McCoy's dark turn called to see how I was doing. "What a tool. But I mean, seriously, so many of them are tools," she said with a laugh. "I had this gross old boss at an ice cream shop who used to quote unquote adjust my T-shirt all the time. Oh, and before that, these pricks at my high school wrote *Loose Pussy* with shaving cream on my dad's Volvo because I wouldn't blow one of them after prom. I mean, hello, this is the opposite of loose, right? Dumbasses."

"Jesus. That's horrible," I said.

She went on: "I'm just saying, who doesn't have at least one story like that? It's just part of life."

If I had to name what I was most grateful for today, it was that Twitter and Facebook and Instagram and 4chan had yet to be born when I was at Dartmouth. My social discomfort there would only have been amplified by so many party photos and group selfies. I might have even leaned more heavily on Professor McCoy for solace.

GLORIA'S HAIR WAS down and uncombed, and she had an angry cold sore at the side of her mouth. For all I knew, she, too, had signed a non-disclosure agreement and had already gotten some kind of reprimand. She took my coat and Lana appeared behind her. "Hi, Allie. We're all in the dining room."

"Hi, okay." I nervously followed her down the hallway.

There had to be a dozen people crowded around that oak table: Shirley; Colin; Gin; Reggie, of the transition glasses; an attractive woman in a taupe turtleneck; a guy with a shaved head who could not have been older than thirty. When they saw me, every one of them set down a phone or ceased talking to each other. I turned to Colin for a sign of moral support, but he only made his mouth into a flat line.

Shirley, in a black blazer and kidney-colored blouse, cleared her throat and said, "We ready? Here's what we know. @deplorablefucker67 is a man named John Lance. John lives in Jacksonville, Florida, and is part of a white male supremacy group—he runs a local chapter. His Aunt Liz used to be a columnist for the *Tampa Bay Times*. She lives in Sebastian, Florida."

If only it were possible to summon a portal to another time and place.

The young bald man said, "Interestingly, Liz and 82 percent of her friends on Facebook are Democrats."

Colin said, "So why would they—?"

The man just kept on. "Allison could have been hacked. We'll check right now," the man said. "Does she even have a protected server? Give me a second and I'll grab her data."

A montage of things that I wanted no one to see flashed through my mind: the naked photo of me that my old boyfriend once took; a picture of me lighting a joint in front of the Grateful Dead house; the snapshot of my coworkers propping me up as I was too drunk to stand outside Clover Dooley's Pub in Manhattan.

"Hold on," Shirley said. "Let's get back to Sebastian, Florida. Specifically, the Whispering Winds condos. Allison?"

How I wished it were just Lana and me sitting across from each other. I kept my eyes on a goblet of water with a dark lipstick smudge near its rim. "Yeah," I made myself begin. "Well, I accidentally told my mother about the book."

Lana nodded, her jaw set.

Gin reached for the goblet.

"Was that . . ." Reggie paused. "Is she Liz Gillis?" He looked down at his phone.

"No," I said. "I don't know who that is. My mother told her friend, a woman named Patty Copeland."

"How many people did you and she tell?" he asked.

"Just my mother," I said, my words slipping down my throat. "I'm so sorry. I can't tell you how embarrassed I am. I swore her to secrecy—I told her there was so much to lose, and she thinks Lana is amazing, by the way, and that it's amazing how I got to work with her. Still, I feel thoroughly terrible. I wish I could rewind time and fix everything."

Colin, bless him, spoke up, "Like you said, it was an accident. It's your mother, not a reporter at the *Times*, right?"

"Of course not," I said, and then, "I still feel like an idiot."

Shirley nodded. "We appreciate that."

Lana did not look appreciative. She looked both flabbergasted and annoyed. Maybe my desperate supplication was irritating to her.

The woman in the turtleneck said, "The damage: Allison's name is out there, as are a ton of photos of Gloria with Norton. People know there's a hands-on nanny and a very, very hands-on ghostwriter. I've been on the phone all morning—it sounds like Remy's team is already spinning this as hypocrisy." Remy Calhoun—former owner of a bottled water empire and current owner of a middling NBA team—had recently announced his candidacy in the upcoming primary. "If anyone knows that poverty is a women's issue, it's Lana. And here she is profiting from the work of a poor single mother. Two, when you count Gloria."

Poor? Were we officially poor? Was I? I looked over at Colin again, but he kept his eyes on the woman who was talking. I had never thought of myself and Cass as poor. "Broke," sure. "Broke" had a whiff of accident to it. "Poor" was what someone else called you behind your back. "Poor" was pitiful, an overly simplistic, old-fashioned word that conjured Dickensian filth and debauchery. I preferred the term "income inequality" to "poverty," and had in fact been careful to avoid the words "poor" or "rich" in Lana's book.

"They're going to call this whole thing 'establishment bullshit,'" the woman said, and used air quotes to add, "'Those big-money Democrats riding the backs of poor people one more time.'"

Reggie said, his eyes on his phone, "Here are some Republican soundbites: 'The tone deafness toward the plight of the working person.' 'This is class appropriation. Breban literally stole her writer's life.' 'Honest Abe never lied.' Oh, and this: 'How is exploiting two poor women considered feminism?'"

Gloria deserved none of this. It was infuriating. And I resented this portrayal of me as utterly powerless. I myself had made the conscious decision to write the pages that I had written. Lana had pressured me, but I had agreed of my own volition.

"Lana needs some distance," Reggie said. "She needs to separate herself from this bees' nest."

A woman said, "Amen."

Chewing his thumbnail, he went on. "What if Lana didn't know about the parts of the book that Allison wrote about herself?"

The parts? At least 80 percent of the book had to have been taken from my life.

Lana watched him. I waited for her to speak.

But he went on: "Allison inserted her own life into this book without Lana even being aware of it. And yes, she saw an earlier draft, but later on, she was too busy to vet the *final final* version. She only learned about Allison adding in her own stuff after the book went to press. I'm just spit-balling. Trying to think of a way to get in front of this—if it's not too late, of course."

"Keep going," Shirley said.

For some reason, his words had not made any meaning to me yet. I could not fathom exactly what he was proposing.

"Allison thought she had more to say about motherhood than Lana did, that she herself was a better mother or something, I guess, since she doesn't have a nanny—I don't know, we'll fine-tune the motive. Allison puts out a statement owning up to everything, all the lies, all the sections that were really about her own life. And maybe Gloria says something too—or no, that'd be too much. It'd be seen as defensive."

A few heads slowly nodded, taking it in.

Everything slid into focus for me.

"And the book?" Gin asked with hesitation.

"Can we pulp it?" the bald man said. Shirley nodded in agreement.

Gin breathed a sigh that I thought would not end. "I'll check. Probably—I'm just not sure how soon."

"Jesus," I said, but no one responded.

They began to work on a statement for me to deliver at a press conference. I'd keep it brief, but try to seem genuine and contrite, a little embarrassed, but most important, I would emphatically assume blame for each and every falsehood in the book. I would then "passionately advocate" for Lana. Shirley and maybe one or two others would stand behind me when I spoke as a symbol of Lana's support for all "poor, exploited women."

It was decided that Lana herself should lay low for a least a few days. Maybe go hide out at a spa, someone suggested. "Self-care is important right now, Lana."

Lana's eyes skimmed past me and dropped.

The gears started moving again in my head: I would no longer be able to ghostwrite. No one would trust me. I wondered if I would be able to complete my revision of *Uncivilized*; how lucky that at least for the moment, I was not broke.

"We'll try to get some media together for a conference tomorrow," Shirley said. "I'll send out a blast to everyone once we know the plan."

Gin said, "I hate to be the bad guy, but what about Allie's NDA? We pulp all those books? Countenance is taking a huge loss here. Technically, we're not the ones at fault."

Shirley raised her brows. "Up to you guys."

I had not thought it possible to feel worse than I just had.

"Let's try to be fair," Colin said. "Allie made a mistake. She didn't do anything malicious, right?"

"I'm just anticipating what corporate will say. I'll do what I can," Gin said. She shot Colin a look. "We'll talk later?"

People began to chat with each other as they stood and gathered their things. I set one hand on my stomach and the other on my heart, and waited for someone to ask me if I was even able to pay back Countenance. And was I on board with the press conference? Did that sound okay to me? I had never spoken publicly, not at Dartmouth, not at any meetings in San Francisco or at the equity firm.

Colin was talking with Gin now, Lana to the woman next to her.

"Excuse me," I said at last.

Shirley looked over at me. "We'll text you the details of the conference tomorrow once we've got them."

A little sick, I got myself together and approached Lana. "You have a minute?" I asked. She turned to look at me. "I just need a minute."

"What is it?"

I lead her into the hallway. "You were the one. You were the one who told me, you know, to ask." My own words were stuck to each other and I could not pry them apart. "To ask for more, for what I am worth."

"Okay?"

"You don't think I'm worth more than this?" It was and was not a question.

She pursed her lips.

"How do you expect me to write such a big check to Countenance? You think all the money's just been sitting in my bank account this whole time? If I go on TV tomorrow, I'm done. I won't be asked to write for anyone ever again. That is, if I'm not too late already." I straightened my spine and tried very hard to appear strong and solid, nothing that I felt. How awful it would be to cry right now.

"Gin just needs to talk to her people. I doubt you'll have to pay them back."

"You don't know that."

"What is it that you want me to do?"

"I don't know," I snapped. "Maybe something to counteract what is happening right now, especially after I did all I did for you."

"You willingly agreed to do it," she said.

I kept my eyes on the floor. "I'm no good at public speaking. I'm not sure you even want me to do the press conference," I said.

"Go ahead—just ask me for this straight out."

What did she think I wanted? A second later, though, I understood. How had I missed the leverage that I did in fact have? I suppose that I had trained myself to be a ghost in uncomfortable work situations. An accommodating subordinate, a person who did what she was told.

Lana looked at me, waiting.

"Okay. If I'm going to talk to those reporters, maybe you can ask Gin or even Countenance to let me off the hook. We both know that they'll listen to you more than anyone else in that room. Definitely more than me." I grew unsteady, and instinctively opened my mouth to back-pedal, but Lana spoke first.

"Fine."

"Fine?"

"I'll put in a good word for you with Gin, and—" Lana looked at me, gauging something in my face. The silence became too much.

"Thank you," I said.

"And I need to talk to Shirley, but maybe there's some work for the campaign, some writing that you could do. Speechwriting? I can't predict what she'll say. I can't promise anything," she said. "This could be a terrible idea. We have no clue how this press conference will be received. I have to be honest—we could both come out of it in worse shape. I don't know how the DNC and the super PACs will react, or how any of it will impact this campaign at the end of the day. I'm just taking it five minutes at a time right now."

I nodded. "I've never been on TV—I've never wanted to be on TV. You're really sure you want *me* doing this?"

"Who else is there?" she said. "It's not so hard. Pretend you're, I don't know, another person, a warrior or a superhero or something. Just fake it. It sounds kind of silly, but it's what I do. If you pretend you are up to the task, you'll start to believe it."

THAT NIGHT, I called my mother and told her everything that happened. "No," she said. "No."

"What do you mean, 'no'?"

"It can't have been that bad."

"That's your response? You don't believe me?" I said. Words flew once again, culminating in my calling her "naïve" and "a lifelong social climber." She fired back with "And you are an ungrateful brat and an anxious wreck."

A hard silence followed. This time, I forced myself not to press End and to see us through to a better place. The alternative would have been too much, given the level of angst elsewhere in my life. "Mom," I said. "It *was* that bad at Lana's. I'm not exaggerating."

"Okay," she said.

"It has been the longest day. I need my mother right now on my side." I heard her inhale and exhale. "Of course."

"I shouldn't have said those harsh things to you."

"Let's forget what I said, too. I'm sorry for this awful trouble I've caused," she said, and then joked, "I had no idea of the destructive powers that I had."

"Congratulations."

"I miss you and Cass terribly. You know what, I'm going to come up there. Let's plan it."

We found our calendars and tried to settle on a date, all the while talking over each other and laughing with lingering nerves and relief.

THE NEXT MORNING as I waited in the lobby of Countenance Books, I took in the posh silver wallpaper, the walls lined with their recent bestsellers; novels, cookbooks, children's books. I thumbed through a sumptuously designed copy of *Mrs. Dalloway*, complete with gold leaf lettering and deckle edges. The receptionist, a youngish woman wearing a silk graphic blouse, peered over at me from behind her hulking half-circle desk. I was glad to note the glint of a tiny nose ring.

Lana and Colin came for me, both somber, and led me down a quiet hallway and into a small conference room. Colin left us alone. "Let's sit," she said, and we chose chairs across a long empty table from each other. "I emailed Gin last night and told her you'd been punished enough. I even said I'd help repay your fee if corporate wouldn't budge. But they'll back down. They'll be embarrassed—they won't want my money and the press that will come from taking yours, believe me. Do you want to see the email?"

"Really?" I half-expected her to laugh heartily, admit that she had been joking, and ask if I brought my checkbook.

But she only went for her phone.

"It's okay. I believe you," I said. "Thank you."

"And in terms of working for the campaign, Shirley wants to wait and see what the fallout is after today—but if everything goes as planned and nothing major happens, she agreed to a one-month trial. She said, 'If anyone knows your voice, and how you think and talk, it's Allison.'"

Even now—even after finishing her book and having known her for a year—I was uncertain of the veracity of this statement. Of course the idea of becoming a speechwriter rather than an underemployed substitute teacher/landscaper was appealing.

"We need to keep this agreement quiet, at least for now."

"All right. I won't even tell my mother," I joked, but Lana just twitched. "I should probably ask you—and you were the one who helped me see the need to ask for this sort of thing! Do you know what I might get paid for this trial for my becoming a speechwriter?" As soon as I had said it, I knew that I had pressed the button under my seat too soon.

"I'm sure we can give you what you need. You'll have to figure that out." She rose. Before she left, she said, "Oh, I almost forgot! Here's *your* speech for today. Don't worry. It's short, and when you're done, just turn over any questions to Shirley." Lana handed me a page with two paragraphs, double-spaced.

It was the first time another person had written my words for me. Seeing them could not have been stranger, like being handed a wildly inaccurate mask of my face. They had me saying a version of what had been discussed in our meeting; I had grown desperate for Lana to win the election, especially in order to help women like me. I had worried that readers might negatively judge her for relying on a nanny—"Women are still, even now, punished for their work-life choices"—and at the last minute, I had stuffed the book full of anecdotes from my own life. I must have thought that these moments needed witness, I would say. After all, the struggles of a person like me were just as important as the struggles of a person like Lana—a belief that she herself had long espoused. "Still, I was wrong. I apologize with all of my heart and take full responsibility for hijacking this project. Without a single reservation, I support Lana Breban, the candidate we need during this challenging time."

It was a lot to digest: this speech, but also Lana's unexpected kindness, a sudden career change, this pivot from the most private form of writing to the most public, that is if everything worked out. I considered what it might be like to write speeches instead of books, to hear Lana say my words in front of crowds of people.

Outside the room, Colin asked me if I needed anything before we began, and I said, "A restroom?"

"You got it."

Behind a tall door was a fawn-colored tiled bathroom. I made sure that I was alone before I faced the mirror, applied some lip gloss, and whispered to myself, "You are a warrior. You are a superhero." It sounded inane, so I tried again. But I felt no better inside, no stronger or abler to handle what was about to occur.

I was, in fact, no warrior. And I was, of course, mortal. How the hell would I get through this? I shuddered at the thought of being seen and judged by so many people, being made so nakedly available like that. So I took a pen from my bag and crossed out each mention of "people like me." I thought it would be enough to admit my desperation for Lana to help women in general. This made me feel better, a little less vulnerable.

The word "after" came to mind. After this conference, after I spoke, after the cameras were turned off, after things settled down and other news inevitably broke and washed over this moment, at that point I might get to write about the importance of family leave and strong nondiscrimination and antiharassment laws. If things worked out with this job, I would no longer have to write about the estate tax or a super-model's diet and skincare regimen or fend off the creepy questions of a long-ago heartthrob. Even better, I would no longer have to wait anxiously for Colin's next call.

"You'll be okay," I told myself in the mirror. "Everything will be all right. Now, go."

It was like jumping off a sky-high cliff into water. I did not die on impact. My bathing suit did not fall off in front of everyone who was watching. In some strange way, it was exhilarating. I read the words that had been given to me and told the dozen or so reporters that Lana had been nothing but gracious and supportive of me, and that she'd had no knowledge whatsoever of my altering her story. There came a heady rush with speaking in front of those dozen people, and admittedly a sense of power in withholding a truth, even if the specifics of the untruth had been generated by someone else. When I had finished, I folded up the paper and said, "Thank you."

The reporters were hungry birds, eager for any bits that Shirley would give them now. "What about Gloria?" someone shouted. "What's going to happen to her? Is Lana going to talk?"

I noticed at the back of the room stood a frazzled woman probably in her mid-thirties, her hair thrown into a bun that was held up by a pencil, an expression of skepticism on her face. She kept her eyes on me.

Shirley announced that she would not take any questions, and thanked them all for coming. I watched the frazzled woman turn and whisper something to another woman. They both craned to get a better look at me. I had the urge to walk over to them and tell them not to pity me. Yes, being outed and publicly ridiculed was nothing I recommended, but I was hardly coming away empty-handed from this mess. I did not feel exploited. Far from it.

Shirley guided me out into the hallway. "Nice job, Allie." She patted the side of my arm. "Listen, I'll be in touch about the speechwriting thing. Lana always wants to help *everyone*. That's what will make her an incredible senator, right?" She looked at me anew. "Hey, I have a question. What's your network like? Do you know people in New York? Do you have any single-mom friends here?"

I could see her mind working, conjuring other financially challenged, college-educated liberal women who might be recruited.

CHAPTER EIGHTEEN

Despite our best efforts to contain bad publicity, Lana's opponents continued to seize on the debacle. She was dubbed "World's Best Mom" with no subtle irony, and she—and I—amassed other epithets that spread throughout Twitter: "Vlana the Impaler," with a nod to Romania; "Rescue Bullshitter," with a nod to Amber from Lifetime TV. Someone had photoshopped me and Gloria onto the cover of *All That Matters,* and within a day or so, the image became a meme: one picture showed a staff of maids squeezed between Lana and Norton; another a butler serving them tea; a third had Louisa May Alcott hovering behind them, a quill at the ready.

The Democratic National Committee put out a short statement claiming that the incident was a "blip, a mistake, and more importantly a distraction from real issues like healthcare and the economy." Gradually, a backlash to the backlash materialized. People railed against this harassment of a successful immigrant woman, and to a far lesser extent, the harassment of me and Gloria, too. A new sentiment was taking root online. Patty Copeland herself retweeted it best: "No human being can be a full-time mother and save the world at the same time. Our expectations of women are, as always, absurd."

Still, Remy Calhoun's campaign held on to what they called Lana's "false feminism," and they painted him as the more trustworthy, predictable candidate. He was a golf-playing father of two and grandfather of many, a stately veteran whose positions ran far more to the center than Lana's. In his speech announcing his campaign, he had already obfuscated on everything from healthcare to gun laws. His campaign released an ad that showed him in jeans and a sky blue button-down shirt, its sleeves rolled up, strolling around in his sprawling back yard, his wife and adult daughter seated in lawn chairs on a patio behind him. Each of them held the leash of a Cavalier King Charles spaniel seated at attention. "I'm a pretty simple and straightforward guy," he said. "In high school, I knew I wanted to fight for my country, so I volunteered to go to Vietnam. When I got back, I knew I wanted to try my hand at running a business, so I started a little water company. Eventually it turned into a bigger water company." His wife had short, copper-red hair and was trim. She wore a cardigan with a tailored white skirt. Their daughter came from a different mold, though, in her oversized black hoodie and multicolored animal-print leggings. I thought she had a shaved head, but it was difficult to be sure; the camera whizzed past her and settled on one of the dogs.

Since the press conference, I had been walking around in a state of high alert, never knowing who had kept up with what news and who might spring their thoughts on me at any given moment. Jimmy began to call *me* "World's Best Mom." A woman I knew at the nursery where I got my landscaping supplies became gruff with me, and soon admitted that she was "no fan of people like Lana," whatever that meant. When I went in for an overdue dental exam and cleaning, Aaron said, "You have this whole secret life I never knew about! Have you worked with a lot of famous people? I bet you have some stories. What's Lana Breban really like? I bet she's kind of a tyrant to work for." I simply gestured for the saliva pump.

I was surprised and relieved to learn that I would be able to continue my work on *Uncivilized*. My client took the news about Lana in stride. "I don't much care about your time before me," he said. "If anything, you'll be more discreet and devoted to me now, right?"

"Absolutely," I said, nervous that his old flirtations might return, but they did not.

POLLS BEGAN TO show Remy Calhoun gaining ground, although he still trailed Lana somewhere between 6 and 8 percentage points.

"Those dumb ads are working," Reggie, whom I now knew as Lana's communications director, complained to me one day over the phone. "Can you believe it? This old dude puts on blue jeans, walks around his yard, and shows off his dogs as if he's the first candidate ever to do these things. I am starting to lose faith in voters. Maybe we should have put Lana's dog on the cover of *your* book," he said with a laugh. "It's a shame we had to get it pulped; I think it might have helped her."

I had no response.

"I don't mean to make you feel worse about that whole thing." Reggie was in fact calling to let me know that they would bring me on as a speechwriter. Ironically, I remained speechless for the moment.

Then a few days later, two of Calhoun's former employees came forward to say that he had sexually harassed them. I watched the press conference on my laptop. He had touched their breasts while reaching for a pen or a cup of coffee. One added that he had slipped his hand between her thighs, and the other described a similar incident at a Christmas party. "I didn't say anything at the time, because I was so surprised," the second woman said. "I mean, this was Remy Calhoun. I had no words." Her conservative blue blouse had been buttoned almost all the way up, and her wire-rim reading glasses sat halfway down her nose. She had to look credible, after all.

"Well then," I said to no one in my kitchen and closed my computer. I wondered if he would drop out of the race.

Reggie told me that everyone at Lana's campaign office was ecstatic about this news. "Not about what happened to those two women, of course. Listen, could you write up a response statement from Lana? I'm going to need a somber tone of concern and disgust."

SHIRLEY'S NIECE VICTORIA, who worked for a firm called character. org, was hired to finally drown out any remaining "Vlana the Impaler" chatter, which had yet to die out even after Calhoun's employees came forward. Colin told me that reputation management firms like character.org were cropping up everywhere. "As a public or even private figure with no image control, you are enormously vulnerable."

"I guess it's far better to construct an image than to be constructed," I said.

Victoria interviewed me about my interests and skills. She created Tumblr and Instagram accounts for me, "BerkshireMama" and "GardenGal." I was instructed to provide her with photos of me raking my yard (actually, it was Jessica's yard, which, Victoria gently pointed out, was "slightly more grown in" than mine), as well as photos of me gazing at a yellow-orange maple leaf and pushing Cass on a swing.

Countenance finally agreed to a pay-back of only a portion of my advance, and Colin negotiated on my behalf to spread my repayment over two years. It could have been worse—but it could have been better. All this because my mother boasted about me to Patty Copeland? Because Lana had not been a hands-on mother to Norton? I vowed that I would never again take the fall for another person's choices or mistakes, or worse.

My mother and Ed came to visit, and I figured that it was time to introduce them to Kurt. That Saturday, Kurt, Cass, and I headed out to meet them at their hotel in Pittsfield. It had been at least ten years since I had introduced them to anyone I was seeing, and I grew frazzled in anticipation.

My mother and Ed cooed over Cass at first. They handed him some citrus candies they had brought from Florida.

"*Ahem,*" I said. "This is Kurt."

Kurt reached out a hand, and I was glad to see my mother take in his face and his height, and flash me an approving look.

We made our way to the indoor pool, and I saw Ed wince when Kurt mentioned his former career on Wall Street. A son-in-law in finance had to be Ed's dream. Overall though, Kurt meshed well with them; he had a lot of experience pleasing difficult people. He asked them all sorts of questions about Florida, their preferred subject. He laughed at Ed's jokes, and kept quiet as Ed and I slipped into an argument about single-payer healthcare.

Cass and Kurt went to splash around in the water while the three of us got caught up in the corner of the humid room.

The next day, we all drove out to a corn maze at a farm. A song about a sexy tractor and a basket of chicken played at a high volume on loop. Someone had the idea to split up and see who could finish first. I told Cass that he and I would be a team, but he disappeared from me in less than a minute, so I called out for him again and again. I waited five or ten minutes for him to return, but picturing the worst, I broke into a jog. I went for my phone, but of course there was no reception here in this massive pilgrim-shaped maze that had been mowed into a field of dried corn. Twenty minutes passed. I pushed through a wall of cornhusks, and assailed a family with a picture of Cass, but they were no help. Finally I found my mother back at the beginning, chatting with a woman she used to know. We began yelling at each other, but then managed to enlist the help of a high school boy dressed as a scarecrow. At long last, we found Cass sitting, sobbing at the top of the pilgrim's hat. We comforted him, and ourselves, and reunited with Ed by the candy apple stand.

Back in the car, I considered the symbolism: the five of us had endured such difficulties coming together today. Life itself was its own kind of corn maze. It was not poetry, but it did have its own truth and felt helpful in the moment. To put words to something amorphous always was. Subtext could be found anywhere if you watched for it, even at Cotter's Family Fun Farm.

A MESSAGE APPEARED on my phone the next day: *Dude. I read about you in the Daily News! Welcome to the land of the fucked. You hanging in there, 'Rescue Bullshitter'?*

The sight of his name on my phone shook me. Wasn't he in jail? I had heard nothing from him since his book was canceled.

It came back to me, that phone call from Colin, all the terrible news, but also the good: his extravagant gifts to me and Cass, his reassurances that I was doing a good job as a single mom and that, anyway, no mom, no *parent* was perfect. I wanted to reply, *Isn't this crazy? Fuck the land of the fucked; I want to go home now.*

I blinked down at his text.

And then a long-ago moment returned to me, a moment from just before I had left New York. A few of my colleagues in the equity firm and I were at the pub, and I'd had a drink or two, no more, although I wish that I could blame my following actions on alcohol. The guys were trying to guess the bra size of my new summer intern, a recent college graduate named Chloe, who was pretty and poised and athletic, far more so on each count than I. One guy said, "I'm going with a D cup. And you know they're real even though she's so thin everywhere else. She's her friends' worst nightmare." Another said, "Get this: she's a Knicks fan. She's seen the Boss live six times." "Bruce?" "No, your boss. Yes, Bruce." "Fuck me. She's perfect," the first guy said. I remembered a flame of panic about something rare slipping away from me as they went on. "Your gay-dar needs tuning up," I said. "No!" someone groaned.

I nodded. "Chloe has a longtime girlfriend. She's firmly on the other team. She called you guys 'overgrown frat boys' the other day," I lied. Three faces froze, confused. One said, "I mean, I *was* in a frat at Florida State." Another said, "Hey, ask her to bring her girlfriend by some day. I'm not opposed to some threesome action." Someone punched his arm and the subject changed, and there was no more talk of my intern. "Hey, Little Tiger," one of them said to me. "You're on a desert island and you have to choose between me and him. Which is it?" He gestured to the junior analyst beside him. "What makes you think I'd go anywhere with you two losers?" I flirted. "But if Chloe were there? No question, I'd pick her." "*Ooooooh!* Nice!" they howled happily, just as I knew they would.

The next morning on my way to work, I bought Chloe a cup of coffee and when I got to the office, asked her to help me with some market research. She was in such a good mood, so full of gratitude for that small deli coffee, so full of cheer and willingness to help me file my reports that I grew claustrophobic. I wanted out not just of my role as her manager (she deserved so much better), but out of writing dull newsletters about equity upsides and flexible capital solutions. Out of this person I became when I was with the guys. Fate took the reins in the form of a phone call from my mother. Ed had just been rushed to the hospital. The decision was easy: I quit, giving no notice, and suggested to my boss that he hire Chloe to replace me. I told everyone I had to move back home, and never spoke to any of them again.

Now, standing beside Cass in his bedroom, I made myself block Nick Felles's number.

IN OCTOBER, AN actress tweeted something that a woman named Tarana Burke had come up with years ago, and #MeToo caught fire. I thought of Nick and Professor McCoy. I thought of Remy Calhoun's former employees. Almost everyone I knew—Jenna Rose, Jessica Garbella, even Maggie down in Bolivia—put forth their #MeToo moments online. Facebook and Twitter became confessionals. I watched, awed by this enormous uprising of bald honesty and courage. I recalled some other incidents I'd had—a flirty high school Spanish teacher, the time I was flashed in New York. The rush of details that spread across the Internet made the long-hidden truth seem even more vivid and devastating. We should not have been so surprised: the long history of the world was built on uneven power dynamics and greed.

In the end, I would not add my voice to the chorus. And not just because I had already been exposed and shamed during the mess with Lana, and I hardly wanted to expose myself further. Maybe I also preferred to stay hidden because of the times I had waded into murky waters myself. It was, of course, an uneasy thought. I told myself that I would do better from now on. I emailed Jenna, Jessica, and Maggie and passed along my admiration and support, but it was hardly enough. I did hope that, in some way, writing speeches for Lana was a start.

She published an op-ed in support of the movement and reaffirmed her concern about Calhoun. She wrote that real and systemic change would only be possible with a widespread reexamination of our current laws, which meant that voters had to show up and make their voices heard. Women and people of color made up less than 20 percent of Congress, and yet this was the most diverse it had ever been. It sounded as if she were watching the movement from afar, chiming in rather than influencing. Maybe even exploiting the national fervor for her upcoming primary. But I reminded myself that her goals were pure. Lately, she was lunching with Reese Witherspoon at Le Coucou, sampling Cool Whip at a factory in Avon, and appearing alongside a group of students near SUNY Oswego hollering, "Never Apologize, Never Compromise, Never Rationalize!" One place where she no longer appeared was Twitter. Reggie and the bald guy, Everett, had taken over her account, and now posted only short videos from her speeches, endorsements, and constant reminders for people to vote.

In my new role, I was getting to know both Reggie and Everett better. Although he was sometimes blunt and always in some kind of panic, Reggie was a good and supportive manager. And I was coming to like the quick turnaround time of speechwriting, as well as the regular pay, although I did not love the way that a portion of each check was handed over to Countenance, or that Shirley occasionally excised any "overly sophisticated language" from my speeches. I learned to refer to people as "folks" and gun control as "gun safety regulation." Government spending was called "investment" and abortion "the right to choose." Speechwriting differed significantly from writing for the page. Sentences had to be shorter now, language overtly inspirational and far less descriptive. I had to cater my words to wildly different crowds; high-brow, low-brow, the political establishment, the disenfranchised.

Unexpectedly, Remy Calhoun's daughter stepped out of the shadows and began to travel with him to campaign stops. Sometimes she even spoke. A glassblower and environmental activist in her late twenties, Andrea Calhoun did indeed have a shaved head, as well as a pierced eyebrow. She gave well-written, impassioned speeches about healthcare. She was diabetic and bemoaned the outrageous costs of insulin and the unholy interplay between big pharma and the government. If they made a strange pair visually, Remy clearly adored his daughter. She had a certain presence and passion, a magnetism that actually brought to mind the old Lana Breban. I thought she added something necessary to his campaign, and soon I was proven right. New polls had Remy and Lana within three points of each other.

When Remy signaled that he might switch his position and favor broadening some restrictions around medical marijuana, Shirley expressed concern to me. "He's starting to look too much like us," she said. "Thank God everyone hates old white men these days."

"They do?" I said, although I should have been used to her generalizations.

"The #MeToo movement? Hello?"

"Well, his own #MeToo moments didn't hurt him."

"This is true. If only more women had come forward and he was more of a, you know. What Remy did looks like Boy Scout fun compared to Harvey Weinstein and those others."

"You're right. God," I said.

CHAPTER NINETEEN

Finally, in November, the evening of the special election arrived. I dressed Cass in a green checked button-down and little khakis. He was put off by all the buttons, as he was used to far more casual clothes. "When I grow up I'm never going to wear anything like this," he said. I saw an adult Cass in loungewear on my couch, enjoying a Happy Meal, watching his third hour of TV. "Yes, you will," I said. "But let's not worry about that right now."

Kurt had found a nice coffee-colored blazer at a thrift store. "You ready for all this?" he asked me.

"No," I said. "Maybe."

We began our drive down to New York to attend Lana's party in Soho. It felt imperative that Lana win tonight; my future employment was now tethered to hers, but of course there were other things at stake. All of us working on her campaign—hell, everyone in New York—were desperate to see a woman, and mother and immigrant, overtake a man like Remy Calhoun and win this seat.

Our hotel was located just a ten-minute walk from the party. In my new black shift dress and heels, my hair blown out with Jessica's help, I hardly felt like myself.

"Lana's got this," Kurt said, as we stepped out of the lobby.

"What do you mean? You saw that poll yesterday, it's not a slam dunk."

"It smells like a toilet," Cass said. One of the many talents of children was to keep you in the present moment.

"Canal Street Station," Kurt said with a laugh. "The nose knows."

I focused on not tripping in my new shoes as we crossed the street and bypassed a group of twenty-somethings speaking French.

We made our way to the party at the other hotel and, inside the crowded lobby, an alternative universe. Clouds, real clouds, hovered near the ceiling. One of the walls was covered in live moss. I took in the throngs of people, the upbeat jazz, the wait staff threading their way through the group with trays full of small, skewered things. More than a few people in the room wore pink knitted hats. I scanned the room, but Lana was nowhere to be seen. Kurt's hand in mine, I tried to let it sink in that we were really here in this boutique hotel in Soho, at a party for Lana Breban.

"What would Jimmy think of this?" I said.

Kurt rolled his eyes. " 'Buncha coastal elites.' "

The mood in the crowded room was giddy, buoyant with a sense that momentarily, we would begin to take back our country, a phrase I had written into Lana's speeches several times by now. A phrase I had written into her acceptance speech. I imagined replaying one of her speeches before Congress on my laptop for Cass. "I wrote those words," I would tell him.

I imagined the words I might use to describe this party had I still been a ghostwriter working on Lana's book. Here we were, moments before all the hard work of balancing motherhood and career would finally pay off, when Lana would rocket upward into her new role as outspoken progressive senator. I might detail the atmosphere of the room, the din of nervous voices, the laughter of others, the soft mossy wall, Coltrane's busy saxophone in "My Favorite Things." I might namedrop: *Hanging on other walls were poster-sized photographs of me with Hillary Clinton, Ellen DeGeneres, and Alyssa Milano. Was that Reese Witherspoon headed my way?*

Cass stayed by my side and poked at the collar of his shirt. Kurt went off to get us drinks.

Shirley and Colin approached. Colin gave me a hug and bent over so Cass could hear him. "Hey little man, you look sharp."

"This is our night!" Shirley said as she hugged me.

"I hope so," I said.

"You know so," she said with a controlled and controlling nod.

The music grew louder, and it became more difficult to hear what she was saying. When Kurt returned, I introduced everyone the best that I could. Shirley gave Cass one of Lana's campaign buttons, and went off to talk to a few actresses whose faces I recognized but could not identify by name.

I took Cass's hand as I wandered the room, enjoying my free martini, and trying to maintain hope for the future of women and democracy. I made myself smile big whenever I remembered.

"I almost forgot," Shirley said, finding me again. She handed me an envelope. "From Lana."

Inside were three tickets for a show of *The Lion King* the next day, along with a card that read: "For Allie. For everything. Whatever happens, I hope you'll keep giving me the right words to say."

"Oh my God!" I said, and hurried back to Colin and Kurt, who were talking now. "This is Broadway. What the hell?"

"Jeez! Cass is going to love that," Kurt said.

"Looks like she wants you to keep writing for her even if she doesn't win tonight," Colin said.

"I guess so," I said. "I mean, who knows where she'll land if things don't go her way? Even the mighty fall. She can't exactly put out another memoir any time soon. I guess she'd still do her op eds—" Colin shook his head. "What the hell am I talking about? She's going to win. And our Allie has good, steady work, and now we need to celebrate, right?"

Someone called out, "We're getting some results!"

People were gathered around TV screens in two corners of the room, and we made our way toward one of them. Still reeling from the gift of the tickets, I watched as a commercial for arthritis medication played. I asked a man next to me if he had heard any of the returns yet, but he shook his head.

Lana sat nearby on a leather couch, flanked by Lester and Shirley. Lana and I locked eyes for a moment, and I held up the envelope and mouthed, "Thank you!"

She gave me a thumbs-up.

More commercials came on, and Cass tugged me back toward a small dance floor. The jazz had ended and someone had put on "Girls Just Want to Have Fun." Kurt appeared and the three of us danced, making faces at each other. Again, I imagined writing deeper into this scene, but this time, from my point of view. I would describe my wild adoration of these two people beside me, now doing a bastard-ized "Macarena," my new appreciation for Lana and her unexpected if complicated generosity, for Colin and his connecting me with her after the bottom fell out with Nick's book. "There were plenty of reasons to despair about our country," I would write, "but here in this room were plenty of reasons to feel lucky."

Someone turned off the music and an abrupt hush fell over the room.

"Ulster and Columbia counties by 3 percent each," Shirley's voice announced. An explosion of clapping and whistling sounded, and we made our way back toward the corner where Lana sat. Cass pulled at my hand. Kurt kissed the top of my head. There it was on the TV screen: she was in the lead, but with only two precincts reporting. Coltrane came booming back on, but Shirley yelled, "Not yet! Keep it down for now," and the music cut again.

The commercial for arthritis medication played again. I leaned over and told Cass that we had tickets to see *The Lion King* the next day, and his eyes went wide. "Really?" he said.

"Really!"

"I'm tired. Can we go soon?" It was growing late.

Putnam County went for Calhoun. This time Shirley didn't announce it, and people nodded grimly. Reggie walked past and we exchanged looks. "To be expected," he said.

Cass pulled at my arm again, and I looked around for Kurt. Maybe he could take Cass for a walk or something during this last part of the night. Where the hell *was* Kurt? I grew panicked about being on my own with my son if, God forbid, the news was bad. In that case, I would be the one who might need a parent.

And then, like the bursting of a dam, St. Lawrence, Franklin, Albany, and Rockland all came in, and minutes later, someone rang what sounded like a cowbell. Everyone began to jump and clap and hoot, hugging each other and exchanging high fives. I scooped up Cass and finally found Kurt making his way toward us. My heart threatened to leave my chest and rise up with those odd clouds near the ceiling. People clustered around Lana and I could hardly see her, until I could, and then I saw her wipe at her eyes and cover her face with her hands. When she removed them, she threw open her mouth and laugh-cried with abandon. I had never seen her face this way, so wide open.

Soon she would make her way to a podium and begin the speech that I written for her. "My friends, my friends! Look at all of us!" she would say. "Look at what we have done. I am so full of thankfulness for every one of you here. You have each worked so hard. You have fought like soldiers in this ongoing war to defend women and people of color, immigrants and working people, LGBTQIA and disabled people. To defend all of the people who have been resisting tirelessly and trying make this country our great home again. That's right. We will make America great again, but on the people's terms, and not the terms of the one percent. Not the terms of the corrupt. And certainly not the terms of the current regime."

I would stand, relieved, with my son and begin to feel more hopeful about the country. I would begin to more fully believe in his future again, as well as my own.

It was as familiar to me as the Berkshires sky, this sort of ending. I had written it how many times? I had written the crescendo, this moment of victory, in whatever form it took. I had written the ensuing denouement, the last sentence.

If I close my eyes even now, I can visualize the rest, both on the page and in person: Lana setting up her desk in the Russell Senate Office Building, Norton seated in the corner doing homework. "Can you believe your old mom is a United States senator now?" Lana would say. "Whatever." But then he would look up and flash her a proud smile.

If only this was what had transpired; if only we could determine the future by writing it first.

SOMEONE TURNED OFF the music as an abrupt hush fell over the room.

"Ulster and Columbia counties by 3 percent each," Shirley's voice announced. An explosion of clapping and whistling sounded, and we made our way back toward the corner where Lana sat. Cass pulled at my hand. Kurt kissed the top of my head. There it was on the TV screen: she was in the lead, but with only two precincts reporting. Coltrane came booming back on, but Shirley yelled, "Not yet! Keep it down for now," and the music cut again.

The commercial for arthritis medication played again. I leaned over and told Cass that we had tickets to see *The Lion King* the next day.

Putnam County went for Calhoun. This time Shirley didn't

announce it, and people nodded grimly. Reggie walked past and we exchanged looks. "To be expected," he said.

Cass pulled at my arm again, and I looked around for Kurt. Maybe he could take Cass for a walk during this last part of the night. Delaware went for Calhoun. I got the creeping sense that Andrea Calhoun may have had more impact than we thought. Or worse, that she was not even needed in the end—and that the electorate had no real qualms with Remy's harassment of his employees. Suffolk and Nassau came in for Calhoun. Where the hell *was* Kurt? Orange and Schenectady went for Calhoun, just as Kurt finally appeared.

"It's not looking good," I said and gestured toward a few people quietly leaving. "Where were you?"

"I ran into an old neighbor. We were out in the hall. I didn't know all these returns came in so quickly."

"Mom," Cass whined.

If we left the party, maybe things would turn around for Lana. If I was not here to witness the worst, then the worst might not happen. The irrational bargains we make when faced with the possibility of grief.

"Let's go," I said.

Kurt looked at me. "You sure? We came all the way here."

"Cass needs sleep," I said.

I found Lana still seated in the corner with Shirley and a few others, and when Lana saw me, her face lit as if she remembered to look upbeat. "Stay optimistic," she said, reaching out her hand for mine.

"You, too," I said.

Back in our hotel room, Cass drifted off just after we set him in his bed. Kurt headed into the bathroom.

I found my laptop and took it to a chair at the side of the room. I pulled off my shoes, tucked my feet under my legs, and opened the screen. A moment later I was looking at a photograph of Remy Calhoun and his wife hugging. My eyes moved down to take in the headline.

"Oh no," I whispered. "No, no, no." I grew a little breathless. There were times I still did not know how to find enough oxygen in this new place, the country as it had been over the past year.

Kurt stepped out of the bathroom and saw my face. "Oh."

I nodded.

He came and sat on the floor next to my chair and wrapped his arms around my waist. "Shit," he said into my stomach.

"What do I tell Cass?" I said.

"The truth?"

"Can't I just lie to him and let him believe it for a minute or two before I tell him what really happened?"

"He's a kid," Kurt said. "He'll love you regardless of whether your team won or not."

"It's not about *that*," I said. The distance between our sexes was too far at that moment: Kurt could not know the disappointment—the outrage—of watching Lana fall to Remy Calhoun. It was hardly Kurt's fault that this pulverizing disappointment might never be as pulverizing to him. But I did not have the heart to explain anything more right then.

About a year earlier, we had raced around my house, tidying up, putting out chips and salsa, some beer and wine. Pete and Sandra arrived first, followed by Jimmy in his red MAKE AMERICA GREAT AGAIN T-shirt. The sight of it had unnerved me more than I would have expected. Kurt had talked me into having this party. "It'll be a way to lighten the moment. You know, remind each other that we're all friends and neighbors, that we still live in the same country."

I had sneaked out behind my house to smoke a quick joint and improvise a prayer for our first woman president.

When I came back, a few results had already come in: he had taken Indiana and Kentucky, and she Vermont. On the *New York Times* website, a forecast needle gyrated across the "tossup" zone.

An hour or so passed, time that I cannot seem to retrieve now.

And then we lost Ohio. Over on the couch, Jimmy dropped his gaze to the floor. When he looked up, our eyes met and something passed between us. He half-smiled, but in a sad way, and I had the sense that he was aware of my thoughts, as if he were my father watching me take in for the first time some hard truth about the world. He appeared nearly contrite. I rose and went to lie down in my bedroom.

After we lost North Carolina, Kurt came in to give me the news. "Is it rude if we ask everyone to leave now?" I said.

"Kind of," he said.

He returned to the other room, but came back a while later to tell me that Utah and Iowa had not gone our way. At this point, I had hidden myself under my blanket, Cass's stuffed hippo curled to my chest. "We were looking everywhere for that when Cass went to bed," Kurt said.

"People are still here?" I could hear a couple of voices talking quietly in the living room.

"Just Pete and Sandra."

It became clear to me that I would not sleep at all that night. At around 2:30 a.m., we learned that Hillary Clinton had just called to congratulate him. His campaign manager described it. "They had maybe a one-minute conversation, very gracious very warm, he commended her for being smart and tough and running a hard-fought campaign."

"Wow. I cannot believe he will be president. I'm kind of numb," Kurt said, beside me in bed with my laptop between us.

I myself was something like a human plasma globe exploding with tiny lightning bolts. I could not stay still, but at the same time, I could not seem to move. There was no way to contain all this electricity, but there was nowhere for it to go.

In our New York hotel room now, Cass murmured something in his sleep and threw off the thin blanket.

Lana would not be a U.S. senator.

"Go to sleep," I told Kurt.

"You sure?"

I nodded. I suppose I wanted some solitude right then. I watched him pull off his undershirt, a sight that once made me quicken. It would again, I knew, at some point.

He climbed beneath the sheets and said, "It's bullshit, isn't it? I mean what happened tonight. She should have won."

"Total bullshit," I said.

By now, Lana would have made her way to the podium and given my concession speech. "My friends, my friends! Look at all of us," she would have said. "I am so full of thankfulness for every one of you here. You have each worked so hard. You have fought like soldiers in this ongoing war to defend women and people of color, immigrants and working people, LGBTQIA, and disabled people. To defend all of the people who have been resisting tirelessly to make this country our great home again. That's right. We will keep fighting to make America great again, but on the people's terms, not the terms of the one percent. Not the terms of the corrupt. And certainly not the terms of the current regime. We will continue in this fight together. Every day. Let this moment only make us try harder."

CHAPTER TWENTY

We made our way down the red carpeted aisle of the Minskoff Theatre, found our seats, Orchestra Right, and marveled at our close view of the stage and the size of the place—it had to hold over a thousand people.

I noticed someone I recognized slouching alongside a group of kids about his age. He wore the same shirt, a red polo, that he had worn on the cover of the book. The group stopped just two rows ahead of us, squeezed past a woman with a toddler, and took a minute to match their tickets with their seats. A girl about thirteen or fourteen years old flicked Norton's arm, and bent over laughing. He said something to her, then turned around. Our eyes met for a second. We had never been formally introduced. I did not know if he could identify me, although I assumed that Lana filled him in on the fate of the book. And it would take someone less than a second to find a photo of me online these days. For my part, I had seen him in person only from a distance at Lana's election night party, that is in addition to the day I tailed him around his Manhattan neighborhood all those months ago.

It seemed a kind of offer from Lana to me: *Here is my son. Here he is in person, a flesh-and-blood boy, just like yours. Remember that I am a mother, too. There was truth beneath the fabrications of our book. It was not all in vain—certainly not for the people who read it.*

Would she have had a better chance at winning if she had kept her hair blue, her accent intact—and if she been honest about having delegated so much of Norton's childcare? Changing her image had in fact meant apologizing for it. I thought back to my first impressions of her on Colbert; "I wanted viewers to see the world as Wanda did. We look at poverty, or at least most of us do, but we need to start looking from it." I would have happily voted for that woman. I had found her boldness infectious. Of course she was not as involved with her child's life as other women, but I would never have expected her to be.

Norton appeared to be having fun with his friends. What did he think of his mother's loss last night? Of course she was not Lana Breban to him; she was "Mom." We can never see our parents as others see them, although we do get glimpses.

Enough people had read *All That Matters* to propel it onto the *New York Times* bestseller list. They had read of my difficulties implementing my birth plan, my awe at my first meeting my son, my challenges breastfeeding. They had read about Cass dropping the replica jaw into the fish tank, and my curdling shame in that waiting room. They had read of a mother's wistfulness when watching her son grow older. Maybe some of those readers recognized their own true experiences parenting. If nothing else, I had written a book that I myself had wished to read.

"Middle schoolers, you think?" I said to Kurt, gesturing to the group. If I wanted to, I could have identified Norton for him, as this of course was no longer confidential information. But something stopped me.

"Looks like it," Kurt said.

I leaned closer so that no one else could hear. "What do you think Cass will be like when he's in middle school?"

Kurt shrugged.

To my left, my son had pushed himself into the crook of his seat and was pulling his jacket zipper up and down.

"It's your first play!" I said, and he nodded eagerly. How many kids could say that their first time at the theater was a Broadway production of *The Lion King*?

I turned back to Kurt. "You're supposed to say that he'll be handsome and poised and amazing."

"He'll be handsome and poised and amazing."

"He'll be happy and interesting and creative."

"He'll be sulky and pimply and awkward," he said.

"Hey."

"He'll be in middle school. Come on."

Late last night, after the results of the special election were announced, I had considered returning these tickets to Lana. Attending a Broadway show had felt wrong now. A somber gong of truth rang over and over in my mind: nothing would change for our country tomorrow, or the next day, or even the next.

I watched footage of Andrea Calhoun hugging Remy, and I hoped that she knew something about him that I did not. Maybe he had been a loving father despite everything and maybe she would nudge him toward a more progressive agenda. I thought about the many U.S. senators already putting up a good fight and the massive Women's March and even the rainbow peace flag that a neighbor had hung on his cracked, rotted fence just the day before. I thought about Maggie, who would return from Bolivia soon, about Luana and Carlos, who were not going anywhere at least for now, and about the fact that I would get to keep writing for Lana, whatever form that would take. Cass deserved to see *The Lion King*. He deserved everything I was able to give him. In the morning, we would go for breakfast somewhere for his favorite, chocolate chip pancakes, and then head up to Central Park. The three of us would wander that grandiose symbol, stop in at the zoo, go model boat sailing, see the Alice in Wonderland statue, maybe make our way over to Strawberry Fields and the Imagine mosaic. We would have a good day—we would have one great day.

As the house lights went dark, I reached for Cass's hand and imagined that I was him, a little apprehensive about what would come next. What would be the first sound? How loud would the music be? The stage lit up in yellow, and someone issued forth a sustained call. His hand squeezed mine.

From a side box, a man with no shirt and a ram headdress belted out an answer to the first call. More lights came on and an enormous sun rose from the stage. Other voices rang out and joined in a complex unity, and a gentle drumbeat began. People dressed as elaborate hyenas and leopards swept down the aisles. Several women in white bird costumes twirled right beside Cass, and his eyes grew large at them.

I saw Norton elbow the boy beside him when an antelope danced past.

Here was the savannah, deafening and harmonious and vivid. Here was the enormous audience, sitting rapt in their seats as the animals made their way forward to gather onstage.

ACKNOWLEDGMENTS

My thanks to the work of Dan Kindlon, Ellen R. Malcolm, Elizabeth Noble, Christia Spears Brown, Michael Thompson, and Virginia Woolf. Thank you, Neil Giordano, for the wiper blades, and needless to say, so much else. For putting me up while I wrote parts of this book, thank you Hemingway House, Emily Franklin, Susan Shepherd, and Wellspring House. For being an unbelievably smart, funny, and kind editor and friend, thank you, Kathy Pories. All my gratitude also goes to Maria Massie, Margot Landsman, Bonnie Hearn Hill, Bret Anthony Johnston, Rachel Kadish, Catherine Knepper, Tova Mirvis, Asata Radcliffe, Joanna Rakoff, Jane Roper, Anna Solomon, Chris Stamey, Sylvia True (I do not know a more generous person), Annie Weatherwax, Roger Wieand, Marisa Wilson, and Laura Zigman. Finally, thanks to Gareth Cook, everyone at the Mount (including the ghosts of Edith Wharton and her dogs), Jennifer 8. Lee, and Yael Goldstein Love for enlarging my horizons.

Impersonation

The Path to *Impersonation*
An Essay by Heidi Pitlor

Questions for Discussion

THE PATH TO *IMPERSONATION*
An Essay by Heidi Pitlor

The year that I switched from full-time book editor to the more part-time work of editing the *Best American Short Stories* series was the same year I published my first novel and had twins. Unsurprisingly, it was a chaotic year. And things began to get pretty tight for us. Twin diapers and twin day care do not come cheap. We lived outside Boston, not the most affordable area of the country, but we wanted to stay put because my father, who was single (my mother passed away when I was young), had some concerning health issues. I found myself shuttling between a fabulous work lunch at the Four Seasons with some well-known writer (thank you, days-of-yore expense account) and a dinner of Kraft mac and cheese—alongside bottles for the babies. I would pray that the twins would sleep at the same time for more than an hour at night. Maybe, just maybe I would finally get some rest and be able to fake the wherewithal to seem awake and alert, even semi-intelligent and literary the next day, so that I could continue to earn a living. When a more financially comfortable friend would mention an upcoming eco-conscious vacation or their locally made toys, I grew frankly jealous. I would have given my left hand for a trip to Costa Rica or a room full of beautiful hand-carved playthings for my kids. I began to wonder if living according to certain ideals was possible only for the economically privileged.

THE NARRATOR OF *IMPERSONATION*, Allie Lang, and I have a few things in common. We are both moms of sons. Neither of us excels at housework, though we genuinely admire those who do. We both work in publishing, and with far higher-profile people. We've both had some financial struggles. We are both mystified by the lasting power of toxic masculinity. Allie is a ghostwriter. I have done a small amount of ghostwriting, and in a sense, my work as series editor of *The Best American Short Stories* is a kind of "ghost editing."

Each year, I read every American short story published in a literary journal, select the top 120, pass these along to my guest editor, and help them choose the top 20 that will appear in the book. The process varies widely depending on the guest editor's personality and availability. While I try not to do my initial reading with them in mind, I am always conscious of their taste throughout our collaboration. So the role of invisible or less visible participant in the workplace has been interesting to me for years.

I set out to write a book that was a little satirical, and I did have some fun at the expense of the publishing industry, as well as the American political landscape and the world of parenting experts. Although the story and characters are all fictional, some of the emotional terrain is not. I wanted to write about a worker bee, a woman who wants to live by feminist ideals but, due to various circumstances, cannot always do so.

In the novel, Allie is thrilled when she meets her new client, Lana Breban, a renowned women's rights lawyer. Ghostwriting for Lana means no longer working for the morally dubious—something Allie has done more often than she would have liked to in the past. Both

Allie and Lana share the belief that women should have equal access to all that men do. Lana proves to be more Machiavellian than she seems initially, though, and the two become foils for each other in ways that neither could have predicted. Allie must eventually learn to assert herself in various aspects of her life: social, romantic, economic. Lana learns a few things too, but no spoilers here.

To me, *Impersonation* is about idealism, authenticity, and privilege. It's about who tells what story—who truly controls which narrative, and how this affects our culture and our lives as individuals. Finally, it's a love story, one about a mother's profound love for her son and her concern about his future.

QUESTIONS FOR DISCUSSION

1. How does Allie's one-night stand with her agent, Colin, affect their future working relationship?

2. How much do you think a ghostwriter should augment or even invent for her client? Where is the line for you?

3. Did Allie reveal too much about her client, Lana, over dinner with her parents? Why or why not?

4. How present are traditional ideals of masculinity and femininity in our country? In what ways do they affect the characters' lives in *Impersonation*? In what ways do they affect your life?

5. Throughout the novel, Allie struggles to read one book—*To the Lighthouse* by Virginia Woolf. How does Allie's life provide a counterpoint to the lives of Woolf's characters?

6. Allie has an arrangement with her elderly neighbor, Bertie, for childcare. How do you feel about this arrangement? Is it wrong for Allie to ask Bertie to look after her son? Why or why not?

7. Is Allie's neighbor Jessica a sympathetic or unsympathetic character? Why?

8. When Allie interviews Dr. Boyle for Lana's book, he says, "I try to caution parents against assigning too much import to a baby's gender in terms of it predetermining behavior." How much does a baby's gender determine, do you think? What is biological and what is learned?

9. Lana ultimately relies on Allie for much more than shaping her prose. On the other hand, Lana's ultimate goal was to help women of all stripes. How did you end up feeling about Lana and her choices?

10. In the scene featuring *Rescue Sitter*, a mother is shamed for not being loud enough with her children. In what ways are mothers shamed by our culture? What about fathers and other parents?

11. Is Kurt a good partner for Allie? Why or why not?

12. Who or what is the real antagonist in this book? Why?

13. What kinds of incorrect assumptions have people made about you? Why do you think this happens? What are the consequences of this?

14. Have you ever made incorrect assumptions about other people? What were the consequences then?

15. How does your public self differ from your true self?

16. How important is authenticity in politicians? What is the most important factor for you when voting for someone?

© ADAM LANDSMAN

HEIDI PITLOR is the author of the novels *The Birthdays* and *The Daylight Marriage*. She has been the series editor of *The Best American Short Stories* since 2007 and is the editorial director of Plympton, a literary studio. Her writing has been published in *Ploughshares*, the *New York Times*, the *Boston Globe*, *Lit Hub*, the *Huffington Post*, and the anthologies *It Occurs to Me That I Am America: New Stories and Art* and *Labor Day: True Birth Stories by Today's Best Women Writers*. She lives outside Boston.